Edward H. Thompson

The Life of the Baron de Renty

perfection in the world exemplified

Edward H. Thompson

The Life of the Baron de Renty
perfection in the world exemplified

ISBN/EAN: 9783337300494

Printed in Europe, USA, Canada, Australia, Japan

Cover: Foto ©Andreas Hilbeck / pixelio.de

More available books at **www.hansebooks.com**

LIBRARY

OF

RELIGIOUS BIOGRAPHY

EDITED BY

EDWARD HEALY THOMPSON.

VOLUME IV.

THE BARON DE RENTY.

THE LIFE

OF

THE BARON DE RENTY;

OR,

𝔓erfection in the 𝔚orld exemplified.

"Hoc enim sentite in vobis, quod et in Christo Jesu, qui......
Semetipsum exinanivit, formam servi accipiens,......et...humiliavit
Semetipsum, factus obediens usque ad mortem, mortem autem crucis."—
Phil. iii. 5—8.

Second Edition.

LONDON: BURNS AND OATES.
1881.

ADVERTISEMENT.

THE materials for a biography of the Baron de
Renty are at once copious and limited. His Life
by Saint-Jure* may be said to be the sole available
authority, as, with the exception of a few scattered
notices in various works, nothing additional can be
gleaned from any other source. That source, however, is one entitled to the fullest confidence. Saint-
Jure was De Renty's director for many years, and his
name stands high among writers of that time on
ascetical and mystical theology. His description of
this remarkable man, considered as the portrait of a
Christian living in the world and giving a high example of Evangelical perfection, leaves nothing to be
desired. The author, indeed, had no other aim in
view than the spiritual profit which might be derived

* It is interesting to note that Jean-Baptiste Saint-Jure,
of the Company of Jesus, was among the ecclesiastics who
came over to England with Henrietta Maria on her marriage
with Charles I. The title of his biography is *La Vie de M. de
Renty; ou, Le Modèle d'un Parfait Chrétien.*

Renty is a bourg in the department of the Pas de Calais,
22 kilomètres (16¼ English miles) from Saint-Omer. In the
year 1533 it was erected into a marquisate by the Emperor
Charles V., within whose Flemish dominions it was at that
time included. The *château* of Bény, De Renty's ancestral
house, was in the neighbourhood of Bayeux.

b

from the full exhibition of such an example; more-over, writing so soon after De Renty's death, he did not judge it fitting to enter into other details, which might at the present time possess considerable in-terest; and so far does he carry this precaution and reserve that, even where it would seem as if no possible injury to any one could have accrued by the insertion of names, he has refrained from giving them. Scarcely a single name, indeed, is mentioned through-out the work when this could be avoided. In the present biography a few have been supplied from other sources.

Although De Renty's brief career was one of con-tinual activity in the service of God and of his neighbour, it did not abound in what is properly termed incident. This circumstance alone necessarily left little room for choice as to the method according to which the life should be written. Chronological sequence, except as regarded two or three leading facts, could not be preserved : it was impossible, then, to allow the individual simply to exhibit himself by means of a consecutive narrative of the events with which he was connected; nor, if this had been feasible, would it have been satisfactory in the case of a life which, notwithstanding his many active employments, was so interior as was that of De Renty. The drama of his life was within him.

But, though deficient in incident, the life of this holy man possessed what must be regarded as of far more importance—because conducing most to spiritual profit—distinctive feature, and that in an eminent degree. The object, therefore, of this biography— grounded as it is throughout on Saint-Jure's detailed and minute description — is to convey a definite portrait of the man himself : of his inner life, of the character of his sanctity, and of the nature of his spiritual attractions.

On this subject we may here make the following general remarks. Although in its essential features the saintly character is always similar (and it could not be otherwise, since Saints are only copies of one and the same Model, our Saviour Jesus Christ), yet we observe in all holy persons, not merely individual peculiarities, as is the case in all God's works, but, as it were, certain distinctions into classes, which may be said to offer a parallel in the kingdom of grace to the divisions of genus and species in that of nature. While, then, the Saints are all copies of Jesus Christ, their Master, yet is there scope in this imitation for diversity of type, by which some perfection of their Divine Model, some aspect or mystery of His Life is peculiarly illustrated and set forth. Thus we can point to those, as a class, who particularly honour the Hidden Life ; not that it has not been, and ever will be, honoured by all devout Christians, but they have been attracted to a special *cultus* of it in their own persons, and have manifested this *cultus* with special prominence in all they have said and done. It has coloured all their devotions, it has interpenetrated all their views, it has been ever on their lips. These persons have usually been remarkable also for what may, for want of a more accurate designation, be called a special devotion to " God Alone" : so that those two words may be said to have been their motto, and the summing-up (as it were) of their whole spiritual life. The connection of the two devotions is easily intelligible; for devotion to the Hidden Life implies a very prominent attraction to the most complete annihilation of self, manifested by a perpetual longing after this total eclipse and extinction of the mere natural man in the abyss of his own nothingness. This spiritual proclivity, which acts as a weight drawing down the creature to its self-annihilation, correspondingly exalts the Creator, and explains the accompanying passion, as we might term it, for God Alone.

Boudon, the saintly Archdeacon of Evreux, may be taken as a striking representative of this class among the holy persons who flourished during the seventeenth century in France. No one who is acquainted with his personal history or with his writings can question his powerful and all-prevailing attraction in this combined direction, evinced, not merely in his published work on that subject, but in all the other products of his pen; and we do not hesitate to class M. de Renty under the same category: for, notwithstanding his active life of charity, he will be found to have been inwardly dragged, so to say, by grace in a direction altogether different from the sphere which he was called to fill; so that in desire alone could he realize his attraction.

Another instance of similar attraction was furnished by a contemporary and fellow-countryman of De Renty, but one whose name is less known, M. de Bernières-Louvigny, Treasurer of France, author of a very valuable work, or collection of writings, bearing the title of *Le Chrétien Intérieur*. As Caen was his place of residence, there can be little doubt but that these two holy laymen were personally well acquainted with each other; particularly as M. de Bernières-Louvigny is reckoned among the peculiar friends of P. Eudes, with whom M. de Renty had also very close relations.

In obedience to the decrees of Urban VIII. and other Sovereign Pontiffs, we declare that in all we have written of the holy life and exalted virtues of M. de Renty we submit ourselves without reserve to the infallible judgment of the Apostolic See, which alone has authority to pronounce to whom rightly belong the character and title of Saint.

CONTENTS.

INTRODUCTION.

Each mystery of the Incarnation has its special transforming power on the soul. Characteristics of Spiritual Infancy. Women often chosen as the instruments of some special devotion. The influence exercised by the Venerable Margaret of the Blessed Sacrament in spreading devotion to the Sacred Infancy. France the scene of its manifestation. How opposed to the evils then dominant in that land. The Incarnation and Redemption specially exhibited in the Infancy. Bethlehem the vestibule of Calvary. M. de Renty the disciple of Margaret. Self-denudation a peculiar grace of the Sacred Infancy. Jesus chose the Crib. Devotion to the Sacred Infancy a peculiarly safe devotion. Self-surrender an effect of this devotion. Close connection between this devotion and that to the Blessed Sacrament . . *page* 1

PART I.

𝔓erfect 𝔠onbersion.

CHAPTER I.

THE EARLY YEARS OF GASTON DE RENTY.

His ancestry and parentage. Has poor people for his sponsors. Receives great graces from his earliest childhood. His superior abilities and energy of will. Has a special turn for mathematics. The Providence of God in the casual incidents of life. Effect on De Renty of reading the "Imitation of Christ." His desire to embrace the religious state. His flight from Paris. His letter to his father. He is discovered and taken to the château of Bény. Explanation of his acquiescence. He is chosen deputy to the States of Normandy. Rebuilds the church of Bény . . . . *page* 19

CHAPTER V.
DE RENTY'S VICTORY OVER SELF.

CHAPTER VI.
DE RENTY'S ESTEEM FOR SUFFERING. HIS DOMESTIC TROUBLES.

CHAPTER VII.
DE RENTY'S POVERTY IN THE MIDST OF RICHES.

PART II.

Active Life of Charity.

CHAPTER I.

DE RENTY A CO-OPERATOR IN GOOD WORKS.

CHAPTER II.

DE RENTY'S CORPORAL WORKS OF MERCY.

CHAPTER III.

DE RENTY'S ZEAL FOR SOULS.

CHAPTER IV.

RULES DRAWN UP BY DE RENTY FOR THE SANCTIFICATION OF CERTAIN CLASSES.

PART III.

Interior and Mystical Life.

CHAPTER I.

MARGARET OF THE BLESSED SACRAMENT.

CHAPTER II.

SPIRITUAL ALLIANCE BETWEEN DE RENTY AND MARGARET.

INTRODUCTION.

JUST as the Passion of Jesus is stamped upon and
acted out, as it were, visibly in some saintly persons,
and is even manifested at times in their very bodies,
so also has the Sacred Infancy given its peculiar
impress to the sanctity of others. Both states are
but the extension and the more perfect realization of
that which is essential to the Christian character.
To all indiscriminately it is said, " Except ye become
as little children, ye shall not enter into the Kingdom
of Heaven "; and conformity to the Cross is declared
by our Lord to be no less indispensable when He
says, " He that taketh not up his Cross, and followeth
Me, is not worthy of Me." But these two conditions
have, we need scarcely say, their indefinite degrees
of perfection, beginning at the bare rudiments of the
state of grace, and rising gradually to that sublime
transformation in which the Saint can exclaim with
St. Paul, " I live, yet not I, but Christ liveth in me."
It is of this stage we are speaking. Each mystery of
the Incarnation has its own specially transforming
power on the soul ; for (as Father Faber has observed)
"every action of our Blessed Lord is so fertile and
exuberant, so powerful to produce its like in others,

B

so full of divine energy and signification, that it is in
itself a creative word, and calls forth in our souls a
perfect little world of mystical and spiritual beauty
and consistency."* Spiritual Infancy is the name
given by mystical writers to a state which the Holy
Ghost operates in certain chosen souls to whom the
Sacred Infancy has been supereminently the subject
of contemplation and the object of devotion. It is
described by them as a state of voluntary humiliation,
which reduces those whom God has led to embrace it
to the condition as it were of children. Its three
great characteristics are a wonderful sense of humiliation and subjection, as respects not only God but
also men; an extraordinary tenderness in what concerns God and spiritual things; and, thirdly, the receiving of sweetnesses and caresses from God similar
to what are lavished on children. These marks were
strikingly exhibited in the Venerable Servant of God
who was raised up in the 17th century, to propagate
devotion to the Holy Childhood, the Carmelite nun,
Marguerite du Saint-Sacrement, and in two saintly
souls upon whom it was divinely ordained that she
should exercise so powerful an influence, that they
may almost in some sense be called her disciples : the
one a priest, M. Olier; the other a layman, the Baron
de Renty. Nor need this appear to us a circumstance
either strange or exceptional. When, in the progress
of His wonderful dealings in His Church, wherein
He has deposited all the treasures of His Revelation,
God has willed at His appointed time to give a fresh
development and impulse to some special devotion,
He has often been pleased, in the first instance, to

* *The Blessed Sacrament*, p. 26.

choose a woman for His instrument, and particularly in these later ages. From the sixteenth century, that dark period of blasphemy and sacrilegious outrage, may be said to date an increased manifestation of the tenderness of Jesus ; what may be called the feminine element in the Sacred Humanity,—an element which is included in the perfect human type,—has been brought with an ever-growing prominence before the mind of the Church. What wonder, then, if it has pleased Him, who has made His Mother the special Mediatrix of His mercy, to select women to take the initiative in the manifestation of the prodigalities of His compassionate love ? What wonder if it please Him to send His sweetest messages by those whom He chose to bring the first tidings of His Resurrection on the Easter morn ? First at His sepulchre with the homage of their loving sorrow, they first heard and were commissioned to repeat those joyful words : "Go, tell My *brethren*, that I ascend to my Father and your Father, to my God and your God." The expansion given to devotion to the Sacred Heart,* to the Adorable Sacrament, and to the Holy Infancy—the second being closely united

* We have not forgotten that P. Eudes, the founder of the Order of our Lady of Refuge and the Congregation of Jesus and Mary, was also a great apostle of devotion to the Sacred Hearts of Jesus and Mary, to which he consecrated his two institutes, and even obtained permission to have a public and solemn office performed in Their honour. This was about thirty years before the Blessed Margaret Mary, the Visitation nun, received a divine commission to spread devotion to the Sacred Heart of Jesus. That the Sacred Heart was honoured before this time cannot be questioned; but neither can it be questioned that she was its first propagator *by a special revelation.*

to the first, and the third having an intimate connection with the second (as Father Faber has so admirably pointed out in the work to which we have already alluded)—has in each case been the fruit of revelations made to women. Not but that men have been their co-operators, and, indeed, have had the largest share in its active promotion ; but the first immediate touch as it were, the first whispered word, has been to the heart of a woman.

Revolutions (observes the compiler of the *Archiconfrérie de la Sainte Enfance*, speaking of the Carmelitess Marguerite du Saint-Sacrement,* have retarded the work of the servant of God, but it has never been suspended. Sister Marguerite herself had foretold that, if it should suffer partial eclipse from evil times, the "King of the Crib" would eventually bring it again to light and cause it to prosper. We seem to be beholding the accomplishment of her prediction, and perhaps we may discern a peculiar opportuneness now, as at its first origin, in the wonderful spread of this devotion. It received its first impulse, as we have said, in the early part of the seventeenth century. France, which seems ever to present an epitome of the Christian world, and to fill in the religious system an office analogous to that of the heart in the human body, lay physically and morally exhausted at the close of the dismal century which had preceded. Faith had become enfeebled by the long course of religious and civil strife through which

* The Association in honour of the Holy Infancy, which owes its origin to Sister Marguerite du Saint-Sacrement, and which was approved by Innocent X. in 1653, and by Alexander VII. in 1661, was raised on December 4th, 1855, by Pius IX. to the rank of an Archconfraternity.

she had passed; society was abandoned to a licentious-
ness of which the court, so peculiarly influential at
that period, gave a shameless example. The provinces,
ravaged by the continual passing and repassing of
armies—and we know how armies victualled themselves in those days — were a scene of frightful desolation. War, famine, pestilence had done their
work; but a greater misery still was the profanation
of holy things and places, the loss of ecclesiastical
order, and that declension in the knowledge and
practice of religion which was the result of all these
combined evils. Corruption had invaded the very
sanctuary; the salt had lost its savour. Suddenly, a
ray of divine mercy beamed on France, and men
beheld a whole generation of Christian souls start, as
it were, into life. The year 1603 seems to mark the
point at which this flow of grace began. St. Teresa
led the way; for this was the date of the introduction
into France of the Carmelite Order, which she had
reformed, by Blessed Mary of the Incarnation
(Madame Acarie), M. de Berulle, and M. de Bretigny.
Twenty-six years later we find forty convents of that
Order in the country; and it is a fact worthy of
notice, that the superioresses of well-nigh every one
of these forty convents are considered worthy of being
candidates for the honours of canonization. In 1610
we have St. Francis de Sales instituting the Order of
the Visitation. In 1611 we see the beginnings of the
Oratory of Jesus founded by Cardinal de Berulle, and
witness the labours of M. Olier, the venerable founder
of St. Sulpice, himself a devout lover of the Infant
Jesus, and to whom also we are indebted for the Life
of Marguerite, which M. Amelote wrote by his
desire. We need but name St. Vincent de Paul, that

apostle of charity, and cannot attempt so much as to
name the many founders of pious institutions, not
priests alone, but holy seculars, both men and women,
who form a very galaxy of sanctity illustrating the
seventeenth century in France.

But the circumstance to which we desire to draw
particular attention is that the special devotion to the
Sacred Infancy, which had so large a share in the
religious regeneration of that country, took its rise
and received its development at a time when every
spirit most opposed to itself was dominant in the land.
To the pride and turbulent habits fostered by war,
was soon to be added all the love of worldly splendour and display, of pleasure, pomp, and prodigality,
which had its focus in the court of the Grand
Monarque. Against all these the simplicity, the
purity, the poverty, the voluntary abnegation of the
Infant Jesus were to contend, drawing hearts to the
love of the very virtues which are naturally least
congenial to the dispositions of an artificial and
depraved state of society; and it was a Carmelite nun
who was to be the first instrument of calling the men
and women of that corrupt and arrogant age to
mingle with the shepherds in adoration round the
manger of Bethlehem, and to learn the simple and
lowly virtues of the House of Nazareth.

With the exception of the Passion, there is no
period of our Saviour's life on earth concerning which
the Gospel has furnished us with such minute details
as the Infancy; and for this there seems to be one
obvious reason which applies to both. The two great
mysteries of the Incarnation and Redemption are in a
special manner exhibited in them. In contemplating
the Infancy and the Passion, the Child Jesus and the

Crucified Jesus, we behold an Incarnate God and a Suffering God. Thus these states proclaim the Man-God and the Divine Redeemer in a manner peculiar to themselves. Accordingly they assume a form of permanence which no other portion of our Lord's life appears so intimately to possess. We listen to Jesus as our Teacher, but we commonly view Him as hanging on the cross, or encircled with Mary's arms. It is there where His Divinity would appear to be more thickly veiled that it is more fully declared and confessed. It is in the stable that He receives divine homage from shepherds and kings, and it is when hanging dead upon the cross that the converted centurion bears witness to Him in words which, while they were a profession of faith, expressed also an act of adoration : " Truly this was the Son of God."

As the two mysteries of the Incarnation and Redemption are closely united,—parts of the same divine scheme, or, rather, the one the condition of the other,—so also devotion to the Passion and devotion to the Sacred Infancy are but varied manifestations of one and the same devotion to the Incarnate God,— God made Man for our salvation. Accordingly we find the two so closely intertwined in the lives of the saints that we cannot separate them, although the one rather than the other may have given its peculiar colouring to the sanctity of each. Bethlehem to the great adorers of the Child Jesus has always been the vestibule of Calvary. So it was with the holy Marguerite, and we find the Divine Spouse of her soul giving her to share alternately the sweetness of the joyful, and the bitterness of the dolorous mysteries. She passed from the Crib to the Cross, and from the Cross back to the Crib ; but it was the

Crib that had led her to the Cross; and it is this
circumstance which specially characterizes the devotion of which we are speaking.

Nowhere were the gifts and graces of the holy Carmelitess more appreciated than at St. Sulpice, which,
through the instrumentality of its holy founder, became
thoroughly penetrated with the devotion she had propagated; and, next to M. Olier, none perhaps had a
larger share in promoting its development than the
subject of the following biography. It was M. de
Renty, indeed, who himself had originally decided the
saintly founder of St. Sulpice to repair to Beaune to
visit the Carmelite nun by whom God was at that
time working such marvels in renewal of devotion to
the Sacred Infancy. This remarkable man was pre-
eminently the disciple of Marguerite. He was already
generally known for the prodigies which his charity
had worked in every corner of France before his relations with Marguerite began. He was the life and
soul of every pious undertaking. A gentleman of
noble birth and ample fortune, a married man, the
father of a family, he had attained to a disengagement
from earthly things which would have been admirable
in a religious, but which in a secular is truly astonishing. In reading the detailed account of his habitual
life, resembling that of an angel more than of a man,
we are led to wonder what more could be added to
him, and to what further degree of perfection it was
possible to attain in the secular state; nevertheless
we learn on his own authority that he was quite
another person after his visit to Beaune. "I was
but as a stone," was his own forcible expression, "before I received help from my sister Marguerite." This
help mainly consisted in leading him to a still closer

union with the Infant Jesus, and, as its peculiar fruit, a still more entire self-denudation.

This self-denudation, this spirit of simple abnegation, which we shall find so strikingly exemplified in the life of this holy man, appears, then, to be one of the leading characteristics of the devotion to the Sacred Infancy. It may, however, be asked, in what does it herein differ from devotion to the Passion, or any other devotion which centres in and draws its spirit from our Incarnate God? Are not these the very essentials of sanctity? and are they not learned at the foot of the Cross as well as in the Stable of Bethlehem? The reply is obvious, and, indeed, is implied in much that has been already said. The devotions are not contrasted, any more than the mysteries of the Nativity and of the Crucifixion are contrasted. They are parts, as has been noticed, of one harmonious whole, like and various at the same time; but a few observations drawn from a letter written by M. de Renty to his director, at the latter's desire, will serve to set the matter in a clearer light. His director had asked this precise question: what he thought of this mystery of the Infancy, and in what its grace consisted? In his reply M. de Renty states that he had recently, while praying in church, been disquieted by a difficulty which occurred to his mind respecting this devotion. The Christian is bound to regard Jesus Christ in His entirety, from His Incarnation to His Ascension to the right hand of His Father, whence He sends down His Holy Spirit upon us; we ought therefore, it would seem, to address ourselves to all these mysteries according to our needs, without attaching ourselves to one especially, since by so acting we appear to dwarf our devotion and limit the extent of divine truths as well as the fulness of grace. Having communicated, and, as usual, cast himself upon God for light, he was inwardly illuminated to behold our Lord in all His mysteries, from His Incarnation to His state of glory; and in particular the greatness and dignity of His Infancy were manifested to him, and how this mystery is the door and the way to our final consummation in glory. It was also shown to him that there is temerity in addressing ourselves of our own movement to any other mystery in the same manner; as, for instance, to ask for crosses, since it is the province of grace to conduct us to them and to sustain us under them; or to petition for Thabor,—in other words, great lights; in fine, that *of ourselves* we must in the first instance seek only the state exhibited in the Infancy, "which places us,"— these are his precise words,—"in ignorance and separation, allowing only such an application to the things of this world as consists in using them simply, according as we need them, or as they are given to us, which keeps us in a great silence, producing a life of death as respects the exterior," while inwardly we are continually making an offering of ourselves, after the pattern of the Soul of our Infant Lord to His Father, to accept with zeal, and love, and obedience all the states through which He has decreed we should pass; and he proceeds to indicate the reason, as it was shown to himself, commenting on the words: "*Semet ipsum exinavivit, formam servi accipiens;*" and those others: "*Factus obediens usque ad mortem,*" * which had forcibly occurred to his mind as furnishing a proof of what he had stated. "They show," he says, "the true

---

* "Emptied Himself, taking the form of a servant." "Becoming obedient unto death." (Phil. ii. 7, 8.)

order of proceeding in Jesus Christ, who in His Infancy reduced Himself to the form of a servant, and
for the rest of His life was obedient unto His Death
upon the Cross, according to the command He received from His Father, and this, not by election and
choice, but by submission and patience." Here, then,
we have the reason for the preference of this holy
man for the Mystery of the Infancy as the way which
for ourselves we ought to choose : he saw that when
Jesus, as the great apostle tells us, annihilated Himself,
it was the Crib He chose, not the Cross. He was conducted to the Cross by obedience. He chose the Crib,
He accepted the Cross to which it led, in order to
teach us to choose this same self-annihilation, and
leave it to God to conduct us, like docile children, into
Egypt, into the desert, to the cross, and finally to
glory. Nowhere, indeed, do we find our Lord speaking
of His own election of the Cross, neither do we meet
with any such expressions concerning Him in Holy
Scripture. "Behold I come to do Thy will": it is
thus that His offering of Himself is prophetically
described. The offering, it is true, includes the Cross,
but it includes it as the fruit of obedience. M. de
Renty accordingly considered that it is safest to follow
our Divine Model ; to *seek* Bethlehem, but allow ourselves to *be led* to Calvary.

Devotion to the Sacred Infancy is also a peculiarly
safe devotion, from the circumstance of its excluding
one great source of illusion, a certain spiritual pride
and presumption, which may possibly creep in and deceive us when carried away by the fervour of our zeal
to embrace crosses in our own strength. For, averse
albeit as is our human nature to suffering, it is also
capable of feeling a strange attraction towards it.

There is to be found in the abasement of crucifying
pains and sorrows an aliment for the subtle pride and
self-seeking of the fleshly heart. Men will secretly
glory in rising superior to that from which their fellow-
creatures generally shrink. We see this disposition
evidenced in the ordinary matters of daily life; it is
very patent; it is not even disavowed; nay, there are
persons who will find a species of satisfaction and consolation in the mere fact of exceptional sufferings, if
they can but get them recognized and appreciated.
The same tendency is to be met with, in a more hidden
form, in the religious affections. Hence it is that we
find a hideous counterpart of the voluntary mortifications of the saints in the self-imposed barbarities of
Pagan devotees. The very Sacrifice of the Cross has
its travesty in many a blood-stained heathen rite, but
the proud heart of the natural man has found no
element to lay hold upon and pervert to its purposes
in the mystery of the Sacred Infancy. Simplicity,
ignorance, and all the helplessness of childhood can
never become objects of ambition. It is not in human
nature to desire to parade the depths of its insignificance and its impotence. Hence there is less room
for self-deception in this devotion than in any other;
for self-deception invariably has its root in self-love,
and self-love can find no support here. Mere *acts* of
humility, it is true, may be dictated by motives not
free from a secret vanity, but the humility inspired by
this devotion is (as Father Surin describes it) an experimental state, in which the soul is placed in an
attitude of humiliation and subjection before God and
men. It does not merely esteem itself to be little;
it feels itself to be little, as does a child, who perhaps
has never made the conscious reflection, and who yet

lives and exists in the atmosphere of its own littleness. We shall find this experimental state exhibited
in a most remarkable degree in the case of M. de
Renty.

Another and a cognate effect of this devotion is the
utter surrender of liberty which it involves, the copy
in spirit of that which is exhibited materially in in-
fants. This surrender is so important a point in the
spiritual life, and is so entirely the condition of the
full carrying out of God's work in the soul, that we
cannot wonder that those who have been most deeply
penetrated with devotion to the Sacred Infancy, as
was the subject of these pages, should have been also
led to the sublimest heights of perfection and to the
closest union with God. The Divine Infant's claims,
although made with such surpassing mildness, are
nevertheless universal, exclusive, imperative. We
embrace Him ; He permits us to do so ; and it is
easier and sweeter to our frailty than to embrace the
Cross ; but then with a gentle despotism he takes
possession of our whole being and draws us on to our
entire crucifixion. If, however, He thus claims our
liberty, He gives Himself in return. P. de Champeaux,
in his *Mois de Marie*, quotes a pretty anecdote related of St. Teresa. Meeting one day in her monastery
a beautiful little child, she questioned him as to who
he was. " I will tell you my name," said the boy, " if
you will tell me yours." " I am Teresa of Jesus,"
said the saint. " Then I am Jesus of Teresa," replied the child, and vanished. Jesus gives Himself
in return for our perfect surrender of self ; and, as it
is His manner to make our dealings with Him a kind
of pattern, wide as must be the difference, of His own
adorable ways with us—according to that promise:

"With the holy man thou wilt be holy, and with the innocent man thou wilt be innocent "*—so it will be observed that the devout adorers of His Infancy have been the subjects of a peculiar class of graces, privileges, and favours, corresponding to the child-like self-renunciations they have made, and to the simple confiding affection with which they have embraced and dedicated themselves to their Infant God.

We have already noticed the close connection which subsists between devotion to the Sacred Infancy and devotion to the Blessed Sacrament, and this is the last characteristic to which we shall briefly make allusion. Father Faber, in his work on the Blessed Sacrament, has abundantly demonstrated this fact, and has indicated the reasons, and drawn out at length the analogy between them. The language of the Church in her ritual (as he points out) bears witness to this near connection, as any one may see by looking at the hymns and offices for Corpus Christi, and by noticing that there is no special Preface for that festival; the one appointed for the Nativity being common to both, as if equally applicable to the two. "Passing," he says, "from the conduct of the Church to the interior life of her children, we find the two devotions to the Blessed Sacrament and the Holy Infancy constantly united and connected, as it were, naturally together. With certain differences, the one seems to produce the same spiritual fruits as the other, to suggest corresponding devout exercises, and to lead to the same ascetical practices."† And then he proceeds to instance Sister Marguerite of the Blessed Sacrament, "whom God raised up to give such an

* Psalm xvii. 26.   † P. 145.

impulse and fresh extension to the devotion to the
Sacred Infancy." Our Lord Himself (he adds) seems
to point out this connection by the manner in which
He has vouchsafed to appear to saints and other holy
persons in the Blessed Sacrament, which, with rare
exceptions, has been so uniformly under the appearance of an infant. Nevertheless the Blessed Sacrament was instituted to commemorate, not the Infancy,
but the Passion, of our Lord. " The time and circumstances of its first institution," says the same writer,
" leave no doubt whatever upon the subject, even
independently of the positive precept of commemora-
ting the Passion thereby. The Mass is itself externally
a sort of drama of the Passion, and internally it is the
identical Sacrifice perpetually and bloodlessly renewed.
Yet, on the most superficial consideration of the
matter, we cannot avoid being struck by the obvious
analogies between the Blessed Sacrament and the
Sacred Infancy; and when we come to examine it
fully, we arrive at the conclusion, that while the
spirit of the Sacrifice is the spirit of Calvary, the
spirit of the Sacrament is the spirit of Bethlehem ;
and the whole character of the devotion resembles,
as closely as two devotions can resemble each other,
the Devotion to the Sacred Infancy." * Jesus in the
manger foreshadows, in every the minutest detail, Jesus
on the altar. This fact cannot but be obvious to all ;
but the more closely it is meditated upon, the more
deeply and fully will it be evidenced to the mind. The
two devotions, it will also be observed, considered
doctrinally, have one and the same special object, the
Sacred Humanity of our Lord—God Incarnate, God

* *Ib.*, p. 144.

abasing Himself to take human flesh and become a
little child, that He might unite our nature to His own,
and again descending to a still lower depth, when He
veils alike His Humanity and His Divinity under
the accidents of bread and wine, that He may become
our food.   Both devotions, in fine, have the wonders
and condescensions of the Incarnation in all its diver-
sified aspects as the peculiar object of their contemplation and loving adoration.   What wonder, then, if
they should seem to blend, as it were, into one, and
should mould the minds which cultivate them to a
similar type!

PART I.

PERFECT CONVERSION.

CHAPTER I.

THE EARLY YEARS OF GASTON DE RENTY.

THE Baron de Renty's family was one of the most ancient in Artois, and had gained additional lustre by the great matrimonial alliances which it had contracted, the honourable offices which at different times had been held by its members, and the heroism of not a few of them on the battle-field. But in the record of one who possessed a title to nobility of a far higher order than any which pedigree could confer, it is more interesting to learn that piety had been a distinguishing characteristic of many of his ancestors; one of whom, named Wambert, in very early times, had won for himself by his charitable deeds the appellation of " the good Count of Renty." He and Hamburge, his wife, bequeathed to posterity a standing testimony of their love of God, in a monastery founded and richly endowed by them, under the name and patronage of St. Denis, and in three other churches which they also built—the first dedicated to St. Peter, the second to St. Martin, and the third to St. Wast. The spirit of this good couple was to revive conspicuously in their descendant.

Gaston de Renty was the only son of Charles de

c 2

Renty and of Madeleine de Pastoureau, who, on the maternal side, was also allied by blood with the house of Renty.   He was born at the château of Bény, in Lower Normandy, in the diocese of Bayeux, in the year 1611 ; and Providence so ordained it that he, who was to be so devoted a friend of the poor and so ardent a lover of poverty, should be held by poor people at the baptismal font.   His biographer does not explain the reason, but it was, no doubt, an act of piety on the part of his parents.   Indeed, there seems reason to believe that it was not an unusual practice with devout parents in France, particularly when we meet with an instance of it in comparatively modern times ; for we find it recorded in the Life of the admirable Madame de Montagu, that the Duchesse d'Ayen, who was afterwards to be one of the victims of the guillotine, had, in the days of her prosperity, diligently sought out a pious beggar-woman to stand godmother to her little girl.   In each case the act seems to have brought down a blessing upon the child, and in particular the grace of a most intense and self-sacrificing love for Christ's poor.   The infant received the name of Gaston, and afterwards, in Confirmation, took in addition that of Jean-Baptiste.

The first seven years of his life were spent in the place of his birth; his mother then took him to Paris, and kept him at home with her for two more years : after which he was sent to the college of Navarre, and was subsequently removed by his parents to the Jesuit college at Caen, probably in order to have him near them on their return to their château.   Here he had an ecclesiastical preceptor, and, as was usual in those times, was placed besides under the charge of a governor.   The choice of this

latter was an unfortunate one, and might have had
most disastrous consequences. He was a heretic, a
concealed one, we presume, or he would never have
been selected for such a trust, and was as corrupt in
morals as in faith. But God, who designed to make
him an instrument of His glory, shielded young
Gaston from the poison of contamination, giving him
His powerful assistance to repel temptation. On this
point we are not left to conjecture, for M. de Renty,
in after years, affirmed that he had received great
graces from his earliest childhood ; so that he might,
with David, say that God had been his helper from
his mother's womb.* He had very good natural
abilities, quickness of intellect, much application, and
an excellent judgment, so that he made rapid progress, and took a high stand amongst his fellow-
students. He was not, however, left to complete his
course of education at Caen, but was sent, at the age
of seventeen, to an academy at Paris, where he also
distinguished himself in all branches, but evinced a
special turn for mathematics. In order that he might
give particular attention to this favourite science,
without neglecting his other studies, he denied himself those amusements which have usually so great
a charm for youth, and attained to such proficiency as
even to compose some original treatises on the subject.
Besides economizing the time which he might have
given to amusement, he saved the money which
would have been thus profitlessly expended, and
devoted it to the purchase of books to assist him in
his mathematical and other kindred pursuits. Whatever he did he did with all the energy of a mind

* Psalm xxi. 10, 11.

capable of strong exertion, and with that resolution and perseverance of will which was one of his marked characteristics.

To such as correspond with the leadings of God's Spirit, and in proportion as they correspond, all the little apparent casual incidents of life, and the thousand circumstances which are continually arising, or into which their tastes may lead them, form a sequence of providential graces, or, rather, bring offers of grace; and happy the soul that understands and accepts them as they successively present themselves : the events of each day become so many golden steps on the heavenward ladder, just as to those who blindly follow the suggestions of mere nature and of their earthly desires, who never listen to the whispers of the Divine voice, all with which they are brought into contact, and every passing daily encounter, become so many lures and bribes of the evil one, pitfalls and snares of Satan ; so that the miserable soul, contemplating its degradation in after years, will accuse, as the cause of its own hard lot, the circumstances, the friends, the position, the inevitable temptations to which it was cruelly exposed ; thus virtually arraigning the Providence of the Most High as the author of its ruin. Yet out of the same or similar materials, with a better will, saints have been formed.

This good will Gaston de Renty eminently possessed. Now it happened one day that the bookseller whose shop he frequented for the purpose of making the purchases of which we have spoken, offered him the "Imitation of Christ," begging him to read it. Gaston, whose attention at that moment was engrossed by some other subject connected with his studies, scarcely gave heed to what was said to him ;

his mind was elsewhere. But there was a great offer of grace lying hid in this little book, and it pleased God that he should not lose it through accidental inattention. On another occasion the bookseller, after laying before him several works for which he had asked, again presented him with the " Imitation of Christ," this time not merely recommending, but pressing him to read it. The young man now consented, and took the book home with him. Perhaps no uninspired work has been so fruitful in vocations to perfection, as that same little work of one who has left no name on earth ; and, in Gaston de Renty's case, its words fell on a good soil, one of that blessed kind which brings forth the hundredfold. In him faith had always been strong, as we have seen, and it had been his constant desire from his earliest childhood to keep God's commandments and serve Him faithfully ; but with the perusal of the " Imitation " his eyes seemed to open to a new appreciation of the value of heavenly things. It was like a fresh Revelation. He now perceived that God deserved not alone to be the first object of a Christian's aims, but was alone worthy to be so ; and in the light of this discovery a new order of thoughts and affections was simultaneously taking possession of him. This is the first step in the road of perfection, the desire of living for God alone. Hitherto he had desired to live blamelessly and to please God, but he had desired other things besides, although in a subordinate degree, with all the strong energy of his nature ; now all that energy is to be concentrated into one focus, and nothing henceforth, however good, however noble, however useful, is to be sought or desired for its own sake. All for God, and God in all.

We are not surprised to find that the immediate effect of this thorough conversion was to kindle in the heart of young Gaston a wish to leave the world that he might devote himself wholly to God. The world is seen by those whose souls have been thus newly enlightened as so utterly opposed to God, and life in its vortex so beset with difficulties and temptations, that it is no wonder if the first movement should be a strong desire to turn their backs on God's enemy altogether, and retire to be alone with Him whom they have chosen for their portion. Accordingly, a wish to enter religion has been very common among aspirants to high perfection, in regard to whom, as their after-career has proved, God had other designs. He allows them, however, doubtless for their greater merit, to entertain the will to make a complete and irrevocable holocaust of themselves, by embracing a life which not only aims at perfection, but engages by vow to the observance of its counsels. In young De Renty's case, this wish was not the result of a mere passing fervour. If his fervour prompted the wish, his reason weighed and tested it; nay, he has himself told us that he resisted and fought against it for a considerable time. He appears to have been about seventeen years of age when he felt himself thus drawn to give himself to God in religion, his preference leaning to the Carthusian order; but, as the reader will anticipate, great obstacles stood between such a desire and its accomplishment. Parents are seldom willing to part with an only son, and in this case it was question of an only child, the heir to a large property, one, too, who gave promise of talents likely to lead to high worldly distinction. Doubtless, Gaston knew well that his parents were

certain to offer no exception to a too general rule ;
neither did he make any attempt to obtain what
he was convinced would be refused.

His resolution, however, remained unmoved ; firmness was one of his prominent qualities; and,
believing as he did that the step he was meditating
was pleasing to God, at the end of two years he
decided upon putting his purpose into execution.
Whether he admitted any one into his counsels we
are not told ; but we may infer with probability that
he took the whole responsibility upon himself of
an act which was sure to excite his father's serious
displeasure. One December day, then, in the year
1630, when crossing the Pont Notre Dame in the
company of his mother, [he requested her to set him
down, as there was something he desired to buy. The
purchase he wished to make was that of the pearl of
great price, but she, thinking her son only wanted to
go into some neighbouring shop, readily suffered him
to alight from the carriage. Profiting by the first
turn that removed him from her sight, he threaded
the streets of the capital with all speed, until he
emerged into the country, and took his way, still on
foot, to Notre Dame des Ardilliers, at Saumur. On
the road he exchanged his dress, trimmed with gold
lace, after the fashion of the nobles of the time, for
that of a poor man ; and a few days after his father
received the following letter from him. It is valuable
as giving an insight into the character of his mind
and the motives which had led to his resolution. The
strong love of God which animated him, and the
detestation which his pure soul felt of all which is
opposed to that love, are revealed in every line :—

"Sir,

"I am well aware that the change I have made will give you pain, first movements being beyond our control, and nature herself prompting us to regret the loss of what we love. But since it is here question of God, I most humbly entreat you to discard all passion from your soul, and to consider calmly what comes from Him. And that is, Sir, that having struggled for two years against myself, and resisted all the inspirations which God gave me during all that time, I have been at last constrained to break through this long delay and to quit the world, confessing that I have not strength equal to the attempt of saving my soul where the contrary to what I fain would do is practised. Such a state is too perilous for one who is weak, and desires to walk safely; wherefore I have judged that it was better to stifle evil in its beginnings than to wait till it had waxed stronger, and then perhaps to find myself unable to cope with it. For the maxims of the world are so different from those of Jesus Christ, that I do not believe that a soul which is fearful of offending Him could live there long, particularly at court, without feeling compelled to abandon it, beholding itself obliged to countenance by its presence all those things which are the result of its corruption, and which it would not become me to specify, since my design is for the future rather to bury in oblivion all these follies than to endeavour to recall them to mind. I wish to escape from this entanglement, although I know that people will say that I might very well live in the world and refrain from doing such evil things as are done there. This I acknowledge; but see what would follow : one must make up one's mind to be the talk of a set of fashionable gentlemen, who will call one a bigot, a clown, a man who wants for wit and conversation, whom everybody feels to be a bore, and a thousand other things of which I have already had too much experience. And, indeed, it would be a good joke to see a young man like me go to court and attempt to play the reformer : would you not, Sir, be the first to ridicule such conduct ? I beg you, then, to reflect what a mortification it would be to a father to see his son at court and in the midst of society only to become a laughing-stock. Not but that a good conscience would esteem it a high honour to suffer all these things for God ; yet I believe that I shall contribute more to your satisfaction by withdrawing ; for at court one must live as people live at court, and, as I cannot serve two masters, I conclude, in accordance with the Gospel, that he who would serve God must follow Him.

"I have ever observed this practice prevail in the world, that when your friend has a quarrel with any one, not only do you not go and offer your services to his adversary, but you also avoid his company : so, in like manner, God and the world being at enmity with each other, I should believe that I committed a very great offence were I not to do for God what I should certainly do for a friend, a mere mortal man. Besides, when we love anything, we do not go and seek out its opposite. Now, the means of avoiding sin is to fly from its occasions ; and are we for the sake of a miserable vanity which prompts us to put ourselves forward and get talked about, to run the risk of losing our soul ? No, no ; and those who now think otherwise will see things very differently when they have to give account to God of their past lives : then truly will they understand what it is to live well or to live ill ; but it will be too late. Wherefore, leaving the dead to bury their dead, let us, if we have been vouchsafed a little light, labour to reform our life, and to do something for the love of God, who has so expressly and so often said that we must renounce ourselves, leave all, and follow Him, that I do not believe you would willingly controvert it.

"You have been the cause of my delay, and my prayers have all this time been directed to prepare for this separation, dreading much your affliction, which nevertheless will soon be moderated, when you reflect that God does all for the best, and that He has perhaps sent you this tribulation to work some good effect.

"Leaving all this to His secret judgments, I entreat you to believe that I shall be able to serve you at the least as well in this new profession as in the one for which you designed me. May God give me grace to do so. I do not as yet send you word where I am, fearing lest passion might impel you at first to come and seek me ; but after a while, when I shall know how matters stand, I will not fail to apprise you. In the meantime I shall pray without ceasing Him whom I have resolved to serve, to be with you, and to convince you with what affection I am,

"SIR,

"Your very humble son and very obedient servant,

"GASTON DE RENTY."

The young man had not in prospect overrated the sorrow of his father, who had no sooner received this letter, which dashed all his fondest hopes to the ground, than he despatched servants in every direction

in quest of the fugitive. God permitted their search
to be successful; and, notwithstanding his disguise,
Gaston was recognized at Amboise, and brought back
to his parents. As much is said of his father's grief,
but no mention is made of his anger, we may conclude
that he did not behave with severity to his son, and
that, satisfied with having recovered him, he spared
reproaches and limited himself to precautions. These
precautions appear to have consisted in taking him
away from Paris to his own château of Bény, where
he would be more under the paternal eye, and, what
was regarded as of no less importance, would be
removed from scenes which had helped to excite or
encourage in him a repugnance to the world and a
distaste for secular life. It does not appear that
Gaston made any attempt to obtain his father's consent to his embracing the religious state, either
because he saw the futility of any such endeavour
for the present or that divine grace at once prompted
him to recognize the intervention of Providence in
the defeat of his design. The high perfection which
he afterwards attained in the world utterly precludes
the idea that he stifled the voice of conscience in
compliance with the will of his father. When saints
or saintly persons have renounced an apparent vocation to religion out of consideration for the wishes of
parents, it is certain that they have done so in
obedience to God's will, clearly brought home to them
in some manner, never as putting filial obedience
before fidelity to the call of their God. They have
given up that higher vocation for the very same
reason that others have pertinaciously adhered to their
resolve, either wearying out the paternal opposition
by a holy obstinacy, as did Aloysius Gonzaga, or

braving it with a generous courage, like Stanislas
Kostka. The thought may, however, occur to some :
if Gaston was mistaken in supposing that God intended him for the religious life, what are we to think
of those inspirations which, he asserted to his father,
had pursued him for the last two years, and which
had prevailed over all his counter-struggles ? Were
these pure imaginations ? Such an idea would be
extremely distressing, for young Gaston was no hot-
headed enthusiast, likely to mistake his own ardent
desires for divine movements, while there can be no
doubt, from the seriousness of his character, and
especially from the profound effect which the perusal
of the " Imitation " had worked in him, that he made
the subject of his vocation in life the matter of
persevering prayer. The reply to this difficulty is
not far to seek. God does not always will to reveal
the whole of His designs at once. He was leading
this young soul to aspire to a life of very great perfection : this, we may believe, was the meaning and
import of the inspirations. Gaston's own conclusion,
and a very natural one we must consider it, was that
such perfection was unattainable or most difficult of
attainment in the corrupt atmosphere which surrounded him. His love of God and his humility both
combined therefore to produce the resolution to which
he came, and which, no doubt, was permitted by God,
as we have already intimated, in order that he might
have the merit in desire of a life to which he was not
to be called.

Gaston's father seems to have behaved prudently
in giving employment to his talents, which were of a
highly practical character; bringing him forward thus
early to take that share in public life, in his native

province, to which his birth and position entitled
him. Those were days in which the Provinces
enjoyed their local administration, instead of being
ruled by the *préfets* and *employés* of a central govern-
ment. A useful career was thus open to such members
of the *noblesse* as had the wisdom to prefer an honourable career of this sort before the miserable attractions
of a corrupt court. Young De Renty's merits were
so conspicuous, that at the age of nineteen, and therefore not long after his return to Bény with his father,
he was chosen as deputy of the *noblesse* from the
Bailliage of Vire to the States of Normandy, held at
Rouen, and presided over at that time by M. de
Longueville. Here, notwithstanding his youth, he
was by no means an inactive member. He spoke
upon several occasions, and so much to the point, that,
we are told, the Three Estates were surprised at the
prudence and knowledge of business manifested by so
young a man.

His father seems also to have been liberal to his
son in the matter of pecuniary allowance; for we
find Gaston, after his return from attendance at the
States, busied in rebuilding the church of Bény.
His own economy, moreover, made the most of the
money with which he was supplied; for none of it
was lavished upon those expensive diversions in which
the nobility of his time indulged,—entailing an outlay
in dress alone which, in these days of more simple
attire (we speak of course only of that of men), seems
quite incredible. Young De Renty's time was as well
economized as his money, and for the same object,
in order to give it to God. Every morning he rose
punctually at four o'clock, and repaired quietly to his
own private room, without rousing his valet (for

nobles of that day had usually a personal attendant sleeping in their ante-room), for the purpose of performing his devotions. After an hour's prayer, he went to Mass at the church, after which he remained until seven or eight o'clock in the evening with his workmen, superintending and joining in their work ; for, not contented with giving his money and his time, he contributed largely in personal labour to the rearing of the sacred edifice. He even caused his meals to be brought to him on the spot, in order to avoid all interruption. No one can doubt but that the zeal with which the young man applied himself to this good work procured for him many and great graces. In these and similar occupations the next four years of his life were passed. But, admirable as was the tenour of a life thus spent, at an age so prone to thoughtlessness, so fond of excitement, we see here but the merest beginnings: only the foundation-stone of the edifice of grace which was to be reared in this chosen soul was as yet laid.

CHAPTER II.

De Renty's Marriage and Military Career.

Although God designed to raise Gaston de Renty to one of the highest grades of perfection, yet He had not destined him for the most perfect state. Christian marriage is a holy state, but the religious life, for which we have witnessed his earliest aspirations, is far superior. Nevertheless, for each individual that

state is the best to which God calls him, seeing
that our perfection consists not in the excellency
of the state which we have embraced, but in our own
perfect conformity to the Divine will, and the excellency with which we acquit ourselves in the station
which He wills us to fill.   M. de Renty, so far from
entertaining any misgiving as to whether God willed
that he should remain in the world and enter the
married state, was heard frequently to declare that he
had an amount of certainty in the matter which left
him no room for doubt.   Yet, though God designed
that he should live in the world, we cannot fail to
see that it was for the express purpose of giving it
the benefit of his shining example.   Moreover, layman as he was, he was to co-operate in the great work
of spiritual renovation carried on in France in the
first half of the seventeenth century by holy ecclesiastics and religious ; nay, he was to have no small
share in the direction of souls in the paths of holiness : such share at least as it is competent to a
layman to take.

But first he was to give, as we have said, a shining
example of the exercise of virtue to a corrupt world,
and in the midst of its opposing influences.   Those
were days when, not only vice flourished in high
places, but the very fountain-head of virtue was
tainted by the general sanction given to evil principles ; the maxims of the world being allowed so
completely to override those of the Gospel as in
frequent cases to make an heroic effort necessary, if a
man, and especially a gentleman, would be faithful to
his Christian profession.   Courage of another sort
abounded, but courage in the cause of God was rare.
Gaston de Renty was to manifest this higher, this

D

sublime valour. Accordingly, in the next five years
of his life—that is, from the age of twenty-two to
that of twenty-seven, when he was to be called to
a still more exalted stage of holiness, and a special
character of grace was to be manifested in him—he
may be viewed as peculiarly set forth for a model to
the Christian man and gentleman in ordinary life ; to
the married, and to the members of secular professions, and even of that which might seem most
ill-suited for the display of the milder and sweeter
of Christian graces, the profession of arms.   In these
states of life Gaston de Renty exhibits a pattern, the
significance and practical application of which there
is no evading. Afterwards he was raised to what
people, considering it as an exceptional state (which
in degree doubtless it was), would be apt to regard as
simply admirable, but unattainable, and therefore not
imitable; so cunning are we, through the sloth of our
natures and the suggestions of the enemy of all goodness, to escape from any inference which may result
in a call on our exertions. We have a trick of
canonizing, so to say, whatever rises above a certain
level, and then of tacitly pronouncing it to have
no practical bearing whatsoever on our own behaviour. Thus the evil one contrives to neutralize
the beautiful example which God's peculiar servants
were intended to present to us, converting our regard
of them into a mere barren admiration. Upon the
futility of such subterfuges of spiritual sloth we may
have occasion to remark by-and-by : meanwhile thus
much may be allowed, that a description of one who
is walking in the higher paths of grace, and is raised
to the sublimer degrees of sanctity, will naturally

have most attraction, and come home with most
profit, to those who are enamoured, be it only as
yet slightly, of the heights, and sigh for the keen
pure air of the mountain-tops.   For the present we
must pause awhile in the valley, to contemplate the
generous beginnings of this great soul.

At the age of twenty-two, Gaston de Renty was
united in marriage with Elisabeth de Balsac, of
the house of Entraigues, daughter of M. de Dunes,
Count of Graville.   She was a lady of great virtue,
and she cordially co-operated with her husband in
many of the good works which he undertook ; but
this is, unfortunately, pretty well all that we have to
tell of her.   She survived M. de Renty, and was still
living when Saint-Jure, our chief authority, wrote
his life.   He refrained, therefore, as he himself alleges,
from saying more of her through respect for her
modesty, leaving her the greater merit for her good
deeds before God, as she should receive the less praise
from men.   Saint-Jure wrote his biography while many
yet lived whom he would naturally have mentioned
in connection with M. de Renty, and for this reason,
he often fails us where we should have been glad
to have more details, which he would have been
so well able to supply.   But when we remember,
on the other hand, that the interest attaching to
M. de Renty's life mainly centres in his personal
sanctity, and that Saint-Jure had an intimate knowledge of that interior in which so many marvels took
place, we must consider that our gain is greater than
our loss.   The price we pay in the shape of omissions
and suppressions is slight compared to the revelations which he alone could make, and which he freely

makes. If we have a history less full, we have a
more perfect portrait; and it is in that light chiefly
that we must regard the biography of this holy man.

M. de Renty's life in the world, for the five
years of which we are now speaking, was not marked
by any singularity, save what was unfortunately at
that time a singularity, that of a young, rich, and
gifted nobleman behaving with consummate prudence,
discretion, and modesty upon all occasions, and refraining from all that not only was sinful, but might
ever so remotely prove the occasion of sin. Nevertheless, no austerity marked his behaviour. He
interested himself in all such pursuits as were good,
noble, and becoming in his station; paying whatever
visits civility demanded of him, never betraying an
unsociable temper, but acquitting himself of these
debts of Christian courtesy in a cheerful and cordial
manner, not as though he were going through a piece
of necessary formality or discharging an uncongenial
obligation. His charity was too pure, and his watchfulness over motives too strict, to allow him to fall
into a temptation of this nature—a temptation which
is apt to assail beginners in a devout life, and which
is sometimes not easy to detect, because it masks
itself under the disguise of that just hatred of the
world and distaste for its ways and its spirit which
must accompany a genuine love of God, and in
the absence of which no true aspiration after perfection can exist in the soul. His gentleness, his
modesty, and his cheerfulness recommended him to
all who were brought into his society; add to which,
he had a certain facility and wit in repartee, which
made his company highly agreeable. This harmless
gaiety, this " seasoning of salt " in his conversation,

of which the Apostle speaks, was all that remained in
him of a strong turn for satire and irony, which, combined with a disposition by nature somewhat prone to
haughtiness, had often led him to indulge in a vein of
raillery, a tendency so difficult to curb or restrain
within the limits of Christian charity.   Grace had
now subdued in him those undisciplined movements,
and taught him to prune away the evil shoots of
nature.   The intellectual gift, however, still was his,
and its legitimate use enlivened his conversation, and
gave point and grace to his remarks.   The king,
Louis XIII., evinced much partiality and a high
esteem for him.   That monarch, who made such a
poor figure on the throne, was possessed nevertheless
of certain virtues, and had higher aspirations than he
had force of character to follow.   Amongst the kings
of the houses of Valois and Bourbon who had preceded and were to come after him on the throne
of France—from that picturesque royal profligate,
Francis I. (the epithet " chivalrous " is degraded by
being applied to him) down to the contemptible
Louis XV., who contrived to wear out the loyalty of
the once most loyal nation of Europe—he stands
almost alone in his respect for purity ; and, whatever
were his faults and deficiencies (and, it must be confessed, they were many), he at least did not dishonour
his high position by immorality, or help on the
deepening corruption of the age by his own personal
vices.   It was perhaps this instinctive leaning of the
monarch to virtue, which in some respects he practised, and which he still loved in its ideal, where
he had not the resolution to aim at it in his conduct,
which caused him to feel an attraction to the pure
and high-minded De Renty, as much as the charms of

the young nobleman's conversation. Louis must have manifested this preference in some marked degree, for the favour shown to him excited the envy of certain courtiers, who, with the meanness of their race, began to watch the object of royal notice very closely, in the hope of detecting something which might furnish an occasion for lowering his credit; but all was so simple, so straightforward, so irreproachable in him, that they were unable after all to find fault with anything but his youth.

The source of M. de Renty's steadfastness in virtue, whilst breathing the unhealthy atmosphere of a court, is to be sought, not in his own firmness of purpose and rectitude of principle, great as these were, but in what may avail and has availed to strengthen even the feeblest,—prayer and the frequentation of the sacraments. Besides acquitting himself with the strictest punctuality of all his Christian duties, he added many voluntary acts and practices of devotion; and, in particular, he was in the habit of saying the Office of Our Lady, often adding that of the Dead, besides other vocal prayers.

But it was not at the court only that he gave this edifying and very exceptional example; his demeanour in the camp was no less admirable. In those days every noble wore a sword, not merely as an honourable appendage, the badge and privilege of his rank, but as a testimony of what was esteemed the chief obligation of nobility, to do battle in the cause and at the summons of his sovereign. Hence the nobles were all military by profession, if all did not actually serve. The policy of Richelieu, Louis' minister, but virtually ruler in his name, which aimed at humbling the house of Austria, had embarked France at that time in a

war which furnishes some of the least creditable pages
in her annals. What has been mildly called "the
policy of equilibrium," of which Richelieu was one of
the great initiators (although it must be confessed that,
like other politicians of his class, he was not by any
means undesirous that the balance should incline in
favour of his own country), overrode in that statesman's mind all other considerations, however just and
weighty ; nay, it seemed to supersede the necessity of
taking them into account.   A selfish policy has been
at all periods too much the mainspring of the conduct
of rulers : ambition is no new passion, and a greed for
territorial aggrandisement no new form of covetousness. Such have very commonly been the causes which
in all ages have led to war.   Still honourable exceptions are to be met with in earlier European history.
The Crusades, for instance, bear witness to the exist-
ence and recognition of loftier aims ; and we shall
observe the same regard and homage paid to superior
motives prevailing in other national undertakings : for
instance, in voyages of discovery, and plans for colo-
nization and conquest, we find the planting of the
Cross and the spread of the Gospel put forward as the
incentive to enterprise, where now we should hear only
of the opening out of commercial prospects and other
temporal objects.   Not that the practice by any means
came up to the profession ; but at any rate the standard of action was maintained at a higher level, and,
above all, it was Christian principle which was thus
upheld and honoured.   It was reserved for these last
centuries to abandon the Christian basis of policy
altogether, in order to erect a low motive of expediency
in its room ; and no one lent his influence more
strongly to this lamentable substitution (although he

did not invent it) than the famous Cardinal Richelieu.
The Thirty Years' War was raging in Germany, and,
to compass his object of lowering the preponderance
of a formidable neighbour, this prince of the Church
had not scrupled to ally himself with the Protestant
princes of the Empire and with the Lutheran Swedes
against Catholic Austria. France, however, did not
intervene directly in the conflict until 1635, when
Richelieu considered that she had gained sufficient
strength to take an actively hostile part. Spain was
Austria's right hand ; and hence a great jealousy had
long subsisted between that power and France, notwithstanding the family tie which connected them.
With Spain, accordingly, Richelieu picked a quarrel :
no difficult matter, considering the hollowness of the
peace between the two countries. This was the first
systematic war (so to call it) on which France had ever
been launched, a war which necessitated operations on
a large scale, and a regular plan of campaign. The
Imperialists had to be dealt with as well as the
Spaniards. No less than four armies, therefore, had
to be equipped to act on four different points : on the
Scheldt, on the Rhine, at the foot of the Alps, and
at that of the Pyrenees.

It was in the second of these armies that Gaston de
Renty served. What were his views and his reflections upon the policy which had entailed this rupture
we know not. Probably the war was simply to him
a fact. He was not called by either his position or
his inclination to be a politician ; and those were not
days of journalism, which now forces the great as well
as little questions of the hour on the attention of all
indiscriminately, whether competent or not to have
an opinion. It had pleased the monarch, or him at

least whose dictation Louis followed, to go to war with Spain and Austria, and his sword was at his king's disposal. But whether or no he had formed any judgment of his own upon the merits of the question, or upon the steps which had brought France into a situation which led her to make common cause with the enemies of Catholicism, De Renty must certainly have had a very strong opinion with respect to the manner in which the miserable conflict had been, and still continued to be, conducted by those with whom he was now compelled to act. In order to attach to his party Bernard, Duke of Weimar, the most able of the generals who had been formed under Gustavus Adolphus, Louis XIII., at Richelieu's instigation, engaged to pay him during the war a large yearly subsidy, and had added the further bribe of the possession of Alsace, which he was to hold with the title of Landgrave, along with all the rights which had appertained to the house of Austria over that province. The duke accordingly hoped, by the aid of France, and in payment for the support which his arms afforded in the strife with Austria, eventually to erect into an independent state for himself the whole of the dominions of the Duke of Lorraine, from which France had ejected that prince, some years previously, on the ground that he had broken his pledge of neutrality and joined the Imperialists in the defence of Catholic Germany against its Lutheran invaders. The miseries to which unhappy Lorraine was a prey during a succession of years have been described by the pen of Protestant as well as Catholic writers, and it does not lie within the scope of the present work to enlarge upon this topic. Suffice it to say, that the picture presented baffles all that has been narrated of the horrors of war even in those pitiless days, when it did not enter into the idea of a commander to spare, as far as possible, the inoffensive and unarmed population of an enemy's country the inflictions which war brings in its train : so far from this, armies systematically plundered, when they did no worse, wherever they passed. Amongst the ruthless commanders who figured in the Thirty Years' War, none has earned a worse reputation than Bernard of Weimar; and it must have deeply pained the soul of De Renty to witness the desolation and misery which his troops inflicted on the regions cursed by their presence or passage. No great forbearance was probably exercised by the French army which co-operated with that general, and to which De Renty was attached; for it was the custom, as we have just observed, in those times, for troops to live pretty much at free quarters when they took the field. This Christian soldier saw the matter in a very different light : no custom, no practice, no precedent, could efface in his mind the essential laws of justice and humanity; and he deserves, therefore, the more commendation for a behaviour which was neither enforced upon him by superiors nor encouraged by their example.

Upon De Renty's talents for the profession of arms we shall not stop to dilate; but we may just observe that his aptitude for all military operations was so remarkable as to attract the attention of the leaders. He had, in fact, made military tactics a special subject of study; so that when councils of war were held, the most experienced captains, amongst whom must be reckoned Duke Bernard of Weimar, whose genius for war was indisputable, expressed their admiration at the knowledge of the profession evinced in the observations he made,—a knowledge truly surprising in so young a man, who besides was making his first campaign. Nor was the science he displayed in council merely theoretical; it was also practically manifested in the field. He foresaw everything; he provided for everything; uniting to considerable bodily strength and great vigour a wonderful activity of mind. These gifts never betrayed him into impetuosity or indiscretion, but were always held in check by a consummate prudence. His spirit was both generous and resolute, and he knew no fear save the fear of offending God,— a fear which nerves the soul against all other perils. But it is more to our purpose to speak of his humanity than of his talents or courage. What was to others a school for the unlearning of every Christian, nay, of every natural, feeling of compassion, was to him a provocative of their greater development. To De Renty might be applied what the Poet of the Lakes sings of the character of the " Happy Warrior " :—

> " Who, doomed to go in company with Pain,
> And Fear, and Bloodshed, miserable train !
> Turns his necessity to glorious gain ;
> In face of these doth exercise a power
> Which is our human nature's highest dower ;
> Controls them and subdues, transmutes, bereaves
> Of their bad influence, and their good receives :
> By objects, which might force the soul to abate
> Her feeling, rendered more compassionate ;
> Is placable—because occasions rise
> So often that demand such sacrifice ;
> More skilful in self-knowledge, even more pure,
> As tempted more ; more able to endure,
> As more exposed to suffering and distress ;
> Thence, also, more alive to tenderness." *

An instance has been preserved in which God rewarded De Renty's kindness by a special deliverance.

* Wordsworth, *Poems of Sentiment and Reflection.*

During the war in Lorraine he commanded a company
of above two hundred horsemen, sixty of whom were
gentlemen of noble birth. On their march they arrived
upon one occasion at two o'clock in the morning at a
village, which they found entirely deserted by the terri-
fied inhabitants. The houses were all empty, so each
had to establish and provide for himself as best he might.
It so happened that the tenement which De Renty
chose for his night's lodging formed an exception to
the rest of these abandoned homes, in that it was
found to contain one solitary individual, a poor old
woman. She was in a dying condition, the result partly
of starvation, partly of illness, and had therefore been
unable to accompany the fugitives. De Renty, full of
the tenderest compassion for this suffering creature,
aided her both spiritually and corporally in this her
last extremity. He watched over her as a son might
have done over an expiring mother ; he fed her, he
comforted her, and, when she had revived a little, he
helped her to the best of his power to make a good
and Christian death.   The poor creature was so
touched by this unexpected charity, that it moved her
to an act of gratitude ; she asked her benefactor if he
belonged to the king's troops or to those of the Duke
of Lorraine.   He, ignorant of her motive, cautiously
asked her why she made this inquiry ; to which she
rejoined, that if he belonged to the king's army he
had better not tarry there long, for the Croats would
certainly arrive in a few hours and cut them to pieces.
De Renty communicated this piece of information to
his fellow-officers, and all thought it most prudent to
get into the saddle again, tired as they were, and
quietly retire on the main body.   It was well they
took this precaution, for three hours later the enemy

marched upon the village in great force, hoping to
surprise them, when, but for the timely advice they
had received, not one of their number could have
escaped death or capture.

Wherever De Renty was in command he used
his whole authority to prevent all acts of oppression,
all excess, all injustice.   He strictly forbade his
soldiers to ill-treat or in any way harass those in
whose houses they were quartered, and enjoined them
to avoid giving the smallest cause for complaint.
But, knowing well how often orders are disregarded
unless means are taken to enforce them, he never
mounted his horse to resume his march without
summoning his whole troop and publicly inquiring
whether any one had suffered damage or injury at the
hands of the soldiers under his command ; and if he
discovered that such had been the case he took
care that justice should be done upon the spot.   One
morning, when about to leave a place where he and
his troop had passed the night, having made his
customary inquiry of his hostess, she complained that
one of his servants had taken a shirt from her.   At
'once De Renty called them all together, and desired
her to point out the offender.   She recognized him,
nor did the man deny the truth of her assertion,
confessing that, in fact, he had the shirt on his back
at that moment.   Immediately his master bade him
strip and return it to the owner.   Some of the officers,
gentlemen of rank, who were present, thought this
proceeding too severe, and would have had De Renty
spare the soldier this humiliation before his companions.   The fault was a very trifling one in their
eyes, and, at any rate, pecuniary compensation might
easily be made ; but Gaston was inflexible where

justice was concerned, and said he would not suffer
a thief amongst his followers.

He exerted his authority in like manner to prevent
every kind of disorder amongst his troops: no easy
matter, considering the liberty permitted by other
officers, and the ill example which they themselves
gave to their men. Gambling, drinking, swearing,
bad language, and the other vices which are their
invariable accompaniments, were common in the
army; and, whenever there was a temporary halt,
many of De Renty's noble companions thought that
the fatigues of a campaign purchased for them the right,
on those occasions, to throw off all moral self-control,
and indulge their inclinations in every possible way.
De Renty's austere and grave bearing was a silent
reproof to them. He never joined them in their un-
hallowed diversions, but lived in a licentious camp
as he had lived amidst the dissipation of a court, and
in the quiet retirement of his father's castle. He
adhered to his stated hours of prayer and usual
devotions whenever his military duties offered no
impediment; when such was the case, he made up for
the omission as soon as he was disengaged. On
reaching his quarters for the night, if there was a
church, his first care was to go and visit our Lord in
His Adorable Sacrament; if there was a religious
house in the town, there it was that in preference he
chose to lodge, and always by himself, in order that
he might cause no inconvenience to the inmates.

Perhaps one of the greatest temptations to which
a man of noble birth, and an officer in particular, was
exposed at this period in France, was that of becoming
engaged in a duel. It is difficult to form an idea of
the frightful prevalence of duelling amongst the upper

classes in the beginning of the 17th century, in spite of
the severe laws which had been promulgated against
it. This barbarous practice was a legacy bequeathed
by the civil wars which had desolated France during
the previous century, and which had occasioned a
complete state of internal disorganization. Law was
in abeyance to a wide extent during those wretched
times, and every one in consequence sought to do himself justice, or what he esteemed such. The contagion
of example converted this sanguinary abuse into a
tyrannous fashion ; and when peace was restored on
the accession of Henry IV., it had become so general
amongst the nobility and gentry, that the judges
either themselves shrank from applying the severe
penalties which the king had at length been induced
to pronounce against it, or weakly yielded to the
solicitations of princes and men of rank in favour of
culprits of high degree. The king himself, who had
passed his life in camps, and who was naturally imbued in no small measure with the spirit which had
reigned there, helped to destroy the effects of his own
law by his tenderness towards the offenders, and by
the indiscreet admiration which he would not seldom
betray for valour displayed in so ill a cause. The
evil accordingly did but increase, and the historian
Loménie reckons no less than four thousand gentlemen
who had perished in single combat during the first
eighteen years of that monarch's reign. This was in
1607. The law we have just mentioned had, it is
true, not been promulgated for more than five years,
but those last five years had furnished their full quota
of victims. At the beginning of 1609 we hear that
not a day passed without one duel or more being
fought, and very commonly in public places, where the

witnesses, often numerous, would join in the murderous
fray and cut each other's throats as furiously as if
they had been mortal foes. France was losing her
noblest and best blood on these ignoble battle-fields.
At last Henry IV.'s eyes were opened, and more
effectual legislation for the repression of this vice was
adopted. Unfortunately it revived with fresh force
under the feeble regency of Mary of Medicis, and at
the period of which we are speaking, the hateful
custom once more flourished in full vigour. In vain
might a gentleman be himself peaceable in his disposition, and unwilling either to give or to take offence ; it was impossible to live amongst a number of
hot-headed, arrogant individuals, many of whom were
touchy in the extreme from their overweening pride, and
never do or say anything which persons of this temper
might not interpret as an affront. Satisfaction upon
such occasions was always sought at the sword's point,
and he who should refuse to give it, or who should fail
to demand it, if himself insulted, would have been
regarded as a mean-spirited coward, who, as such, had
disgraced his birth and rank. We are all aware how
the code of so-called honour has maxims utterly repugnant to those of the Gospel, and how hard it is
found by those who mix in the world to shake off its
influence. It tyrannizes over noble spirits by means
of some of their noblest natural qualities, and it needs,
in somes cases, a moral courage of a very high order
to disregard its verdicts. Seldom, indeed, do mere
good principles supply the necessary fortitude. For
this triumph the powerful action of Divine grace is
needed.

In the early part of his campaign M. de Renty had
a difference with a brother officer, who had one of

those touchy temperaments to which we have adverted.   The disagreement came to the knowledge of
their superiors in command, who, hoping to put a
stop to what might not unlikely lead to one of these
"affairs of honour," interfered, and represented to
De Renty's opponent that he had in reality no just
cause for complaint.   The pride of this man prevented
him from acquiescing in their judgment; and he proceeded to require that satisfaction which, according
to the world's wretched maxims, he was entitled
to claim.   He challenged M. de Renty, who calmly
replied to the person who brought him the hostile
message that the gentleman was in the wrong, and
that he had given him every satisfaction which he
could justly desire.   But the duellist was not to be
put off by an answer of this kind; he was determined
to make De Renty draw his sword.   But even when
thus urged, the Christian soldier had the courage
to send a decided refusal; a proceeding the more
meritorious on his part, as he was not only young in
years, but, having only recently joined the army,
he had as yet had no opportunity of proving his
valour in the field.   His reply was to this effect:
that he was resolved not to fight, since God forbade
him to do so, as did also the king; for the rest,
he wished his adversary to know that if he had used
his best endeavours to satisfy him by other means,
this was not from any fear he entertained of him, but
solely because he feared God; adding that he should
continue as usual to go every day wherever his duty
and his affairs called him, and, should this gentleman venture to attack him, he would have cause to
repent it.

His enemy, finding that he could not provoke him

E

to an open duel, watched his opportunity, and, observing him one day walking with a friend, came upon him suddenly accompanied by a brother officer, both with drawn swords. In those days gentlemen had such a passion for this barbarous custom, that the seconds, who had no manner of quarrel with each other, used to take an active share in the fray. De Renty, thus put upon his defence, was not slow in unsheathing his weapon, hastily enjoining his companion, who did the same, to beware of killing his adversary. De Renty was strong and active, and, although he placed himself strictly on the defensive, while his opponent fought with all the reckless freedom which indifference to consequences allowed to his movements, he had soon disarmed him; and his friend was equally successful in his combat with the second. Both principal and second had received but slight wounds; De Renty, true Christian as he was, having fought without anger or animosity, and inflicted no more hurt upon his adversary than was necessary for the purpose of disarming him, now evinced nothing but tender compassion for the wounded men. With the assistance of his comrade he carried them to his own tent, dressed their wounds, gave them wine, restored them their swords, and, adding to charity and generosity that humility and modesty which always marked his actions, he kept the whole affair a profound secret, never alluding to it again even to the friend who had acted as his second, whom, moreover, he requested not to mention the circumstance to any one. His refusal to fight had of course been known, and had exposed him to unfavourable comments; but his brave and successful encounter, which in those days would have been

regarded as no contemptible feather in a young
officer's cap, was veiled from public knowledge, so
far as it lay in his own power to conceal it.

This was not the only occasion upon which he
became an object of unreasonable displeasure to associates through no fault of his own, or himself had
just cause to complain of the treatment he received.
But the prudence, patience, forbearance, and charity
which guided his behaviour in every case, through
God's blessing, extricated him happily from all difficulties without any compromise of conscience. It
is in circumstances of this kind that the valour of
a true soldier of Christ is brought to the proof. The
world's bravery is often sheer cowardice; and De
Renty was in the habit of telling his servants that
there was far more of courage and generosity in
bearing an affront or an injury for the love of God
than in repaying it; more in endurance than in
revenge; because this was far the most difficult of the
two. "Bulls," he would say, "may surpass men in
boldness and daring, but theirs is a brutal courage;
ours ought to be reasonable and Christian."

CHAPTER III.

A Second Conversion.

In the preceding chapter we have given a slight
sketch of De Renty's life while his feet were yet only
on the lowest steps of that ladder to whose heights he

was to climb. It is very common in the progress
of great souls to meet with certain epochs in their
inner life, when such a notable change is recorded to
have come over them as might almost be likened to
a fresh conversion. In others the grow this more
equable, and no such dates in the spiritual progress
can be discerned. Nevertheless, it is still perhaps
true of all who make advance in the life of grace that
there is something analogous constantly occurring
within them, realized by themselves with more or
less distinctness, although it may not outwardly
appear in any perceptible change of their mode of
life. Each illumination of grace vouchsafed to the
soul, each touch of God's hand upon the heart (and
such illuminations and touches are sure to be the
reward of fidelity to previous light and impulse
received), is like to a new revelation of God's perfections to that soul, a new call to His service, a renewed
desire imparted to it to give Him its whole affections.
Doubtless it was the experience of one of these converting effects of grace which elicited the " *Nunc
cœpi* " of David. The soul at these times seems
hitherto to have done nothing ; all is to begin afresh :
and is there not something parallel to this in God's
own dealings with those who follow after perfection?
The Holy Spirit seems to erect in order to pull down,
and to be ever beginning His work anew after a more
perfect plan. Yet what seems to be pulled down has
not been wasted ; it has done its work, and has
placed the soul in a state wherein it becomes capable
of sustaining higher operations, and operations sometimes not only higher in degree but of quite a different
order.

A **very** remarkable change of this nature took

place in De Renty's spiritual state when he was twenty-seven years of age, having then been married five years ; and we are therefore led to regard this period as that at which it pleased God to call him to enter on the ways of high perfection. Hitherto, virtuous as he had been, assiduous in the practice of devotion, and estranged from the spirit of the world and all its maxims, so that he may well be held up as a model to Christians engaged in the secular life, still there was nothing which can be characterized as extraordinary in his state. It was singularly perfect in its own order ; but that is another thing. Some, perhaps the large majority, are called to nothing superior. God has not imparted to their souls the capacity for any higher state, and their own special perfection is accomplished within the humbler limits which Divine Wisdom has assigned to them. Such calls and impulses of grace of which they are the recipients, find their adequate result in the more exact and perfect fulfilment of their Christian duties on this lower scale ; and we must await the great day of account fully to know the merit which can be earned by fidelity to the small trust, and the value which the All-just Judge sets upon the perfection with which these humbler vocations have been ful-filled.

De Renty, however, was now to be called to a life of singular and extraordinary holiness. The Fathers of the Oratory gave a Retreat in the year 1638, at a place distant some seven or eight leagues from Paris. This celebrated Congregation founded by the Cardinal de Bérulle, which, after initiating a great work parallel to the reforms introduced by St. Philip Néri and St. Charles Borromeo at Rome and Milan, was, before

long, to degenerate and become infected with Jansenism, then stood at the height of its well-merited
celebrity, and numbered in its ranks a band of apostolic men destined (to use the words of a contemporary writer), as so many new Noës, to repeople the
Church of France after the deluge of evils which
in the preceding century had overwhelmed it. This
seems to have been the mission of the Oratory. It
was to be the nursery and the school of the men who
were destined by God to execute the great work of
ecclesiastical reform, and who were to go forth to
evangelize France and bid its wildernesses and desolate
places blossom and bear fruit once more. Moreover,
the Oratory, besides itself training so many admirable
priests, had communicated its spirit to many others,
chosen souls who had resorted thither for a while to
sit at the feet of its saintly founder, and were afterwards to be distinguished by their labours in the
cause of holy reform. St. Vincent de Paul spent two
years under the Cardinal de Bérulle's discipline, seeking, as he averred, in the person of that holy priest,
a visible angel to guide and direct him, and to help
him to discover what God required of him. Nor was
he disappointed in his expectation. The venerable
De Bérulle discerned the Saint's future vocation, and
even, it is said, foretold to him the abundant fruit
which should crown his labours in the raising up of
a Congregation of faithful and zealous priests. Père
Eudes, the founder of another Congregation devoted
to a similar object,—the education and training of
priests, was in like manner himself formed by De
Bérulle : who also in his case foresaw the great
services which he would render to the Church. From
the same school came forth M. Bourdoise, the in-

stitutor of the Community of St. Nicolas, who himself trained so many ecclesiastics afterwards employed
in the seminaries.

The Cardinal de Bérulle had a successor equal to
himself, if he did not even surpass him, in the gift of
guiding and training souls, Charles de Condren, one
of the holiest of that uncanonized multitude of holy
persons who form the true glory of France in the
seventeenth century. St. Jane Frances de Chantal,
indeed, did not hesitate to affirm that that if her holy
founder had been raised up to direct men, P. de
Condren seemed fitted to guide, not only men, but
angels. "*Non est inventus similis illi*," were the
words which St. Vincent de Paul used concerning him
after his death. De Bérulle, who had himself received such rich gifts of grace, and who was so
enlightened in the science of the saints, would sometimes, as he passed Père de Condren's room, stoop
to kiss the floor which his feet had trod, and used
reverently to write down, on his knees and bare-
headed, words which had fallen from the lips of his
own disciple. "God had made P. de Condren for the
saints," writes one of his historians, "and had fitted
him to guide them to the most sublime perfection ;
nor was there any way of sanctification, however
extraordinary, which he did not immediately understand." The great reputation which he had hence
acquired for deep discernment of all the secrets of the
spiritual life, caused numbers of holy souls to have
recourse to him ; and we are told that he was in
consequence acquainted with so many and such various
vocations to high perfection, that he believed that
saints were as numerous in his day, although more
hidden, as in the first ages of the Church. Amongst

those persons of eminent sanctity whose peculiar
vocation he discerned, was M. Olier, the future founder
of St. Sulpice, who was by him hindered from accepting a bishopric, a step which would have interfered
with God's designs in his regard; thus proving his
possession of light which in this instance had been
withheld from M. Olier's own director, St. Vincent
de Paul. This striking circumstance serves to show
how great was the insight vouchsafed· to this holy
man into God's dealings with souls, and his high
capacities for spiritual direction. His penetration
might be said almost to resemble sight; it was as if
he beheld through a transparent glass the special gifts
which the Holy Ghost was dispensing to each, and the
peculiar character and impress of sanctity which He
desired to stamp on their several souls. As others see
at a glance and can describe the outward man, and
can readily judge of the natural temperament from
certain external indications, so he seemed to behold
in each the new man in Christ; his form, complexion,
and stature, in fine, the type after which, according to
the divine predestination, the Holy Ghost was moulding him.

He would sometimes, in intimate conversation with
M. Olier, advert, with the utmost simplicity, combined
with the most unhesitating confidence, to the result
of his observations in a region so closely hidden from
the eyes of men, and, though supernaturally unveiled
to a few, yet usually in very reserved measure. One
day, after alluding to the special character of grace in
several persons, he said, " I have that of Infancy:"
" and, in fact," adds M. Olier, in relating the conversation, " the Infant Jesus was his great object of
devotion, and he was himself quite a child in his

whole behaviour, by his simplicity, innocence, candour, and humility." M. Olier then inquired what was *his* particular grace, and P. de Condren told him that it was akin to his own. Upon another occasion P. de Condren told M. Olier that he would be one of his heirs, not of perishable goods, but of spirit and graces. "Would to God," adds that pattern of humility, "that I might possess one small spark of his pure love!" He allows, however, in his autograph memoirs, that he had no doubt but that he was drawn by our Lord to live without care or reflection, in all simplicity, like a child cradled in its father's arms, with no other thought but to love, admire, praise, and please Him, and that it was impossible to express how much confirmed in this disposition he was after P. de Condren's death. It is, indeed, commonly said that this holy man, like another Elias, bequeathed his mantle to his disciple. This spirit of infancy, with which that of entire self-abnegation is so intimately associated, M. Olier propagated in St. Sulpice, and it constituted one of the leading features of the character formed by his teaching and example. Such also was the distinguishing spiritual characteristic of the holy man whose life we are recording, the foundations of which P. de Condren was the instrument of laying, although it was reserved to a humble religious, and that a woman, to give it a further and most powerful impulse, and thus to be the means, in God's hands, of promoting its more full and complete development.

It was, as we have said, during a Retreat, to which we have alluded, given by the Fathers of the Oratory in the year 1638, that De Renty first was brought into communication with P. de Condren. He undertook this exercise in a spirit of deep humility, always so strong in him as to give its peculiar form to all his actions. Upon this occasion it was noticed that he walked the whole way, some three or four and twenty miles, certainly not for want of an easier mode of conveyance. His first act was to make a general confession after a most searching preparation, and the abundance of grace which he then received, made him ever look back to this period as the beginning of his entire conversion to God and perfect consecration to His service. He did not trust, however, to the fervour of those resolutions, so often formed during seasons of Retreat, but so apt to cool down after a return to the world and to our ordinary occupations, but, being determined to provide against any relaxation in his spiritual course, he took P. de Condren as his director. Death deprived him of that holy man's guidance two years later, but he had made such great advance during that time, and had manifested so great a capacity for the sublimest perfection, that the discerning eye of his director foresaw the heights to which he would attain, and said to another in confidence, "M. de Renty will be one day a great saint."

De Renty's first step was to break entirely with the world. The court is not a place in which high sanctity can well thrive. Such miracles may and do occur when duty detains a person unwillingly within its atmosphere, but no duty of this kind bound him to it, and so he bade it an entire farewell. In like manner he renounced every employment which had only worldly honour and advancement for its object, in order to devote himself altogether to those which directly concerned the glory of God and the good of his neighbour. He gave up all visits in themselves unnecessary, those visits of pure civility which are justifiable, and often, in a measure, even incumbent upon those who occupy a certain position in the world. He increased his hours of prayer, and began the custom of regularly saying Office, rising even in the night to recite Matins, which were followed by an hour's meditation. Not less than two, and often three, hours were nightly, and that even in the depth of winter, given to the exercise of prayer. Twice a day he made his examen of conscience, the one before the mid-day meal, the other in the evening, scanning his smallest defects most rigorously. Twice a week he went to confession, and communicated three or four times. On one day of the seven he repaired to the Hôtel Dieu to instruct the sick; another he devoted in like manner to the poor of his own parish; another was allotted to prisoners; and on the remaining days he attended meetings for different pious objects. With all this activity in outward acts of charity, his own family, so far from being neglected, was the first object of his care. His solicitude was not confined to his children, but extended to all his servants and dependents. Every evening a bell summoned them all to meet for the purpose of making their examen and joining in the Litanies of Our Lady and other devotions; and on the Saturdays, his wife and children being also present, as usual, he gave his whole household a familiar explanation of the Gospel of the coming Sunday, a practice from which they all derived much edification and profit.

The common worship of the family was not interrupted by the journeys which they were occasionally called upon to make. Travelling was a great under-

taking in those times; but, whether the movement be
slow or rapid, whether, as now, the distance traversed
in an hour exceeds what in the seventeenth century
was often a laborious day's journey, it will be generally
admitted that the act of moving and the change of
scene and place are apt to bring distractions, in the
spiritual acceptation of the word, partly from those
very circumstances of change and variety, partly
because travelling disarranges that more or less regular
disposition of occupations which is so favourable to
recollection of mind and to the punctual observance of
stated devotional exercises.   Hence the behaviour of
persons on travel is a great test of their solid advance in
the Christian life, as, on the other hand, the sanctification of that time is a great security against the deteri-
orating influences of change and irregularity.   Accordingly we find saints and saintly persons adding to,
rather than curtailing, their exercises of piety when
necessitated to travel.   Thus their journeys became a
sort of pilgrimage, so many stages of progress in the
spiritual life, instead of seasons of mental dissipation
and of retrogression in holy habits.   Such was M. de
Renty's practice.   Every morning, before leaving the
place where they had passed the night, he and his
family heard Mass.   As soon as they were seated in
their carriage and had started, the first thing they did
was to say the Itinerary.   This he himself never
omitted, were the journey ever so short; whenever, in
fact, any business took him beyond the immediate
precincts of his place of residence, or outside the city,
if he were staying in Paris.   Then followed the Litanies of Our Lord, succeeded by meditation; after
which he would say a portion of the Divine Office.
When these different devotions were concluded he

would enter into cheerful conversation, either himself
introducing some subjects which tended to raise the
mind and affections to God, or profiting by passing
scenes and the little incidents of the way for the same
purpose. Yet all was done so naturally, not as though
he were aiming to teach, but as one who spoke out of
the abundance and overflowing of his own heart, that
no one ever wearied of hearing him recur to the same
theme. Everything spoke to him of God, and so he
could not but speak to others of Him. Wide and far-
stretching plains filled his thoughts with the grandeur
and immensity of the great Creator. Mountain-ranges
told of Him who stands round about His people as
their fortress and defence. Rich and smiling valleys,
fields enamelled with flowers, and rivers winding their
pleasant course amidst luxuriant verdure, were to him
suggestive of that Paradise of beauty whose ineffable
charms are to gladden the Christian's glorified senses
in his everlasting home, and to form a portion of his
accidental joys. Sometimes he would even break forth
aloud in acts of faith, hope, charity, or other virtues,
as if, like the breathings of the material frame, they
could not be repressed. His hearers were much edified on these occasions, as people ever scarcely fail to
be at a spontaneous manifestation of deep feeling.

On approaching the place where they were to dine,
he invited his companions to make their mid-day
examen ; and the moment he alighted from the carriage, before entering the inn, he hastened to the
church to pay our Lord a visit, which was also his
constant practice on reaching the halting-place for the
night. If he found the door of the sacred edifice closed,
and no one at hand to admit him, he would kneel down
close to it to adore the Blessed Sacrament within. This

done, he would inquire if there was a hospital in the place, in order that he might visit and tend his Lord in the person of His suffering members. On returning to the inn, his first act was to kneel down in his room and adore God, praying fervently for all who dwelt in the place, or might journey that way, and begging forgiveness for all the sins which had been committed there. If he saw anything unbefitting written on the walls, he would efface it, and write something good and holy in its place; and, before resuming his journey, he always sought an opportunity to address, if it were but one or two words of advice, to the servants of the inn, as was his practice also in regard to the poor who fell in his way, in order that, after the example of his Lord, he might pass through no place without doing good.

The afternoon portion of the journey had also its allotted order. First, after re-entering the carriage, he passed some time in interior recollection; then followed the recreation, in which cheerfulness was always accompanied by a certain seriousness and modesty, which his example instilled into all who surrounded him. They all then sang Vespers together, after which succeeded the liveliest hour of the day, when the father encouraged his children to indulge in that innocent mirthfulness which, so far from being adverse to the Christian spirit, is its most congenial accompaniment. De Renty knew that with the young especially the bow must be sometimes unbent, if it is to retain its elasticity and vigour. Joy is an instinct of the youthful heart, as it is of every living thing fresh from the creating hands of Him who is the fount of all joy; and it can find no more suitable and agreeable outlet than in song. " Is any cheerful in mind," says St. James, "let him sing." De Renty had considerable taste for music, and would himself lead the family choir, taking special delight in singing with them the Creed in the vernacular to a suitable air of his own selection. At four o'clock they sang Compline, and again he withdrew inwardly to meditate and pray ; on arriving at their night's resting-place, his devotional exercises were similar to those we have already described.

It will be seen from this sketch of the order observed by De Renty in his journeys that, since what may be called his second conversion, he not only lived the life of a good fervent Christian—this he did before — but lived wholly and exclusively for God. He was correspondingly anxious to train his children in the ways of holiness, but he had too much prudence to run the risk of overshooting his mark through indiscreet zeal, or of interfering with the vocation of God in their regard by rigidly exacting practices of perfection to which they might not be called. His family was a model of regularity, and he required the strict observance of every religious duty, so far as respected the exterior. As for the interior, he endeavoured to inspire his children with a great fear of offending God, a deep horror of sin, and a thorough disesteem of the world, showing them how opposed were its maxims to the spirit of Jesus Christ. He ever taught them that true nobility consists in virtue : this is the highest distinction for all, rich and poor, high and low alike. Yet he did not require them to despise their own rank in society ; only he would have them live as became it, not from pride of birth and station, not according to the world's ideas of

greatness, but from the desire to glorify God in the
state of life in which He had placed them, and to let
their lives bear witness to Whose they were and
Whom they served. The following remarks, extracted
from a letter of his, written to a lady, will show his
general notions on the subject of education.

"In regard to the education of children, God, by
making a difference in their conditions, would seem to
teach us that there must also be a difference between the
rearing of one of low estate (*"un roturier"*) and that
of a gentleman, who, being born to wear a sword,
certainly ought not to be put into a cloister to be
trained for a monastic life. But to such a pitch has
corruption now arrived amongst us, that all the
principal instructions we give them, and which those
we set about them give them, serve but to kindle an
infernal flame of vanity in hearts where there is
already only too much of it ; impelling the young by
pagan comparisons to endure nothing, to aim always
at what is most lofty, and to employ for its attainment those means which are most approved by the
world, albeit forbidden by God. But if persons do not
go so far as that, at any rate no pains are taken to
plant Christian maxims in the heart of a well-born
youth. For instance, you are aware how young men
are universally infected with the vice of duelling :
now, tell me, how many fathers will you meet with
who would wish their grown-up sons not to fight, if
challenged, particularly if they could be certain that
they would not be wounded and would come off
victors ? And what is the consequence ? That
perhaps not one of these fathers will ever in express
and deliberate terms condemn duelling. Yet it is
the more incumbent on us to do this frequently and

forcibly, pointing out at the same time the miserable consequences which flow from this vice, because inclination, example, worldly approbation and honour, all combine to draw men towards the practice, and to engage them in it. If by chance a spark of that furnace we carry within us escape from the lips of a youth, the parent will say, in a laughing tone, ' Oh ! that is not right ; God forbids us to do that.' O yes, forsooth ; but please to observe, is this the way you would go to work to prevent your son growing up with crooked legs and a distorted body ? "

Such were his sentiments. De Renty did not fall into the mistake of either, on the one hand, supposing that all were called to follow the evangelical counsels, or, on the other, consenting to reduce and tone down the precepts of the Gospel for the use of seculars. To uphold and enforce the observance of those precepts, and to inculcate a great reverence for them in all who came within his influence, and especially such as were subject to his control, this was his rule and the method he pursued. We find him dealing in the same spirit with his dependents on his estates, and with those whom he had set in authority over others, recommending to them particularly the virtues of justice, charity, and mildness. He wished as much good as possible to be done to everybody, and as little suffering as was possible to be inflicted in any case. Faults, of course, must be corrected and evil prevented ; but where his own interests were concerned, he detested any excess of zeal, and preferred rather to err on the side of leniency. He writes as follows to rebuke a person in his employment who had given way to anger, and had been guilty of some scandal. The particulars are not related, but we gather from

what is said that the individual in question had
inflicted some excessive chastisement on an offender,
and that in a cemetery, which is consecrated ground.
"I have heard with pain of what you have done,"
writes his master, "and although I am unwilling to
give credit to all the reported details, yet sufficient
still remains to convince me that you have acted
under the dominion of passion. If I employed you
in my service simply for the sake of myself and my
interests, I might wish you to exterminate all who
seek to injure me ; but with you and me it is a
question of living like good Christians, or else of
being damned. If such be not our belief and our
desire, let us profess ourselves Turks and barbarians at
once. If you could see how displeasing such actions
are to God, and what scandal and hurt they cause to
men, your heart would soon be changed. I pray God
to bring this to pass, and I offer Him my goods, my
blood, and my life to obtain for you this grace,
whereon your salvation depends ; but anyhow, I
implore you as a brother, and enjoin upon you as a
master, to make reparation for the wrong you have
done to God, to the holy place, and to your neighbour.
I would rather that utter ruin should fall upon my
house than that you should again proceed to such
extremities. I am bound to regulate my natural
feelings, and my desire to preserve my goods, by my
conscience and by the love of God who bestowed
them on me. I own that practically this involves a
difficulty, seeing how great is the malice of men nowadays, and seeing also that sometimes the oppression
of the weak and the perpetration of injustice may be
prevented by recourse to extraordinary measures (of
severity) ; but when our self-interest is implicated in

the matter we must restrict ourselves to ordinary measures—first of gentleness, then of justice; and if these do not succeed, then we must practise patience : there it is that our virtue is called into exercise. I do not place much value upon certain formal devotions, but I respect the maxims of the Gospel, which teach us the way we ought to go."

The whole letter is characteristic of the man ; of his uncompromising hatred of sin, his zeal for God, his generous contempt of self-interest.

Such, then, was De Renty after his second conversion, both in his capacity of a father of a family and in that of a master. To complete the general picture of its results, we will now take a glance at him in the regulation of his ordinary day. We will quote his own words, in which he gives an account of himself to his new director, a Father of the Company of Jesus, probably Saint-Jure, who succeeded P. de Condren in that office, and who had told him that it was necessary for him, upon undertaking the charge, to be acquainted with his dispositions and the rule of life he was in the habit of observing. This circumstance fixes the date of the letter, as P. de Condren (as we have said) survived the Retreat which was the means of bringing De Renty into connection with him for a period of two years. We shall note in this account the strong bent of his attraction, which was to receive a fuller development in proportion as he advanced in the ways of grace, and particularly after it had pleased Him who causes all things to work for the good of His elect, to make a very distressing affair in which M. de Renty became involved, the occasion of taking him into the vicinity of Sister Marguerite of Beaune, who was to be the instrument of leading him on to that extraordi-

nary conformity to the Infant Jesus which afterwards
distinguished him ; a conformity which was displayed
in herself in so supernatural a manner that it may
rather be styled a species of transformation.

"I have delayed a few days," writes De Renty, "since
receiving your injunction to send you an account of
how I employ my day, with the view of endeavouring to understand something about it ; but I cannot
observe anything of a plan, or anything which can be
put on paper, because all consists in an abandonment
of self to God, and in following the order which He
intimates ; and this results generally in some variation, the ground, however, remaining always the same.
As regards the exterior, I rise usually at five o'clock."
(This, it may be observed, was after passing a portion
of the night in prayer.)   " Upon waking I inwardly
annihilate myself before the Majesty of God ; I unite
myself to His Son and to His Holy Spirit, to pay
Him my homage.   Having risen, I take holy water,
and, kneeling down, I adore the benefit of the Incarnation, which gives us access to God and reconciles us
to Him.   I abandon myself to the Infant Jesus, that
I may enter into His spirit.   Sometimes I salute my
good Angel, St. John Baptist, St. Teresa, and some
other Saints, and then I recite the *Angelus*."   He says
sometimes, not because he was apt to fail in attention,
or was addicted to change, for he was extremely punctual in performing all he had undertaken ; but the
application of his mind to God was so close and intense, often even arriving at the passive state, as to
disable him from diverting his attention from the immediate object of his contemplation.   He continues:
" I am not long dressing, and then I go to the chapel,
passing on my way through a little room on the man-

telpiece of which I have installed, as Mistress of the house, the Blessed Virgin with her Son in her arms. I kiss the ground before her, and say, '*Monstra te esse Matrem*,' &c., dedicating myself anew to her service, and offering to her my whole family,—my wife, my children, my servants,—an oblation which I have been moved for a long time past to make to her, that through her means they may be a perfect holocaust to God. As I rise I say, '*Mater incomparabilis, ora pro nobis*.' I then enter the chapel and prostrate myself in adoration before God, abasing myself before Him, and making myself as little, as naked, and as empty of myself as I can. And thus, by faith, I keep myself united to His Son and His Divine Spirit, in order that I may do whatsoever He wills I should do, and so I remain. If I have any penance to perform, I acquit myself of it at about half-past six, and then I read two chapters of the New Testament bareheaded and on my knees. At seven I go up to my oratory, where I have three stations : the first to the Blessed Virgin, the second to St. Joseph, the third to St. Teresa, to all of whom I pay my little devotions. After that I attend to any business I may have to do ; but if there be none requiring immediate attention, I place myself on my knees before God until I go to hear Mass, and remain in the church until half-past eleven, except on those days on which we give the poor a dinner, when I return at eleven. Before dinner I make my morning examen, and offer some prayers for the Church, for the propagation of the Faith, and for the souls in Purgatory, after which I say the *Angelus*. I dine at mid-day, and during dinner I cause some one to read. From half-past twelve, for about the space of an hour, I speak to persons who come to me on

business, and this is the hour I appoint for seeing me.
I then go out, and proceed whithersoever it may please
God to send me. Some days have their regularly
fixed work, the others have their employment determined from week to week. If it so happens that I
have no other call upon me, I go and pray in some
church; but in all cases I endeavour never to miss an
afternoon visit to the Blessed Sacrament, and an hour's
meditation in the evening. About seven o'clock I
recite a few vocal prayers, and then we sup. During
supper some one reads a selection from the martyrology
and the life of the Saint who is to be honoured on the
morrow. When supper is over I talk to my children,
and say something to them in the way of instruction.
At nine o'clock the bell rings for prayers, at which the
servants all attend, and then every one retires. For
myself, I remain praying in the chapel until ten
o'clock, when I go to my chamber, and, having offered
and commended myself to God according as I am inwardly moved,* to the Blessed Virgin, to my good
Angel, and to certain other Saints, I take holy water
and lie down in my bed. There I repeat the *De Pro-
fundis* for the dead, together with a few other short
prayers, and compose myself to sleep.

"This is about the usual order of the day as regards
the exterior. But as to the interior, I have none, so
to say; for since I gave up saying Office, which will
be a year next Holy Week, all my forms and all my
methods (*pratiques*) have abandoned me, and, instead
of serving me as helps to draw near to God, they
would now act as hindrances. My usual state is this;

---

* "Selon le fond que je porte": an expression which M. de
Renty frequently employs, and which it is not easy to render
cacurately in English.

but I am guilty of so many and such great infidelities in all that I am about to say, that I write it reluctantly, because I am nothing but vice and sin. I have within me an experimental realization of the presence of the Most Holy Trinity, or of some mystery which raises me by a simple view to God; yet I continue the while doing whatever Divine Providence enjoins me, not regarding the things themselves, whether they be great or little, but simply the order of God and the glory which they may render to Him. As respects the examens and other exercises in common which I have noted above, I am sometimes unable to attend to them. I acquit myself of them externally for the sake of observing regularity, but I follow my interior attraction without disturbing it, for when one has found God there is no need to seek Him elsewhere; and when He is occupying us in one way, it is not for us to choose some other. The soul knows well what inwardly makes it pure and simplifies it, and what it is that causes multiplicity.* As regards the interior, then, I follow my attraction, and, externally, I discern the Will of God which makes me follow it, and which inclines me to regulate myself thereby in simplicity by the light which His Spirit affords me. Thus, by His grace, I enjoy in all things a great interior silence, joined with a profound reverence and a solid peace.

"I usually confess on Thursdays, according to the direction I have received, and communicate almost daily, feeling that I am attracted to do so, and that I have a great need thereof. In one word, the abiding attraction manifested to me (*le fond qui m'est montré*)

* "L'âme connaît bien ce qui lui fait son fond plus net et l'unit, ou ce qui la multiplie."

is to give myself to God through Jesus Christ with a purity which aims at adoring God in spirit and in truth, with utter despoilment, loving Him with all my heart, with all my soul, and with all my strength, and in all things seeing and adoring the leadings of God and following them : this alone remaining in my mind, all the rest is blotted out.

"I have no sensible experiences, with the exception of some occasional passing impression ; but, if I may venture to say so, when I sound my will, I find it sometimes so ardent that it would consume me if the same Lord who animates it, unworthy as it is, did not restrain it. A fire seems then kindled within me, and to my very finger ends I feel that everything in me speaks for its God, expanding itself far and wide in His immensity, in which it is dissolved and loses itself for His glory. I cannot express this as it really is ; I do not, however, dwell upon what passes within me, but fall back always into my own nothingness, where I find the pure act of elevation to God which I have described above."

De Renty concludes this report of himself in these words : "I beg pardon, Reverend Father, for any want of order and connection ; I have written it all just as it came into my mind. I should be truly glad if you could know all my miserable defects, for you would pity me much."

Such was the account which this holy man rendered to his new director. Comment would be superfluous. Both what we understand in it and what soars beyond our full apprehension serve alike to indicate the height of spiritual perfection to which he had already attained.

CHAPTER IV.

The Source of De Renty's Virtues.

If we now proceed to examine the source and principle of those virtues which shone so eminently in De Renty from the very beginnings of his full conversion of heart to God, we shall find it to be close union with our Lord Jesus Christ, to which all his aims were directed, and the all-importance of which had been deeply impressed on his mind by P. de Condren. We do not speak here of that union with the Head which is essential to constitute an individual a member of His Body, that union which by sanctifying grace is imparted to each Christian in Baptism, and, when forfeited, is restored through the Sacrament of Penance, a union by the loss of which a man becomes a dead branch, separated from the Vine and the life-giving sap which it infuses : this is a union common to all true Christians ; but we mean that union of conformity which operates an entire transformation in the whole being, which is the perfect end of our predestination in Christ, in whom we are "called to be saints." Just as without Christ in our souls we are altogether dead, since He is the Life, so also whatever part of us is not reformed and informed by His Spirit is also dead, though we ourselves live ; it is the hay and the stubble which are devoted to the purgatorial flames, but which, while we are "yet in the way," might be meritoriously mortified and consumed in the fire of that Divine Charity which has come to unite us to

Itself. Christ has come to suffer and rise again in each of us, but few indeed permit Him to accomplish this perfect work. The great bulk of Christians aim only at saving their souls and avoiding grievous sin, while by far the greater number of those who have worthier and better aspirations can scarcely be said to set before them as an attainable object that complete union which makes a man, so to say, another Christ.

As this perfect union with Christ is the end at which we ought to aim in aspiring to perfection, so also is union with Him the means; for He is the Way as well as the Truth and the Life. Hence P. de Condren, that admirable director, impressed most strongly on De Renty's mind from the first the necessity of a constant application to Jesus Christ, both as our Divine Model in the regulation of the exterior, and as our guiding and informing Spirit interiorly. We have here the key to this wonderful man's sanctification. He did not multiply himself in aspirations, desires, practices; he did not aim so much at severally producing in himself those virtues which make up the character of the perfect Christian; his religion was altogether personal: he set Jesus before him at every moment; he kept close to Jesus; copying His features, drinking of His spirit, learning in His school, clothing himself with Him, "putting on" Jesus, as the Apostle exhorts men to do.* He had no other occupation. It was by faithfully following this recommendation of his director that he attained in a few years to such singular perfection; but from the very beginning the likeness he sought to reproduce in himself was, so to say, complete as a sketch, which he

* Rom. xiii. 13.

was continually filling in, as the painter keeps working up his portrait, adding fresh strokes day by day. In the last years of his life the likeness of his Lord had become so marvellously stamped upon him, so interpenetrated was he by the life of Jesus, that, as St. Paul says of himself,* it seemed that he no longer lived himself, but that Christ lived in him. Writing to his director about the year 1646, he employs a somewhat similar expression, although with no intentional reference to the Apostle's words. "I feel," he says, "a great need of Jesus Christ, but I am bound to tell you, both from gratitude to the mercy of God and from the certainty of its truth, that I feel that He is more dominant in me than I myself. I know, indeed, that in myself I am nothing but sin, but withal I experience our Lord within me, who is my strength, my life, my peace, my all."

This expression of the "great need" he felt of Jesus Christ is to be found more than once in his letters to his director. It had a deep meaning as he employed it. It did not simply convey a judgment of his mind and a profound and heartfelt conviction—in that sense all good Christians could adopt and use it— but rather an intimate craving of his soul. Nothing could exceed this longing of his whole being, this instinct of the new man who alone was allowed to energize in him (so completely did he keep in check every mere natural movement), except his thorough confidence in this good Saviour and his abandonment to Him. "I do not know what to tell you," he writes on another occasion, "for all things are effaced in me as they pass." To this phenomenon of his

Gal. ii. 20.

spiritual state we shall allude again hereafter. "I
can retain nothing but God, and that only in a certain
blind manner, by a naked faith, which, while it
manifests to me the bad nature which is in me (*le
mauvais fond*), at the same time always imparts to me
strength and great confidence by the way of abandonment to our Lord Jesus Christ in God." And then
he quotes St. Paul, where he speaks * of the confidence we possess in Christ; "not that we are sufficient to think anything of ourselves as of ourselves,
but our sufficiency is from God." The sight of his
own poverty and of his riches in Christ were ever
simultaneously before him as co-relatives, so that he
could always say with the same Apostle, † " When I
am weak then am I powerful;" and, "I can do all
things in Him who strengtheneth me." Again he
writes thus :—" About a fortnight ago these words
were suggested to me without any contribution on
my own part : *Quære venam aquarum viventium*—
'Seek the source of the living waters;' and at the
same time my mind, like to one who should trace back
the whole course of a river to its source, went to seek
and follow Jesus Christ from the commencement of
His life on earth to the summit of His glory, where
He sits enthroned at the right hand of His Father,
and whence He sends down His Spirit to vivify His
Church and those who are His. I perceived that
here was the source from which the streams of living
water flow to us, and it is to this we must address
ourselves."

The same idea is recurring always under various
forms and aspects. So filled was he with the en-

.　　　* 2 Cor. iii. 5.　　　* *Ib.* xii. 10; Phil. iv. 13.

grossing view of Jesus Christ as not only the End but the Way, that not merely in his letters to his director, where we naturally expect to meet with the exposition of his spiritual experiences, but in such as were addressed to secular friends, it is his frequently occurring theme. As he himself loved and thought of nothing but Jesus, as he performed all his smallest actions in union with Him, so he could speak of nothing else. " Let Jesus Christ," he writes to a friend, " be the bond, the soul, and the life of us all, even as He is our pattern; looking closely at this holy Original, let us enter into His maxims, adopt His desires, execute His works, so that men may know that we are Christians." To another he says, " I adore and bless with all my heart our Lord Jesus Christ in that He is opening His heart to you, that He may wholly possess yours. He will cause it to die, and reduce it to a holy poverty, in order that you may taste the true life and all riches, and will make you confess that to belong to Jesus Christ is a great mercy. I beseech Him to impart to you the most sanctifying of His graces, and enable us to die well and live well by His spirit. Let us enter into this spirit, which will give us the sentiments and the energy of children of God. Every other exercise of the presence of God and application of mind to the Divine Majesty, which is not made in union with the Soul of Jesus Christ, is that of a creature towards its Creator, which indeed implies respect, but does not impart the life and the movements of the children of God towards their Father ; it is by joining ourselves to the interior operations of Jesus Christ that we acquire the affections of true children, which we cannot have save in union with the True Son."

The testimony which De Renty's letters give of himself on this subject was confirmed by all who had merited to enjoy his confidence. An intimate friend, speaking of him after his death, observed that his tender and ardent love towards our Lord Jesus Christ was manifest in all that he said; his conversation being always directed to the one end of leading souls to the true and solid knowledge and love of our Lord. Frequently indeed had he acknowledged to him that he had no relish for anything in which he did not find Jesus. All else, however innocent, however good in its way, was to him tasteless. Jesus was the savour of all things to him. "As for a soul," he would say, "which does not speak of Him, or in which one does not feel the effect of that grace which flows from His spirit and is the principle of all solid Christian acts, whether interior or exterior —do not talk to me of it. I might see in it miracles, prodigies, but if I do not see Jesus Christ nor hear anything of Him, I reckon all to be mere trifling, waste of time, and a dangerous snare." And again, the same friend avers that he would often say to him, " Let us love Jesus Christ, let us unite ourselves to His spirit and to His grace ;" adding, with his characteristic humility, " as for me, a miserable sinner, who do not love Him, I shall at least be glad to see my deficiency supplied by others who love Him ardently: but I am too unworthy to procure anything so great and in which I have so little part."

Having this strong perception of Jesus as the Way, he was as profoundly convinced that out of this Way, that is, apart from a close union with Him who is our strength, our efforts, however well meant, avail little to advance us in the path of holiness. He considered that sufficient scope was seldom left for God's work in us. " Ah ! my Father," we find him writing to his director, " the great imperfection of souls is not to wait enough upon God : the active nature, unsubdued, seizes on fair pretexts to intermeddle, and thinks it is doing wonders ; and yet this is what stains the purity of the soul, troubles its silence, and diverts its eye of faith, trust, and love : whence it results that the Father of Lights does not express in us His Eternal Word and does not produce in us His Spirit of Love. The Incarnation has merited all, not only for the abolition of our faults, but also for all those dispositions of grace to which Jesus Christ desires to associate us ; the chief of which is, even as it was in Himself as Man, to do nothing of ourselves, to speak and act according as we receive, knowing that we are not alone in performing our work, but that the Holy Spirit, who is the Spirit of Jesus Christ, which ruled Him in all His ways, is in the midst of us ; who would make His impressions in us, and give us life, the real and experimental life of our faith, if, patiently enduring, we would wait for His operation. Here it is that I feel my infirmity, and here nevertheless is my attraction."

These are very remarkable words as coming from one who spent so large a portion of his time in active works of charity, and speak volumes, not only for the principle from which they all sprang, but for the unmixed purity of intention with which they were carried out. Hence it was, as we shall find, that he was as much recollected, and as much alone with God, in the midst of his manifold and laborious works of mercy as if living a life of cloistered contemplation. We have perhaps all of us had occasion to see some-

thing of what we may call charitable bustle in many
excellent persons, but have withheld our tongues
from criticism out of respect for an indefatigable
kindness and zeal in good works which, conscious of
our own inability to imitate, we have felt it would be
ungracious to depreciate. , Yet can there be no question that without great watchfulness a certain distraction and dissipation of mind is commonly incidental
to those engaged in much active work, however good
and holy its object ; and this even where their duty
and unmistaken vocation call them to it, much more
where it is self-elected : a temptation so well known
to interior souls, and so much apprehended by them,
as often to cause them secretly to complain, with the
spouse in the Canticles,* "They have made me the
keeper in the vineyards : my vineyard I have not
kept." When, therefore, we meet with one who, like
the subject of this biography, could thus combine the
contemplative and the active, we may rest assured
that he is very highly advanced on the scale of
perfection, that mystical ladder which is Christ Himself. All his acts are done, not *for* Jesus only, but *in*
Him ; so that between action and repose there is no
difference. In action he is resting in God ; in the
repose of contemplation he is but pouring forth acts
of love. His life, in fact, is a life of love, indescribable
by human terms. De Renty, so precise and sober in
his expressions, so utterly a stranger to what may be
called flights of language, cannot find words to explain
his state. "I see," he writes in the letter from which
we have just quoted, "what I cannot say, for I
possess what I cannot express ; and the cause of my

* i. 6.

brevity, Father, springs from my ignorance, and also from a too great liberality of Divine goodness, which produces in me what I am unable to tell. The effect is a fulness and a replenishment of truth and of the brightness of God's magnificence, of the greatness of Jesus Christ and of the riches we enjoy in Him, and of those of the Blessed Virgin and the Saints : the soul beholds all praise and adoration, and is plunged in it." It is as though he had enjoyed a glimpse of the beatific vision. " I seem," he continues, " in saying this to say many things to you, nevertheless all is but one simple and powerful view in the superior part of the mind : thus I am no ways distracted thereby in my external acts ; I hear all, I see all, and I execute, albeit badly, all that I have to do."

We have observed that he did not so much endeavour to acquire certain virtues because they form a necessary part of the Christian character, as that he did all with an eye to a personal conformity to Jesus. It was the Man-God he had ever before him, not an abstract idea of goodness, however Christian in its type. Undoubtedly it is well to see the beauty of virtue, and to aim at cultivating it in ourselves, and if in doing so we have the right intention of pleasing our Lord, we act meritoriously, and shall reap our reward ; but better far, and a nearer road to holiness, as all the experience and example of the Saints demonstrate, is it to imitate Jesus Himself, and keep a simple eye on our Model. " Learn of Me," He says. Imitation is the shortest road to experimental science even in natural things, and so it is in spiritual. For this end De Renty made the New Testament his constant study. Here, in the record of Christ's sayings and doings when He abode amongst men, he

sought his pattern and rule, and particularly in the
practice of charity towards his neighbour.   He considered all that Jesus did and endured for men, the
ineffable affection and tenderness He had for them :
how He sought them, conversed with them, instructed,
reproved them, bore with their defects, and held them
all, so to say, clasped in the embrace of His love.
Then he weighed all that the Saviour said of charity
to our neighbour : how He constituted it at once the
foundation and the perfection of the New Law ; how
He enjoined it as a " new commandment," stamped
with His own special authority as the God-Man—"A
new commandment I give unto you."   He noticed
how our Lord urged on us the observance of this commandment in a most special manner ; how He gave
His own practice of charity as the measure of what
ours was to be, and declared that it should be the
distinguishing mark of those who were His true
disciples.

M. de Renty accordingly, having determined with
the whole force of his strong soul, and in the strength
of divine grace, to become a perfect imitator of his
Lord, embraced this doctrine of fraternal charity
without reservation, and resolved to love his neighbour,
so far as was possible to him, according to the measure
and in the spirit of his Divine Model.   His own
words will again best describe his sentiments.   " I
have so great a perception," he writes to a friend, " of
the goodness, love, and all the different effects of love
in the Most Holy Soul of our Lord, that this Interior,
all clemency, kindness, and charity, has made me
comprehend quite otherwise than I had ever previously done, how we ought to live by this Divine
love towards God and towards man, and how, in fact,

it is in Him that the law is perfectly accomplished."
And again he exclaims, " Ah, how good is the desert
when, after Baptism, we are led thither together with
our Lord by the Spirit of God! It was from thence
that our Lord went forth to converse with men, to
teach them, and work their salvation. Since with
Him we form but one Jesus Christ, having the honour
to be His members, we ought to live by His life, adopt
His spirit, and walk in His steps." And that which
he thus earnestly recommended to others was his own
fervent and persevering practice. He strove to unite
himself most closely to our Lord in all his conversation and dealings with men ; he placed himself in
His hands as an instrument to help them, and he
was continually beseeching Him to animate him with
that spirit of charity which He had inculcated. On
every occasion, and in every doubt, he consulted Him
as to what he ought to say and what he ought to do
for their good : when he should speak, when he should
be silent ; when act and when abstain from action ;
that so he might perfectly accomplish the work which
his Lord was pleased to do by his means. Hence it
was that De Renty never looked at his fellow-creatures
with a purely natural eye, nor did he esteem them
according to the qualities with which they were
severally endowed by nature. It was from a much
higher point of view that he regarded and estimated
them : it was as creatures of God, made to His image
and redeemed by His Blood ; it was as his brethren
and co-heirs, purchased at the cost of the bitter
Passion and Death of Jesus, whose they were, and to
whose Heart they were inexpressibly dear. Here
was their title to his love ; and here we may see the
reason why his active life of charity was, as we have

observed, no occasion of spiritual distraction to this good man, but served only to unite him more nearly to Him whom he alone regarded in his neighbour. It was the source also of the blessing with which it pleased God so abundantly to crown his labours, a blessing at once the reward and the fruit of purity of intention : the reward, because God is wont to send His benediction on him who does His work lovingly and simply, without any eye to self or secondary objects ; its fruit, because the whole behaviour of one who acts with this pure supernatural motive is free from those vicious imperfections which mar the work of him whose zeal for God is mingled with human alloy, and because his words, all instinct with the charity of Jesus, have a powerful grace to draw others to the love of God.   It is needless to pursue this subject further here, as the conformity to Jesus which was the ruling attraction of De Renty, and the ground of his perfection, will be abundantly exemplified in the detailed consideration of his virtues.

CHAPTER V.

De Renty's Victory over Self.

It is common for those who treat of the spiritual life to divide it into three successive stages : the Purgative, dedicated to the extirpation of vices ; the Illuminative, in which the acquisition of virtues is the principal work ; and the Unitive, in which the soul, now brought to a state of greater purity, is capable of that close union with its God for which the two previous states were but the preparation. Yet this division can have but a general application, for it would be quite impossible to separate these stages of progress by rigid lines of demarcation. The first two, especially, must more or less proceed conjointly, though the first will predominate and give a special character to the earlier stages of the spiritual career; and for this simple reason, that vices are eradicated in order to the planting of virtues by the Divine Gardener, our vices forming the sole obstacle to this work. Nevertheless, He does not wait to sow and cultivate till the ground is all cleared, but in proportion as we set our hand heartily, with His help, to make room for His Divine operations, the fruits of holiness begin to spring up in the liberated soil of our souls. Neither, on the other hand, when they have grown, and flourished, and matured, and filled the place of those bad plants which formerly encumbered the ground, can there be a truce to the war against the evil seed, whose germs and roots remain in us so long as we are in this mortal flesh, ready to spring up anew if not continually kept in check. It is not as with Ismael, the son of the bond-woman, the type of the old nature, who, when cast out in order that the son of promise, the true heir, might grow up free and unthwarted, never returned. Our Ismael, albeit cast down, nay, cut down, is not yet cast out. For this reason, the Purgative way, in one sense, can never cease here below; while, as regards the Unitive way, although God does not commonly raise souls to that state until they have merited it by their fidelity to grace in the previous stages, and after passing through many trials and temptations, still He is sovereign, and can do what He will with His own. He is bound by no rule or method in His dealings, and can, when He sees good, impart to souls in the earlier stages of conversion a share and a taste of those gifts which are not ordinarily bestowed save on the perfect.

Nevertheless, the division is in its general sense perfectly accurate, and from the very nature of things must be so. To do penance is the first cry of grace to a soul awakened to the desire of a more perfect sanctification. Victory over the old Adam must always be an indispensable condition of the growth and triumph of the new man Christ in us. Accordingly, we find the Spirit of God usually inciting newly-converted souls to the diligent practice of mortification. The unruly and rebellious passions are the first enemy with which they are brought face to face in the spiritual warfare on which they are entering; and, as the flesh is the stronghold of the passions, so also do these souls commonly feel an attraction for corporal austerities. De Renty formed no exception to this rule; and, as we might have expected from his courageous and resolute temperament, and from the firm and entire purpose with which he had turned to God, he was not disposed to treat with tenderness anything which could offer an obstacle to his purpose, and to the reign of Christ over his whole being. He began at once to treat his body with much rigour. He made a continual fast, eating but one meal a day, and in this practice he persevered for several years, until he was ordered by his director to take more nourishment, in order to support him under the excessive fatigues which he underwent in the prosecution of his charitable labours. He wore for a portion of each week an iron girdle, with a double row of very long points, and an armlet of the same description; he was wont, besides, to discipline himself often very severely ; at times he added a hair shirt to his other inflictions, and always bore on his chest and stomach a bronze crucifix of great length, the nails of which pierced his flesh. He was so mortified in the matter of food that he not only ate little, but always chose the worst, ever bearing in mind that our fall was the consequence of eating a delicious fruit. Dining in company on a day of abstinence, a guest at the same table took occasion to watch him, and noticed that he partook of nothing except some peas ; and, moreover, it was evident from the modesty and recollection of his behaviour that his thoughts were fixed on God, not on his meal. Like the great St. Charles Borromeo, it pained him to see a board laden with viands and delicacies to do him honour. A friend of his, who was a man of piety, asked him to dinner one day at Caen. The table was furnished in a style which this gentleman considered due to De Renty's rank and position ; but when this great lover of frugality and simplicity saw the ceremonious preparation made for him he became silent, and was observed to eat very little. Indeed, as he afterwards declared, his mind had been filled the whole time with shame and humiliation at the thought that Christians should feast in this luxurious fashion ; adding that a little suffices, and that it is very painful to have to take part in a meal where so many dishes are set before you, and where everything is so opposed to the poverty of Jesus, which nevertheless ought to be our rule. He used often to say, " a little bread, bacon, and butter is quite enough for any one." His friends, when they had become aware of his strong feeling on this point, ceased to torment .him with good cheer ; and, when he dined with them, instead of adding to the bill of fare, they were rather careful that the dinner should be more simple than usual.

It was not, as we have seen, solely from the desire to mortify the taste that De Renty preferred a simple and frugal diet, but from his extraordinary attraction towards the poverty and humiliations of Jesus. This it was, as well as his love of mortification, which led him when on travel to take his meal, if possible, in the kitchen with the inn servants and inferior guests of the house. He had a further motive, which his insatiable charity never failed to suggest. This practice gave him the opportunity of speaking a few words of edification to these poor people. When evening came, he made some pretext to dismiss his own attendants, and would pass the night in an arm-chair or throw himself on a bed without undressing. On one occasion, when a lady of Amiens and one of the principal people of that city received him in her house, and, in her desire to do him all the honour she could, allotted him a handsome apartment containing a magnificent bed, he was much displeased, and would not make any use of it. He slept on a bench, and the next day his friend received reproaches instead of thanks for her splendid hospitality ; so that, finding that if she was to enjoy the blessing of lodging him, she must give him another room more to his taste, that is, less luxurious and comfortable, she hastened to meet his wishes.

Some persons may be disposed to question the discretion of so marked a rejection of all the comforts

and conveniences of life on the part of one whom
Providence and his own voluntary election retained
amid worldly cares and duties. They may say that we
are bidden to conceal our austerities, no less than our
alms; that all singularity is best avoided, as savour-
ing of affectation, or, at least, as being open to the
suspicion of secret ostentation; and, at any rate, that
the marked refusal of what might innocently be used
is an implied censure on our neighbours who act
differently. Undoubtedly we can imagine cases to
which these observations would apply. They would
apply, in fact, very generally to all whose grace does
not lead them to anything extraordinary : everything
which goes beyond our grace brings peril with it;
and all singularity, whether of devotion or austerity,
in which those may be tempted to indulge whose
habitual imperfections give good reason to themselves
and others to class them with ordinary Christians, must
especially be regarded with mistrust. But De Renty,
in acting as he did, was not going beyond but following his grace, which led him to live in the world as
not of the world, and thus condemn by his austere
example its lax and self-indulgent practices. No one
less courted observation either for his good deeds or
for his acts of mortification than did this saintly man;
for his humility was as deep as his love of poverty
and spirit of self-denial, and the impression he produced on others may be said indeed to have been the
last thing present to his mind : one thing alone was
present to his single eye,—the Will of God; one
motive alone actuated him,—the desire to follow and
be swayed by every breath of His grace. This is the
key to the understanding many actions of the saints,
and, we may add, of those saintly persons who bear

so strong a resemblance to saints that we only with-
hold the appellation from them because the Church
has never passed any judgment in their case. When
De Renty was alone and free to please himself, or,
rather, to obey without reserve the inclinations which
were supernaturally imparted by the Holy Ghost, his
total neglect and disregard of even his bodily needs
were much more remarkable than in company, where,
from motives of charitable complaisance, he had to
put a certain restraint upon himself. His meat and
drink were the accomplishment of God's will and his
sweetest refection. How often, when some work of
mercy had taken him on foot to a great distance from
Paris, so that it was impossible for him to return
home for dinner, would he rejoice to step alone and
unknown into some little wayside inn, where he
would get a scrap of dry bread and a draught of
water, like some poor man who could afford no better
fare, and then pursue his way with a gaiety of heart
unknown to either rich or poor,—not to the rich, who
usually rise after satiety ; not to the poor, who seldom
convert their abstinence into merit by the willing
acceptance which sanctifies it.

What he practised in respect of eating and drinking, he extended to the gratification of all his other
senses. The Carmelites at Pontoise, where he used
to lodge on some of his journeys, related how, arriving
one very cold day, he begged the Tourière neither to
light a fire nor to prepare a bed for him, for he
should not require either ; then, after speaking to
some of the nuns, he took his leave, saying he must
go and pay his little visits. These visits, we need
scarcely say, were not to personal friends of his own,
but to God's friends, the poor of Christ, and, specially,

the bashful poor, whom he assiduously sought out,—
the sick, the sorrowful, and the prisoner. Returning
to the convent at nine o'clock, and finding the
religious about to say Matins, he refused to eat, and
went into the church, where he remained at his
prayers till eleven, when he retired to his fireless
room. And yet he was one who suffered much pain
and inconvenience from cold : this, however, only
furnished him with an additional reason for not warm-
ing himself, for he was ever on the watch, as it were,
to seize some opportunity to mortify his body; acting
towards it like a spiteful enemy, always engaged in
inflicting some pain upon it, or, at any rate, depriving
it of some pleasure, a work at which he was positively
ingenious. It was sufficient for him to perceive that
his natural inclinations bore him in one direction,
instantly to do the precise contrary; so that in all
things he acted in an abiding spirit of self-sacrifice,
making no use of his senses nor following his natural
feelings save with an eye open to detect the malignity
of nature and check its activity.

In fact, so thoroughly was he enlightened to discern
the enmity of the flesh, and its undying opposition to
the work of grace in the soul, that he had a perfect
horror of anything that could content the senses;
and although he seldom spoke of himself save to his
director, yet one day, when talking confidentially
with a very intimate friend, the confession escaped
his lips that God had given him a great hatred of
himself. This hatred of the old Adam—for "no
man" (as the Apostle says) "ever hated his own
flesh,"* — cannot certainly be excessive, but the

* Eph. v. 29.

severities to which it sometimes impels those who intensely love God in themselves and themselves in God only, may no doubt become excessive; so judged his director, as we have seen, and so also judged Sister Marguerite of the Blessed Sacrament, with whom, as we have already noticed, De Renty had a most intimate union of grace, and who, divinely enlightened, as we may believe, reproached him for his too great rigour towards himself. He had so high a veneration for this holy woman, and placed so much confidence in her, that he deferred to her advice, and relaxed a little in a few particulars, though he complained to an intimate friend that he really could not "see the reason for humouring so lazy a beast, who rather needed urging on."

From the truceless combat he waged against his senses, he arrived at last at such a state of mortification that he was, as it were, insensible to outward impressions; whether that his mind was so abstracted from the body that he scarcely adverted to its sensations, or that, from lack of indulgence and satisfaction, those natural tastes and desires, the gratification of which, in some form or other, constitutes no small portion of the occupation of the great mass of men and women, perished and died away in him. He lived, if we may so express it, as if inhabiting a dead body; thus truly "bearing about" in it "the mortification of Jesus Christ." * There is a blunting of the taste which proceeds from over-indulgence. The glutton and the epicure, to their regret, cease to relish what they do not cease to love and to desire; but there is also a blunting which comes eventually of lack of

* 2 Cor. iv. 10.

supply to the cravings of the natural inclinations, when such lack of supply is a voluntary act. Hence it was that De Renty at last scarce knew what he was eating : all things, he confessed to a friend, tasted alike to him, or, at least, he had no preference whatsoever as respected food ; and, as he ate without relishing, so also he may be said to have seen without seeing, and this even in cases where he might reasonably have been expected to take a peculiar interest ; as, for instance, when, after spending a long time in churches magnificently adorned, and being questioned whether he did not admire them, he was compelled to own that he had seen or, at any rate, had observed nothing.

It will the less surprise us to find De Renty arriving at so high a point of mortification in so short a time, and without those special aids which the religious life affords, when we remember that from the very moment of his complete conversion of heart he directed his generous and unrelaxing efforts to this object, the suppression of all his desires and the putting to death of corrupt nature. Days count for years when a soul works with persevering energy and fervour, and corresponds so faithfully to grace. The entire diversion of the mind from his senses, and from creatures which, through the channel of the senses, come to occupy the attention and fill the heart, was accompanied by an abiding application of his soul to God. The one, in fact, implies the other. If we make room for God by banishing creatures, He will enter to fill it. De Renty's mind was so fixed on God, that even when suffering sharp pain during severe illness he did not bestow a thought upon what he endured : nay, he seemed scarcely to advert to it, but behaved as one who is

insensible. No one, indeed, was so reserved at all
times in alluding to his own discomforts; for he was
aware that nature finds a great alleviation in uttering
complaints, and in the consciousness that sympathizing
friends know what it suffers. This consideration was
alone sufficient to make him deny himself the satisfaction : thus he added to his involuntary sufferings the
merit which belongs to voluntary inflictions, by bury-
ing them in silence and offering them to God. The
persons who knew him most intimately, and who had
studied his behaviour on all occasions most attentively,
testified to never having heard him complain on any
occasion, whether in sickness or in sorrow ; not even
when he lost a very dear son, did his affliction betray
itself in word or look. His brow was ever serene,
unfurrowed by any line of care or of displeasure. His
manners were always even, and his words few ; the
expression of his countenance a mixture of innocence
and confidence, such as we may note in children, upon
whose young faces anger, fear, or sadness has as yet
engraved no mark.

"He who is baptized," he used to say, "ought to
be dead in Jesus Christ, that he may live a life of
suffering and of application to God. Let us be ever
aiming at one end, which is sacrifice in everything
and in the manner which God wills. Let us be victims in union with the interior dispositions and the
sentiments He had from His Conception until His
Death, and the final completion of His immolation."
" Death, sacrifice, union," were words which he would
often repeat ; meaning thereby that we ought to study
and strive to die in all things to ourselves ; and,
in order to this, to sacrifice to God our mind, our
judgment, our will, our thoughts, our affections, our

desires, our passions, and all in union with and after the pattern of Jesus Christ. He had a great devotion to those words sung by the four-and-twenty ancients whom St. John beheld in vision prostrating themselves before the throne of the Lamb : " Thou hast made us to our God a kingdom and priests, and we shall reign on the earth." *   " For this Divine Lamb," he said, " establishes the kingdom of God in us, in that He reigns in our souls and in our bodies by His grace, and makes us Priests to offer ourselves to Him in sacrifice ; and consequently we shall reign eternally with Him in the land of the living."

This continual sacrifice of self had resulted generally in a species of holy insensibility akin to that which we have noticed with regard to his senses. So completely had he subdued all his passions, affections, desires, and even the first movements of nature, that he came to feel neither conflict, nor opposition, nor repugnance of any kind within him to anything whatsoever, however disagreeable or painful it might be ; so that, writing to his director, to give an account of his spiritual state, we find him saying that he could no longer comprehend what mortification was ; for in fact, where opposition and resistance cease, mortification also ceases, as the act of dying and its pains cease when death has taken place. Thus when familiar friends would evince their regret at some distressing circumstance which had befallen him, and which was calculated to inflict a deep wound on his feelings, De Renty would laugh unaffectedly, and say that all went well with him ; adding that we ought so to conquer ourselves, that nothing should any longer be able to mortify us. Few

* Apoc. v. 10.

perhaps could succeed so perfectly in thus deadening themselves as he certainly did; and that, not only because few can be found to act with such persevering energy, but also because, where such may be met with, this insensibility cannot be obtained at will. Neither does failure in this respect diminish merit, such immunity from inward repugnances and rebellions being a grace which God gives or withdraws at His pleasure. He pledges Himself to give us grace to surmount temptation, but that is all which we can presume to reckon upon, however long we may have battled with our old Adam, and however completely we may seem to have subdued him. Nay, Saints far advanced in holiness have been permitted, for their greater humiliation and the increase of their merit, to suffer much through the renewal of temptations from which they had long been free, and from which their repeated victories over self would appear to have for ever secured them.

De Renty, so far as we know, never passed through a phase of this kind in the spiritual life; perhaps God was pleased signally to reward in him the generosity and fidelity with which he had fought; for we must bear in mind that the man who arrived ta this state of holy insensibility had had to combat a nature which, so far from favouring his efforts, must in the outset have offered a fierce opposition to coercion. De Renty had many fine natural qualities; he was brave, true, upright, generous, liberal, just, compassionate to the poor; but those who knew him in his early youth speak of counter-balancing faults, describing him as passionate, hot, impetuous, intolerant, arrogant, and satirical. Of what may be called the nobler virtues he possessed an abundance, but in

the sweeter, the gentler, the lowlier, he appears to
have been by nature deficient ; and although the fear
of God had always operated to keep his defects within
certain limits, and had made him, after he had taken
the care of his soul seriously to heart, exercise a great
degree of self-control, it had left them potentially
alive and active ; and there is a wide interval, we
need scarcely say, between such a qualified restraint
of the passions and their extermination, between
holding nature in check and waging a war of persecution against it. This was what De Renty in the
strength of divine grace undertook and carried
through; and what a victory it was that he achieved !
So moderate, patient, humble, and respectful to his
fellow-creatures of all ranks and degrees did he become, that any one who had not been previously
acquainted with him would have imagined that his
natural dispositions had been the very opposite to
what they really were. Perhaps the victory is seldom
so complete as it is in such cases. Generous souls are
stirred up by the consciousness of their own defects
to use violence, and the Kingdom of Heaven, as we
know, is won by violence. De Renty was strongly
impressed with the needfulness of this violence if we
would arrive at perfection, and frequently warned
others against confiding in an easy spirituality, trust-
ing in their round of devotional acts—perhaps, after
all, very imperfectly performed—and in their speculative views of virtue. Victory over self he regarded as
the sole measure of progress ; but he was aware that
few, comparatively, address themselves in earnest to
the task of self-mortification, for that even with the
greater number of the piously disposed it is apt to
remain a matter of approbation, of desire, and, it may

H

be, of aspiration, scarcely a step being taken towards its actual realization. "We adore Jesus Christ in the morning," he writes to a friend, "as our master and director, and our life throughout the day is none the better directed; we take Him as the rule and regulator of our senses, and nevertheless we do not sacrifice our appetites to Him; we set Him before us as the model of our conversations, yet for all that they are not the more holy; we promise Him to labour and to conquer ourselves, but it is only in idea. Certainly, if we do not know our devotion more by the violence we do ourselves and by the amendment of our conduct than by the multiplication of our spiritual exercises, it is to be feared that these very exercises will prove our condemnation rather than our sanctification; for, after all, what is the good of all this if it be not followed by act, and if we do not change and destroy what is vicious in our nature? Otherwise we are like an architect who should collect a quantity of materials for erecting a fine building, and yet never begin to build: to this the work of Jesus Christ has almost come in our day." He considered that this speculative and merely appreciative way of viewing Christian virtues was a very common snare. Persons confound their own esteem and love of holiness with the possession of it, making herein a most lamentable mistake; for "our Lord," he says, "assuredly designs that His followers should enter into the solid practice of His divine virtues, especially those of mortification, patience, poverty, and self-renunciation; and the reason why there are so few souls truly Christian and solidly spiritual, sometimes even in religious communities, is because they content themselves with remaining at this first stage."

Amongst his conquests over self none was more remarkable than that which he achieved over a naturally impatient and intolerant spirit. Although temperament may have its share in fostering this spirit, yet, viewed in relation to the will which acquiesces in its indulgence, pride undoubtedly is its great root, that prolific source of many more vices and imperfections than we are apt to suspect, and of some with which at first sight we do not always see its close connection. Patience under sufferings of all kinds is distinctive of the truly humble man ; and this is easily intelligible, for, after all, impatience and every species of intolerance proceed, in persons who have attained the full use of reason, chiefly from reflection on what they suffer, rather than from the irrepressible and instinctive outbreak of pain and distress. The humble man is patient because he reckons that he deserves all he suffers, and much more. This sense of unworthiness, the fruit of grace, silences a thousand utterances of an impatience which has its hidden source in self-esteem. Again, it is pride and self-love, in some one of their forms, which make us desire to have our sufferings appreciated ; and it was the profound humility of this servant of God, as much as the desire to offer a willing sacrifice of all he endured to God, which made him refuse himself the solace of human sympathy and consolation. His humility will deserve a separate notice ; we therefore only allude to it here as the basis of that virtue of patience which he so eminently possessed. Not to speak of all that he had continually to try it in the laborious works of

mercy which he undertook, in the prosecution of
which he encountered cold, heat, hunger, fatigue, and
other corporal sufferings, which were the necessary
accompaniments of work performed as he performed
it, who was to himself the severest and the most
pitiless of task-masters, we have but to observe the
manner in which one of a spirit naturally lofty bore
the contempt and insolence of which he was often the
object, to see how thoroughly he had subdued all the
rebellious risings of proud nature.

The following example will show how he behaved
under provocations of this kind. On certain fixed
days he was in the habit of going to catechize some
poor people in a hospital. An official of the establishment felt annoyed and irritated at seeing a man
of his rank performing such an act of humility and
charity ; in fact, he did not like the intrusion of a
gentleman, and the usurpation, as he deemed it, of
his functions. Narrow-minded persons of this stamp
may not unfrequently be found among underlings,
who will much prefer to see their superiors idling
away their days in luxurious self-indulgence to being
annoyed by their presence in what they reckon their
own domain, however admirable may be the motives
of their visitors. It is a sort of interference with
their independence in their own little sphere, and
they do not like it. One day, then, this official,
being determined to bear the encroachment on his
territory no longer, came forward while De Renty
was in the midst of a circle of poor sick folk, and
addressed to him in their hearing some very offensive
and insulting words. De Renty listened without a
shade of emotion on his countenance, and then replied, in a tone of much humility and respect, that if

he desired himself to give instruction to these poor people, who much needed it, he on his part would not return on the accustomed days; but if he did not wish to undertake the task, he prayed him not to hinder their receiving so great a benefit. The man would not bind himself by any such engagement; nevertheless, on four successive days, as soon as De Renty had begun to catechize, he came and took his place: an impertinence to which that holy man submitted with a meekness and patience truly admirable. It will enhance his merit when we remember that those were days when the lines of demarcation between classes were much more rigidly defined than now, and when the nobility were a privileged class and held their heads very high.

De Renty practised the same forbearance in all the vexations and annoyances of life, small and great; and perhaps the small, by their very insignificance and frequency, are the most trying. "As I was praying before the Blessed Sacrament," he writes in one of his papers, "a poor man came and begged for alms. I was in the act of trying to put myself in a state of recollection; and we are apt to feel annoyance at such little interruptions, as, indeed, the term we commonly use implies, for we speak of the *importunity* of beggars. But instantly it was given me to understand that, if we were well enlightened, we should never consider ourselves to be importuned by anybody, or hindered by anything, because we should look at the order of God conducting all things for our advantage; that even as we ought patiently to endure inward distractions, so also ought we to bear such as come from without; the trouble, disquietude, and impatience which these little incidents cause us pro-

ceeding from our ignorance and want of mortification.
Not but that we ought to avoid such things as may
disturb us, but when they come we must regard them
as ordained by God, receive them in a spirit of sweetness, and endure them with humility and respect;
thus, whatever happens to us, and in whatever
manner we may be interrupted, the order of God is
not interrupted in us, but we follow it ; and this
is the treasure and the great secret of the spiritual
life : it is, so to say, Paradise on earth."

It was in this manner that the servant of God
made gain of everything, for in everything matter for
patience and endurance will occur, because nature is
sure to find itself thwarted in some way or other. It
was the same where his best and highest projects
were concerned : if they failed and were defeated,
straightway he set himself to use this disappointment
as a personal means of advancement in grace and perfection, by possessing his soul in patience, and thus
keeping it in peace. Solomon says,* " The patient
man is better than the valiant ; and he that ruleth
his spirit than he that taketh cities." Patience is
truly the highest form of courage when it flows, as it
did in De Renty, from a supernatural motive ; and it
is also the strongest of virtues, since it requires much
more force to endure than to do. *"Passio est consum-
matio fortitudinis;* endurance is the perfection of
fortitude," says the great St. Ambrose ; to which
may be added the testimony of the Angelic Doctor:
*"Principalior actus fortitudinis est sustinere quam
aggredi;* it is a higher act of fortitude to endure than
to assault." The Christian's victory, to be perfect,

* Prov. xvi 32.

must be after the pattern of his Lord's, who triumphed over sin and death, and worked our Redemption,. not by what He did, but by what He endured..

CHAPTER VI.

DE RENTY'S ESTEEM FOR SUFFERING.   HIS DOMESTIC TROUBLES.

DE RENTY'S patience was not based on his deep humility alone, but sprang from the esteem in which he held suffering, to which the Passion of Jesus has given a supreme value.   He knew that, rightly accepted, sufferings become sources of life eternal, mines of heavenly treasure, seeing that they are participations in the Cross of Jesus, which God has made the source of our salvation, and to which all who would be saved must therefore unite themselves. " God is fashioning you for Himself," he writes to an afflicted person, " by uniting you here below to the suffering Jesus. Ah, what a grace is this, and a greater than people think !"   And to another, " What a blessing is yours that God should make you suffer while the world laughs ! If they of the other side had their eyes opened, as you have, we should see a delightful wonder ; for we should behold you laughing while you suffer, and them weeping because they do not suffer. You have a grace which these men despise, because they know it not, and the poor creatures reckon themselves happy for what is their misfortune."   This high esteem which he had for

sufferings made him thirst for them, so as to exclaim
with the Saint for whom he had so great a devotion,
"Either to die or to suffer!" "There is but one
profitable thing in this life," he says, "and that is
to suffer: all consolation, all sweetness, all joy is an
anticipation of the recompense, which is not due to
criminals, who sojourn on this earth only in order to
purify themselves and do penance; and to this consolations, sweetness, and joys bring some modification,
and, no doubt, prevent the requisite penance from
being so complete, and ourselves from attaining as
high a degree of perfection. Not but what," he adds,
"these things are at times necessary for our infirmity,
which needs for its support to be propped up on all
sides." The beauty of suffering, as assimilating and
conforming us to our Crucified Head, was always
present to his mind, and he never ceased exhorting
his friends to love and recognize this grace, which
imprints on us the characters of the Passion of Jesus
Christ, and becomes a pledge of future glory; "for
who can doubt," he says, writing to a person in affliction, "that in proportion as we shall be fashioned to
the likeness of the Death and Sufferings of the Son of
God, in the same degree we shall be made partakers
of His Glory?"

But notwithstanding all his attraction to suffering,
he never ventured to ask for it. It was equally part
of his attraction to refrain from doing so. To this
he alludes in several of his letters to his director. In
one of these, for example, we find him dwelling on
the longing desire he felt to suffer, giving as his
reason that whereas in other things we are recipients,
in this case, albeit we receive the grace of suffering,
nevertheless suffering itself is, properly speaking, that

which we can give to God, and the greatest pledge and proof of our love; but he immediately adds, "not that I therefore myself elect sufferings, but I feel myself interiorly drawn towards them. 1 am conducted thus far, and there I am stopped." How strongly he at times experienced the attraction to which he here alludes he instances in the same letter, where he says, "About a fortnight ago I was impressed with so strong a feeling of love and gratitude for our Lord Jesus Christ suffering and immolating · Himself to His Eternal Father, and allying us to Himself that with Him we may be one same love and one same sacrifice, that I felt myself instantly, and for an instant, fastened to His Cross, as by an alliance of love—an inexplicable alliance, the effect of which I still experience." All eminently holy persons have undoubtedly felt attracted to suffering in some form or other, but all have not asked for sufferings. Such a prayer, without a special movement of the Holy Ghost, might perhaps imply a certain presumption. St. James * bids us count it all joy when we fall into divers temptations, yet nowhere are we enjoined to pray for them; nay, our Lord taught us daily to pray not to be led into temptation. Now, sufferings are trials, and trials are in a sense temptations; true, we are made perfect by passing through them, but, unless moved to make choice of them by the Holy Spirit, the Christian soul prefers to abandon itself to God's will and appointment in this as in all other things.

We find De Renty describing his own sentiments on this subject in an account which he gave of his interior dispositions to his director in the Lent of 1648. "It came into my mind," he writes, "that one

* i. 2.

means of making me pass a very severe Lent would
be to set me before a well-filled board, and compel me
to make good cheer; to throw me into the midst of
gay worldly company, and force me to talk and laugh;
to take me to promenades and places of public resort;
for all this would be to me a little hell, not to speak
of the sin there might be in it, the sole thought of
which makes me shudder with horror; for true it is
that solitude, fasting, and those other things which
are called penance, are my attraction." And then
he goes on to say, "Although I experience all this,
nevertheless I know what I am, and in the midst of
all my attraction and desires *I am mindful not to ask
for the least suffering :* when I have done so from an
impulse of my own I have afterwards revoked my act,
as being that of a madman. I have too much experience of my feebleness, and so I only give myself to
God for all that He desires of me, from the height of
heaven above to the very depth of hell below; I will
all that He orders for me; with Him I can do all
things; and what He ordains is always accompanied
by His grace."

He laid great stress on the manner in which
sufferings were borne, considering that the grace to
accept them in a truly Christian spirit and render
them fruitful to their full extent is far from common.
"The beauty of suffering," he writes to a friend, "is
in the interior, in the holy dispositions of Jesus Christ,
who is (and this is what we must particularly remark
and always closely study) the model as well as the
Head of all who suffer." And again, "It is a great
grace to suffer; people are mistaken in supposing
that this is a very common grace: it is very rare. It
is true that we can say that many suffer, but few suffer

with the dispositions of Jesus Christ; few suffer with a perfect consent to what God ordains concerning them; few without some uneasiness and some application of mind to their suffering; few who commit all events to God's disposal without making reflections on them, so as to give themselves entirely to His praise, and leave him free to exercise in their regard all His rights over them." Writing to encourage a lady who was in much trouble, he says, "Few understand the secret of Christianity: many call themselves Christians, but few have the spirit of Christians; many in their prayers and ordinary affairs look to Heaven, but in cases of importance they are children of nature, regarding earth alone; or, if they raise their eyes to Heaven, it is to lament themselves, and to beg God to condescend to their desires, not to accept His. They give small things to God, but they wish to retain those to which love attaches them; and if He separates these from them, it is as though they were suffering a violence and a dismemberment, to which they cannot consent; as if the life of Christians was not a life of sacrifice and an imitation of the Crucified Jesus. God, who knows our misery, takes away from us that which is the cause of evil to us, for our greater good—a relation, a child, a husband—that by another evil, which is affliction, He may draw us to Himself, and make us perceive that all attachments to anything whatever which separates us from Him are obstacles of so much importance, that the day will come when we shall confess before all creatures that the greatest mercy He ever showed us was to have set us free from them: it is as wormwood, bitter in the mouth and to the taste, but salutary to the heart. It kills Adam that Jesus Christ may live. It is like a severe winter,

which secures the beauty of the other seasons; but we
must diligently watch lest what is presented to us by
grace should be received by us as a casualty or as a
misfortune, for this would be to convert a remedy
into a poison, and to receive a grace only to drive it
away. Let us enter into the holy and adorable disposition in which Jesus Christ ever was, to suffer voluntarily for the honour of His Father and for our salvation. Is it not strange that men should perceive that
the road which Jesus Christ followed to arrive at
glory was ignominy, pain, and the Cross, and that they
who call themselves His disciples and imitators should
expect and ask another for themselves? Is the
disciple above his Master? And if the Head has
willed to pass by that way, what must be the consequence as respects the members? Must not they
follow Him? Let us, then, go after Him, and let us
suffer after His example. Blessed be sickness; blessed
be the loss of honour, of goods, of our nearest relatives; blessed be our separation from creatures,
which kept us bowed down to earth! These afflictions raise us up and make us lift up our eyes to
Heaven, and enter into the designs of God towards
us. Blessed be pestilence, war, and famine; and
blessed, without reserve, be all the scourges of God,
which produce these effects of grace and salvation
in us!"

One of the greatest, perhaps in many ways the
greatest, trial which De Renty was called to endure
was that which arose from the trouble caused him by
his mother. Whether that lady was actuated by
prejudice against her son, caused by vexation at
seeing him carry his devotions to what she deemed
extravagant lengths, spending his time in hospitals

and prisons, engaged in what the world judges to
be mean and abject employments, unworthy of his
birth, and that she would willingly have seen him
occupying some distinguished post, such as his ancestors had filled, and of which his own talents rendered
him well worthy; or whether she was impelled by
bad advisers, or moved by a covetous spirit, or in-
fluenced by all these motives combined, so it was that
at the death of her husband she set up exorbitant
claims over his property, to the detriment of her son's
lawful heritage. De Renty, as may be supposed, was
not a man to stand upon his rights, even if filial
affection and respect had not combined in this case to
make him entirely averse to any contention for their
maintenance. Had no other interests been at stake
than his own, gladly would he, in whose eyes worldly
goods and worldly cares were a painful burden, have
yielded to all her demands, however manifestly
groundless and unreasonable. As it was, he gave
her not only what was her due, but beyond it,
treating her throughout the whole affair with the
utmost deference and submission ; but this failed to
content her : she made further claims, and when her
son, after taking good advice, became aware that he
could not comply with her wishes and renounce his
own rights without doing a wrong to his children,
whose interests he was bound to consider, he did not
feel it to be just to take upon himself the responsibility of conceding what she required. He accordingly resolved to refer the matter to arbitration,
allowing his mother, for her more complete satisfaction, to choose the umpires herself, and to select any
persons of her acquaintance of acknowledged probity
and competence, although they might be personally

unknown to him. Further, he desired that these
arbitrators should decide, not what in justice he could
claim, but how much he could in conscience surrender
to his mother. As soon, therefore, as they had been
appointed, he went to see them, in order to beg them
to satisfy his mother in all that was possible, without
any regard to his interests.

The day being arrived upon which these gentlemen
were to give their judgment, while they were shut up
in consultation, M. de Renty's mother was awaiting
their decision in another room. In what manner she
passed the anxious time we have no record, but how
her saintly son, whom she had the misfortune not to
appreciate, was employed we know on the authority
of a lady, a friend of him and of his wife, who was
with them in another part of the house. She afterwards related that De Renty was engaged the whole
time in praying that the result of the affair might be
for the glory of God and the promotion of peace;
and with this intention he asked his two companions
to recite some hymns with him. While they were
thus occupied, the document that had been drawn up
was brought for him to sign. It was first read to
him, and he listened with the most imperturbable tranquillity, although it was far from being favourable to
him. Moreover, it had been decided that a considerable sum should be forfeited by whichever of the
parties should either go back from the engagement
or appeal against it. This was for the purpose of
binding both sides more securely by the decision,
which, it will be remembered, was not the sentence
of a law court. De Renty himself was the only party
in the transaction who could have reason to demur to
the judgment; he, however, affixed his signature at

once without a moment's hesitation; and, now believing that his mother would be fully contented, he returned to his own house, where his first act was to collect all his household to sing the *Te Deum*, himself leading it in a loud and jubilant voice, expressive of his unfeigned joy and gratitude at a resolution which he was persuaded would prove a bond of peace between him and his parent for the remainder of her life.

But in this confidence he was much mistaken. His trials were not ended, and God, for his greater purification and increase of merit, had a heavy cross prepared for him, which he was to bear for several years. Madame de Renty, against all reasonable expectation, was not satisfied with the decision of the arbitrators, and, having discovered some subterfuge which enabled her to evade the payment of the sum which was to be forfeited by the appellant, she resolved to prosecute her assumed rights before the Parliament of Dijon. In vain did her son employ every means he could devise to soften her heart and divert her from this project; in vain had he recourse to all those supernatural helps upon which he placed far more reliance than on his own efforts. He made long prayers with this object, and, adding penance to prayer, he fasted with extreme rigour, and used other great austerities, hoping that God would have regard to his supplications and the sincerity of his intentions. After a course of these penitential exercises and fervent petitions, he again sought his mother, and, kneeling at her feet with the deepest reverence and submission, implored her with many tears to give up her design of going to law. He, at the same time, made a most generous offer, which practically would have conceded to her all that she asked. He was ready, he said, with his whole family, to go and live under her roof, she maintaining them exactly as she judged fit, and to resign to her the management and administration of all the·property which his father had bequeathed to him. But, strange to say, this impracticable woman hardened herself against this touching appeal of her son, although it was repeated in the same manner more than once. She would accept of no concession, however ample, but insisted on obtaining by regular course of law the full amount of her claims. It was suggested to him, as a last resource, to throw a legal difficulty in her way, by refusing to go to Dijon to plead ; this expedient, it appears, was free to him to adopt, and would have had the effect of defeating her intention. But his filial respect for his mother was so great, that he did not consider himself at liberty to refuse her any satisfaction which he could conscientiously afford her. She desired this lawsuit, and he would not therefore hinder it. He would go to Dijon, since she wished it ; and to Dijon he did go.

He undertook this journey in a spirit prepared to suffer confusion and humiliation, which in fact awaited him in that city. The world, we know, is very hasty in its judgments, and very hard and unkind, even when not actuated by malice. People readily take up a prejudice, and thereupon form an opinion, without so much as giving themselves the trouble to ascertain if it rests on any solid grounds. It would seem, indeed, that the world has a special repugnance to examining or weighing evidence before giving its verdict. It likes decided and sweeping views; it loves to praise and admire in an unqualified manner, or to censure and condemn without reserve and without mercy. This falls in alike with the vanity, shallow thoughtlessness, and love of excitement natural to the human heart. Here was a man who, by his actions and the habitual tenour of his life, made a high profession of piety, and yet he was actually engaged in a lawsuit against his own widowed mother ! This was really very shocking, and the good gossips of Dijon felt it to be so. It is very comfortable to some persons to feel shocked, and here was a good opportunity; and perhaps we do not wrong the little world of Dijon in suspecting that not a few of those who were loudest in deploring the " scandal " contrived to extract some small amount of satisfaction from a circumstance so levelling to a great reputation ; for the world everywhere and at all times resembles itself. Anyhow it is certain that De Renty had been already tried and condemned before the tribunal of public opinion ere he arrived. He accepted this humiliation, however, not with patience only, but with joy, welcoming it as a means of sharing in the opprobrium which for our sakes the Son of God endured by taking the likeness of sinful flesh and appearing in the character of a criminal, He who was Innocence Itself. And as a criminal De Renty was indeed regarded in a matter wherein, so far from being open to blame, he was all the while performing acts of virtue which may truly be deemed heroic.

A letter of his to his director, dated July 24th, 1643, will give an insight into his feelings under this distressing trial. " I am at Dijon, then," he writes, " since so it has pleased God ; and I was aware, from the previously conceived opinions with regard to me, what it was that God designed me to draw from my

I

sojourn in this place.   He meant me to live a hidden
life here, unknown to men, in a spirit of penance. The
report which had been circulated concerning me, that
I was a bigot, with only the artifices and externals of
devotion covering my inward malice, has made me
keep very retired in my room, lest by showing myself
I should rather give scandal than a good example. I
found a Community here actively canvassing against
me, which for several just reasons was the very one
from which I had rather cause to expect support. God
has made this the channel of many graces to me. I
went to see them, and the humiliation I received at
their hands was a great joy to me.   I took care not
to make any communication which might recommend
me in their eyes. I only stated with reference to my
business what truth demanded, and then accepted all
the rest to my confusion and condemnation, as I
ought.   I regard myself here as one excommunicated,
the scapegoat of the old law, driven into the wilder-
ness for my enormous sins, for which it has appeared
to me that God-willed that I should do penance, not
by simple sufferings, but by sufferings which bring
shame with them.   I tell you this merely to render
you an account of myself, not dwelling upon it any
further, my single aim being to love God and to
condemn myself."

We cannot help pausing a moment to notice the
many admirable things contained in these few words.
We gather from them that he refrained from every
expression which might tend to justify him and remove the peculiar odium attaching to covetousness
and to deficiency in filial affection and respect.   This
abstention was surely in itself a very heroic act; but
the act is further enhanced by the simplicity with

which it is done, a simplicity which quite obscures its merit in his eyes. He regards himself and his spiritual health as under the treatment of the Great Physician; and, just as a person might speak of being sent by the doctors to the seaside or to some baths for his bodily health, so he regards his visit to Dijon as a divine prescription. It is a simple fact in his course of treatment. Again, the confusion which he has to swallow there is not something to be avoided if possible, and submitted to resignedly if unavoidable : it is the dose he has to take ; he wishes to take it ; he thinks, indeed he knows, that it will do him good. He does not value himself for doing so, nor does he perceive aught that is admirable in the act, any more than the sick man thinks himself praiseworthy for taking his nauseous potion. Then he keeps himself from the public eye, not·to shun scorn, but because he is profoundly convinced that, thinking of him as men do, he will be a scandal and a detriment·to religious interests. Any other motive does not so much as suggest itself. Let us mark·also what we may call the thorough objectiveness of his mind, which is one of the childlike characteristics of this strong man. If he makes any reflections upon what passes in him, it is in obedience to his director and for his information ; otherwise his single eye is ever fixed on God, that he may love Him ; and when he gives a thought to himself, it is only in a general way, as something sentenced to condemnation,—the body of sin which is to be destroyed to make way for the reign of Christ, his true life. It is a very simple affair with him, and precludes a world of reflections, difficulties, and vexations.

We are apt to consider saints and saintly persons

as too far beyond us in the spiritual course to be objects of imitation. When we read of their austerities, their incessant self-denial in even lawful things, their marvellous acts of charity and devotion, their long hours of prayer, their vigils, their cruel penances, our hearts will sometimes sink within us, and we say to ourselves that these things are too far above us to be either a pattern or a guide for our practice. Certainly many acts of these great servants of God are beyond our poor efforts, and are not, even as acts, proposed for general imitation ; yet, paradoxical as it may seem at first sight, it is nevertheless true that that which is most admirable in the saints is also just that which is most imitable, and which, indeed, we all ought to strive to imitate. We mean the spirit in which they performed their actions, the motive which determined the attitude, so to say, of their souls. This is always imitable to a certain extent, yet it is also that which gave its real value to all their deeds ; both those in which we may copy them, and those which materially we are not called to copy. To study, then, the leanings, teachings, and workings of grace in eminently holy souls, is one of the best means of promoting the accomplishment of its full and perfect work in ourselves, however inferior may be our calling.

In the many letters of De Renty to his director which have been preserved, we are fortunate in possessing a complete key to his acts, and a beautiful analysis of the work of grace in his soul. Saint-Jure also diligently collected from the numerous survivors —and they were very numerous, for De Renty died while still young—many authentic anecdotes which help to complete the picture which has been bequeathed to us for our edification. We subjoin a few connected with the affair of which we are speaking. The superioress of a religious house at Dijon communicated to him all the bad reports and strange stories that had been circulated concerning him in that place, where, as there was no one personally acquainted with him to undertake his justification, the calumnies remained uncontradicted and met with general credence. De Renty listened to all without showing any emotion, and then replied in terms which manifested at once the elevation of his soul to God, and his entire acceptance of the humiliation to which he was subjected. He did not shrink from it; on the contrary, his heart seemed to dilate to receive and drink it in. He evidently felt it to be his gain as well as his duty, not merely to bear it as well as he could, but to taste its full bitterness. This was implied both in his countenance and in the few words he uttered. The superioress, much edified, proceeded to inquire whether it was true, as report affirmed, that documents had been published reflecting injuriously on his mother. This he denied, adding that lawyers sometimes would say more than you wished them to say; but that he had himself seen all the papers relating to the suit, and none of them departed from the respect which a son owes his mother. Desiring to read further into this pure soul, she then asked him if he did not feel much displeasure at her conduct towards him, which certainly appeared at once strange and unkind. " No," he replied, " because I so adore the order of God in my regard, that I cannot feel displeasure at what happens to me by His permission. I am a great sinner, and therefore, not my own mother only, but the whole world ought to rise against me." So sincere and genuine was this

sentiment, that he never was heard to utter a single
complaint against his mother for her ill-treatment of
him, but attributed all to his own sins. The same
nun, whose testimony we have quoted, further remarked, that so impracticable was this lady on the
subject, that although many persons laboured to persuade her to come to some compromise and amicable
arrangement, they had the greatest trouble in per-
suading her even to entertain the proposal ; and at
last, when every difficulty seemed to be smoothed
and the whole affair settled in a manner calculated to
meet her wishes, she would raise fresh objections and
start new difficulties. While these negotiations were
going on, the superioress said one day to M. de Renty.
"Sir, I will willingly say a *Te Deum* when I shall
hear that your business is concluded." At length
there seemed to be a fair prospect of its happy ter-
mination. Articles had been drawn up and mutually
accepted, and a day had been fixed for signature, when
Mdme. de Renty, suddenly changing her mind, broke
off the treaty. On that same day her son appeared
at the convent with an extremely cheerful face, and
begged his friend, the religious, to keep her word to
him. "The time is come," he said, "for the *Te Deum*
which you had the goodness to promise me ; but might
I venture to ask to be allowed to say it with you!
Oh ! what a great and good God we have, who well
knows how to dispose things, not according to our
impatience, but in His own order, which is our sanctification." His request was of course granted, and he
sang along with the nun a most jubilant *Te Deum.*
It was enough to hear and see him to be convinced
that his spirit was all filled with God. When the
thanksgiving was over he said, "Well, nothing has

been done, but it was right to say the *Te Deum*, to
thank God for having done His own will and not that
of a sinner unworthy to be heard or regarded." · The
religious, as may be supposed, readily forgave him
what may be called his pious stratagem, and felt all
the more admiration for him, as it was believed that
the negotiation was now irretrievably broken off, and
the business really concluded, though in a manner
quite contrary to his hopes.

Saint-Jure adds his testimony to that of the Dijon
nun as to De Renty's utter silence concerning his
mother's behaviour. This was the more remarkable
as, when giving an account of his interior to his
director, he might not unnaturally, and without
suspecting his own motives, have taken the opportunity to unburden his mind of the distress which
his mother's unkindness must have caused him, and
thus, indirectly at least, to pass some judgment on
its injustice. But no ; he never uttered one single
word respecting either the affair or his mother to him
who had his whole confidence, save to recommend both
the one and the other to his prayers. Once Saint-
Jure informed him of some suggestions which had
been made by persons desirous to serve him. De
Renty thanked him and the individuals in question
with much cordiality for their good-will, and then,
pursuing the subject no further, began to discourse
about God, and never opened his mouth on the
subject to him again. We learn from the same
source that this business continued to furnish constant matter for trial and endurance to De Renty up
to the time of his mother's death, and even after that
event, which bequeathed to him a legacy of embarrassments. But his biographer gives us no further

details, contenting himself with remarking that the heroic patience he displayed throughout all these transactions was the wonder of all who had the opportunity of observing it; and that, since, considering his eminent virtues, there was every reason to believe that De Renty was now in the land of perfect charity, he doubted not but that he would approve his resolve to say no more, but to practise some reserve in speaking of a mother for whom through life he had entertained so much love and respect. Enough, however, has been told us to exhibit in a striking light the value which this servant of God set upon sufferings, and his admirable behaviour under their pressure.

CHAPTER VII.

DE RENTY'S POVERTY IN THE MIDST OF RICHES.

THAT De Renty had no attachment to the goods of this world would be sufficiently proved by his behaviour during the long course of time in which his possession of the greater portion of them was at stake. But his virtue extended far beyond these limits. He had entered deeply into the comprehension and love of the eight Beatitudes, and had vividly realized, as we find him writing to a friend, that there were none other; for, had there been, our Lord would have told us so; and that therefore they ought to constitute our whole study. He followed after them accordingly with all the eagerness and assiduity with which men of the world pursue its so-called blessings. In particular that Beatitude which heads the list, "Blessed are the poor in spirit," was profoundly rooted in his affections. Like the seraphic Saint of Assisi, he may truly be said to have been enamoured of poverty. "I never saw any one"—these are the words of a person who knew him intimately—"who so perfectly possessed poverty of spirit, or who so longingly desired to experience all the effects of poverty. In the ardour of this desire he would beg me to obtain for him by my prayers that he might be able to change his mode of life. "When shall you obtain this for me from God?" he would exclaim : "this attire and these goods are very irksome to me."

Saint-Jure says that after his death he was speaking about him to a religious to whom De Renty had communicated the attraction he felt to renounce his earthly possessions. The Father told him that De Renty one day suddenly consulted him on the subject, throwing himself on his knees before him with his face bathed in tears. He felt moved to surprise and admiration at seeing so pure a love of poverty in one of the rich of this world; it was the work of Him to whom all things are possible. De Renty confessed that so powerful was the attraction by which God drew him to separate himself from creatures and renounce the mode of life suitable to his birth, that if another divine attraction had not at one and the same time held him back he would have forsaken all, and, following the example of St. Alexis, would have gone forth to live a life similar to his ; but that God, while imprinting in his heart this desire of poverty, withheld its effect, in order to retain

him in the state in which He had placed him, and
this was no slight cross to him, because in proportion
to the impossibility of attaining a desired object is
the torment and pain of the soul which vehemently
longs for it. Yet, as in all things he conformed
himself absolutely to the will of God, he bore this
cross, repugnant as it was, not to his natural inclinations alone (that would have been little to one
whose daily habit it was to trample with joy on
nature), but to a supernatural inclination infused by
the same Spirit which imperatively forbade its indulgence, and bore it with that peace of mind and perfect submission to God's decrees which he so uniformly
displayed. "He often told me in confidence," says
an intimate friend of his, "that he felt ashamed, when
he entered the doors of his house, to see himself so
well lodged in this world, and that one of his great
distresses was the possessing so much, and being so
much at his ease; that he would have been enchanted
to be reduced to penury, with nothing but bread and
water for his fare, and even to have to earn this
bare subsistence by toil and the sweat of his brow.
Having asked him one day how he could always be
so tranquil under the many sufferings he had to
endure, and amidst all the distressing affairs which
beset him, he answered that he would tell me, provided I would keep his secret; and proceeded to confess that by the mercy of God his mind was as peaceful and undisturbed in the midst of afflictions and
troubles as in joy; that he was never moved to fear
anything or desire anything: and I myself," adds the
person whose words we are quoting, "noticed this to
be the case on many occasions, and in particular when
he was in peril of losing the best part of his property.

Since God,' he said, ' has laid on me the charge of
these possessions, I will do what is fitting for their
preservation; but after having bestowed the care
which He requires of me, it is the same to me whatever may be the result.' "

" He possessed the virtue of evangelical poverty in
its perfection," says another friend of his, " being
entirely removed in mind, thought, heart, and
affection from all the goods of this world : he told me
that he had no greater cross than those goods, and
that it would have been the greatest joy to him to be
a beggar unknown to all men, if only such had been
the will of God." In desiring this condition himself,
De Renty was actuated by a simple, unfeigned love
of poverty as the state which the Son of God chose
for Himself. He looked at the poor with a kind of
holy envy, and would sometimes ejaculate with a
heartfelt sigh, " Ah ! why am I not as one of them ? "
Hence it was that he so loved and honoured the poor,
treated them with so much endearing sweetness, and
would often serve them on his knees. All this was
not the mere result of his humility ; it was the expression of his genuine esteem for their state, which
more favourably disposes for the perfection of the new
law, and assimilates a man more closely to the likeness of Jesus Christ.

But let us hear his own sentiments, as expressed in
a letter to Sister Marguerite of the Blessed Sacrament. Of the union of grace which subsisted between
De Renty and this holy nun we shall speak more
fully when we come to treat of his devotion to the
Sacred Infancy, which gave its character to his whole
spiritual state in the latter years of his life, and of
which P. de Condren had laid the first foundations in

him. "My dear sister," he writes, "my heart tells
me that the Infant Jesus desires something of me;
that He wishes me to ask it of Him, and dispose
myself to obtain it; and I confess to you that the
more my worldly goods increase the more clearly do I
discern the malignity which clings to them, and the
more clearly do I realize that they produce nothing
but embarrassments, while they scarcely bring any
greater facilities for good. My heart is powerfully
attracted towards an actual renunciation of all these
things, in order to follow Him alone, since He is my
way, as the poorest and most humble of His disciples.
And if I did not know that it would be a presumption in me to think myself capable of this state, and a
temptation to contemplate it, tied as I at present am,
I should have a longing desire for it. What I would
draw from this is that, in my ignorance of God's
purposes, and not knowing what He may have in
preparation for me in the future, I should offer
myself meanwhile for whatever may please Him,
being assured that with Him I can do all things,
even as without Him I can do nothing and will
nothing. My very dear sister, I stand much in need
of doing penance and of being humbled; I feel greatly
ashamed at my condition and at what I am: I live at
my ease and have an abundance of worldly goods (for
my family and the state of things do not allow of its
being otherwise), and I see both churches and poor in
want of everything, though I would fain pour all
I have upon them—at least all that in justice was
possible—or be as poor as the poor themselves, that I
might not have reason to be ashamed of being better
off than they are."

The feeling which he here so simply and candidly

expresses was always manifesting itself in some outward act; not merely in those overflowing alms and works of charity, for which alone he seemed to possess the goods which so oppressed him, but in the daily increasing retrenchment of all that could minister to personal comfort, convenience, or recreation. His love of poverty was shown, for instance, in the simplicity of his dress ; and it must be remembered that at that period the dress of the nobles gave almost as much opportunity for display as did that of their wives and daughters. He wore no gloves ; and, indeed, his hands were always so busily employed in some act of mercy that he had little opportunity for their use. He parted with various books on account of their rich binding ; he reduced his retinue, which in those times was considered one of the necessary appendages of the rich and noble, until he dispensed with it altogether. "I have seen him," says Saint-Jure, "first go about in a carriage with a page and a lackey ; then in a carriage with a lackey and no page ; next without a carriage, on foot, with a lackey only ; and after that alone without a lackey ; and finally — without himself." Much was meant by these last words. The interior despoilment of this good man was far more complete than the exterior, which was but a faint image of the other. God, in fact, had given him such an ardent desire for poverty, that not being able, circumstanced as he was, to satisfy this attraction, resign his possessions, and follow in the steps of Jesus Christ, who made Himself poor for our sakes, he endeavoured to content himself, at least in some small measure, by parting, not with superfluities alone, but with everything which was not strictly necessary. When he was going about the country by himself, it was a great enjoyment to him to be able to do in this respect just as he pleased; but he found his greatest solace in a device which he had discovered. This consisted in an interior renunciation of his whole right of property in his possessions, of which he thenceforth regarded himself simply as the depository: he was now but their administrator and dispenser; they were not his; and what he was obliged to use for his food and clothing he received as an alms from God through the hands of those who supplied them to him. Thus, as poor men sometimes amuse and solace themselves with the waking dream of being rich men, De Renty consoled himself in his riches by a mental process of the opposite character; only with him it was no dream, but embodied itself in the form of a serious and solemn act.

We have found him alluding once or twice to the ties of duty towards his family, which bound him to devote considerable attention to his property. It seems, in fact, that although he was in affluent circumstances, the estates had been neglected, and many buildings in particular had fallen into complete dilapidation. De Renty felt it to be incumbent upon him to set all these things in order, as affecting the interests both of his children and of his numerous dependents. For business of this character his natural abilities eminently fitted him, but it was most repugnant to the tastes and inclinations with which grace had imbued his soul. It brought him into contact with secular concerns, and obliged him to bestow much of his time and attention on matters connected with mere temporal interests; and although, in thus employing himself, he was convinced he was doing his duty and therefore serving God, because accomplishing His will, nevertheless such employment was not the direct service of God, neither was it that labour which, as we have seen, he deemed blessed, the labour of the poor, by which they earn their daily subsistence. We transcribe the act written with his own hand by which he endeavoured to spiritualize more fully these avocations.

"I resolve, in the presence of my God, to look to the repairs, manufactures, markets, and leases which are needed in the management of the property of which He has given me the administration ; and so much the more as He has vouchsafed me the grace to resolve to make the total renunciation both of it and of all that I am, on the great day of His Nativity now approaching, and so to dispose myself as that He shall be the proprietor and I His steward and servant to distribute it, holding myself in perfect readiness to relinquish it at the least intimation of His will. I acknowledge, then, to-day through His divine mercy that being, as a Christian, one of low and mean estate (*roturier*), I am bound to apply myself to these things as much as need shall require and opportunity permit, and even to work at them, as likewise at the meanest occupations, such as digging, reaping, &c., since He has been pleased to impart to me the knowledge of some of these arts ; and I must esteem these employments as highly as the care of souls, not looking at things as they are in themselves, but at the will of God and what in His good pleasure He may require of me. I beseech this Lord of my heart to forgive me my shortcomings hitherto in this respect. I write this memorandum, in accordance with the light He has given me, this 5th of November, 1643, that it may serve to remind me of my obligation."

We have here his resolution and his promise, nor have we been left without proofs that they did not remain a dead letter, the product of a mere passing effervescence of fervour. He built a great deal at Citry, one of the demesnes he possessed in Brie. A letter of his to Saint-Jure, written on the spot in the midst of this work, evidences the purity of intention and disengagement of affection with which it was prosecuted, and the elevated thoughts which his very employment, secular as it was, suggested. "Our great God be for ever blessed through our Lord Jesus Christ and all the just who are filled with His Spirit. I believe that it is in the order of God that I should be engaged in this exterior employment among a number of workmen, since necessity requires it. I am bound thereto as father of a family, seeing that the house was of importance to my children, and was in jeopardy, in consequence of long neglect. I confess to you that my heart longs for a far other edifice than that which is built up with earthly stones ; but I regard this as a dispensation of God's justice, who, since the sin of the first man, has condemned him and all his offspring to labour. Wherefore I revere labour, and give myself heartily to it, while deeply humbling myself under a penance which has little affinity with the life of the Spirit. We have seen some of our earliest Popes, who were great saints, condemned to take care of mules ; and I, who am a very great sinner, and deserve rather to be in hell, am treated so leniently as only to be sent to the quarries, not in exile and want, like our primitive Christians, but on an estate *which seems to belong to me.*" These last words show us that his interior renunciation of property had continued to be a practical reality with him. "Often in the course of the day, it will occur to me that this is a very ungrateful toil, and I say to myself, 'Of what use so many houses, which we must leave so soon, and which will themselves be destroyed?' I am humbled at the thought of the work itself, but not at being set to this work." Here again we have a remarkable illustration of what we asserted just now, that what is most admirable in the saints * is also the most within reach of general imitation : not that it is easy for any one to perform his daily work in as holy a spirit as did Gaston de Renty, but all are capable, if they will, of imitating it, and aspiring to it in their measure; for there is nothing to render it unsuitable to Christians following the commonest avocations of life, and with no call to any higher.

But let us hear his own account of his sentiments : —" This time," he writes a little later to his director, " is very precious to me, regarding it as I do as a small portion of the penance due for my great sins. If grace did not sustain me by means of this perception, I should suffer much from being engaged in a work so ungrateful and so little worth as that of building a mere secular's house, and bestowing my time on this business, which requires constant attention. But I feel that it is by God's disposal, and I quit, as it seems to me, Magdalen's state to embrace that of Martha, accepting this humiliation with self-abasement, and as a homage to the Divine justice. What makes me know more surely

* It is scarcely necessary to observe that in using this appellation we use it subject to the same reservation with which Saint-Jure applied it to this holy man: as signifying that he exhibited virtue far from what is ordinary amongst Christians.

that this is God's appointment, is that from time to time, and on festival days and Sundays, the mercies of the Lord are so great towards me, that I feel more recompense in a single instant than all the patience and humiliation of a sinner could merit for him in the course of a whole life. He communicates Himself to me in such wise that my hard nature is softened, and I am constrained to melt into tears; often I am so penetrated with love, veneration, and gratitude for the effects of His goodness, that they are ready to overflow my eyelids if I did not restrain them; indeed He manifests to me His inexplicable dealings with me in a way which I have no words to tell.

"Hereby I know how great a grace it is to follow God's order, and not our own, at the suggestion of the human spirit and a secret pride, which often, under the pretext of advancing the glory of God, lead us, without our perceiving it, to dispense ourselves from working at laborious and mean occupations appertaining to our state of life : nevertheless our Lord blesses these, not according to our choice of them, but according to His own appointment; and our fidelity does not derive its value from our doing this or that, but from being exact in doing that which He requires of us, and in our abandoning ourselves to His good pleasure. I perceive that a great dying to ourselves and a great fund of self-annihilation are needed in order to follow grace thus purely, and belong not to our own will but to God's Will."

Less than a month later we find the same ideas uppermost in his mind. "I am still in all the turmoil of business, which takes up much of my time, and indeed nearly all; but I should not venture to turn to anything else; I can only humble and submit myself to the Divine appointment. It was a very vulgar employment for Jesus Christ to have to converse with men who were ruder and harder than these stones of mine, and who offered more opposition to His purity than do these materials to my workmen; yet He suffered all, bore all, and converted very few. I entreat you to obtain for me a participation in His obedience and patience in fulfilling the behests of His Heavenly Father." Similar sentiments are expressed in a letter to a friend about the same time. " I am here," he says, " with four or five bodies of workmen, occupied in rebuilding on this property a family house, which was falling into ruins. What part can the soul take in such an employment, which, according to the spirit of faith, ought to be a pilgrim and stranger upon earth? Doubtless it groans much; not at the order of God, but after its true country, in the midst of occupations which are hampering to its liberty. We must do penance by labouring; it is the sentence of God passed on the first sin." Such was the spirit in which De Renty not only engaged in building, but performed every other work, whatever might be its immediate object. This spirit he also endeavoured to communicate to those over whom he had influence, and whose spiritual director he may be said to have been, so far as that office could be filled by a layman.

We conclude with a quotation from a letter of his to a lady who was endeavouring to advance in the paths of perfection. " Come," he writes, " let us die to the world in good earnest, and search out the obstacles which it throws in the way of our perfection, in order to condemn them, and live in the world, after the Apostle's manner, as not living therein, and possessing as if we possessed not. Let us manfully

expel from our minds the complacency and attachment we feel for our fine houses ; let us destroy the
beauty of our gardens, burn our woods, exterminate
the vain prospects we harbour for our children, in
whom we have hidden away our own self-love, which
seems dead in ourselves, and which makes us desire,
esteem, and approve in their persons what we condemn in ourselves—the show and lustre of the world.
I know that there is a difference in stations, but all
ought to reject the appendages which are reckoned to
belong to high birth and noble blood ; I mean those
maxims of aspiring to what is loftiest, and putting up
with nothing.   These are the maxims which our children derive from the birth we have given them ; but
that second birth which we procure for them from
Jesus Christ ought to repair all these disorders. If
we set before them vanity of mind, and all the ways
of a human policy ; if we offer them the examples of
those great men in history whose punishment in hell
is now as signal as was their presumption on earth,
we should be leading them on to make a similar end.'

It would appear that his energetic language had
somewhat alarmed his devout correspondent, who had
understood his advice about destroying in a literal
sense, for we find him explaining his meaning in a
subsequent letter. "My object," he says, "was not
that you should demolish your walls, and let your
gardens run to waste, in order to give yourself more
perfectly to God ; I simply meant the detachment
and demolitions which are to be effected interiorly,
and not to be executed upon insensible matter, whose
sole value is in its form.   When I said that you must
set on fire and consume all, my idea was to follow
the admirable spirit of the Apostle, who would have

us poor in the midst of riches, and stripped of every thing in the midst of possessions; he would have our minds truly purified and separated from the creatures of which we have the actual enjoyment, because the Christian who aims at perfection does himself a great wrong when he stops at these amusements, and admits into his heart other inclinations than those of Jesus Christ, who looked upon the world without destroying it, but also without attaching Himself to it. The desire to do His Father's will, and show forth His glory, was His life; the windings of rivers, and the beauties of the country, presented Him only with passing considerations, not with occupations. This is what I desire to arrive at ; I do not ask for more."

Sublime as is the example here presented to us, it will be seen at once that it is particularly suited to persons living in the world, and that imitation is within the reach of all. Yet it would be a delusion to suppose that such imitation could have any serious results without much previous struggle for the attainment of disengagement of heart, and, above all, apart from the great means which De Renty employed, the assiduous practice of prayer. For it is in vain that a man intellectually knows (as none, indeed, can but know) that the goods of this world are intrinsically valueless ; that he *may* lose them any day, and that some day he *must* quit them ; in vain does experience tell him that they are unsatisfying to the soul ; in vain does faith tell him that heavenly treasure is alone worthy of a Christian's solicitude ; notwithstanding all this, he will more or less cling to earthly things until a powerful ray of divine grace illuminates his inward eye, and makes him see them as they will appear at the hour of death. He will never realize

experimentally and effectually the relative value of
earth and heaven, or, rather, that there is no relative
value between them—that the visible is the shadow,
and the invisible the substance—until the scales fall,
and he beholds things as they are in the eternal light
of truth.   God, indeed, has been sometimes pleased, in
His inscrutable mercy, to grant this strong and vivid
perception in a moment of time even to great sinners;
but, ordinarily, it is the fruit and reward of diligent
prayer, and the seeking of His Face ; and it is for
want of this seeking that the knowledge possessed of
divine truth remains in the mass of Christians so
barren and unproductive.   It is not because they lack
the high vocation of men like De Renty, but because
they themselves are slothful and ungenerous, that the
talent committed to them remains profitless in their
hands.

CHAPTER VIII.

De Renty's Solitude in the midst of the World.

If De Renty was poor in the midst of riches, he was
also solitary in the midst of the world.   As God had
not willed that he should despoil himself in effect of
his property, but gave him the rare grace of being
inwardly stripped of his wealth, and as poor in spirit
as a perfect religious, who has renounced all by
vows; so also, whilst retaining him in the world, He
bestowed on him the grace of utter separation from

it. De Renty was a solitary in desire. It was not his love of poverty alone which made him long, as has been already told, to follow the example of St. Alexis, but his no less powerful attraction to the hidden life. Urged by this love, he was frequently heard to say that, if God had not bound him to the state in which he was placed, he would have gone away into some distant land, there to abide hidden and unknown for the remainder of his days. One of his most ardent wishes, one of those wishes with which grace inspired this holy man, and then forbade him to gratify it, was that he should be not only completely unknown to any one, but entirely banished from men's hearts and thoughts, so that they should not so much as know that he existed. This propensity was always active in his mind, albeit God denied him the field for its indulgence which his spiritual nature would have craved ; so that, just as we see persons who have neither the opportunity nor the ability for display on a large scale, but entertain for it an habitual longing in their souls, seizing every little occasion to put themselves forward, be it in ever so trifling a matter, so also those who observed De Renty might note how sedulously he withdrew himself, so far as was possible, from notice, while those who were intimately acquainted with his interior sentiments were well aware that he never performed any of his actions with a view to the smallest return of love or gratitude from others.

The more he advanced in light and grace, the more noticeable was this disposition in him, which sprang not only from the purity of intention with which he desired to consecrate all his actions to God alone, but from the longing of which we speak, the longing for a

life hidden from men ; and this he himself attested to
a friend five or six months before his death. This
was part of the grace of the devotion which drew him
towards Nazareth. He beheld our Lord remaining
there thirty years in obscurity, appearing only once
during that time for a brief space in the Temple;
and yet not only was there no peril for Him who was
Sanctity Itself in mixing amongst men, but rather
nothing but the very greatest good could accrue to
them from His converse with them. Had He not,
moreover, come down on earth expressly to instruct
them? And yet the Light of the world hid Himself,
as it were, under a bushel; the Eternal Word made
Himself dumb for thirty years ! From this he passed
on to contemplate the Ever-Blessed Triune God,
whom the prophet emphatically styles the Hidden
God,* who in effect was for an eternity hidden
within the depths of His own mysterious Being, and
who, although He has now revealed Himself externally, is incomparably and infinitely more within
Himself than what He has manifested of Himself
without. On these sublime models this servant of
God formed himself.

In one of his reports to his director, we find the
following remarks, dated March, 1645 :—"Some time
ago, finding myself in a street in which carriages were
passing to and fro, a doubt crossed my mind whether,
since I was in a quarter of the town in which I had
acquaintances, I ought to look at the passers-by or not;
and whether, if I never turned my eyes to glance at
them, but went on looking straight before me, I might
not give occasion to observations." (Here we see a

---

* Isaias xlv. 15.

momentary contention between his love of concealment and that humility which led him to shun all
singularity, dispositions usually coinciding in the
course they dictated.)   "Instantly," he proceeds,
"these words were suggested to my mind, and in such
a manner that I cannot doubt but that they came
from God : 'Care not to be known, and do not stop
to know.' These few words brought so much light
and power with them that for eight days I continued
to discern in them the greatest aids in the spiritual
life, and I still feel their influence substantially remaining in me. It is certain that, since the greater
part of our evils and imperfections proceeds from our
desire to be seen and to see, this must be a practice
fraught with poison as regards the progress of the
soul, though often it does not perceive the injury it
suffers therefrom, and is insensible to the wound
inflicted. What impairs the purity of our devotional
acts is that self-love of ours, which is well pleased that
they should be known and we ourselves become the
objects of remark. We always show what is best in
us, we conceal our defects and the reverse side of our
character, and our whole exterior is so well composed
that our interior is frequently more occupied therewith than with God ; and there are few persons who
do not take a large share, passively or actively, in the
vain regard of creatures. How these words seemed
to create in me a great separation from the world !
What a purging and purifying of the soul, to be on
earth only to behold God ! Oh ! .assuredly he who
should live as if unknown of all, without regard to
what the world says or thinks of him, choosing
neither to know nor to be known of any one, either
by name, following, or appearance—known only to

our Lord—how naked, pure, and free in spirit would
he walk! I was in the streets, in the midst of all
their hubbub, pressed upon by the crowd, jostled, but
as tranquil, as much united to God, and occupied with
Him as if I had been in a desert ; and ever since that
day it is in this manner I pass through the streets,
my eyes nevertheless retaining their freedom to see
what I ought to see, yet without my attention
being engaged ; and on needful occasions these words
are again suggested to me, and they protect and preserve me in God." Yet even here his humility makes
him, as usual, find matter for self-accusation ; for he
adds, " I am very unfaithful, however, to this grace ;
but its substantial truth is not effaced within me,
which makes me much more culpable."

His love for a life severed from all communication
with creatures is exhibited also in the following
passage, quoted from a letter to a lady of his acquaintance :—" Let us animate ourselves to lead this life,
unknown and hidden from men, but known to God
and intimately conversant with Him, stripping ourselves of all, and banishing from our mind all those
useless things which, trivial as they are, do us so much
injury, because they occupy it in the place of God.
For when I reflect upon what it is which interrupts
and cuts up into so many fragments this sweet and
delightful union which we ought to have abidingly
with God, I find that it is a Monsieur this, or a
Madame that,—a conversation, in short, which for us
is a folly, but which nevertheless robs us of so precious
a time and a society so holy and so much to be desired. Let us leave this off, I beg of you, and learn
how to pay our court well to our Master ; let us well
understand what our world is,—not this world which

we renounce, but that world in which the children of God pay their homage to their Father."

It seems almost superfluous to add of one whose whole heart and thoughts were in this invisible region, and who would gladly himself have been invisible to mortal eye, that his contempt of the world equalled his love for the hidden life, and formed indeed an integral part of it; for we do not wish to quit what we esteem. But as he was unable to quit the world save in desire, his actions were continually marking how thoroughly he despised it. In this way he not only renounced it daily, but daily trampled it disdainfully under his feet. We shall defer our notice of some of these actions till we come to speak of the extraordinary humility which distinguished him, and limit ourselves at present to a few more quotations from his letters, which exhibit his views with respect to contempt of the world and all exterior objects.

He seems on another occasion to have heard one of those interior words, the crucial test of whose origin, we are told by spiritual writers, is to be found in their substantial and abiding effect upon the soul. In the November of the year 1644, finding himself in a chapel richly ornamented with sculpture and bas-reliefs, he began to observe them with some attention. He had considerable knowledge of the decorative arts as applied to building, which rendered him able to appreciate the exquisite workmanship displayed in the tracery, where the hard and unyielding stone was made to simulate the graceful and delicate forms of nature. All of a sudden these words were put into his mind : "The original of what you behold would not engage your attention." "At once," he says, "I became aware that I should never have bestowed any

attention upon those blades and flowers had they been
real; and that all the ornaments which architectural
art invents are very mean works, made up almost
entirely of leaves, fruit, branches, masks, scrolls,
harpies, and chimeras, things which in part are common or paltry in their nature, and in part sports of
the fancy; that nevertheless man, who is caught by
everything, becomes enamoured and enslaved, so to
say, by the skill of a good workman, who copies and
imitates these fiddle-faddles.   I was thus enlightened
to perceive how easily man is deceived, amused, and
turned away from his Sovereign Good; and I have
never since been able to stop to contemplate such
things, and, if I did, I should feel inwardly reproached.
When I meet with them in churches and elsewhere
immediately these words come into my mind : 'The
original is nothing; the copy, the image, is less still;
all is vanity, except occupying ourselves with God
only.'"   It may be well to add, as a qualification to
what may appear like despising and undervaluing the
labours of art as applied to the decoration of the sanctuary, that such was far from De Renty's meaning,
who would have had all that was beautiful and glorious
in nature or art brought to minister to the honour
and splendour of God's service.   Rightly to understand
the import of such observations in the mouths of eminently holy persons, we must remember how exalted
was their grace,—a grace which led them to practise
a species of renunciation the most refined; so that for
them it was good to turn away from and despise what
others, lower down in Christ's spiritual school, may
be invited to contemplate and admire to their own
improvement.   Yet something also may be gathered
here which is of general application; for, although

beauty of architecture and splendour of ceremonial
tend to raise the heart to Him whom they are designed
to honour, nevertheless a subtle temptation often lurks
beneath them. There is danger of art being loved and
admired for its own sake; there is fear lest the impressions of the imagination should be mistaken for the
genuine sentiments of fervent piety.*

De Renty's contempt of the world, and the source

* "The Church of God by its history bears witness that the
service of God in spirit and in truth requires no external
splendour. It accepts, indeed, all that the art of man can do
in architecture, in painting, in sculpture, in music, because all
these come from God and ought to be consecrated to God. The
warning of the Lord by the prophet rings in the ears of Christians: 'Is it time for you to dwell in ceiled houses, and this
house lies desolate?' (Aggeus i. 4). It is true of us also that
the wealth spent upon the private dwellings of men exceeds
ten-thousandfold that which is spent upon the honour and
worship of God. The Church, therefore, both consecrates all
things to God's service, and also sustains the same spirit of
austere interior worship as in the beginning; and the Church
has, in all ages, by its chief Orders, kept up its testimony that
the worship of God in spirit and in truth does not need external
splendour. St. Francis laid down as the law for his children
—the most numerous family in the Catholic Church—that
upon the altar there should be candlesticks of wood, and that
the vestments of the priest should have no silk. You will not
misunderstand me, then, when I say that the spirit of the
world will often enter into the splendour of the sanctuary, and
that the sounds which fill the ear, and the beauty which fills
the eye, may take away the heart and mind. Unless there be
a spirit of prayer and union with our Divine Lord in the heart,
men may come and go without worshipping God in spirit and
in truth. This is one of our most subtle dangers. Satan knows
how . . . . . to make even the splendours, sweetness, beauty,
and majesty of Catholic worship a fascination of the sense and
a distraction of the soul."—*The Four Great Evils of the Day,*
by the Archbishop of Westminster, pp. 62-64.

of that contempt, his vivid realization of the inappreciable glory of our union with the God-Man and our divine inheritance in Him, are well expressed in the following passage from a letter addressed by him to a lady :—" I would say to you that, as we are Christians only in virtue of our union with Jesus Christ, our dependence upon Him, and the life we derive from Him, I marvel, and can in no way comprehend, how a thing so little as man, drawn out of nothing in his first origin, infected with the sin of his first parent, and with his own, and raised to so high a degree of honour as the Christian alliance confers on him, even that of forming but one Christ with the Son of God, ot being His brother and co-heir in the world to come—I say that I marvel how, after being invested with such admirable prerogatives, a man should hold this world in esteem, and take account of its vanities. Can any one fix his heart on them and belong to this life after these considerations? The things of this world, of which also death will despoil us, and for ever, shall they constitute the fulness of our heart during the brief time that we have to be here for the purpose of securing our salvation, acquiring the treasures prepared for us, and rendering thanks to God for His mercies? Ought we not to manifest to God and to men the most lively faith, freely forsaking whatever appertains only to this world, its false, or, at any rate, its useless, empty honours, its perishable works, its extravagant opinions, and all which will pass away like a dream, even as our great-grandfathers have passed away and are forgotten? Their ups and downs, their satisfactions and their dissatisfactions, which they took so much to heart, and which they found so difficult to accommodate at once with the law of Jesus Christ and the spirit of their times— all this has vanished away. Have we not good reason to judge that they were wanting in wisdom if they had regard to anything save God in their actions? And so it will be with us : all will pass away, and God alone will remain. Oh, how good it is to attach ourselves to Him only ! "

This was the one longing desire and aim of his life. It was this absorbing object which effaced the world from his sight, and made him pass through it, and mix with it, like one in a dream, whose body is present, but whose spirit is living in another region. Something parallel in the natural order we may not unfrequently observe amongst men whose intellectual or scientific occupations so engross their whole attention and regard, that whatever has no reference thereto, they see and hear as if they neither saw nor heard, the senses conveying no corresponding impressions ; so much so, that we characterize this state as absence of mind. In De Renty, however, the condition we have described was not the result of a mere natural pre-occupation of mind, but the supernatural effect of the reign of grace in his soul ; that same Holy Spirit who is the author of order, not confusion, enabling him to give as much application and attention to necessary affairs as if they had filled his heart, and formed the staple of his thoughts. But to this subject we shall again recur, when we come to speak more particularly of his interior life, and of the character imprinted upon it by his peculiar devotion.

CHAPTER IX.

DE RENTY'S HUMILITY IN THOUGHT AND WORD.

IT would have been impossible to proceed thus far in the portrait of De Renty after his perfect conversion of heart, without often alluding, directly or indirectly, to his humility; but this virtue, which in every Christian must be the basis of the rest, if they are to possess any value or solidity, was so peculiarly remarkable in this great servant of God, that it merits a special notice. We lay the foundation deep when we mean to raise a magnificent edifice thereon; even so, the Great Artificer, designing to build up in this chosen soul a sublime superstructure of perfection, gave him the grace of a most profound humility. God shows to such, in the illuminating light of His Spirit, the transcendent beauty of this virtue, which has a special prerogative for bringing men near to God, on account of its relation to truth. To them He reveals the true nature of humility,—a knowledge hidden from the great mass of men, who are acquainted with it only superficially, and in its more palpable outward effects. To see it in its true nature, is to perceive its priceless value; but pearls are not cast before swine, and it is therefore but an elect few, known in the counsels of God, who receive this precious grace: the vision is for those who will be obedient to It, special illuminating graces being generally reserved for those who the All-seeing knows will correspond with them. Herein we may trace the marks of His mercy and love, for such special light brings great responsibilities. De Renty had been thus divinely enlightened to see the beauty and value of humility. He no sooner saw than he coveted; he no sooner coveted than he strove to obtain. There were no lingering intervals with him; he lived his life of grace fast. Words could not express what was his love for this virtue, or the greatness of his desire to acquire it; not only was he unceasingly praying for it, but he was continually beseeching others to join their prayers to his to obtain it for him from God. He never believed that he possessed it; his own progress in this virtue, and the very light he daily received respecting it, helping to conceal from him his advance. Yet, though unconscious of his own progress, or esteeming it as little, from the fresh manifestations made to his soul, and the fresh insight ever granted to him into those two abysses, the nothingness of the creature and the greatness of God, he was fully conscious of his attraction, and how, with all the weight of his desires, he tended towards that nothingness which is the truth of the creature—its centre, where it finds God.

These two conjoint sentiments are evinced in the following extract from a letter to a confidential friend: —" Have pity on me," he writes ; " I am more unfaithful than any creature in the world: I cast myself on my knees before you to beg you to believe this. If our Lord did not show me what I am, Lucifer would have a rich prize in me; but this good Lord in His mercy always manifests to me my nothingness ; it is thither that grace draws me." Many other passages might be quoted from his correspondence testifying to this attraction ; and we must understand this attraction, not merely as a strong desire to possess

L

the virtue of humility, but as a positive drawing towards that nothingness and self-annihilation which is its ultimate goal. He indeed loved the virtue of humility with all his heart, and chiefly because it was the special virtue of Jesus Christ, his pattern in all things, and the virtue which our Lord peculiarly appropriated to Himself, and proposed to the imitation of His followers. But, further still, he loved it with a vivid perception of what it effects, namely, the emptying, as it may be called, of the soul to give place to the operation of the new creation, which, like the old one, requires nothingness for its field of action ; not, however, voiceless and passive nothingness, but a poverty and an emptiness, and withal a hunger, which cries out to God to supply and to fill it ; that poverty, emptiness, and hunger which is the burden of the *Magnificat*, the song of the Mistress of humility.

We have here De Renty's views of this virtue :— "Humility is the basis which sustains and supports the whole work of God in us ; it renders the creature so naked and separated from itself, that it leaves it no power to cast a look upon itself, and is so occupied with the greatness of God, which annihilates it, that it is lost in reverence and abasement. This is the grace of Christian pilgrims, who, naked and despoiled of all, esteem themselves as nothing, a mere breath of being, which, possessing only what it has received from God, turns instinctively to God alone. It is a beautiful humility to perceive in oneself this utter void : the soul that perceives this void in itself sees nothing there but nothingness ; and, seeing nothing in itself, it finds there nothing to arrest its regard, and thus is directed always to God. Such a soul resembles a needle which

has touched the magnet, and, having been swathed in
many wrappers, should be at last set free ; immediately it would turn to the north, and there would
remain fixed, however much the winds and the tem-
pestuous sea might toss and agitate the vessel." Such
was his conception of humility, the two views combined
of our own nothingness and God's greatness, which
reciprocally act on each other ; for if the sight of God's
infinite greatness plunges the soul into its own nothingness, so also it is only through the perception of its own
nothingness that it can attain to its elevation in God.
A paper which remained in Saint-Jure's possession
when he wrote the biography of this holy man contains
these words penned with his blood :—" I give Thee
my liberty, O my God, and ask from Thee nothingness, to which the Christian must arrive in order to
raise himself purely towards Thee.—GASTON JEAN-
BAPTISTE."

Humility is usually regarded under three aspects :
humility in heart and thought, humility in words,
and humility in act, though, properly speaking, they
are all one and the same, resolving themselves into the
first, which is the source of the other two ; yet, commonly, the only means we possess of inferring the
presence of this virtue is its outward manifestations ;
and these, taken separately, sometimes deceive us,
from the many counterfeits, conscious or unintentional,
which are to be met with in the world, owing to the
countless reasons which men have to conceal their self-
love, and wear a certain humility of exterior. Still,
when any person for a length of time, and under all
circumstances, has given very remarkable external
tokens of this virtue, we may have a moral certainty
of its sterling reality. This proof De Renty's conduct

abundantly supplies; and we have further the exceptional advantage derived from the preservation of his
correspondence with his director, to whom he unveiled
his inmost self, whereby we obtain an insight into his
interior which we never should otherwise have possessed,
and which can so seldom be enjoyed in any case.

We have seen what were his general views of the
nothingness of the creature. To these were joined the
most profound conviction of his own individual worth-
lessness, intellectual and moral; it would, indeed, be
difficult to express the very poor opinion he in every
way entertained of himself. He sincerely reputed himself the most unworthy of men, taking this title in some
of his letters; but "a sinner and a very great sinner"
was what he most commonly called himself; and he
was not the man to use such expressions if he had not
been deeply convinced of their truth. One who knew
him intimately for nearly six years said that, although
he had been acquainted with other holy souls, he had
never met with any one who lived in such a perpetual
state of self-abasement before God and before creatures.
The greatness of God humbled him to the very depths.
He said to this person one day, "Is there anything
great in presence of this Greatness? I see myself before It so little, so little, so little—and nothing at all."
Then penetrated, as it were, by this sentiment, he
added, after a pause, "An atom in the sun is very
little, but I am very much less in the presence of God,
for I am nothing." Again he paused, and seemed to
gather fresh matter for humility from the consideration of himself. "Alas!" he exclaimed, "I am too
much; I am a sinner, an infidel, and anathema for
my crimes." Another time he wrote to this same
person, "I feel as if I crushed myself before God,

like an egg upon which I should stamp with all my strength : must I, then, speak to you of myself? must I so much as have a name? It seems a strange thing that I should."

De Renty had, as we have before observed, high natural abilities ; they were moreover very various ; there seemed to be nothing to which he could not readily turn his mind or his hand, from the most abstruse scientific study to the meanest handicraft. Abilities of this multifarious order, covering so large an extent of ground, and, from their practical character never, so to say, leaving their possessor at fault, are perhaps more apt to foster self-confidence and self-sufficiency, than is great genius in some one or two departments, which is often accompanied by palpable deficiencies in other more ordinary talents. Nevertheless, so far from having a shade of self-reliance, De Renty was always in an attitude of genuine self-humiliation before his fellow-creatures. He would sometimes say with tears in his eyes, that he quite marvelled at people's kindness to him and their toleration of him. He wondered how they could endure him, and would have been far less surprised had he been pelted with mud, and driven out of their company. This mean opinion of himself made him feel that it was great boldness of him to speak at all, and that it was an act of sheer compassion in others to endure his conversation, which he deemed tedious and irksome. Yet at no time of his life could these epithets have been applied to him, for never had he been inclined to prolixity, and his words had always been singularly to the point.

" I have often seen him," observes one of his intimate friends, "humble himself to the very ground

when he spoke to me of God, saying that it was not
for such a one as he to speak of Him, but that he ought
rather to refrain himself in silence ; and, as a matter
of fact, he never did speak of God, except when he was
specially moved by our Lord to say something for the
good of his neighbour or the Divine glory : when he
had no such inward movement, he remained silent
through humility, as if he had not a word to say on the
subject." To him the attitude of humility was the
attitude of truth. It is, indeed, difficult to speak much
and often and yet faithfully to preserve this attitude,
although our lips may utter nothing but what is good
and true. " Let us live on truth," he writes to a friend,
meaning, as the context shows, let us abide in humility.

The perception of his own weakness was always
present to him, a perception which he confessed came
to him, not through search or study or reflection of his
own, but by divine light vouchsafed to him, which,
leaving a deep impression, kept him in a state of self-
annihilation and of profound self-mistrust: "nevertheless," he said, "I place my whole confidence in God and
in His Son, our Lord. If I were but faithful to this
state, it would keep me in a marvellous littleness.
There are moments when it seems to me that my
whole body is crushed, ground, and annihilated, and
my interior far more so." These wonderful flashes of
grace, revealing to him at one glance the greatness of
God and the littleness and vileness of His creature,
and the effect they worked in him, remind us of holy
Job, when he exclaims,* "With the hearing of the ear
I have heard Thee, but now mine eye seeth Thee.
Therefore I reprehend myself, and do penance in dust
and ashes." The same light which illuminated him

* xlii. 5, 6.

to perceive the feebleness of his nature made him also lynx-eyed to discern his faults. "I assure you," he writes to his director, "I have plenty to humble me and set me working in good earnest to correct myself, albeit with patience; for I experience and clearly see that, although we labour and desire to rid ourselves of our imperfections, our Lord leaves us in them some-times for a long time, to make us know our weakness, and to humble us." This patience with himself proves that the humiliation which his shortcomings produced in him was of a healthy kind, and free from that self-love which is often more or less masked under its sem-blance, or which is so apt to mingle with and impair its purity. But what is better evidence of humility than the acknowledgment of faults, is the way in which blame is accepted. De Renty desired to be apprised of his defects and reproved for them. After his call to a state of higher perfection, he got his director to bid a person watch him, and warn him if he did anything contrary to the spirit of perfection. The monitor thus selected was much his inferior in every way, which would naturally have rendered the rebuke more distasteful; but it was far otherwise with De Renty, to whom a greater service in his estimation could not be rendered than to help on the work of purification in his soul. When his censor told him of some failure, however light it might be, the mere shadow commonly of a fault, he listened with the greatest respect and grati-tude, and humbled himself as much as if he had been guilty of some grave offence. He would also be the first to accuse himself of any failure, kneeling down and declaring that he was a miserable sinner; that he had committed such or such a fault, which very often was one nearly imperceptible to less enlightened eyes.

If his imperfections or his faults furnished him with matter of humiliation, such he also found in those distinctions and social advantages which so often feed the vanity or bolster up the self-esteem of men. The same spirit which, as we have seen, had made him in heart reject all worldly greatness, honour, and praise, made him also ashamed of those things; and he would often groan, prostrate before the Majesty of God, because he had a high and noble position in the world, he who, as he said, occupied so low and vulgar a position (*si roturière* is his significant expression) according to the spirit of Jesus Christ: this thought covered him with shame and confusion. He had made a solemn renunciation of his nobility in the hands of our Lord, as we have seen him do in the case of his property, and he told a holy person in confidence that our Lord gave him His own in return: that is, He gave him His love, which has the power to transform the man into God, because it makes him die to himself, and leaves God alone living in him and reigning; thus exalting and deifying him and bestowing on him the highest degree of nobility to which he can be raised. Ever after this act it was with great difficulty that De Renty could endure hearing himself called "Monsieur." In these days the appellation is a mere courtesy, which all who are respectably clothed may reckon on receiving. It is no longer a distinction, which it was at the period at which De Renty lived, and, as such, it pained the ears of him who had "chosen to be an abject."[*]   "I am a fine Monsieur indeed, am I not? the name suits me well," he would sometimes say ironically, when conversing with familiar friends, veiling his annoyance with a pleasant laugh; but in

* Ps. lxxxiii. 11.

his letters he would seriously remonstrate with them
for giving him this title. In one of them we find
his humility suddenly taking another turn; so fearful is he of anything like pretension, that he adds, "I
beg of you to believe that I am a pitiable creature.
I take back the 'Monsieur' which I had rejected;
my pride ought to have all these appendages rather
than impose on your candour, which might lead you
to mistake in me a bit of glass for a diamond." The
Emperor Charles V. had raised Renty to the dignity
of a marquisate; at his father's death, therefore, the
title of Marquis de Renty devolved on his son, but
Gaston would never assume it; allowing himself,
however, to be called Baron de Renty, the name by
which he was popularly known.

The same humility which he manifested in regard
of his personal endowments and social advantages, he
equally or, rather, still more strongly, evinced with
reference to his high spiritual gifts and graces. When
these gifts and graces are received into a soul thus
admirably disposed, they both exalt and abase it at
one and the same time; for while they raise it to God
they humble it in itself. The first strong impulse of
a soul thus favoured is to hide its treasure, like the
man in the Parable who had found the pearl. Several
motives prompt to this holy instinct of concealment,
and among them one of the chief is humility. De
Renty was so studious to conceal God's gifts and
his own good deeds that, doubtless, much that was
most admirable in him has been buried in secrecy,
never to be known until the day when all hidden
things will be made manifest. His letters and reports
to his director give us, it is true, an account of his
interior states and of the graces he received, but even

here he was evidently parsimonious of his information, limiting himself to what truth and frankness absolutely required in treating with his spiritual guide. All that goes beyond this limit is, as it were, surprised from him by the swelling gratitude of his heart to God for His superabundant liberality. Since the singular graces which he had received could not remain concealed, and the fame of his good works spread wherever he went, he often found himself treated in consequence with much honour; but he had so vivid a perception of the incapacity of the creature, and could so clearly discern between the precious and the vile, between what was God's share in all good works and what man contributes of his own, that he was not tempted to take any of the credit to himself, but straightway referred all to God as the source: thus he preserved heart and hands clean and pure in the midst of all the temporal and spiritual goods with which God enriched him.

But if we stopped here we should say far too little; for he was, moreover, exceedingly desirous that others should make the same distinction, and should have no consideration for him in anything he said or did, but should regard God alone. Persons sought his advice eagerly, and he was compelled, as we have said, to exercise in many cases a kind of spiritual direction. This was a great and peculiar honour to a layman, and with not a few might have proved a subtle temptation to self-satisfaction. But with him it only furnished a fresh motive for humiliation, and we find evidence in his letters of the distress which the respect with which he was treated occasioned to him. " It is with difficulty I endure the value you set upon my visits and conversation :" thus it is he writes to one of these self-constituted disciples; "let us look much to God, let us ever unite ourselves to Jesus Christ, in order to learn of Him the deepest self-abasement. O my God, when shall the time come that we shall have no eye for ourselves, we shall no longer speak of ourselves, and all vanity shall be destroyed in us?" To another he writes in the same strain : "I beseech you to regard in me nothing but my infirmities and a frightful fund of malice and pride which I have within me. It is of this that I need the world should speak to me, and punish me for it."

But he not only felt shame before men that they should praise in him the gifts of God—for this, as he never appropriated them to himself, he felt to be a robbery and a sort of sacrilegious injustice—but he also confounded himself before God on their account. He could not be ignorant—indeed he was not ignorant— how abundant were the graces of which he was the recipient, and so low was his own self-estimation that he judged himself utterly unworthy of the very least of them ; as for the greater, they put him beside himself, like the chief Apostle when he beheld the miraculous draught of fishes. Moreover, this bounti- fulness of the Lord threw him into a perplexing state of embarrassment, as it produced a conflict between his gratitude to God, urging him to publish His great mercies, and his humility, which not only would have made him conceal all that was advantageous to him- self, but would have prompted him never so much as to mention anything which personally concerned him. On this subject he thus writes to his director :— "I have at the same time two contrary movements : the one is to confess to you with sentiments of grati- tude that God fills me with the effects of His goodness

and the impressions of His kingdom; while the other
urges me rather to condemn myself than to contemplate these things in me; for, after all and notwithstanding all, I am a pitiable creature." And again,
in another letter, after having spoken of the great
lights and admirable sentiments which God had communicated to him, he says, "I do not dwell upon
all this, I only tell you what has occurred in order to
report it to you, making use of my own judgment
only to condemn myself for my vices, and in every
other case keeping it in suspense and referring it to
God." With others he was usually much more
reserved, yet he was fain to speak sometimes. We
may observe in the following quotation from a letter
to an intimate friend, how he takes refuge in the
plural pronoun as a slight shelter to his own personality. "The gifts of God," he writes, "are sometimes so great that they put us beyond ourselves, so
to say, and if we could recede still further than
nonentity itself, we should do so. You may notice
among men that if something proportionate to his
condition is given to any one, he returns thanks, and
great thanks, for the present; but if a prince were to
give to a beggar according to the greatness of his own
power, whether it were a sum of money, or some
official post, you would see the poor man draw back,
and say, 'Alas! my lord, I think you do not know
me: this is too much for me, I am unworthy of it.'
There are, in like manner, good things which,
far surpassing our expectations, make us recognize
what we are, and not dare even to lift up our eyes,
so dazzling is their brightness, so alarming their
grandeur."

The gifts of God were likewise a source of humi-

liation to him, because he was persuaded that he
corresponded so very ill with them, and thus wasted
their efficacy to a great degree. This abiding conviction he shared with all the saints, and it goes far to
explain what would otherwise be well-nigh incompre-
hensible,—we mean the genuine conviction invariably
to be met with amongst persons of eminent sanctity
that they are the greatest of sinners. Such De Renty
judged himself to be, and in holding this opinion he
did not regard merely his past life before his conversion, but his actual state, when he appeared to
others to be living a life of consummate perfection,
and when he could not even himself deny that he was
strenuously aiming at what was highest and most
perfect. He is ever recurring to the same topic, " the
fund of malice and horrible pride " within him. In
vain had he by God's grace crushed that old nature
under his feet : there it lay, the old Adam, but it still
clave to him,—that " body of death,"* from which he
was not yet freed, and which might at any time
revive. This consideration alone, apart from his supposed present shortcomings, was enough to keep·him
plunged in an abyss of humility.

The sight of his natural corruption animated him
with a holy hatred against himself and a strong
desire for contempt, always, however, moderated and
kept in check by that childlike abandonment to
God's disposal which, excluding the disquietude which
arises from personal wishes, was the source of peren-
nial peace to his soul. " If," he used to say, " I could
desire anything, it would be to be greatly humbled,
abased to nothing, and treated as " off-scouring " by
others : this would be a joy to me, but I do not think

* Rom. vii. 24.

that I deserve so great a grace." Had he not been restrained by weightier considerations, we know that he would have done strange things for the purpose of drawing down on himself contempt and confusion. In the fulness of his heart he said one day to a friend, "It would be a great pleasure to me to be allowed to run about Paris in my shirt, that people might despise me and think me an idiot." Saint-Jure in relating this circumstance makes a most just observation. "Two things," he says, "we learn from this: first, that God at times imparts to holy souls thoughts, affections, and desires so much raised above the common order and above human reason as to appear extravagant, like this desire which he gave to De Renty, and which our holy founder, St. Ignatius, had experienced before him; secondly, that we must not put these desires into practice before they have been well examined and duly weighed in the balance of charity and regard to our neighbour's edification."

To love contempt is the highest degree of humility; and when it comes to us without our seeking, and we receive it, not with patience only, but with joy, there is then no room for doubt or suspicion. We have seen how sincerely De Renty loved abjection, by the manner in which he accepted the trying humiliation to which he was subjected by the lawsuit into which his mother forced him. A further proof that the movement which prompted him to court ridicule and confusion was a genuine inspiration of grace, is to be found in his constant solicitude to avoid all singularity; so averse was his sensitive humility from anything which might possibly afford a harbour for vanity. He used to say that in those exercises which appear to have in them a higher perfection,—*e.g.* fasts,

penances, and the like,—surpassing what others ordinarily practise, there is frequently less than in the
more common ; for the least of these is rewarded by
the death of nature, which often seeks itself in the
extraordinary and the singular, feeling a secret pleasure in excelling and not being sorry to be noticed
and spoken of with esteem.

There is perhaps no greater proof of the solidity of
humility than its continual action on the behaviour
and bearing.   Every Christian will feel the necessity
of checking pride when he perceives it, and of performing from time to time certain acts of humility ;
but few, unfortunately, are they who detect it in its
more secret folds, as giving the tone and the turn to
much that they habitually say and do : here it evades
the sight of all whose eyes are not enlightened by
grace to discern it ; we deceive ourselves, and, what
is more strange, we deceive others, who do not remark its presence unless it lead to either arrogance of
manner or to what is commonly called affectation, for
the lighter shades of that pest of the polished world
pass unobserved, veiled by the polite conventionalities
of society.   Amongst the educated and the refined
this snare to humility is, in fact, the most dangerous ;
the poor have their special temptations, but to this
they are less subject ; the counterfeit of humility
which polished manners supply is much more rare
amongst them, and, moreover, the incentives to pride,
as well as the materials of its nourishment, are happily
more lacking to them.   De Renty had been in early
life of an arrogant temper, and, although ever since
his conversion he had repressed his nature in this
respect and brought under control the irony of his
tongue, as we have already noticed, yet the victory

was not thoroughly achieved until later, when his spiritual eye became so enlightened that he was enabled to surprise his old enemy and pursue it to the death in its most hidden recesses. Not a word, not a look, but was now all "steeped," to use Saint-Jure's forcible expression, in humility and modesty. He always took care to use the simplest and most moderate terms in expressing himself, so as never to draw attention to himself as the speaker; a merit which is perhaps more rare than one might suppose in those who can talk well, and who, if they keep themselves in check, commonly do so rather from natural tact, and the polite fear of wearying, or from the instinctive feeling that a certain modesty and reserve enhances agreeability in discourse, than from any desire to humble and eclipse themselves. De Renty was particularly careful, when discoursing of spiritual things and the deep mysteries of the faith, to be very sparing of grand or unusual terms; not because the subject was not worthy of them, but because, esteeming himself so unworthy, he dreaded conveying the impression that he was something when he was nothing. If by chance some expression fell from him which departed from what was simple and ordinary, he would immediately show that he used it with regret and only because he was unable otherwise to make himself understood.

The same refined humility would have prompted him never to speak of himself at all, even for the purpose of self-depreciation. Indeed, such was his general determination, believing as he did that, save upon exceptional occasions, there was more of self-annihilation in saying neither good nor evil of ourselves; nevertheless, it is certain that he was quite

unable to carry out this resolution ; and, as he never
suffered himself to be vanquished where natural inclinations were his sole obstacle, it is clear that he
yielded to One stronger than himself, and acted by
an inward movement of the Holy Spirit, when he so
constantly spoke of himself in language of the profoundest self-abasement. He was a sinner, and a
great sinner, a coward, a traitor, perfidious, ungrateful, ignorant—his letters are full of these self-accusa-
tions ; indeed it would be difficult to select one in
which there is not something of this kind. Though
driven to repeat himself, he is nevertheless quite
ingenious in the variety of his abusive vocabulary :
he is an " idiot," " a poor layman and a sinner," " a
wretched straw," " a plebeian in grace and condition
in God's Church," " one undeserving even of a name."
He often applied similar epithets to himself in conversation ; in fact he could not help it ; the sense of
his vileness and his utter self-contempt would burst
forth in spite of all his previous resolves. A friend of
his one day told him that it was not well to be so
continually speaking ill of himself ; he took the
rebuke with his accustomed meekness, struck his
breast, and confessed that he was very wrong. Undoubtedly there are persons who talk humbly of
themselves in order to get the credit of humility, or
simply moved by a secret wish to hear themselves
contradicted: this system of self-depreciation is, speaking generally, a practice exceedingly irksome to
hearers ; and perhaps the chief reason why it is dis-
liked is that we secretly mistrust the entire sincerity
of the speaker, and feel that a little praise or consolation is being extorted from us by a kind of stratagem.
None, however, experienced this weariness in De

M

Renty's case; his words had the genuine accent of truth, and men felt that, so far from laying himself out to be contradicted, it would much pain him to have his word doubted. He had also a certain pleasant way of expressing himself, which imparted a natural charm to all he said; moreover, the grace which prompted and accompanied these utterances of self-humiliation gave them an indescribable efficacy, and many persons bore testimony to having experienced in their own souls, while listening to his words, kindred sentiments of humility and a lively realization of their own littleness.

Whenever, by a particular movement of the Holy Spirit, De Renty spoke of the graces, mercies, and liberalities of God to his soul, it was never without accompanying testimonies of profound self-abasement. In one of his letters, after making some communication of this kind, we find him instantly adding, "I am but a sinner, have pity on me, adoring for me the goodness of God and of our Lord, who, as we learn from the Gospel,[*] sometimes makes Himself the guest of sinners. With Zacheus I can give some news of Him; but I confound myself at not producing in my whole life what love and gratitude effected in him in a single moment."

These quotations might be multiplied, but the last trait which we will here add of his humility in word is that which he exhibited towards those with whom he was associated in pious and charitable exercises; associations, be it noted, of which he was himself the originator. Far from stepping into the position to which this circumstance entitled him, his demeanour

---

[*] Luke xix. 7.

amongst them was that of the most retiring modesty. " If I might venture, I would beg you to salute them in my name " : such are the terms in which he would send his remembrance to them ; and again, " I reckon myself to be very happy to be the last of this company ; I am quite incapable and unworthy of it ; and I shall be condemned by you all, if you do not take pity on me and obtain my deliverance from my miserable imperfections." Is it possible, we shall almost feel inclined to ask, that he should in the bottom of his heart have really ranked himself thus low, as compared with the very men whom his own burning charity and zeal had prompted him to collect and animate to a participation in his acts of self-denying love ? To this there can be but one reply : Yes, it is possible, and it is true ; for De Renty would have sooner allowed his lips to be seared with a hot iron than have suffered one word to pass them which was not the faithful transcript and exponent of the genuine thoughts of his heart.

CHAPTER X.

De Renty's Humility in his Actions.

De Renty's humility in his actions was in keeping with all we have related of his expressed sentiments and general demeanour. Instances will be constantly occurring when we come to speak of him in his active life of charity, for humility was so interwoven with

M 2

his every action, so thoroughly was every virtue he practised hedged in (if we may use such a simile) and guarded by it, that it is scarcely possible to speak of him at all without speaking of his humility; we will here, however, specify a few examples which will not so naturally find their place elsewhere.

There was one practice of humility which, from the moment of his special vocation to the service of God, he immediately adopted. Forced to retain some of the marks of secular rank in the world, he at once flung them aside in presence of his God, in whose sight all are equal. He refused to accept any of the privileges which the rich enjoy in the house of God. In those days noblemen, when they went to church, had their footstool borne by their attendants, if there was not one already provided for them. This distinction and accommodation he refused; but, not content with thus foregoing what without the least ostentation he might have retained, he used to mingle with the crowd of workmen and common people, seeking to be hidden and despised. As his dress was of the simplest and plainest, this was easy, at least in places where he was not known; he was often therefore jostled and inconvenienced in no small degree; and this he relished as a great satisfaction. Like the Publican, he took his place afar off, at the lower end of the church, and at the Ursuline Convent at Dijon the portresses often perceived him quite at the bottom of the sacred building, among the poor, where, after they had retired, he would remain praying with his arms extended in the form of a cross; often, indeed, he would pray before the closed door, that he might not, as he said, trouble any one to open it to a poor sinner. The offertory was made in those days, not by means

of a bag or plate carried round, which is a substitute
for the more ancient practice, but by each person
at the altar. De Renty always went up with a very
poor man, who was also his frequent companion in
following the Blessed Sacrament through the streets
when borne to the sick. Often might he be seen thus
associated, and unaccompanied by any person of his
own class.

During the civil troubles, when war was raging in
and about Paris, he used every day to go and buy
bread for the poor and distribute it with his own
hands at their houses to the extent which his strength
permitted. During that unhappy period he undertook the custody of the church plate belonging to
a convent of nuns ; and would fain have. carried one
very large and heavy vessel in his own hands through
the city to his house: it was humility which prompted
a request which discretion, however, induced the religious to refuse. He used often to visit these nuns,
and, as the distance was considerable and the streets
of Paris deep in mud, they would ask him why, when
he did them the favour of coming to see them, he did
not at least make use of his carriage ; to whom he
would smilingly reply that he was not fond of going
in a carriage, it savoured too much of the "Monsieur,"
and we ought to make ourselves as little as we can.
Sometimes, when they saw him preparing to return
in the evening of one of those short winter days when
a thaw had converted the mud of the badly lighted
streets of the city into a species of quagmire, these
nuns could not suppress the expression of their distress at the thought of the more than discomfort
he was about to face, not to speak of the plight
in which he would arrive at home, which most men

of his condition would have esteemed derogatory to
their rank in those days of state and of marked social
distinctions ; and he would reply by reminding them
that our Lord endured far greater humiliations, pains,
and fatigues, when He trod the way seeking souls;
and that Jesus was his pattern.

One day, having to visit a person of high rank with
reference to an affair which concerned God's glory
(and in no other affairs did he interest himself), as
the rain was descending in torrents, those about him
tried to persuade him to go in his carriage, particularly
as it was necessary to traverse nearly the whole of the
city in order to reach his destination ; but all argu-
ments were vain. It was then suggested that at least
he should allow a footman to accompany him with
a cloak, which he could exchange for the one he wore
when he arrived, and so avoid the impropriety of
appearing all dripping wet before a person of quality:
this was a happy device, moreover, for substituting
a more creditable garment for his interview. But he
was not to be thus cheated of his humiliation ; accordingly he accepted half the offer, dispensed with
the lacquey, put the good cloak over his shabby one,
and by this means was enabled to reconcile humility
with a regard to decorum ; for on reaching the hotel
he took off the wet cloak and made his appearance in
his own ordinary garment. These may seem trifles,
and some persons may even regard them as censurable
singularities : it were better, they would say, in indifferent things to fall in with the customs of our
equals, a condescendence in which vanity can find no
place, and which might rather be viewed as a tribute
to courtesy and the respect which we owe to each
other. All this may be true as applied to those whose

grace does not lead them any further, and these will
no doubt always constitute the majority. For any
one in a mere spirit of imitation to wear a shabby
dress on an occasion where the usages of polite society
required an attire becoming his station in life, and
think that by the mere act he was practising a
counsel of perfection, would be to fall into palpable
error, only excusable from the heavier charge of a
vain love of singularity by the good faith in which it
might be done. But it must be remembered, in the
first place, that De Renty had openly and uncompro-
misingly broken with the world, as much as if he had
taken monastic vows : he was not living in society, as
it is called, though he had not retired into cloistral
seclusion ; and in the second place, that he was moved
by grace to these particular acts, in which he combined self-humiliation with a protest against the
luxury and pride of the age.

To such as reckon these acts of self-denial and self-
abasement to be things of small account, implying no
high degree of sanctity, because they feel as if with
no great effort they could do similar acts themselves,
it may be replied that, taken singly, they may indeed
be accounted trifling : to be dressed ill on this or that
occasion may be no great subject of mortification ; to
be accidentally mistaken for a person of inferior class
may even be matter for amusement ; but habitually
to act in a way which in worldly estimation is derogatory to our station, and thus degrading, is assuredly
no trifle, and we deceive ourselves greatly if we
imagine it to be so. It is unquestionable that good
and suitable dress inspires a sense of self-satisfaction
in most people, quite apart from any sensible vanity ;
and there is a corresponding uneasiness accompanying

the consciousness of cutting a sorry figure, or of being
dressed beneath our rank in society, when brought
into a position where this inferiority will be noticed
and condemned, or, worse still, ridiculed.   The exceptional persons who brave these considerations will
be found to do so either from eccentricity or from
some secret form of pride, or from sheer indifference
to such things, an indifference which may be a happy
peculiarity but certainly does not in them arrive at
the dignity of a merit. If, however, want of reflection
or defect in self-examination keep us ignorant of the
general prevalence of a deep-rooted love and value for
the dress and other appendages of our class in life,
and the consequent mortification involved in re-
newing them, saints at least were better informed, and
were also keenly alive to the fact that by the association of ideas, if nothing more, the garb reacts on
the man.   Let us hear how De Renty writes to
his director on this subject :—" Walking through the
streets of Paris one of these Lent days, being very
meanly dressed, and having besides got very dirty,
I entered into the sentiments of the Apostle when he
said* that he was made as the refuse and offscouring
of the world ; and, as it seemed to me that I was in
this despised condition, I returned blessing for cursing,
and for the remainder of my walk, during which my
soul entered into a passive state, actively, however,
receiving light to understand and strength to do,
I comprehended how neatness and new things, even
one's very boots,† a mere glance, or expression of

* 1 Cor. iv. 13.

† This allusion recalls a little incident related by Boudon
of P. de Condren, whose spirit De Renty had so strikingly
imbibed. The author of " The Hidden Life," deploring that

countenance will wound, if we do not take great
care, the simplicity and dignity of this Christian self-
abasement ; and I saw that it was a great temptation
to wish to keep up a state of grandeur and distinction
for the purpose of giving more weight to one's example, and adding to our influence in the service
of God.   It is a pretext of which our weakness avails
itself at the beginning ; but perfection draws us at
length to Jesus Christ humbled and made the last of
men by the Cross.   What an honour to keep Jesus
Christ company, who is so left alone and so little
followed in His ignominy and humiliation !   It is
one of my terrors that I have not yet begun in good
earnest."   De Renty had such marvellous impressions
of the littleness at which the true children of God
and the perfect imitators of Jesus ought to aim, that,
pressed by his inward fervour, he used often to
exclaim, " Let us be little, and very little !   Oh, how
great a thing is holy littleness ! "   Deeply convinced
that nature is always discovering some hidden stratagem by which it may make a return upon self, and
this even in what is most spiritual and holy, he reso-

"we are ever wishing to hold a place in the mind and heart
of creatures, and to be esteemed and loved by them, although
those minds and hearts ought to be filled with God alone,"
proceeds to say that P. de Condren was so penetrated with
this truth, that while still very young, perhaps about seventeen or eighteen years of age, accidentally overhearing, as he
was passing an inn door, a servant-maid remark, " What
well-made boots that young gentleman has on!" seized on the
moment with a zeal all divine, he cut the heel off one of them,
in order to spoil its appearance, exclaiming, " O my God, is
it possible that I can allow such a thing as a boot to occupy
the mind of a creature who ought to think but of God
alone ? "—Part I. chap. xii.

lutely set his face to choose always what was vilest, that he might follow the grace of Jesus Christ, which always inclines to a choice which was His own.

The following incident will serve to exemplify this same spirit of humility, which urged him to decline what others would have thought it prudent to accept for a good object. In a letter to his director, dated December 20th, 1646, he writes : "Madame la Chancelière sent me a packet the day before yesterday, which I found to contain letters from the King, appointing me a Counsellor of State. This was altogether unexpected by me. I replied that I would do myself the honour of seeing her to return my thanks, and that I had too high a value for whatever came with the King's signature not to receive it with respect ; but that I had a humble request to make of her, which was that, living as I did in a simple and common sort of way, I hoped she would not take it ill that, while still considering myself greatly obliged by these letters, I should not feel myself bound to accept them, and if she would allow the matter to drop without notice. It was urged upon me that occasions might occur in which a 'Committimus' might be necessary to me, and that two thousand livres of yearly pension would add to my means for giving alms. To the first point I replied that by God's grace I had not any of what are called 'affairs' on my hands, and that as for a 'Committimus,' the power was often a very vexatious one for those against whom it was employed ; that our part is to bear our little crosses in the ordinary way without laying extraordinary ones on others ; that as for the second point, God having given me more means than I personally needed, I did not think I ought to seek an increase, but remain content with my moderate condition. And so the matter stands. I may add that the appointment cannot take effect unless I assume the title of Counsellor of State, and am registered by the State as a pensionary of the King. You will have seen, by a paper which I sent you some time ago, that I have resigned my earthly nobility to God, and this proceeding would be inconsistent with that act; moreover, it would be a step pledging me to I know not what, something I do not clearly see, and do not wish to see, having other things to think of. My disposition in matters of this nature inclines me to have nothing to do with them. If compulsion is put upon me, and the thing is done in spite of me, it will be a real cross to me; which, however, our Lord will then give me grace to bear. In fine, *Elegi abjectus esse in domo Dei mei; et absit mihi gloriari, nisi in cruce Domini nostri Jesu Christi*:* this is what I feel." He concludes with what is another mark of humility : " I have kept the matter secret to avoid ostentation, which is often exhibited in the refusal of things which confer distinction and attract notice." It seems, however, that, in deference to the judgment of persons whose opinion he respected, he was afterwards induced, for the forwarding of an affair which much concerned God's glory and which would minister greatly to the relief of the poor, to accept these letters and the privileges they conferred.

Nothing, perhaps, places his humility in a stronger light than his perfect submission to his director. Indeed, where not coupled with the virtue of obedience,

---

* "I have chosen to be an abject in the house of my God; and God forbid that I should glory save in the cross of our Lord Jesus Christ."—Ps. lxxxiii. 11 ; Gal. vi. 14.

the genuineness of humility is always more than sus-
picious. Many persons will renounce everything
except their own judgment, and pride, driven out
of all its other intrenchments, will take up its
quarters there, as in a last and, too often, impregnable
fortress. De Renty was one who, possessing by nature
much perspicuity, a cool head, and a very clear judgment of his own, might have seemed less than most
persons to need advice.   Add to which, he had remarkable decision of character, a strong will, and a
pertinacity of purpose, which might easily, but for
God's grace, have assumed the form of obstinacy.
Again, the plenitude of that very grace with which
his soul had been enriched, the lights so abundantly
vouchsafed to him, the spiritual impressions of which
he was the passive recipient, and which appeared to
leave no room for misgiving and almost to preclude
the necessity of any external guidance, might have
led us to think, and, were it not that saints always
mistrust themselves, might, one would fancy, have
led him to think, that he needed not to ask counsel of
man at every step, but might safely follow in general
the leadings of the internal Guide.   But De Renty
did not argue thus.   He knew that in referring to his
director he was not asking counsel of man, but was
securing his own more perfect conformity to the
Divine Will, as well as performing an act of Christian
humility.   It has certainly pleased God to place many
of His most saintly followers in situations where they
could not possibly enjoy the advantage of direction:
where such has been the case, He has Himself been
the immediate Director of their souls, for He needs
not the ministry of any instrument; yet, generally
speaking, few souls attracted to any high degree of

perfection have been left entirely without direction, but at some period of their spiritual course, if not habitually, have been led to seek for guidance in the ordinary way of God's appointment.

De Renty was never without a good director after his call to perfection. First he enjoyed the direction of that marvellous man, P. de Condren. He had afterwards the advantage of that of the eminent Jesuit and spiritual writer, Saint-Jure, who was both his director and the depositary of his papers, and who wrote his life ; but whether he was the immediate successor of the P. de Condren, is not stated by the biographer. It was certainly a Father of the Company of Jesus, for this he expressly asserts ; and we have every reason to believe that this individual was himself. The numerous letters which he quotes as written by De Renty to his director, and which range over the series of years which fill up the period intervening between P. de Condren's death and his own, were, it can scarcely be doubted, all addressed to Saint-Jure. The only fact which appears at first sight to militate against the conclusion which this suggests, is the assertion which we meet with in the Life of M. Olier, that some years after P. de Condren's death De Renty sought the guidance of the great founder of Saint-Sulpice. It is quite possible, however, that although he obeyed the orders of M. Olier, at whose service he had placed himself and whose co-operator he became in works of charity and zeal, this was in no way to the prejudice or interruption of his spiritual relationship with his regular director. We have a letter of De Renty's to M. Olier, written after the death of Sister Marguerite of the Blessed Sacrament, through whose intervention he had obtained the favour to which he refers, in which he says, "I owe her no small obligation for having begged you to tolerate me. You will also do this for the love of our Lord and for that which you bear to this holy soul; and towards you I shall feel penetrated with all the respect that I owe you, or, at least, with all that my weakness will allow of my paying to the reign of God in you. I pray you to endure the alliance of this sinner." These expressions seem to accord with the idea we are disposed to entertain, that it was rather as his leader and guide in external works that M. de Renty here adopts M. Olier than as his personal spiritual director, although he may doubtless often have consulted him in spiritual matters.

It is question here, however, not as to who was this holy man's director at any given time, but as to what was his behaviour towards the guide of his soul. On this point no question can in fact exist. He did nothing of the smallest importance without referring the decision to him, by word of mouth, if in his neighbourhood, but, if at a distance, as, fortunately for us, he frequently was, then by letter. Here we find him always stating the subject under consideration in terms concise, clear, and dispassionate, as one who most sincerely desired to elicit an unbiassed opinion, not as one who was seeking to incline another to his own view, as is too often the case with people even while asking for advice. The tone is invariably that of profound respect and the most childlike humility and trust; he asks his director to make known to him his opinion and his will, and to give him his blessing on the resolution he should take in conformity therewith. Nor were these mere words; for no sooner did he receive his answer than, without discussion or reply, he proceeded in all simplicity and with all equanimity of mind to execute the instructions he had received, whatever their tenor might be. His humility is also shown in the manner in which he acquits himself of the obedience laid on him to detail what passed in his interior.   It transpires everywhere through the frankness which makes him disguise nothing in speaking of those graces of which his spiritual guide had required an accurate account. The very simplicity and purity of his intention, which at other times sealed his lips, here opened them without hesitation.   He was a man of but one desire, and that desire is thus expressed in one of the letters to which we are alluding :—" I breathe only to find God and Jesus Christ with as much simplicity as truth ; I have no other aim in this world, and, apart from that, I desire nothing." Yet this very man, so submissive, so docile to his director, who with a truly touching reiteration is continually begging him to be convinced of his great imperfection, incapacity, and sinfulness, was one who not only, as we have said, was possessed of a very remarkable and clear-sighted intellect and was gifted with singular prudence—not to speak of what he was in addition by virtue of the illuminating grace of God—but was recognized and honoured as a very high authority in spiritual matters by those who knew him or had heard of him, and who was daily receiving letters consulting him on these subjects from all quarters, and from all classes of people—men and women, high and low, secular and religious—ecclesiastics themselves not disdaining to ask his advice, and even his guidance, in affairs which seemed to be their own sacred and exclusive province.

All this, however, moved him not the least, because

he had his eye ever fixed on Jesus, and on Jesus especially in the House of Nazareth. Jesus was the model for his imitation and the 'light to his steps in the submission He paid to St. Joseph; and he took a wonderful delight in contemplating his Lord during those years of His Life of Obedience. One day in particular is recorded, when he had been praying in the church of the Carmelites of Pontoise; and, as it happened that there was a person there to whom he could charitably and prudently speak out of the abundance of his heart, we have thus become incidentally acquainted with the subject of his contemplation on that occasion. "It is true," he said, "that I received this morning a great grace, when meditating on the subjection and dependence in which the Son of God willed to be towards St. Joseph, to whom He was subject and obedient as a child to its father. What grandeur and what grace in this Saint! but what virtue and self-annihilation in Jesus Christ—the Son of God, equal to His Father, subject to a creature, and submitting Himself to a poor carpenter, as if He had not known how to guide Himself! It was given me to know how by this example of the Son of God we receive a striking instruction, and in a manner worthy of such a Master, with regard to the dependence in which creatures ought to be on God, and the strict obligation which binds us to submit to the sovereign power which He has over us and to the direction of men; so that our heart may find no repose save in this self-subjection, united to that which Jesus manifested towards a creature. Oh, how deep is this mystery, and how greatly it touches me!" He here paused as if he had thoughts too deep for utterance, and as if his whole soul was absorbed in contemplation of the greatness of this mystery. The person who had been listening to him began to feel, as it were, an influx and communication of the same grace, and, having expressed as much to De Renty, the latter knelt down, as did his companion also, and together they prayed awhile in blessed union of spirit, adoring Jesus Christ in this state of dependence and submission to a creature, and giving themselves to Him to follow His example.

PART II.

ACTIVE LIFE OF CHARITY.

N 2

CHAPTER L

So far we have endeavoured to give a portrait of De Renty after his call to perfection ; in so doing we have necessarily often touched upon those active works of charity to which his life was devoted. It will now be our special object to view him more particularly as thus engaged, and brought into relation with his neighbour. We shall thus be continuing to fill up the picture of this great servant of God, which, rather than any consecutive history of his career, is what our materials furnish us with the means of presenting.

In speaking of the source of his virtues, which was union and conformity with his Lord, we observed that fraternal charity in him knew no other pattern or measure than that of Jesus. He desired " to compre-hend what is the breadth and length and height and depth " of that "charity of Christ"; and, knowing well that, as the Apostle says, it " surpasseth all know-ledge,"* he was intimately persuaded that there was no other way of becoming His perfect imitator than by giving to charity within ourselves and in our degree a like latitude and longitude. And so he threw down,

* Eph. iii. 18, 19.

as one may say, all barriers of exclusion, and loved all
men, and desired to do good to all and evil to none.
He loved the present and the absent, servants, friends,
strangers, the good and the wicked; none were shut
out from his affections; he esteemed all and honoured
all in their several measures, and spoke respectfully
and kindly of all.   Had not God made them all? and
had not Christ been made man and died for each and
all?   There was no charitable work of any importance
either in Paris or the provinces in which he did not
take a part, and a very great part.   Of many of these
he was, not the ardent promoter alone, but the
originator.   Wherever any meeting or assembly was
held for devising or carrying out in concert some good
and pious object, there was sure to be found the Baron
de Renty, at once the very soul and right hand of the
association.   Moreover, letters poured in upon him
every day from all parts of the kingdom to ask his
advice in any case of difficulty which had arisen in the
establishment or management of hospitals, seminaries,
confraternities, and the like.   It is difficult to conceive how he found time to attend, and to attend well,
to all these calls, as abundant testimony proves that
he did; and, what is still more extraordinary, to
attend to such multifarious interests without internal
distraction or withdrawal of his eye from God.

The following quotations will serve to show that,
numerous as were the demands on his time and attention, he was able to acquit himself of each as if he
had nothing else to divide his care.   "M. de Renty,"
writes a respectable citizen of Caen, "was our main
stay and constant resource for the execution of all
plans that concerned the service of God, the salvation
of souls, and the relief of the poor, and of sufferers of

all kinds. We were continually writing to him on such subjects, whether it were for the establishment of a hospital, or a house of refuge for penitent women, or to obtain help in repressing the insolence of heretics, who openly manifested their contempt of the Blessed Sacrament. In short, we derived assistance and counsel from him upon all occasions, and he invariably displayed the greatest zeal to maintain the glory of God, and to extirpate vice. Since his death we have never been able to find any one to whom we could have recourse in like manner in matters relating to God." Dijon furnishes another testimony to the same effect:—" M. de Renty," writes an inhabitant of that place, " did the greatest good wherever he went in this province, and exceedingly promoted every pious work. It may be said truly that his days were filled with the plenitude of God, and we do not think that he ever wasted a single moment of time, performed a single action, or said a single word, but to serve a good end."

Caen was in De Renty's own province, and as such would have had special claims on his charity ; but he was also the great friend and assistant of P. Eudes, who has been called the Apostle of Normandy, of which he was a native, and which he evangelized for many years. That holy man, after passing twenty two years in the Congregation of the Oratory, was called by the manifest will of God to leave it for the purpose of founding seminaries, the absolute necessity of which in his long exercise of missions had daily forced itself more strongly on his mind. These institutions for the training of zealous and devoted priests were the pressing need of the day, and had, in fact, been the object contemplated in the formation of the congregation of the Oratory, from which primary purpose it had, however, been diverted, although Providence ordered that it should indirectly forward its accomplishment. "The Congregation of the Oratory," we read in M. Olier's Life, "although created for the express purpose of spreading such establishments in the kingdom, was wholly taken up with missions, the care of parishes, and, above all, with the direction of a number of colleges; and it was P. de Condren, its second General, who carried out the designs of Divine Providence, not indeed by himself founding seminaries, but by training those whom God called to lay their first foundations. . . . . He lived surrounded by a crowd of priests, whose enthusiasm he kindled by his sublime ideas on the priesthood, whilst he renewed and transformed their hearts, and whom he sent forth burning with zeal to the conquest of souls." Amongst these was P. Eudes; whom the enlightened and, there is reason to believe, prophetic eye of P. de Condren had singled out as one of the future great instruments in the work which he had so much at heart.

"De Condren," says the author * of the recent Life of St. Vincent de Paul, "the great man and true saint of the French Oratory, understood sooner and better than any one the urgent necessity that existed for the reformation of the clergy, and the part which the Congregation, of which he was the second General, was called to fill with regard to it. One feels surprised at first that, with this keen perception and deep feeling of the needs of the Church, he did not directly apply

* The Abbé Maynard. This highly interesting work is the most complete history of St. Vincent de Paul and his times that has appeared.

himself and those whom he ruled to the work ; but, in
the elect of God we must suppose, besides a clearer
view of the present, a sort of second sight of the future.
There can be no question but that De Condren had a
presentiment more or less distinct and conscious of the
approaching fall of his Congregation into the errors of
Jansenism.   Hence he discerned that the Oratory, in
itself undertaking the education of the clergy, would
but open a corrupted source to the sacerdotal spirit in
France ; and that he ought therefore, by a kind of
derivation, to communicate its grace to others while
it was as yet pure.   For we repeat, Condren was a
saint, and that is to say, a *seer.*"   Accordingly, on
his death-bed, he had told P. Eudes that at last the
time was come, it was God's will, and the men were
ready :   possibly, indeed,   he   had   spoken of that
Father   to   Richelieu,   for   not   long   afterwards the
Minister   summoned   him   to   Paris,   in   order   to
confer with him on the subject of seminaries ; and
we   are   told   that   he   was   so   struck   with the
wisdom,   firmness,   and   prudence   of   this disciple
of De Bérulle and De Condren, that he applied to
him   the words of the King of Tyre to the am-
bassadors of Solomon :   " Blessed   be   the   Lord God
this day, who hath given to David so wise a son."
Cardinal Richelieu had two sides to his character,—
that of the statesman and politician and that of the
churchman.   In the former—whatever we may think
of his talents—his worldliness, his craft, his hardness
and severity, and, above all, his preference of supposed
national interests to those which ought to be dearest
to the Catholic heart, repel us,—nay, often excite our
strongest reprobation ; but, as a prelate of the Church,
he must be allowed the praise of at least favouring

many measures calculated to promote the interests of religion, and to have been in particular desirous to aid in the much-needed reform of the clergy. He died in 1642, and one of his last acts had been to enjoin the Archbishop of Paris and the Bishop of Bayeux to expedite to P. Eudes the king's letters patent empowering him to purchase or build houses to be endowed with the same privileges and rights as were enjoyed by similar houses and communities in the kingdom.

It was in Caen that P. Eudes resolved to open his first seminary, and it was there that in 1642 he established his new Congregation, the constitution of which was modelled on that of the French Oratory, its object being to conduct retreats and other exercises in seminaries ; and thus to aid in the training of good ecclesiastics, and in keeping alive the spirit of Christianity amongst the people by frequent missions. It took the name of the Congregation of Jesus and Mary, because it was opened on the 25th of March, the festival of the Annunciation, and it was consecrated—1. to the Holy Trinity, as to the beginning and last end of the Episcopal dignity and sanctity ; 2. to the Holy Family, Jesus, Mary, and Joseph, whom they were to take as their rule and model ; 3. to the Divine Heart of Jesus and the Sacred Heart of Mary. Had the saintly De Condren been alive, he would have beheld with unmingled joy the initiation of these good works, although they were not founded by the Oratory, but by a disciple who forsook that Congregation in order that he might be better able to carry out its original design, from which, to the regret of both De Bérulle and his successor, it had swerved.

Unfortunately all good men cannot attain to this

generous and truly evangelical spirit, not even all those
who have renounced the world, and seem to have
thoroughly renounced themselves.   Self-love seeks a
last hiding-place in the love of their own religious
institute, and in a narrow jealousy for its honour.
The great St. Vincent de Paul, when in his old age
he called his children round him to expound to them
the spirit of the rules he had given them, warned
them against this delusive temptation.   " Is it not a
strange thing," he said in his own homely but none
the less striking language, " that it is well understood
how the individuals of a Company, how Peter, John,
and James, ought to fly from honours and love to be
despised ; but the Company, the Community, it is
said, ought to acquire and preserve esteem and honour
in the world ?   For, I pray you, how is it possible
that Peter, James, and John should truly and sincerely
love and seek contempt, while the Company nevertheless, which is composed only of Peter, John, and
James, and other individuals, is to love honour, and
to seek after it ?   The two things, it must be allowed
and confessed, are incompatible."   This was the judgment of a saint, and yet it is not rare to meet with
this inconsistency even amongst those whose very profession binds them to aspire to perfection.   We have
perhaps, therefore, scarcely reason to be surprised
when we find that, although so long as P. Eudes was
a member of the Oratory, and his labours were a thing
of its own, in which it could take pride and satisfaction, his merits had met with a thorough appreciation,
yet when that Congregation beheld him about to
found a new society, a society designed to meet a need
which, from one cause or another, the Oratory had
failed to supply, a sense of irritation was roused in its

bosom. That such a feeling should exist would have
been sad enough ; but this was not all. It exhibited
itself in deplorable acts.   P. Eudes was openly treated
as a deserter, and his name erased from the list of their
members ; * and, what was still worse, the animosity
with which the Congregation pursued the new Institute, an animosity sharpened by the Jansenistic leanings which about this time began to infect the Oratory,
created suspicion and excited opposition to it in other
quarters, and was the cause of its being beset with
difficulties and crosses for more than thirty-six years.

Père Eudes bore the unmerited treatment with a
heavenly calm and the sweetest charity, and in speaking of his now bitter enemies of the Oratory, he used
simply to call them " his former friends."   Meanwhile
these "former friends," in a memorial which they
addressed to the Queen, designed to thwart a request
which he had presented, described him as "a poor
youth of low extraction, destitute of temporal goods,
and one of little learning."   They invariably imputed
the step he had taken to presumption and vanity,
and moreover propagated calumnies concerning him,
for the purpose of lowering his reputation.   These
manœuvres too surely began to work their effect, for
the esteem in which the Oratory was held necessarily
lent great weight to the opinion and judgment of that
body.   Many did not so much as think of questioning

* This was very rarely done. The famous P. Quesnel,
who had joined the Oratorians in 1657, and who subsequently
quitted France in consequence of his implication with
Jansenism, was not excluded from the Congregation of the
Oratory until he had been for years in a position of revolt
against the Church. But the sympathies of the Oratory were
by that time entirely with the insidious promoters of this
heresy.

the justice of its verdict, and the consequence was that P. Eudes often met with most contumelious treatment from men high in rank and position, their very servants being ordered to drive him from the door, as if he were a despicable vagabond. Some of his bitterest adversaries were amongst the clergy, whom he sought to reform; but his worst trial was the desertion of his friends, who were either deceived and carried away by the general belief, or, if they did not altogether credit the worst that was alleged, were at least ashamed of him, and did not dare to utter a syllable in his defence. In the midst of the almost universal abandonment which followed on his quitting the Oratory, three alone stood by him—Monseigneur Cospéan, Bishop of Lisieux; Monseigneur d'Angennes, Bishop of Bayeux; and the Baron de Renty.

How painful to De Renty was the spectacle offered by this lamentable exhibition of jealousy on the part of the members of the Oratory can well be imagined, so utterly opposed as it was to his own spirit of charity and humility. One of the great fruits of charity is union and concord, and he had ever laboured to preserve them in his own person and to promote them in others. Hence he had never fallen into the errors of partisanship, and had known how to refrain his lips even from good things where they could only serve to widen a deplorable breach. It had been his aim to live on the most amicable terms with all, with seculars, ecclesiastics, and religious alike; he respected all, spoke well of all, and, when any difference arose amongst them, he felt it most keenly and used every means in his power to pacify minds and bring them to agreement. But this love of peace was in him indissolubly joined to the love of truth, without which it is mere softness of temper, not a Christian virtue; and he knew upon occasion how to speak as well as how to be silent. He saw justice as well as truth outraged in the treatment of P. Eudes; not satisfied, therefore, with adhering to him personally, he published a letter, in which, while recording his own sentiments of esteem and friendship for the holy missionary, he exculpated him from all the charges which his enemies had brought against him, and which had been too lightly credited by so many.

While P. Eudes was thus assailed by calumnies and persecutions, the missions which he continued to give were blessed with the most marvellous success. Of many of these the expenses were paid in whole or in great part by M. de Renty, some being undertaken at his own earnest request. Amongst those of which he defrayed the entire cost were one at his own Castle of Bény, in Normandy, and two in Burgundy; one being at Arnay-le-Duc, a small town five or six leagues from Autun, the other at Conches, in the same diocese. Attacked by fever and worn out with fatigue, P. Eudes at last fell dangerously ill, and had received the Last Sacraments, when an interior voice bade him remove to a distance from all to which he felt bound by any tie of attachment. Accordingly he made a vow to leave his beloved Normandy for some time, and go and labour in Burgundy, where as yet he had only made a temporary appearance. His health was immediately restored, and in 1648 he repaired to Autun. Here again we meet with his indefatigable co-adjutor, M. de Renty; and ten or twelve days later the Father, at his special entreaty, gave a mission at Beaune, to the expenses of which, as to those of the former, De Renty mainly contributed. An abundant harvest of souls was the result, and from this place the zealous missionaries hastened to Citry, of which De Renty was the lord, and where ere long he was to find his last resting-place. He had preceded them in order to prepare for their reception; and from thence we find him writing to Saint-Jure, "The Pentecost mission has been begun here, and has been favoured with an extraordinary benediction; hearts are so touched with sentiments of compunction that tears flow abundantly. Many restitutions are made, and prayers in common and in public are the uniform practice in all families. Swearing and blasphemy are heard no longer, and people flock hither from a circuit of three or four leagues." No doubt the missionaries found a powerful aid in De Renty's own example.

After performing his vow of evangelizing Burgundy, P. Eudes returned to Normandy. His good friend and protector, Monseigneur d'Angennes, had died in 1647, but his successor, Monseigneur Molé, did not come to take possession of his see until the year 1649. This prelate was unhappily opposed to everything and everybody that had met with the cordial support of his predecessor; and although a brief from Rome of the 23rd March, 1648, had confirmed the establishment of the Seminary at Caen, and a second brief in the following month had confided to P. Eudes and his associates the mission of Normandy, that Father being himself designated by name as the head, so violent was the prejudice which Monseigneur Molé had conceived against him, that he peremptorily prohibited them from exercising their

functions in his diocese. Monseigneur de Matignon,
who, with the late Bishop of Bayeux, had used all his
efforts to obtain from Rome the recognition of the new
Congregation,—efforts which were defeated at that
time by the intrigues and calumnies of the Oratorian
body,—now invited P. Eudes to labour in his diocese
of Coutance. During that summer he gave four
missions there, the last of which, at Saint-Sever, had
been undertaken at the earnest petition of De Renty,
who was most anxious for the reform of the Bene-
dictine Abbey at that place. In this delicate and
difficult work, which was happily effected, De Renty
doubtless aided by his prayers before the throne of
God, for he was already gone to his reward.

To conclude our notice of his co-operation with
P. Eudes in the work of missions, we give the following extract from a letter which possesses the remarkable interest of being penned a few days before he
was attacked by his last mortal illness. The immediate subject was a mission at Dreux, in the diocese
of Chartres, which he had been planning. The terms
in which he offers to serve the Father breathe that
true spirit of humility which characterized all he said
and all he did. "I have seen a few persons," he
writes, "with a view to engaging them to unite for
the purpose of securing a yearly mission ; and for
ourselves we will be there as much as we can, to serve
you, visit the sick, and relieve the poor, and for this
end to form associations of persons whom the word
of God has converted. We have already pledged our
hands to each other ever since our Lord touched our
hearts,* and my wife and two more along with her

* "Nous nous sommes déjà touchés tous dans la maic, de-
puis que Notre Seigneur nous a touché au cœur."

will be of the company, in imitation of St. Magdalen, St. Joanna, and St. Susanna, of whom St. Luke records that they contributed of their means to the preaching of the kingdom of God : we will endeavour to do this without display, and without being known, taking a little retired lodging." " See," he continues, " my very dear Father, whether you cannot this year in the course of the autumn dispense the Bread of Eternal Life to those who reverently beg it of you. I beseech you with tears in my eyes to listen to us and to grant our petition, touched with the need of our poor brethren, and by the charity of Jesus Christ, who desires to unite us all in one heart, which is His own, that in It we may live before God. My very dear Father, I place this deposit in your hands ; it is for the Spirit of God to render it fruitful in you and in my very dear Fathers, your brethren. I hope that our prayer will be granted, and that we shall see an abundance of mercies. I await your sentiments thereon, both as respects the thing itself and fixing the time ; keep the affair, however, if you please, secret among yourselves." To the subject of missions we shall again have occasion to allude when we come to speak of his zeal for souls.

We have already mentioned how De Renty placed himself also at the service of M. Olier, who stands next to St. Vincent de Paul in the work of the reformation of the French clergy. It does not fall in our way to enter particularly upon that painful sub- ject, the degraded state of the priesthood in France during the first half of the seventeenth century, a state which was the result in a great measure of the want of ecclesiastical seminaries. For the establish- ment of these in every diocese the Council of Trent

O

had given full and precise injunctions; but the
obstinacy of the French Parliaments in resisting the
adoption of its disciplinary decrees had thrown a fatal
impediment in the way of this most essential step
to any thorough reform.   No seminary could be
opened without letters patent from the King, and the
matter was thus removed beyond the control of the
bishops.   We allude to this circumstance simply in
order to say that De Renty's deep grief at beholding
so many faithless shepherds, so many consecrated
priests of God and ministers of the altar given up
to idleness and dissipation, when not directly dis-
gracing their holy calling, caused him night and day
to pour forth his supplications at the throne of grace
and ardently beg of God to send truly Apostolic men
into His vineyard.   We may imagine therefore with
what a good will he enrolled himself under the banner
of the great Sulpician, and became his active co-
adjutor.   No secular was more serviceable to M.
Olier than this devoted man, for to his own zeal he
added the talent and the grace of kindling zeal in
others, of giving it a right direction, and combining
them in united action.

There was one young nobleman in particular, the
Marquis de Fénélon,* over whom he had much influence, and whom he induced to join him in many of
the good and pious undertakings of which he was
either the originator or the chief supporter.   Fénélon
had been a distinguished officer, and was a man of
chivalric courage, but a great duellist; and so per-
verted had his moral sense become on the subject, that
he not only abandoned himself to this prevailing vice,

* Antoine de Salignac, Marquis de la Motte Fénélon. He
was uncle to the celebrated Archbishop of Cambrai.

but attempted to justify it on principle, even after
his conscience had been awakened to the necessity
of amending his life.   Christian sentiments, however,
had at no time been entirely extinguished in his heart,
and, while living the dissipated life of the camp, he
was often seen to go back to the battle-field after
an engagement, and, under the enemy's fire seek for
wounded men, whom he would bear on his shoulders
within the lines, that they might not die without the
Sacraments.   M. Olier converted him, but would not
undertake his direction until he promised to renounce
duelling, which he at last resolved to do, and,
generously abandoning the brilliant prospect of promotion held out to him, quitted the army, and devoted
himself altogether to the affair of his salvation.   Not
contented with giving up the detestable practice by
which he had so often imperilled his soul and the souls
of others, he made the heroic amends of allowing his
name to be placed along with that of another reformed
duellist, the Maréchal de Fabert, at the head of an
association of gentlemen who bound themselves by
oath never either to accept a challenge or to act as
seconds in the duels of others.   M. Olier, seeing how
insufficient were the penalties of the law to deter men
from this sanguinary mania, had conceived the happy
thought of thus opposing the solemn obligations of
true Christian honour to the tyranny of false honour.
The association was to consist of officers well-known
for their valour and intrepidity ; and, in order to
confer the greater publicity and solemnity on their
engagement, as well as to draw down the blessing of
God upon it, they made it in the hands of M. Olier on
the feast of Pentecost, in the chapel of the Seminary
of St. Sulpice, amidst a crowd of distinguished wit-

nesses. Fénélon was soon called to give proof of his
fidelity by his deeds; for, being challenged not long
after, he nobly manifested the same true courage for
God which we have seen his friend De Renty exhibit
during his military career and under circumstances
in one respect more trying; since, without detracting
from the merit of Fénélon's act, we may be allowed to
think that the young De Renty's had in it a special
generosity: Fénélon's reputation for valour was too
well established for a shade of suspicion to attach to him,
and, in fact, the Court looked on with admiration and
applauded this new heroism, although it excited the
enmity of some individuals. Nothing, indeed, more
signally contributed to cause a reaction in the minds
of the nobility against the unworthy bondage in which
they had hitherto lived to a false point of honour,
while it powerfully served to accredit the protest
which M. Olier shortly put forth against duelling,
and which was soon universally accepted and approved;
marshals of France being the first to affix their signa-
tures to it, and exhorting all the gentlemen of the kingdom to follow their example. We need hardly say
that amongst those who strenuously exerted themselves under M. Olier's leadership to combat this crying
evil of duelling, was he who had once almost stood
alone among the gentlemen of his time in protesting
against it, and who had dared for God's sake to risk
what, when he made the sacrifice, was doubtless
dearest to him of all earthly possessions, his reputation
for courage.

There was another important work taken in hand
by M. Olier, in which De Renty was a zealous agent,
we mean the reform of the old guilds or confraternities.
Almost all the trades in the Middle Ages entered into

these associations, with a widely different object however from that of our modern trade unions, namely, the promotion of brotherly charity and devotion, and the increase, not of temporal, but of spiritual gains, although, incidentally, many advantages of the former order accrued from the practice, as is ever the case in any union based on sound principles. These confraternities still existed at the period of which we are speaking. Paris abounded in them, and in particular the Faubourg St. Germain, which M. Olier found in such a fearful state of corruption and degradation, both moral and religious, when he first entered on his labours in that quarter ; but, as may be imagined, they had utterly degenerated from their primitive intention, and only furnished a pretext for every species of riot and disorder on the recurrence of the festival days of their respective patron saints. With these excesses were combined a few superstitious observances, so that these institutions, formerly means of sanctification, had now become nothing but sources of sin and occasions of scandal. M. Olier, however, did not wish to do away with them, but rather to purify, to breathe a fresh spirit into them, and restore them to their true original purpose. His successful labours were, as we have said, admirably seconded by De Renty, who took such a warm personal interest in this charitable work, that we find him even establishing fresh associations of the kind on high principles of perfection, as we shall hereafter notice.

P. Eudes and M. Olier were not the only great Missioners of the day with whom De Renty zealously co-operated. We must add to their number the saint whose very name seems to embalm that century of restoration and reparation in France to which he so

largely contributed, Vincent de Paul.   De Renty was
in frequent communication with this saint.   How,
indeed, should it be otherwise with one so devoted
to missions, seminaries, and every work of mercy?
One while we find him sending to St. Vincent persons
whose lives hitherto had too often been a scandal to
the most sacred of professions; for De Renty, notwithstanding his secular condition, took a very active
share in the recall to virtue or conversion to a holy
life of many ecclesiastics.   He was, it is almost needless to observe, too humble and too well persuaded of
his unfitness, as a layman, for a work of this kind, not
to consider himself as a simple pioneer, a guide to the
true and legitimate guides, although not a few priests
persisted in seeking his counsel on the deepest spiritual
questions.   Such, however, was not his own wish.
No sooner had he obtained access to some erring or
imperfect soul and won its confidence, than he hastened
to bring it to the true pastor of the sheep.   To use
a homely comparison, he aspired to no higher office
than that which the dog fulfils to the shepherd, or the
pointer to the sportsman; but much more devolved
upon him, and nothing, perhaps, is more remarkable
than the exceptional part he was called to play in
the direction of souls.

Again we meet with him co-operating largely with
St. Vincent in works of charity, and not co-operating
only, but the first on more than one occasion to direct
the saint's special attention to them.   To direct St.
Vincent's attention to a need was sufficient to make
him take it up at once with all the zeal and fervour of
his loving heart.   No matter to him how many other
undertakings he had on hand; no matter how empty
was his purse—did he not serve a rich and liberal

Master who would provide? And truly De Renty
was a worthy co-labourer, animated with the same
spirit. The first of the two works we are about to
mention was the relief of the refugee nobility of Lorraine. Crowds of poor from this ravaged province
had resorted to Paris, drawn thither by the charity of
that saint, who had been and still was the ministering
angel of their country. His efforts had been taxed to
the utmost to relieve the necessities of these starving
immigrants, while still continuing to supply the urgent
needs of the desolated province; but a fresh appeal
was now to be made to him, and it was made by
De Renty. He, too, knew something, and too much,
of the miseries endured on the theatre of that frightful
war, in which he himself, as we have seen, had served,
and now his compassion was deeply moved by observing the struggling life of poverty which a large
portion of the refugee nobility of Lorraine were leading in the great capital. These gentlemen lived at
first on the remnants of their fortune, which they had
saved from the wreck of their property, but these
scanty resources were soon exhausted, and then they
sank into a state of misery far more pitiable than the
poor by condition are called to endure. For men of
their class are unable to dig, and to beg are ashamed;
and so it was with the proud nobles of Lorraine, who
were resolved rather to die of starvation than extend
the hand for charity. De Renty, who was always on
the look-out for sin and sorrow, having discovered
their extreme destitution, went at once to St. Vincent
de Paul with a view to proposing some measure for
their relief. "O Sir," was the immediate reply of the
saint, "what pleasure you have given me! Yes, it is
indeed just to assist and relieve these poor nobles in

honour of our Lord, who was at once both very noble
and very poor." At the moment when St. Vincent
thus responded to an appeal which necessarily involved
much outlay, the treasury of St. Lazare was quite
empty, and he had pretty nearly exhausted the purses
of his best friends. This was a consideration of no
weight whatsoever with the saint. The thing was to
be done. Accordingly, after consulting God in prayer,
he proceeded to draw up a plan which obviated all
difficulties. No retrenchment was to be made of the
alms which were being continually poured into Lorraine, and upon which the lives of thousands depended;
neither was any fresh call to be made upon the "As-
sembleé des Dames," the pious associates, who, with
much charity but with no little difficulty, were aiding
him to carry on the works he had already on hand.
The thought had come to him of assisting the nobles
of Lorraine through the instrumentality of their peers,
and he formed the project of an association of gentlemen who should make it a duty of religion and a point
of honour to relieve those who were members both of
Jesus Christ and of their own order, and who thus
were their brethren by a double title. He began by
enrolling seven or eight of this class; De Renty not
only was of their number, but was his main instrument in collecting the associates and in communicating
to them a portion of his own zeal. The first resolution taken was to draw up a statement of the respective numbers and circumstances of the refugee
families. De Renty undertook this task, and upon
his request the associates taxed themselves to furnish
for the ensuing month a fund to meet the necessities
of the sufferers, in the distribution of which De Renty
took an active part. At the end of each month they

again met at St. Lazare to make a fresh estimate.
This charitable work, which De Renty had so large a
share in promoting and carrying out, was indefatigably
pursued for eight years, as long, in fact, as it was
needed ; and even when most of the Lorraine nobility
had returned to their country, it continued its labours
for many years, varying its scope and object with each
fresh necessity that arose in those troublous times.

The other work to which we have alluded, and
which De Renty had the merit of initiating, is one
that gives him an especial title to our own grateful
remembrance. Numbers of Catholics, driven by the
persecution of their faith from the British Isles, had
taken refuge in France. To religious persecution in
those days political had been added, for it was the
period of the civil war which ended in the dethrone-
ment and decapitation of Charles I. The Catholic
nobility and gentry of England, Scotland, and Ireland
had all fought for him with a loyalty and devotion
which had its source in the highest principles ; for
assuredly the sovereign had small claim on their
gratitude. Nevertheless they fought and bled and
suffered confiscation and exile for him, and Paris was
now full of refugee royalists, many of whom also were
Protestants proscribed for their loyalty alone, but
who were at any rate noble sufferers in a generous
cause. These were by no means excluded from De
Renty's sympathy, for his charity was large and comprehensive, but it was the brethren in the faith, the
suffering Catholics, who had the first and greatest
claim on his assistance ; they were, moreover, mostly
not mere political refugees, but victims of fanatical
intolerance and persecution, confessors as well as
exiles. De Renty brought their condition under the

notice of the great apostle of charity, St. Vincent, and together they addressed the association of gentlemen (of which we have just spoken) on the subject, and inspired them with the resolution to do for the English nobles what they were already doing for those of Lorraine. De Renty here also lent personal as well as large pecuniary aid. Every month he used to go on foot, almost always unaccompanied, to the most distant quarters of Paris, which he had selected, according to his usual practice of choosing whatever was most inconvenient, as his own department. On entering he accosted the poor exiles with expressions of the tenderest sympathy, and after a while would produce the alms he had brought, folded up in paper, and present it with a manner so considerate and respectful that he seemed like one who was asking rather than conferring a favour. On one occasion, when a friend was with him, as they were returning he said, " These are good Christians, who have left all for God; what are we in comparison with them, we, who have lost nothing and want for nothing? They are contented with two crowns a month, after having possessed their fifteen or twenty thousand livres of rent, and they suffer with patience this cruel reverse of fortune. As for us, we have abundance of goods and scarcely a little charity. Ah, Sir, it is not in externals or in words that Christianity consists, but in heart and in deeds." In 1649 the English nobility lost their generous benefactor, but St. Vincent continued to assist them until the restoration of the Stuarts, eleven years after De Renty's death, recalled the greater part of them to their country.

The missions in foreign lands also received much assistance from De Renty, and especially those of the

Levant; the Church in Canada was likewise much indebted to him. He was besides a fervent fellow-labourer in another of St. Vincent's great charities, that of the redemption of captives from Moslem slavery, and the provision for the spiritual wants of the many thousands of Christians who languished in fetters in the Barbary States, suffering untold barbarities and exposed to the most frightful temptations to abjure their faith. But we must cease our enumeration, for it would be almost as difficult to specify all the good works of the day in which De Renty co-operated as to single out one in which he did not more or less actively interest himself.

CHAPTER II.

De Renty's Corporal Works of Mercy.

De Renty could not be, as we have seen him, so great a lover of poverty without being also a great lover of the poor. Both loves were the fruit of his all-absorbing love for Jesus Christ, if they may not rather be said to be a portion of it. In poverty he saw the election of the God-Man, in the poor He saw His representatives, His very Self. In serving the poor, the thought that he was serving Jesus was never for a moment absent from his mind. Hence the squalor, the rags, the filth, all that is offensive, not to the sight only, but to other senses whose repugnances it is hardest perhaps to overcome, made

no impression on him. With the eye of faith he
penetrated beneath all to discern his Saviour present
under this disguise. Until Jesus is thus discerned
as the object of charity in the poor, as well as recognized as the motive to that charity, it will always
be difficult at times for the kindest persons to overcome certain physical sensations of disgust which will
arise in spite of themselves. Where love is strong, we
know that not only is the victory accomplished every
day over such sensations, but they are often not so
much as experienced, so powerful is even natural
human affection ; but it is hard for any one to love
with such intensity a poor beggar, who is not only a
stranger to his benefactor, but possibly has nothing to
recommend him to his love, while not seldom he may
even be at once both morally and physically dis-
gustful. We may deeply compassionate such a one,
and do all in our power to better his condition, and
this for the love of God, who has enjoined us to
be pitiful towards our suffering brethren, but the
tenderness which overcomes every rising of sensitive
repulsion is inspired only by regarding Jesus in their
person,—Jesus, as we have said, the object, not the
motive only, of our charity.

In 1641 De Renty began the practice of giving
a dinner in his house to two poor men twice a week,
on Tuesdays and Fridays ; and his aim being always
to combine spiritual with temporal alms, he used to
seek out in particular such individuals as were likely
to need instruction. His custom was after Mass to go
to the Porte St. Antoine, by which numbers of poor
country people were in the habit of entering Paris in
the hope of finding employment or relief ; the probability being that the misfortune of ignorance was

superadded to that of want. Then and there he would make his selection of two, whom he would kindly accost and take to his own house. If it was winter he brought them to the fire, and when they were warmed and comfortably seated he took a chair also, and sat down to converse familiarly with them. His face on these occasions—and nature had gifted him with a very prepossessing countenance—is described as beaming with such cordial affection, and his whole manner as fraught with such winning sweetness, that no wonder he engaged the attention and captivated the hearts of these poor people, as he expounded to them the chief mysteries of the Faith, speaking to them of the Blessed Trinity, the Incarnation of our Lord, and the Most Holy Sacrament of the Altar. He would then proceed briefly to teach them how to make their confession, how to communicate well, how to live well ; and when the instruction was ended he brought them water to wash their hands, and made them sit down to table, serving them himself bare-headed and with the utmost respect. The servants and his children brought the dishes to him, his wife also often assisting, but he put them all on the table himself. During dinner he enjoined silence on all who were thus engaged, in order that his guests might eat undisturbed, to whom, when the repast was finished, he gave alms, and conducted them to the door of his house, bowing to these dirty and ragged beggars with as much civility as if they had been the first gentlemen in the land, and accompanying his parting courtesies with a few words of salutary advice.

He continued this practice for five or six years, when the great press of occupation which his other charities brought upon him obliged him to content himself with giving only one dinner in the week, generally on the Thursday. To make up for this, he added a third to the party, and never intermitted the custom so long as he lived; only when he was quite unable personally to attend, Madame de Renty took his place, substituting poor women for men. He used also every year to give a dinner at Christmas to a child about ten or twelve years old, in honour of our Lord's Infancy; and on the Epiphany he entertained a poor woman with her infant, to honour in like manner the mystery of that day, when the Kings brought their gifts to Jesus as He lay in Mary's arms. On the festival of his patron, St. John the Baptist, he fed twelve poor men, and the same number on Maundy Thursday, after washing their feet.

But, besides these charities to the poor, and many more of which his own house was the theatre, he might be said to have undertaken the care, so far as was possible to him, of all the poor in Paris, not to speak of the other towns he used to visit; in addition to which, he kept up a correspondence with persons in other places, who informed him of any cases of destitution occurring there. He did not wait for the poor to seek him out, he went in quest of them, and never did a beggar look out for relief with more solicitude than his charity searched for its objects. Not satisfied with relieving the wants of the indigent, he loved to minister to their necessities with his own hands; moreover, he endeavoured to put them in the way of earning their own livelihood, and induced others to interest themselves in their behalf. He sought employments for them adapted to their respective capacities, particularly in the case of children and poor girls ; and often, when he could not provide them at once with work or suitable situations, he lodged and maintained them for a length of time under his own roof. And again, he used to furnish poor artisans with tools, or would redeem their own out of pawn, if distress had obliged them to pledge these essential means of making a living. This done, he would supply them with materials for their work, in order that they might profitably employ themselves without delay, furnishing them with food until they could find purchasers ; and, if such were not forth-coming at once, then he himself would purchase their handiwork ; continuing at the same time to visit, en-courage, and give them wholesome advice. But this was not all ; that he might the better assist and direct them in their business, as well as teach other poor people a way of earning their bread, he did not think it beneath him to learn some of their humble trades. Extremely quick at acquiring knowledge of all kinds, and endowed with much natural skill, he did not dis-dain to employ that dexterity which had often won him admiration in noble exercises in the manual occupations of the working classes. Every talent he possessed he knew was from God, to be used to His glory and the good of his neighbour, and not one did he leave idle.

One day he took a friend down into a cellar to visit a poor man who made osier baskets and paniers called *hottes*.* After addressing a few kind words to the tenant of this dingy abode, De Renty, to his companion's no small surprise, set to work himself at

* The "hotte" is a kind of stout deep basket fitted to carry on the back.

an unfinished *hotte*, which, it seemed, he had begun on a previous occasion. When completed, he left it as a present to the poor man, besides paying him for having given him a lesson in his trade. De Renty was desirous of teaching this art to the poor country people, in order to give them some additional means of subsistence. How many more such instances of his charity must have occurred but have remained unknown, for it was seldom that this holy man allowed others to witness his good deeds if it was possible for him to perform them unobserved!

But a large proportion of these, from their nature and from the scene of their performance, could not remain concealed. We must content ourselves with glancing at a few which testify to his loving care of the sick. For twelve years he constantly visited the Hôtel Dieu, the great Hospital of Paris, as well as the Hospital Saint-Gervais, which received the destitute poor and such as we should now call vagrants, giving them bed and supper for a certain period.* Scarcely anything, we are told by Saint-Jure, which is related of the tender and heroic charity of the greatest saints towards the sick and suffering but found its parallel in his practice. Great indeed was his love for the poor, but his love for the sick poor may be said to have exceeded all bounds; and the reason of this was that in them he saw his Lord doubly represented, in His sufferings as well as in His poverty. The following attestation was given in writing after his death by the superintendents of the Hôtel Dieu :—" We have seen M. de Renty visit here with great assiduity for above twelve years. Both at coming in and going out he

* There were some years during which this splendid Institution had afforded hospitality to no less than 36,000 persons.

always went straight to the church, and there, before the Blessed Sacrament, he remained a long time, the sight of him inspiring devotion in all who saw him: on entering, it was to offer his action to our Lord and ask of Him the graces he needed; at his departure, it was to beseech Him to bless it and give it efficacy. On reaching the hospital wards he exercised his charity towards the sick from two o'clock in the afternoon till five, instructing them as well as tending and assisting them in all their necessities. We have seen him dress their wounds, apply medicaments, and cleanse their sores and ulcers. We have often seen him kiss their feet, and help to bury the dead. Moreover, he had the kindness to show the nuns how to compose an ointment which they were unacquainted with, and to make it up before them. He generally came alone, but occasionally he was accompanied by some lords of high rank, who, animated by such an example, insisted on imitating him and taking part in works so holy."

So far the hospital report. It was the same everywhere; and so notorious was his charity for the sick that he used to be literally besieged by crowds of such as were able to walk or to drag themselves along in any fashion. This touching spectacle might often be witnessed at Dijon, once the scene of his humiliations, but which became before long the theatre on which his virtues were signally displayed, in consequence of the prolonged stay which his distressing lawsuit with his mother occasioned. And again, during a four months' residence in 1642 on his property in Normandy, he was almost incessantly employed in acting as physician and surgeon to multitudes of ailing poor, who came from all parts of the country round and

P

crowded about him the entire day. His biographer, Saint-Jure, says that he could not help thinking of how the lame, the blind, and the sick thronged round Jesus, and how impotent folk who could not walk were brought and laid before Him by their friends, that He might heal them. His servant could not, it is true, make them whole with a word, like his Divine Lord, whom he so faithfully imitated; nevertheless, what he could do he did, and God largely blessed his endeavours, and, if he could not relieve the suffering, he had at least a kind word of consolation and encouragement to give, an alms to bestow, some alleviation to minister in one form or other to their pains, so that none were sent away empty and sorrowful. And then the very sight of him, with that large and sublime Christian charity which animated him, that charity which never querulously upbraided, expressed on his calm countenance—with that patient endurance of importunity which the bowels of mercy and of pity, the fruit of close union with our compassionate Lord, can alone enable a man to maintain in unruffled serenity—was in itself sufficient to comfort the hearts of the miserable and inspire holy and edifying thoughts. Thus, if the bodily relief he bestowed was considerable, the spiritual benefit accruing from these ministrations was far greater. He had, however, taken every opportunity to make himself practically acquainted with the medical and surgical art. In 1641 he learned how to bleed and perform other operations; he was always collecting recipes, and got a doctor to give him some general instruction in medicine. But as practice, not mere science, was his object, he not only stored his mind with knowledge, but took care never to be unprovided with the means of beneficially employing it. Accordingly he was in the habit of going about with his pockets full of medicinal powders, carrying besides a small case of instruments for bleeding, lancing, and other surgical purposes, in which his decision of hand and skill, it is said, were admirable. At the same time he was very careful not to venture beyond his knowledge.

When he visited the sick at their houses, there was no service he could possibly render them which he omitted. He would make their beds, light their fires, clean their poor plates and cooking utensils, arrange their rooms, and perform the meanest offices for them; to all which he was prompted, not only by that sweet pity which had its abode in his breast, but by the desire to insinuate himself into their hearts, that he might more easily console, advise them, and win them to God. Nothing pleased him more than to meet with persons like-minded with himself. In the year 1640, having gone to visit some poor people in the parish of St. Paul in Paris, he encountered the Sister in charge coming out of a house. On asking her whom she had been seeking there, she replied that she had been seeking Jesus Christ, and that she had just left a room where there was great need for the exercise of charity. Her answer touched him extremely, and he manifested great pleasure, saying that he also was seeking Jesus Christ ; whereupon they both went together to the room, where there were several sick people whom he had already visited earlier in the day, and for whom he had prepared some soup, given them their breakfast, and made their beds. The Sister and he did not part here ; she took him to several other places, where he instructed and relieved the sick ; and from this time forward they used every week, generally

on the Friday, to repeat these visits in company. It
is by this means that we incidentally learn much concerning his behaviour on such occasions. The Sister
related how he would bleed, or give other surgical
assistance, and then wipe his hands on any rag he
could find, betraying none of the delicacy or repugnance which might have been expected in one brought
up as he had been; moreover, how he never lost
sight of the higher spiritual needs of these poor sufferers, consoling and cheering them, and teaching
them how to make a good confession; how he would
inquire if God were well served by the inmates of
that house, and whether there were any dissensions or
quarrels amongst them. Should he find that there
existed any ill-will of this sort, he at once applied
himself to reconcile their differences and restore
fraternal charity. The blessing of the peace-makers
truly rested upon him, for he never let slip an opportunity of labouring in this cause; and even when he
saw people quarrelling in the streets he would stop to
give them a salutary word of advice, and, if possible,
make them friends again. The Sister bore testimony
also to the peculiar gentleness and respect he used in
his dealings with the poor, and particularly the sick
poor; how he never seemed in a hurry, notwithstanding the multitude of affairs which pressed upon him;
how he listened to them patiently and sympathetically,
giving them time to explain themselves and tell their
story in their own way. An invincible patience, as
we have already observed, always marked his behaviour, and no circumstance, however trying (and
we are sometimes conscious of more strain upon us in
the exercise of this virtue on minor occasions than in
great afflictions, where all good Christians recognize

the hand of God), ever threw him off his balance, or elicited the slightest manifestation of excitement or annoyance.

De Renty's castle of Bény was the refuge of the indigent, and when he visited it, it became a hospital as well as a poor-house and the scene of the sublimest exercises of charity. He had a cheerful and comfortable apartment provided for such as were suffering from the itch and other contagious cutaneous disorders, and here he himself fed, nursed, washed, and cleansed them, performing for them the office which Job on his dunghill performed for himself, and applying the needful remedies until he sent them away cured. He used besides to visit a hospital in the Faubourg St. Germain where these poor creatures were received. He seemed to seek and single out with particular tenderness whatever was most repulsive, and that because shame and reproach were here superadded to bodily pain ; and wherever he saw more suffering he saw Jesus more perfectly. He remembered Him who in the person of the royal Psalmist* described Himself as "a worm, and no man: the reproach of men, and the outcast of the people" ; and of whom the prophet Isaias said,† "We have thought of Him as it were a leper, and as one struck of God and afflicted." When Jesus healed the leper, we are told‡ that He at the same time touched him, although one word would have sufficed from His divine lips ; and so De Renty shrank from the contact of no misery, but loved for Jesus's sake all that human nature usually turns from with disgust. "Upon entering the hall at Bény one day"—these are the words of an eye-witness—"I found him

* xxi. 7.　　† liii. 4.　　‡ Matt. viii. 8.

dressing a cancer which no one could look at even from a distance without recoiling with horror and aversion. Nevertheless he, stifling every feeling of the kind, was acquitting himself of this revolting task with a countenance full of joy and respect."

No disease could, in fact, be so loathsome, no sufferer so degraded, but De Renty would devote himself to tending the afflicted creature with a compassionate love, which could find no parallel but in that of the saintly Sister of Charity. When moral was added to physical disease and degradation, his pity became only the more intense. The Ursuline nuns at Dijon relate particulars concerning the care he bestowed upon a poor wretched girl of whose miserable state they had apprised him, which it might possibly revolt our delicacy too much to see detailed. Suffice it to say that, though her neighbourhood was almost intolerable to those whom De Renty had paid to nurse her, he would with his own hands give her food, and sit by her for a long time, reading to her some devout book and instructing her, betraying the while not the smallest manifestation of those involuntary rebellions of sense which the most charitable persons and those most inured to this peculiar class of trials cannot in extreme cases repress. Perhaps, as a guerdon for his victory over nature, he did not experience them, and what was to others so offensive was with him, as his biographer expresses it, converted into " the sweet odour of Jesus Christ." The poor girl by his assiduous care recovered, and afterwards led a very Christian life, never ceasing to speak with the deepest gratitude of all she owed to M. de Renty's charity. This was not a solitary instance. He frequently exhibited the same generous charity in the hospitals and elsewhere;

and so great was the interest he felt for persons
afflicted with humiliating complaints, that he was extremely desirous to see a hospital established in France
exclusively appropriated to scrofulous patients.

The success of the remedies he applied in treating
the sick was wonderful. Plainly it could not all be
attributed to his peculiar skill, but was the fruit
of God's blessing ; nay more, it was sometimes so
astonishing and so inexplicable by mere natural
causes, health being promptly restored by altogether
inadequate means, and this in cases which had been
supposed incurable, as to suggest the idea of miraculous intervention. This occurred so frequently during
the time he was in Normandy and surrounded with
the sick and infirm, as we have already described,
that the opinion that he healed them rather by grace
and supernatural assistance than by the virtue of his
medicines became very prevalent. We find the same
belief existing afterwards at Dijon, and originating
from the same cause. We can only chronicle the
fact, without presuming to hazard an opinion ; it is
fair, however, in confirmation to a certain extent of
the popular persuasion, to notice a conversation which
took place between himself and the Mother Prioress
of the Carmelites in that city, which, besides, illus-
trates the simplicity and humility of this extraordinary man. He often saw this good Religious,
and was on very confidential terms with her. One
day he told her that he had been called to visit a
poor woman at the point of death. The doctors had
left her, considering that their office was over, but
her friends hoped that he might be able to administer
her some medicine to alleviate her sufferings in this
extremity. " Well," he said, " I made her up one

which I knew perfectly had no curative virtue for such a malady as hers; but as I had nothing better by me, I prayed God to give His blessing to it, if it would be for His glory and the patient's good. My prayer was granted; for I have just returned from seeing her restored to health." As he mentioned this circumstance not at all as one who was relating anything specially extraordinary, it occurred to the Mother Prioress to ask him if he often acted in this way; to which he replied that he did so on similar occasions, when begged to prescribe. "For you see," he added, "these are poor people who are destitute of anything they can apply to their relief; and so am I: our Lord is not bound to remedies; we must have faith where there is nothing we can do; and God in His goodness has given me this faith." She replied, "But then it is a miracle?" "Well," he answered, "and does He not work miracles for us daily?" "Then you work miracles for the poor," she again rejoined; to which he replied simply and naturally, "My Mother calls what our Lord has done a miracle; as for me, I have no share in it, except so far as giving what I have to give to the poor; take it as you will; I make no further reflection upon it, except to thank our Lord when they are cured." Whether or no De Renty worked miracles of healing, we can at least say that it seems far from improbable that God rewarded so much faith and humility by bestowing at times a supernatural efficacy on his naturally inefficacious remedies.

M. de Renty was as indefatigable, however, in preparing the remedies he administered, and in enlarging his pharmacopœia, as if he had not relied with such perfect faith on the power and goodness of God to give

his medicines their curative virtue. He was also eager
to seize any opportunity of imparting his little stock
of knowledge to others ; and having heard with great
pleasure, while at Dijon, that the Ursuline nuns, whom
he so much loved, gave away a great deal of medicine
to the poor, he hastened to add to their means of alle-
viating suffering by teaching the Sister Infirmarians
how to concoct certain "excellent compositions which
had a wonderful efficacy in giving assured relief to the
sick in a very short time." They described afterwards
how he would himself mix and prepare these drugs,
and set them to boil, hanging over the vessels to watch
the process, in spite of the abominable smell which
they generally exhaled and the heat of a blazing
kitchen fire ; retiring from his work, when finished,
with his face all in a flame and bathed in perspiration,
and yet not making the least remark or the slightest
gesture indicative of discomfort. Such offices certainly
did not involve as much self-sacrifice as those we have
previously noticed ; but to a gentleman, reared as he
had been, they must have been not a little trying.
So thought the good Religious, and they did what
they could to persuade him to allow the lay-sisters to
help him and relieve him of, at least, part of his labours,
but he found so many good reasons why the whole
business should be left to his personal care that they
were compelled to desist. He only begged them to
let him know the hours in which the community said
office, and he so arranged his occupations as not to
fail punctually to join them at the appointed time.
This was his way in all things. Consumed by the
inward fire of charity, he could not rest unless he was
spending himself in some way for his neighbour.

Before leaving this branch of our subject, we must

briefly allude to his fulfilment of another of those
works of charity which will receive their special reward when our Lord shall sit upon His throne of
judgment. "I was in prison, and ye visited Me."
The prisoner, no less than the poor, the sick, the
naked, or the stranger, represents Jesus, who was
bound and led away before an unjust judge and condemned to an ignominious death for us. Hence
Christian charity has always been peculiarly directed
to the succour of those who suffer bonds and imprison-
ment and are condemned to undergo the penal sen-
tences of the law. De Renty was a frequent visitor
to the prisons, where he consoled and relieved the
miserable inmates, and not seldom was the means of
procuring their release. That he should be able to do
so may seem strange to us nowadays, but we must
recollect the different state of things which existed at
that period in France. The privileges of rank and
station were very large. Interest and favour, which
often could override justice, could also succeed at
times in procuring the liberty of persons unjustly
committed to prison through the private animosity of
some influential person, and not seldom detained there
for years. The same kind of interest, exerted in
favour of those who in the first instance had been
incarcerated for some better reason, might accomplish
similar results. De Renty, however, acted with much
discretion and discrimination in this matter, and, instead of yielding to a mere natural unreflecting compassion, he considered first whether it would be
expedient for the prisoner's eternal interests that he
should regain his freedom. That with him was the
great, the absorbing interest; and once, when he was
requested to exert himself for the deliverance of an

individual who had been confined for some years, he replied that often persons were freed from prison who made use of their liberty only to offend God and destroy their own souls ; and that it would have been more for their good to have left them there. This answer, however, was only dictated by caution, previously to making himself acquainted with the facts ; for when he had visited the prisoner and ascertained the real circumstances of the case, he exerted himself strenuously in his behalf.

The case was one of the character to which we have alluded. The man was a native of Lower Normandy, who had been committed to prison without any other offence but the having given some cause of displeasure to an individual of influence in those parts. Here he had lain for years, and was reduced to great misery and want. Many persons had endeavoured to obtain his release, but found their efforts unavailing against the superior interest of the prisoner's enemy. M. de Renty having now taken the matter in hand, his first attempt was to effect the poor man's deliverance by expediting his trial, which was pending before the courts of justice, but might pend for as many more years as it had already pended if so it pleased those who had interest and power to delay the course of law. He also provided him with a good and able advocate, and himself undertook the whole charges of the trial. Still the affair dragged on, while the poor man continued to languish in all the misery attendant on incarceration in those times. De Renty now resolved on endeavouring to move the adverse party to an amicable compromise. He wrote to him accordingly, begging him to refer the affair to him, adding that he was about to proceed to Normandy and hoped to arrange matters to his satisfaction. Thither he proceeded at once, and having installed the mission at Bény, of which we have already made mention, he repaired, accompanied by one of the Fathers, to the town where the prisoner was confined. The news of his coming having spread through the place, the streets were thronged with people to welcome him, blessing God for his arrival, for the object of his visit was well known. Many loudly declared that he alone could achieve the deliverance of this poor sufferer, and offered up fervent prayers for his success.

It was indeed one of those difficult enterprises in which few but saints succeed. He had to move a selfish and prejudiced man to forego his resentment and supposed interests, a man whom nine years had hardened in his pitiless state of mind ; the wretched victim of his animosity having been unjustly detained in captivity for no less a period. De Renty went first to the prison, where the Father, who accompanied him, gave an exhortation to the prisoners to console and fortify them ; after which De Renty distributed alms amongst them, and then, taking his poor client aside, he told him that he was going to see his adversary and endeavour by reasoning and, failing this, by entreaty, to consent to his release. He bade him meanwhile pray for a blessing on the undertaking, assuring him, however, that by one means or another he would, with God's good help, deliver him. From the prison he went straight to the adverse party, and, having used every argument which suggested itself, he added the most touching solicitations. Such an appeal, made by one whose words Divine grace powerfully accompanied, had never yet been addressed to this gentleman's heart. He hesitated, and seemed disposed to yield, alleging, however, certain difficulties, which De Renty hastened to remove by returning to the prison for further instructions. Here he found the prisoners engaged at their evening prayers; he therefore waited, although it was then late, and after obtaining the necessary information returned to his own home, which was six miles distant, and which he did not reach until night had long closed in.

The mission, it will be remembered, was going on at his castle of Bény, so that he did not wish to be absent for many hours. It had been a day, however, like all his days, well employed, and the next morning found him again in conference with the prisoner's adversary, whom he successfully brought to terms; then, repairing to the gaol, he liberated the captive, and took him at once to Bény. His soul had now to be cared for, and De Renty urged him to go at once to confession and communion in gratitude for God's mercy to him. He then kept him eight days at his castle, that he might profit by the remainder of the mission. Every evening he used to go and visit him, in order to enforce with good advice the lessons which the day had furnished, and exhorting him to live henceforth a truly Christian life. When finally he bade him farewell, he insisted on his going to see his late enemy as a mark of perfect forgiveness. The man consented, and found him who had been his cruel persecutor for so long now as mild and gentle as a lamb; so wonderful a change had De Renty's charity worked in him. Truly saints carry a sweet infection about them. The liberated prisoner afterwards became a priest, and said his first Mass in the church of Bény for his liberator's intention.

CHAPTER III.

DE RENTY'S ZEAL FOR SOULS.

IN the last chapter we viewed De Renty's charity chiefly as exercised in the corporal works of mercy. Great as was that charity it was far exceeded by that which he displayed in the spiritual works of mercy, for charity in him was well-ordered. As he was not moved by mere natural and sensitive compassion, which is always more affected by what it can see, and often will weep over the wounds and diseases of the perishable body when it has not a tear to bestow on the terrible maladies of the immortal soul, but by supernatural love, and was spiritually enlightened to discern the value of even one single soul, made for God and redeemed by the Blood of a God, no comparison could possibly exist in his mind between the charity which confers only bread, money, health, freedom, and that which labours to render the soul capable of grace, glory, and the eternal possession of God. Moreover, as he was all on fire with the love of God and of His Son Jesus Christ, his intense desire to see Them loved and honoured, and everything removed that could offend Them, was continually urging him on ; while, on the other hand, knowing the ineffable goodness and tenderness of God towards souls, and how dear they are to Him and to the Sacred Heart of His Divine Son, he entered into Their affections, and not only loved souls after Their example, but loved them in, and in union with, his Lord. All this, indeed, will have been abundantly evidenced in much that has been already stated, but the subject deserves a separate notice.

The universality of his zeal is the first thing which strikes us, marking its source in the love of Him who gave Himself to die for all. We have already adverted to the largeness of his charity, and we may here add that it was so great, that he said to an intimate friend (and he was one who never over-rated or overstated his feelings) that he was ready to serve all men without exception, and, if need were, to give his life for any one of them. He longed to enlighten all men with the knowledge of God, and make all burn with the love of Him, to convert, in short, the whole world ; and as Paris was a kind of epitome of the world, this explains the quasi-ubiqui-tous nature of his labours there, and how he was constantly threading its streets in all directions to see what there was of evil that he could remove and of good which he could effect for the glory of God and the salvation of souls. The Holy Spirit who led him on this search blessed his labours and ministered to him grace to direct and strengthen him in their performance : all that he accomplished in this way alone it would be impossible to recount. It might be rash, however, in most persons to strive to copy him in this respect, as in most cases there would be a risk of effecting little or nothing by attempting too much ; it is best for us, speaking generally, to do what comes to our hand, and bestow our chief labours on a more restricted circle and what seems our more immediate calling. Nevertheless the spirit of the charity which urged him to this course is well worthy, not only of our admiration, but of our imitation ; we mean its largeness. For narrowness

can introduce itself even into charity, and zeal which
is apparently all divine can contract a taint of self;
so that men will sometimes come to love their own
special charities a little in the fashion that parents
love their pet children, more for themselves than for
God.

The field of De Renty's zeal was, as has been seen,
not the capital only ; he had an intense charity for
the poor ignorant country-people.   Hence the many
missions to which we have already adverted, undertaken at his request and given at his expense:
missions in his lands of Normandy and Brie ; and,
again, others in quarters where he had no possessions—in Burgundy, Picardy, the Pays Chartrain—
to which he contributed largely when he did not
exclusively bear the cost.   Never was there a state of
things more imperatively calling for this potent
engine of conversion, instruction, and renewal of
fervour than that which had existed in France at the
beginning of the seventeenth century and still to a
large extent existed.   The ignorance and relaxation
which were so lamentably prevalent in the ranks
of the clergy had rendered them unable to fulfil the
Apostolic work which the condition of the people
loudly demanded, in whom corruption and oblivion
of the truths of Christianity were making daily and
rapid progress.   "A half-century of political and
religious anarchy," writes the author* of a recent Life
of St. Vincent de Paul, " had effected a complete
overthrow, if not an entire destruction, in all that
belonged to faith and morals.   Dragged in opposite
directions by a thousand different leaders, the people
no longer knew which way to turn.   The ' yes ' and

* The Abbé Maynard, vol. ii. p. 380.

the 'no' which, right and left, they heard uttered to the same questions bewildered their minds. The admixture of those populations which had remained outwardly faithful with those which Protestantism had already seduced, by degrees entailed first a practical indifference, to be followed by theoretic indifference, the prelude to atheism. The mischief spread above all in the country places, which were even more destitute than the cities of able and vigilant pastors, and consequently more liable to yield to the suggestions of heresy and the encroachments of ignorance and moral disorder." Hence it was that St. Vincent de Paul turned all the energies of his Apostolic zeal to the conversion of the country-people; indeed, this was, we may say, his own proper and exclusive work; his labours to introduce a reform in the education of the clergy having been subservient to this end : viz., to provide the rural districts with faithful pastors. Every one who is conversant with the life of M. Olier will remember his ardent desire to evangelize poor districts, and his own laborious exertions in the missions before he was called to his work of the seminaries.

It was not merely the greater spiritual destitution of the country places which fired the zeal of St. Vincent; it was the conviction also that the harvest was there more sure and more abundant. "Benedictus Deus! Benedictus Deus!" he writes to the priests of Saint-Lazare from one of these country missions, requesting the assistance of more labourers —"Blessed be God! who communicates Himself so liberally to His creatures and, above all, to the poor. .... O Sirs, do not refuse this help to Jesus; there is too much glory in working under Him and in

contributing to the salvation of souls and to the glory
He is to reap from them to all eternity. You have
begun happily ; the example you first set me has made
me quit Paris ; persevere in these divine employments, since it is true that on earth there is nothing
like to them. Paris ! Paris ! Thou beguilest men
who might convert whole worlds. Alas ! in that
great city how many good works without fruit, how
many false conversions, how many good discourses
wasted, for want of those dispositions which God
communicates to the simple. Here, one word is a
sermon ; the poor of these countries have not despised the voice of prophets, as they do in the towns ;
and hence with very little instruction they become
filled with benedictions and graces." It will be
observed in like manner that the missions undertaken
at De Renty's desire were chiefly in small places.
We may, indeed, regard as a peculiar appointment of
Divine love and mercy to France that great movement for the evangelizing of the population of the
provinces which St. Vincent de Paul had the glory
and merit of initiating, and which was so zealously
carried on by his sons * and by other holy Communi-

* Forty missions at least were given between 1617 and
1625, while St. Vincent was still an inmate of the family of
Gondi, and a hundred and forty during the time he and his
community occupied the College of Bons Enfants, that is, from
1625 to 1632 ; while from 1632 to 1660 (St. Vincent died in
1658) the number given from the house of Saint-Lazare alone
exceeded seven hundred ; to which must be added the
number, impossible to calculate, given in more than twenty-
five dioceses of France, and in foreign parts, by the colonies
of missionaries sent out from the parent house.—(See
Life of St. Vincent de Paul by the Abbé Maynard, vol. ii.
p. 420.)

ties, seconded by the admirable clergy whom the seminaries had been the means of forming. It is mainly owing to their labours amongst the populations of France, pursued down to the disastrous days of Revolution, that so large a portion of her peasantry are still so profoundly Catholic. Had the scoffing scepticism of the eighteenth century, the era of Voltaire and Rousseau, which culminated 'in the overthrow of civil order and the abolition of religion in France, come at the commencement of the seventeenth, it is frightful to imagine what must have been its results in extirpating the Faith in that land. It is owing, then, in a great measure, to the Apostolic men whom God bestowed in such abundance on France at the period of which we are speaking and to the disciples whom they formed to tread in their steps, that those whom the "liberals" of this day have contemptuously styled the "rurals" still form the heart and the hope of poor France.

But to return to our more immediate topic. The zeal for souls displayed by De Renty in the missions which he procured or promoted struck all beholders. Not all his humility and desire to escape observation availed to conceal the fire which burned within him. We have already quoted a portion of a letter he wrote to his director from Citry, in which he gives full expression to his joy at its abundant fruits. He exults especially, in the same letter, at the reformation worked in a poor girl who had been leading a bad life, and who had now openly returned with a sincere conversion of heart to God. We are led to infer that he was himself the instrument of this blessed change, and his remark thereupon shows the value he set on one soul, and how largely he shared

Q 2

the spirit of the Good Shepherd, who returns rejoicing
with His one strayed sheep on His shoulders. "I
know now," he says, "that it is for this reason that
our Lord made me come to Citry, and has caused me
to remain here." The joy of his soul was so irrepressible on such occasions that it was fain to overflow in
outward demonstrations. Marking how his eyes were
swimming in tears, a friend who was present at this
same mission asked him the cause ; when he candidly
acknowledged that they had their source in the excessive joy he experienced at seeing so many persons
giving sure proofs of conversion, by restitution of the
goods of others, reconciliation with their enemies,
burning of bad books, renouncement of the occasions
of sin, and the beginning of a new life. This same
eye-witness relates how he observed him, transported
with zeal and fervour, sweeping the church and
cleaning it with his own hands, and then ringing the
bell to summon the people. For most of these
missions he availed himself, as we have already indicated, of the assistance of P. Eudes' Congregation,
who lived in community at Caen ; and several letters
of his to the Father remain as memorials of his zeal
in this cause. For they are full of entreaties, en-
couragements, and information respecting the quarters
where missions might be undertaken with prospect of
fruit, as well as of advice and directions as to the
means to be taken to insure their success. But he
was also in constant correspondence with persons
throughout the kingdom for the same engrossing
object, the glory of God in the salvation of souls.
Wherever his influence could be brought to bear, he
induced people to combine for this purpose, and meet
together to forward their own personal sanctification

and employ themselves in works of mercy and piety.

"Here I am," he writes to Saint-Jure on the 20th September, 1648, "returned, as it has pleased God, from Burgundy. Our visit has been pretty full of occupation in aiding the formation of various associations of men, as also of women, actuated by a great desire truly to serve God." From the account to which we have alluded, furnished after his death by the city of Caen, we learn that in that place likewise he had been the means of establishing many similar societies, the members of which met together every week for the purpose both of assisting the needy and hindering offences against God; and it states that the plan was wonderfully fruitful in good results. He used also to recommend the country gentlemen to meet from time to time in order to animate each other in the pursuit of Christian perfection, and to make solemn profession of their determination never themselves to fight or take a part in any duel. Where he could not directly co-operate in any work for God's glory in the salvation of souls, he would nevertheless associate himself, heart and soul, therewith: "I united myself very closely to you last Sunday," we find him writing to the head of a mission, "which I believe was your opening day;" adding, "I beg you very humbly to believe that if you consider that I might be of any use towards the close of the mission in getting together a small body of gentlemen and forming an association in the town, as we do both in the smaller places and the larger *bourgs*, I will do my best to come; but I should do more harm than good." Saint-Jure gives his own testimony, as an ocular witness, to all he saw him accomplish at Amiens, one

of those places which were specially filled with the
odour of his good works. It would be going over
ground already trodden to recapitulate these; suffice
it to say, that during two visits he made to that city
he succeeded by his example, advice, and exhortations
in associating a large number of the chief burgesses
in the practice of certain stated exercises of charity.
These good men responded with so much zeal, and
embraced the rules he gave them with so much
resolution, that they continued steadfastly to adhere
to them after his death, as Saint-Jure tells us.

De Renty's great desire was to introduce the true
spirit of Christianity into families, so that all in their
several conditions should truly serve God and apply
themselves to the one important affair of life. He
would have wished to multiply himself in order to
instruct all in their duties: fathers, mothers, children,
masters, mistresses, and servants; and this, not for
their eternal interests only, but also for their temporal
good, as subservient to that higher end; for who, he
would say, could place trust in any one, man or
woman, who does not fear God, inasmuch as by
offending Him who is our Sovereign Lord and breaking faith with Him, a person gives us reason to
believe that if interest, honour, pleasure, or profit
attracted him, he might well act in like manner
where it was question only of a servant of that
Sovereign? Thus every motive, the glory of God,
the salvation of men, and the common good of all,
combined to make him ardently desirous to see all
men virtuous, and to labour by every means at his
disposal to render them so. Feeling strongly convinced
of the importance of a good example on the part
of those whose high position made them conspicuous,

and whose influence was wide in proportion, he drew
up a code of rules for such persons, as also for ladies,
which Saint-Jure found among his papers, and which
we shall give in the next chapter, as illustrative at
once of his zeal for the sanctification of all classes and
of his practical views on the subject.

His zeal to rescue from sin was as active as that
which moved him to untiring efforts for the sanctification of those who were in God's grace, and to preserve
them from all occasions of offending Him. We have
already alluded to his peculiar charity towards poor
girls who had been seduced from the paths of virtue,
or were in danger of falling into sin. It would be
impossible, says his biographer, to calculate the number of poor creatures whom he was thus the means of
saving from ruin, temporal and eternal. Many of
these he placed in religious asylums appropriated to
the reception and reformation of penitent women;
others he consigned to the charge of virtuous persons
with whom he was acquainted; and, besides the time
he gave to this work of mercy, he assisted largely in
the way of money. He never despaired of any one;
his was the charity which hopeth all things; and
cases which would have discouraged the efforts of
almost any one who had not possessed this virtue
in so supereminent a degree only seemed to stimulate
him to more persevering exertions. The unhappy
civil wars of France had produced a great moral disorganization in society, and the license and violence
consequent on the presence of an unbridled soldiery
roving about the country had resulted in deeds of
untold wickedness and outrage. The miserable victims
of so wretched a state of things were very numerous,
and De Renty sought them out and followed on their

track with an unwearying compassion which nothing could repel or dishearten.

An instance illustrative of what may be called the heroic determination of his charity for souls is related by Saint-Jure. An unhappy girl, who had been the victim of the cruelty and wickedness of a near relative of her own, had fallen into such a state of despair as to have become a prey to infernal suggestions. Under the influence of these temptations, she conceived an intense hatred and resentment against God, as the author of her calamities. To satisfy her impious rage, she was in the habit of going from church to church and, dreadful to relate, communicating several times in one day, in order, by thus insulting our Lord, to draw down His anger upon her, that so He might make an end of her, and complete her destruction as, she blasphemously averred, He had begun it. The fact became known, and M. de Renty, having been apprised of it, was transported with a double zeal, both for the sacrilegious outrage offered to our Lord in the Sacrament of His Love, and the miserable state of this poor creature, thus rushing headlong to the abyss of hell; for, albeit she was now what might be called insane, nevertheless her mind had become deranged, not by physical causes over which she had no control, but by a wilful yielding to Satanic suggestions. Without losing a moment's time, De Renty set himself vigorously to find her, for with the cunning so frequent in mad persons she was very skilful in evading detection. For eight days he made continual visits to all the surrounding churches, and at last he found her in the very act of making one of her sacrilegious communions; when he at once summoned witnesses, and had her apprehended and taken to a lunatic asylum. Most persons would have imagined that after securing and arranging for the care of the wretched creature and, moreover, undertaking the charge of her maintenance, all had been accomplished that was possible under such circumstances ; not so De Renty. He reflected that her state was the result of a moral derangement and perversion of the will; it was a kind of mental, not bodily, possession. But Satan cannot force free-will, which is God's inalienable gift, and which He Himself respects ; the strong man armed, it is true, was keeping his goods, but there was a stronger than he, who could take them from him, if only the criminal captive could be moved to desire her release. Accordingly he addressed himself to the apparently hopeless work of her conversion, in which he happily succeeded ; for after a while she was brought to a thorough sense of her past wickedness, and detested and renounced it with many signs of the sincerest repentance ; her restoration to grace being at the same time a restoration to a sane mind.

We have already mentioned, when speaking of all that De Renty's charity for the poor prompted him to do for their relief at the Hôtel Dieu, that his care included that of the soul as well as the body ; this was ever, indeed, the main object of his solicitude, to which all else was subservient. We alluded also to his visits to the Hospital of St. Gervais. One day in the year 1641, when passing by that establishment, he inquired as to its object, and expressed much pleasure on learning that poor wayfarers were hospitably lodged and fed there. But as he continued to reflect on the subject, and considered that these poor people were often very ignorant and that their worst privation remained unrelieved, he felt moved by God

to supply this deficiency. Accordingly he went to the
superintendent of the institution, and humbly begged
to be allowed to go of an evening to catechize the
poor inmates when they were all assembled together.
His petition was readily granted, although he did not
mention either his name or his rank, and indeed he
was able successfully to conceal both for the first six
months that he frequented the Hospital. His visits
were as regular as his other charitable engagements
permitted, for, as there were fresh comers almost
every day, and many did not remain long, he was
desirous that none should escape him. In all seasons,
in all weathers, on the darkest winter nights, he
would take his way to this receptacle of poverty.
After catechizing its inmates, he would kneel down
with them to make the examination of conscience;
then followed prayers, after which they sang together
the Commandments of God; and, these devotions
ended, he distributed alms amongst them.

But this is but a meagre description, the mere
skeleton, so to say, of the actual reality. Adequately
to appreciate the charity which informed these acts,
it needed to witness the inexpressible tenderness with
which he treated these poor creatures, the homeless
poor, the refuse, as the world esteems them, of society,
whom he had never seen before, whom probably he
would never see again. If he encountered one of
them at the door, he respectfully saluted him, drawing
back to let him pass, for the poor were his lords, and
he felt them to be so; and he never spoke to them
but in terms of unaffected respect, always uncovering
his head to them. He had nevertheless the utmost
cordiality and frankness of manner in addressing
them, alike removed from the stiff pomposity of some

benefactors and the over-strained and exaggerated familiarity which others, with the best intentions, are apt to assume in their intercourse with inferiors, but which, be it remarked, those inferiors do not value, and often even dislike, for they are conscious that such bearing is assumed, and are thus only painfully reminded of the very distance which it affects to disguise. De Renty assumed nothing; charity was his interior teacher, and his outward behaviour was its perfect exponent. His familiarity was the expression, not of condescension, but of love; and so warm was that love that it often prompted him even to embrace these ragged and dirty wanderers as though they had been his dearest friends.

Much of all this, doubtless, is not generally imitable, simply for the reason just indicated, that it would not be natural, and not being natural—that is to say, not being the genuine representative of the inward feeling —would fail of any good effect; would probably be misunderstood, and therefore positively injurious. To behave exactly as De Renty behaved one must have De Renty's overflowing charity. But *he* was not misunderstood: as the outpourings of his tenderness came from the heart, so they went to the heart. These poor people were deeply touched by the charity and humility of one so much raised above them in birth and station, and the grace of God which accompanied all his acts combined to awaken their better nature and to produce in them sentiments of profound contrition. You might see them, with the big tears rolling down their cheeks, cast themselves on their knees before him, acknowledging the sinfulness of their past lives, protesting their resolution to amend, and beseeching him to counsel and assist them in the

task. Many would hasten that very day to make
their confession, and communicate on the morrow.
When they threw themselves on their knees De Renty
would do the same, in order to unite in supplication
with them or direct all their reverence to God, for
the act, though devotional, was often in a measure
addressed to himself.   One day in particular, a poor
man, after attentively considering him, recognized him
as the lord of the place where he had himself been
born.   Touched at seeing this nobleman employed in
such humble acts of charity, he ran and cast himself
at his feet to do him obeisance.   Instantly De Renty
was also on his knees, and thus they remained for a
long time, for the poor man would not move while his
lord was kneeling, and De Renty would not rise so
long as the poor man continued to do him homage.
It was a dispute which the angels must have looked
on with complacency, called as they so often are to
witness far other contests for precedence in the world.
De Renty knew of no other than what is implied in
our Lord's words, when He declared that he that is
greater than others should become their servant, even
as the Son of Man came not to be ministered unto
but to minister.

After he had visited this Hospice regularly for
several years, some good ecclesiastics, moved by his
example, undertook the care of it.   Another good
effect produced by the sight of his zeal was that which
was worked in the nuns who attended this establishment.   Their own charity caught fire at the flame of
his, and henceforward they resolved to discharge their
office in a very different manner from what had been
their practice hitherto.   For the future they would
go to the Hospital every day, to provide not only

for the material but for the spiritual needs of the poor inmates. Besides repairing their previous neglect, they were led, by thus witnessing the zeal and devotion manifested by a secular, as well as by their conversation with him, to reflect on their own other shortcomings, who by vow and profession were dedicated to God, and bound to follow after perfection. At De Renty's suggestion they adopted several measures for the better internal regulation of their convent, besides profiting by his counsels in many respects regarding their own personal advance in holiness ; so that, as De Renty's biographer asserts, the change wrought in this religious house was most striking, and it became remarkable for the fervour with which God was served within its walls, and for the admirable charity it displayed in external works.

De Renty's zeal for souls was not, however, satisfied with the many regular fields of exercise which it had found or made for itself. It was always on the lookout, and let no, so-called, chance opportunities escape it. We have an instance of this in the account which is given by a friend of his who accompanied him on one occasion to Montmartre, to which holy locality De Renty had a great devotion. On coming out of the church about mid-day he retired to the most solitary part of the hill, which at this period presented very different features from what it does now, near to a little fountain at which, tradition asserted, St. Denys was in the habit of quenching his thirst. Here he knelt down and spent some time in prayer; then he ate a morsel of bread and drank of the holy stream ; this was his whole dinner, and, after returning thanks, he again betook himself to his devotions, opening his New Testament, which he carried about him, and

which, from a motive of profound respect for the Word
of God, he always read on his knees and bareheaded.
While he was thus occupied, a poor man approached
saying his rosary.   M. de Renty rose to salute him,
and began to talk to him about God, and this with
such force and holy energy, that the man commenced
vehemently striking his breast, and then prostrated
himself on the ground in profound adoration, praising
God and making aloud such fervent acts of charity,
that even De Renty, used as he was to witness the
impression which his words produced, was moved
to wonder ; much more his friend.   Scarcely was this
man gone when a young girl came to draw water at
the fountain.   De Renty asked her what was her
condition in life, and upon her replying that she was
a servant, he said, " But do you know that you are a
Christian, and for what end God has created you ?"
He then proceeded briefly to give her the instruction
which she greatly needed, and with such simplicity,
clearness, and persuasiveness, that the girl, after
acknowledging her previous ignorance, frankly confessed that she had never hitherto given a thought to
the salvation of her soul, but now she should take it
seriously to heart ; and she promised him, moreover,
to go to confession.   How often similar instances
occurred it would be impossible to calculate, for De
Renty had not always a witness to give evidence.   Of
one thing we may feel pretty sure, that he neglected
no opportunity, and to him well-nigh every seemingly
casual encounter was an opportunity.   Thus, when
returning from Dijon after his first visit, two devout
persons of some standing in that city, who chose to
accompany him four or five leagues on his way, testified that he stopped no less than three or four times to

catechize poor wayfarers; and once he went some
distance off the road to perform the same charitable
office for a number of labourers, and to teach them
how to sanctify their daily toil.

The zeal which made him intent on the salvation of
all within his reach was not limited to any particular
spot, or to those works in which he could take a
personal share, but went forth to embrace the whole
human race. The interests of Christendom were
specially dear to his heart, and if anything menaced
them he took fire instantly. Thus, upon hearing that
the Sultan was about to make war on the Knights of
Malta, and send a powerful fleet against their island,
he wrote twice to Sister Margaret of the Blessed Sacrament, recommending them to her prayers. The
confidence he had in her intercessory power made him
feel that he could not procure them more effectual aid.
"I recommend to you," he says, "and to the Holy
Family, the Knights of St. John of Jerusalem, for the
Order is at present in great danger, which threatens
also the whole of Christendom; and what the enemies
of the faith may endeavour to do I know not, for they
are very strong. The little Jesus, who is all love and
power, will know how to derive glory from all this : I
pray you to recommend it to Him." And again he
writes, "I supplicate the power of the Holy Child
Jesus to protect His own in the midst of crosses, and
to purify them, enabling them to accomplish His
work; this is what I ask for our brethren of the Order
of St. John of Jerusalem."

CHAPTER IV.

Rules drawn up by De Renty for the Sanctification of certain Classes.

Amongst the papers which De Renty left, Saint-Jure, as we have said, found some rules which he had drawn up for the sanctification of the higher classes. The following seem to have been intended for the guidance of a person of rank occupying a post of authority : they are headed, " A few notes to remind a person of quality of the obligations incumbent upon him as respects his family, his estates, and his subordinates."

" 1. The first and most important obligation for the regulation of a family is a good example, without which the blessing of God cannot rest upon it. Let therefore the whole household and family, from the highest down to the lowest servants, give an example of modesty, whether at church, or when engaged in their respective callings and duties, or when executing commissions and having to converse with those without; so that all may recognize in the harmony outwardly manifested that God is the prime mover of what takes place within, and that nothing reprehensible is there permitted.

"FOR THE OFFICIALS.

" 1. You ought to inform yourself, in detail, if the officials, such as judges, fiscal-procurators, registrars, sergeants, and others, acquit themselves well of their charges ; and you should have an able and confidential person to ascertain this and to suggest the means to remedy abuses.

"2. You ought to examine prudently and quietly if there be any reasonable cause of complaint on the part of the people of injustice or corruption.

"3. Also whether the police regulations are observed according to the ordinances.

"4. Whether the taverns are frequented during the Divine Office on Sundays and Feast Days.

"5. Whether the Festival Days are violated by labouring and carrying without real necessity.

"6. Whether public crimes are punished, and blasphemy and usury repressed; whether drunkards, fornicators, and defrauders of the poor are corrected; and if measures are taken to banish those women who are a scandal and an occasion of sin.

"7. Whether there be libertines who make a mock at religion and priests, and who neglect the fasts of the Church.

"8. It would be well, should there be any one who is notorious for his vicious behaviour, to begin, if possible, with him, in order to show that vice will meet with no toleration; for this will prove to every-one with what firmness you are prepared to act, and will restrain the licence of others. Zeal and firmness are needful, and sometimes also clemency towards those who promise amendment and give good hope of repentance.

"9. One who is invested with full judicial power can on his own authority, and without any other formality, punish a blasphemer or any other individual guilty of any notable vice, by sending him forthwith to prison for twenty-four hours on bread and water, with a warning that, if he should persist in his offence, he will be proceeded against in due course of law.

"10. Some persons dread the loss of their goods more than corporal chastisement; for their punishment, therefore, it is well to condemn them to fines without remission.

"11. Likewise, when persons of known bad character are concerned with others in any affair, it is not desirable to extend any favour to them, but to tell them plainly and openly that it is on account of their evil living that they are severely dealt with, and that they will always be prosecuted in the same manner. On the other hand, you must prove that you value good and simple souls who fear God, and that on this account you are ready publicly to show them favour and accord them protection.

"12. Offices ought to be conferred gratuitously, in order that fitting persons may be selected for the administration of justice, and that you may retain your right to insist upon the fulfilment of this duty.

"13. You must yourself give the example, by never accepting presents from your subjects for exemption from military liabilities, or from those who are pleading a cause before you, or from the poor; but must show yourself to be disinterested, generous, and incorruptible. This will give you much more authority, and more power to enforce respect and hold in check both the officials and the nobles who depend upon you.

"FOR THE CHURCHES.

"1. It will be well to go and visit Messieurs the Curés, that the people may know the esteem in which you hold them, and thence learn how they ought to regard them; and to inquire of them whether any abuses exist in which the temporal power ought to intervene; moreover, to ascertain with what reverence or irreverence persons behave in church; if the people come to hear the sermon; if they are careful to send their children to catechism, and also attend themselves; and you and your servants ought likewise to attend.

" 2. You should see if there be money in the treasury and for defraying necessary parish expenses; if the wardens give in their accounts punctually, and hand over every year all they have received for the profit of the church; if the church money is diverted to pay taxes or for public affairs; and should you find this to be the case, you must not only put a stop to the proceeding, but inform the Bishop; for the treasurers, who are responsible for this money, have no right to consent to such appropriation of it.

" 3. You must look over the accounts of past years, and allot any sum which may have been economized for the purchase of what is most needed for the church. For instance, you will see whether the sacred vessels are of silver; whether there is a proper and decent Tabernacle, and the requisite ornaments.

" 4. You must learn from M. the Curé who are the poorest persons in the parish, take down their names, and assist them in preference to others.

" 5. If I were you, I would never take precedence in walking before priests, particularly in presence of the people.

· " These, as I think, are the main points which are obligatory on one in your position. I may add, a Mission is an excellent thing to infuse a Christian spirit into the people; every one will thus learn his duty and the means of acquitting himself well of it.

R 2

"Gentlemen can agree to meet once a month, to confer on their obligations, and animate each other to the fulfilment of them. In towns, small associations of devout persons may be formed to keep a watch on abuses, remove occasions of sin, and relieve the bashful poor. Charitable confraternities of women might also be established, for the instruction, consolation, and temporal succour of the sick poor; and, above all, an association of good ecclesiastics, who might assemble once a month to consult as to the means of performing well the functions of their ministry, whereon all the good of the people depends."

"RULES FOR LADIES, MARRIED AND UNMARRIED.

"1. It is part of God's ordinary dealings to cause grace to superabound where sin has abounded. The first woman introduced death into this world, and it is through the Blessed Virgin that the Church sings that it was a "happy fault," since it has given us the alliance of her Son, and her Son that of God. But this is not all : if the first woman was the cause of all the ills in the world, it would seem as if God would make use of woman to repair them, having in His wisdom disposed that it should be they upon whom devolve the education of the children and, generally speaking, the care of the family. Men, as the strongest, applying themselves to outdoor affairs, the women lead a sedentary life, and attend to those of the household, so that they see all, know all, and direct all.

"Thus, as in all orders, whether of the Church, the nobility, the magistracy, or the people, the members are drawn from families, which are their nurseries.

we may say that God has intrusted women with a charge of the highest importance; that is to say, to bring up for Him and nourish souls in the spirit of their baptism, disposing them like stainless mirrors to receive the impressions of His will and the vocation of the state to which He calls them for His glory and their salvation. It is, then, of the utmost consequence that they should reflect that the predominance of good or evil amongst men depends in a measure upon them, and that God will require an account thereof at their hands.

" 2. Wherefore let them diligently attend to the instruction of children from their tenderest infancy, repressing by firmness and gentleness whatever their nature manifests that is deserving of censure, and remembering that most vices come from its being supposed that anything children may do is of little moment, and even matter of amusement; but when these same children have grown older and the passions are in all their strength, they, having never been used to subdue and mortify them, will then be incapable of correction.

" 3. Let them attend also to the instruction of their servants, and close the doors of their houses against blasphemy and impurity, immodest games, and all other vices.

" 4. Let them see that their valets do not frequent taverns, or behave insolently to the people.

" 5. Let them see that they be charitably tended when sick, and themselves visit them, as being our brethren and fellow-servants with us of God our Father and common Lord, and at all times provide them with what is needful, so as to remove all temptation to dishonesty or discontent.

" 6. Let them endeavour to introduce both in their own houses and in their neighbourhood, wherever they can, the practice of evening prayers in common; and if the master of the house is unable to be present, let them assemble the household and pray with them.

" 7. Let them be always occupied during the day, in order to render their lives useful and to prevent idleness laying hold on themselves and their households ; remembering that saying of the Apostle, that if any one will not work, neither let him eat. This habit discreetly followed will prove a remedy for many irregularities, and a barrier against much evil.

" 8. Let them from time to time visit poor families, to console them and encourage them to live virtuous lives.

" 9. Let them see to the repairing of the ornaments and linen of their churches ; for want of a little zeal in this matter, we do dishonour to our faith in the Holy Mysteries, and in the end entail much greater expense on a church.

" 10. Let them hold priests in high esteem, not regarding them according to what may have been their extraction by birth, but the dignity to which Jesus Christ has exalted them, and let their behaviour to them be regulated by this consideration ; they are bound to this both that priests themselves may not forget what they are, and to teach the people by their example what reverence they owe to the ministers of the Lord.

" 11. Let them receive visits in a spirit of hospitality, with much charity and with all Christian courtesy, and let them beware of losing the fruit they might reap from these occasions by receiving them in a mere conventional way, or in a worldly spirit; and, above all, let them shun all pagan superfluities.

"12. Let them not tolerate in their houses any pictures which make an improper display of the naked figure, still less let them offend thus in their own persons; let them endeavour with all prudence to banish all affectations and frivolities of dress, which betoken hearts devoid of the spirit of contrition, and which can have no other effect but to foster corruption in souls and turn them away from God."

Such were the salutary counsels he gave to women, and, in particular, to those who were heads of families and had households to guide. But he was also extremely solicitous, and considered it as matter of the highest importance, to promote a reform in all corporate bodies, because here also the influence exerted is far more powerful than in the case of isolated individuals, although the sphere of each person's example for good or evil is really much wider than men usually care to think. We have already (when speaking of De Renty's co-operation with M. Olier's labours in that direction) touched on the subject of the reformation of the trade-guilds and associations, once so powerful an engine for good, but at that time lamentably deteriorated. Not satisfied, however, with the removal of abuses from these confraternities and their restoration to their primitive Christian end, he conceived the idea of establishing others on a more perfect basis. Not that he believed that all were capable of systematically following the Evangelical counsels amidst the engagements of business, or, indeed, in any other situation, but because he felt sure that many are thus capable, and that their fidelity to their superior calling not only is of untold profit to

themselves, but serves to animate those who have not
an equally high vocation to a faithful discharge of the
precepts of the Gospel.   It is difficult to estimate the
evil effect produced on whole classes in the way of
lowering their standard of good by the absence of
such examples. The pattern offered by Religious is
set aside as entirely inapplicable to the guidance of
the man whose daily task is to labour at some business for the support of himself and family ; and the
absence of everything like lofty Christian aims in his
brethren in trade leads practically to the feeling that
such as they have no higher calling than to earn their
bread, and make their fortunes, if possible ; that their
Christian duties are chiefly limited to the negative
order ; that, if they abstain from the vices to which
they are from their state in life more peculiarly liable,
and are honest, sober, industrious members of society,
more cannot be expected from them, nor need they
aspire to anything beyond.   They consider that they
have neither the time nor the means for becoming
saints : that must be left to the Religious by profession, and to a few men and women who have
sufficient leisure to cultivate extraordinary devotion.
Aiming, then, at no more than just saving their
souls, and conceiving nothing higher to be possible of
attainment to them, what wonder that they so frequently fall even below their own low standard ?

De Renty considered within himself that what was
possible to the great body of the early converts to
the Faith, who assuredly were not drawn, generally
speaking, from what are called the easy classes, must
still be attainable by some at least of every class and
occupation in life.   Manual labour is no obstacle or
hindrance to devotion ; nay, it is one of its best

material helps: hence its assiduous practice in several austere religious orders. Accordingly he directed his endeavours to engaging some among the artizans to enter into his views, and was successful in discovering several who had secret aspirations after a higher life than they knew how to realize, and more still in whom it was easy to awaken the desire. He prevailed on these men to put all their gains into a common stock, and, after distributing amongst themselves what was needed for their respective families, to bestow the rest on the poor. Thus was reproduced in the seventeenth century that admirable life of entire disengagement and fraternal charity which was exhibited by the converts of Apostolic times. It was an example given to the world of perfect Christian Communism. De Renty founded two of these corporations, one of tailors, the other of shoemakers, and accepted the office of superior to both. In Paris each was divided into two separate bodies, on account of the size of the town, and similar associations of the two trades were formed at Toulouse. These men did everything in common, got up and retired to rest at the same hour, worked together, and prayed together. Besides the morning and evening prayer they went through some exercise of piety at the beginning of each hour of the day : they sang a hymn, or recited a portion of the rosary, or read a passage out of some book of devotion, or conversed awhile on some portion of the Catechism. They addressed each other as Brothers, and their lives offered a pattern of the most complete union and concord. In concert with a few other devout persons, whom he consulted, De Renty framed rules for the guidance of these associations, and in his capacity of superior used to make them

frequent visits. If he found them engaged in some
spiritual exercise he knelt down with them, and
would not allow them to make the least interruption
for the purpose of saluting him. In all things he
ever made himself as one of them ; and this, indeed,
came quite naturally to him, esteeming himself as he
did the last and least of all. The example of these
good artizans operated most beneficially upon the
men of their class throughout the different trades,
and numbers of them were continually applying to
De Renty for advice, instruction, and help in their
needs and difficulties. He received them all with the
same sweet charity and cordial affection, answering
their questions, solving their doubts, and teaching
them what they ought to do and what to avoid in
their several employments in order to secure their
salvation.

These associations* long survived their founder,
and still existed at the close of the eighteenth
century, when they were swept away by the great
Revolution. During all that time they doubtless
bore much fruit in the salvation of souls, and in
the increase of the merit and future crown of a
large proportion of their members, whom the faithful
fulfilment of their holy rules raised to a degree of
sanctity they would otherwise never have attained.

* De Renty's active co-adjutor in forming the association
of shoemakers was Henri-Michel Buche, commonly called
le Bon Henri, who was himself a shoemaker, and a native of
the duchy of Luxembourg. Coquerel, a doctor of the Sorbonne,
assisted De Renty in drawing up the regulations. Hélyot, in
his *Histoire des Ordres Religieux*, gives an account of the two
Confraternities of tailors and shoemakers, with a picture of
the dress worn by the Brothers.

CHAPTER V.

QUALITIES WHICH DISTINGUISHED DE RENTY'S ZEAL.

THERE is no virtue, perhaps, which requires more accompanying qualities to support, modify, and direct it than zeal. It cannot, so to say, be left to itself, and even when in intention it is pure, in lacking these it will lack all that could render it fruitful for good. First and foremost we may note, as indispensable adjuncts, courage and patience. Both these qualities De Renty possessed in an eminent degree. That he was brave in the best sense of the term, that is, that to physical he had always added moral courage of the highest order, we have already seen. Nature had moreover endowed him with a vigorous temperament, a strong will, and an active mind ; and when Divine grace had touched his heart all these energies were devoted to the cause of God. Saint-Jure says he performed any affair he had undertaken as if he had possessed three bodies instead of one, and accomplished more in half-an-hour than others could in several days ; and this, not only from his great capability of bearing fatigue and the unsparing manner in which he taxed his strength, but also because he possessed the other very valuable qualities of promptness, rapidity, and decision. His mind once made up, no pause was suffered to intervene before action, neither could he be diverted from his purpose, for he saw with a very quick intuition the true merits of a case, and was a stranger to that weakness which can be unnerved or turned away from what is right and just by the fear of false imputations or a possible misconstruction of motives.

The following may serve as an instance. A lady of high rank had constituted him the executor of her Will, containing several charitable and pious bequests; and being informed that the relatives, who were influential persons, manifested a marked dissatisfaction at this testamentary arrangement, De Renty replied with true Christian courage, " I never asked this lady to make any charitable bequest, nor did I suggest it to her, but, since her devotion has prompted her to do so, I will spare no pains to carry out her wishes. I shall take care that her Will is executed, and moreover I am not afraid of anything. If judges have to be solicited, then I will solicit them, in behalf of the poor and those for whose benefit she has bequeathed these legacies, and that she herself may be relieved in her state of suffering, if she be still detained therein."

His zeal was bold and enterprising, and he shrank from nothing where it was question of God's glory and the salvation of souls. He was not the man ever to shirk danger or trouble under the specious plea that the matter was no business of his, or that interference would be reckoned officious, or was certain to be useless, and might be perilous. Allusion has been already made to his practice, when he saw a street-quarrel, instead of turning aside to avoid it, of instantly plunging into the midst of the fray, to try and reconcile the disputants. One day, having chanced upon several men who had just drawn their swords and begun a furious combat, he rushed in between them and with his powerful hands laid hold on the two who appeared the fiercest of the party.

The irritated men were about to unite in turning their rage against the intruder, when suddenly, struck with the dauntless courage with which he persevered in his struggle to separate them, and his evident determination to suffer anything rather than permit them to cut each other's throats, their anger cooled down, they desisted, and listened to what he said to them. The result was that then and there he made them all friends again.

We will give another example of his boldness combined with that no less necessary accompaniment of zeal, patience. Having discovered a man who had been bribed by the heretics to go over to them at Charenton, and who was so bent on his purpose as to be resolved to drag his unwilling wife along with him by force, De Renty sought him out for the purpose of reasoning with him, and dissuading him from his wicked purpose, and by all means, at any rate, of hindering his violent proceedings towards his wife. The man became very angry, would not hearken to a word, and proceeded to use grossly insulting language. M. de Renty, knowing right well how unwise it is to interrupt if you desire to gain a point, particularly with a person already in a state of great irritation, let him have his talk out, and discharge all his fury to his heart's content ; and when he had done, for anger, however fierce, at last exhausts itself, if fresh fuel be not supplied, he was able, by the sweetness which was habitual to him, and which always exercised so potent a charm, to bring him back to a quieter state of mind, and obtain a hearing. The result was that he succeeded in opening the misguided man's eyes to his folly and to the fearful gulf of error and perdition into which he was rushing. He repeated

his visits several times, and at length had the happiness
of seeing him perfectly undeceived and re-established
in his faith. But this was not enough to content his
zeal; he had torn the prey from the jaws of the wolf,
but the wolf was still prowling about, ready to enter
again into the fold, so he sought out the seducer and
threatened him with the strong arm of the law if he
continued his attempts at perversion. What is called
in modern jargon "liberty of conscience," which
practically means liberty to the sectaries of error and
infidelity to pervert and molest the adherents of
the true faith, together with the absence of all legal
protection to that faith, did not, as is well known,
exist in Catholic countries in those times; so that
although the French Protestants were secured in the
free exercise of their own religion by the Edict of
Nantes (not as yet repealed), an endeavour to seduce
and draw away Catholics rendered them amenable to
punishment. De Renty's decision and firmness so
worked on the sectary's fears, that he desisted from
his manœuvres and withdrew from the district; and
thus were a whole family, and possibly others, saved
from perversion.

Zeal is very commonly accompanied by courage, for
it almost belongs to its nature to enlist that quality
in its service, so as to produce at least a temporary
ebullition of valour, if no more, in the most timid;
but patience is a virtue for obvious reasons less akin
to zeal. Yet, in order that zeal may be of the right
sort, forbearance and patience are most needful. The
Sons of Thunder were full of zeal when they asked
our Blessed Lord if they should call down fire from
heaven on the villages which refused to receive Him,
yet He told them that they knew not what spirit they

were of. The Prince of the Apostles was surely animated with the most ardent zeal for his Lord when he drew his sword in His defence and cut off Malchus's ear; yet our Lord bade him sheathe his weapon, telling him that whosoever took the sword should perish by the sword; that is, whoever took it without His sanction, for Peter had indeed asked his Lord's sanction, but, in his precipitate zeal, had not waited for it. De Renty's zeal was patient; for the fervour and force with which he acted were not a natural effervescence or, as with many in whom grace nevertheless operates, mainly the product of human indignation or eagerness. In him they proved themselves to be the genuine fruits of grace, not only by their own constancy, but because they always left full scope to the action of other qualities which had the same divine source. Of these qualities none, perhaps, is more required than patience, if any one would exercise a beneficial influence on his fellow-creatures and aid them in the affair of their salvation; because, if you would influence minds, it is essential first to win hearts, and this cannot be done by an impatient person. However anxious he may be to do good he will waste his efforts; souls will obstinately block themselves up against him, and not a door or an avenue of entrance be left open to persuasion. To win souls, a man must first conquer his own; for he will find it necessary continually to renounce himself in a thousand ways, subdue his repugnances, bear all things, keep silence, even at times from merited reproof, accommodate himself to the most difficult tempers and the most intractable natures, give up his own will, enter into the feelings and views of others, however different from his own, so long as he can innocently do so; in short, he

must make himself as far as he can like to those whom
he would move, so that his heart and mind may be
felt to touch theirs at as many points as possible.
This is what St. Paul meant when he spoke of making
himself all things to all men. Then again, patience is
required in the matter of waiting, whether conversion
or improvement be the object sought. It is difficult
not to suffer discouragement to creep over us and
paralyze our exertions when, after a long time and
much labour expended, no fruit as yet appears. But
De Renty's patience was fed by the sublime hope
which always animated him; besides, he worked in
and for God, the God to whom it appertains to give
the increase in His own good time; so he knew not
what it was to faint or flag at his work. The work
which his large charity entailed on him was indeed of
a very trying character, for he had not only to bear
the contrarieties and disappointments to which we have
alluded as the inevitable portion of those who in any
measure give themselves to the task of gaining souls,
but, in addition, the complaints and the importunities
of so many poor, and not seldom the anger, the dis-
dain, the abuse of the mean and low, who, in common
with those who call themselves their betters, will
sometimes resent nothing more than an attempt to
benefit their souls.

It was a beautiful sight to witness his equanimity
amidst all these troubles and annoyances. His heroic
charity not seldom triumphed over the hardest hearts
and subdued the fiercest spirits. One day he went to
see a man who had conceived some jealous suspicions
against his wife; he had in consequence cruelly ill-
treated her, and had gone so far as even to wound
her with a knife. As might be expected, De Renty

was very ill received, and no sooner had he begun to remonstrate with him than the man burst forth in the most abusive and threatening language, and, raising his hand, as if about to strike, endeavoured to drive him by violence out of the room. But De Renty quietly kept his ground, without uttering a single word or making the slightest gesture either of alarm or of displeasure. The infuriated man paused : he had made his attack, and it seemed foiled by the impassibility of its object. De Renty was now in his turn to be the aggressor. Drawing near, he threw his arms round the miserable man and embraced him, speaking at the same time words of such touching tenderness that the evil spirit within him was vanquished by this assault of love. In a moment all anger had melted away ; he was appeased, and ready to listen to reason. After visiting him several times, De Renty prepared him to make his confession, which he had neglected for twelve years, and also perfectly reconciled him to his wife. The change was solid and lasting, for the man led henceforth a good and Christian life.

We will add one more example of the success of De Renty's patience and forbearance. Visiting a sick old man, he attempted, as was his constant practice, to speak to the sufferer of the affairs of his soul. The poor creature, however, whom sickness, old age, and poverty had soured and rendered querulous, became extremely cross, and, instead of hearkening, told De Renty that he knew more than he did, and could instruct him if he would listen. De Renty replied that this he would most willingly do, and in point of fact he not only allowed the man to have his way, and to run on with a string of ignorant and

S

impertinent remarks, but listened attentively, so that when at last the discourse came to an end, he was able to take an adroit advantage of some of the man's own words and, under the semblance of commenting thereon, to introduce what he had himself desired to say, to impart some profitable instruction, and finally to bring conviction to his mind and touch his conscience. So well, indeed, had he succeeded that before he left the room the old man had resolved to go to confession, and for the rest of his days, attended assiduously to the business of his soul's salvation.

De Renty exhibited the same patience and forbearance in many cases towards the faults of his neighbours ; for, far removed as he was from the spirit of compromise, he knew that, even as the Divine Husbandman does not at once pull up the cockle, so after His example it is sometimes well to endure evil, though never to come to terms with it. His patience was but another phase of his force and strength, after the same divine example. God is strong and also patient, and patient because He is strong. De Renty would sometimes be consulted by zealous persons as to what ought to be their behaviour under special circumstances, and not seldom we find him recommending the wisdom of moderation. We have in particular a letter of his to a good ecclesiastic who had asked his advice as to the manner of dealing with certain gross offenders who were able to evade punishment, in which he says that we ought to have recourse to God by prayer to obtain from His goodness that such sinners might have light and strength to correct themselves ; adding, " It is very difficult to prevent these evils ; our Lord did not remove all the evil from the earth when He abode on it, and we also must needs leave much; and God permits this some-times, as much to exercise and purify the good, as to punish the wicked." The same ecclesiastic apprised him of two other things which had disturbed and per-plexed him. One was some serious faults which he had observed in a priest who had undertaken the direction of souls; the other was that a canon had given a box on the ear to a priest engaged on a mission because he had administered to him a de-served reproof. In reply De Renty writes, "I thank you very humbly for having taken the trouble to inform me of the principal occurrences of the mis-sion:" we may notice here the turn which his humility gives to the communication, for the priest had written expressly to ask his counsel, and this he very well knew, as is proved by what he proceeds to say. "You are all servants of God who know how to respect each other's graces, and who know also that St. Peter, albeit an Apostle, and replenished with graces, was subject to blame on one occasion, as St. Paul testifies. We must excuse our neighbour's faults and pass over all. The work of God which is carried on in souls has its witness in true self-abasement, of which patience and charity are the fruits in His saints, and these are shown to the world in their outward effects; beg the increase thereof for those who stand in need of it. It is a great scandal to see a priest strike a priest; but they were priests who compassed the death of Jesus Christ, and there are many still at this day who partake more of the old than the new law, which consists altogether in alliance and union of charity in Jesus Christ."

He always endeavoured, if possible, to say a word in excuse or palliation, not of the offence itself, but of the guilt of the offender. If personally interested he was sure to adopt a lenient view, and, with the charity that hides a multitude of sins, to overlook injuries of which he was himself the sole object. Thus, when some one pointed out to him a fraud—not, however, involving any very serious results—which was being practised to the detriment of his cause in the lawsuit which he prosecuted at Dijon, he took no notice of it, only saying with his customary humility, " Ah ! it is I who am a defrauder, and who deceive my God ; " and then began to speak of something else. But if De Renty thus bore with the faults of others and specially with those against himself, it was not for the sake of that false peace which sometimes makes the slothful, the timid, and the idolizers of their own comfort appear charitable and forgiving: it was always with the view to their better correction, as was clearly evidenced by the energy he displayed on other occasions where no restraining motive existed to make it advisable to pass over an offence. Yet even then it was admirable to see how many devices he would employ for rendering counsel or reproof less unpalatable. Sometimes, when about to administer a fraternal correction, he would begin with accusing himself, in order by this act of humility and confession of weakness, as it were, to dispose his listener to receive favourably what he was going to say ; or, again, after having mentioned what he had noted as reprehensible, he would beg the person to discharge the same kind office towards himself; and all this was done with so good a grace, that Saint-Jure says that at the time he wrote there were many who still experienced the good effects of this truly charitable correction, and in whom the memory of it would never be effaced. One day, purposing to offer some advice to a person who needed it, he began to discourse on the union of minds and the freedom we ought to manifest in speaking the truth to one another; adding that otherwise we remain ignorant of it, and thus grow old in our vices, which we carry with us to the grave; that for this reason he felt very grateful to any one who showed him this charity. Moved by these remarks to open his mind, the individual addressed begged him to say whether he saw anything in himself which it would be desirable that he should know, and then De Renty told him.

But although, generally speaking, he thus endeavoured to sweeten and recommend the advice or reproof which he administered, he would at other times, when he saw the necessity, speak in a very different tone, and rebuke a sinner with a crushing severity. He knew well how to discriminate when men were to be borne with and when sternly withstood. Thus he said one day to a friend, speaking of a certain individual, "Have a care not to humble yourself before that man ; your self-abasement would do him harm and injure the cause of God ; speak strongly to him." In short, he clearly perceived the difference between the patience which in his own person a Christian ought to exercise, and the force he ought to bring to bear where the honour of God or the good of his neighbour was concerned, and had an unerring judgment as to which of these virtues— virtues which ought ever simultaneously to accompany zeal—was to be allowed the apparent prominence on any particular occasion.

Two other qualities of zeal may be mentioned, which the instances we have already given in illustration of his courage and patience have indirectly evidenced—frankness and prudence. How far a frank, cordial, and fearless manner will go to render acceptable what otherwise might be resentfully rejected the experience of most of us will attest. De Renty was singularly frank : his countenance, his manner, and all he said bore testimony to the candour and sincerity of his soul. He was an utter stranger to the spirit of dissimulation and of human policy. It is true that in regard to himself he used much reserve, and from humility concealed his good actions as much as he could, and his interior sentiments to a very great degree ; yet even his humility, or, rather, the reticence which it would have prompted, was occasionally laid aside at the suggestion of pure zeal for God's glory and the advantage of his neighbour. Under the influence of these motives he would, with a holy simplicity and sincerity, confess the gifts and graces with which God had enriched him ; sometimes, however, using the third person, as did St. Paul when speaking of his revelations, and as many saints have also done, their humility leading them to take refuge under this transparent veil, and thus to shun the form, at any rate, of making self the object of notice.

We will here quote some striking observations on the subject of frankness in spiritual matters written by him to a lady in the year 1640. "You will allow me, madam, to mention to you a thought which occurs to me with regard to the liberty we ought to have freely to communicate the gifts which God bestows on us to those persons who may desire profit from being acquainted with them, instead of keeping what comes from on high shut up within ourselves ; because this would be to stifle the second effect which God looks for from His graces, viz., that, after having benefited us, they should also do good to others; desiring that we should communicate them charitably and discreetly, in order to render them profitable to our neighbour, and that they may be as a seed cast into good ground, which may bring forth much fruit. I should desire that we might regard ourselves in this world like a crystal, which, placed in the midst of the universe, should transmit all the lights which come to it from above; and that by good example, by esteem of virtue and censure of vice, by consolations, conversations, and other acts of piety, we might impart a share of the talents which we receive from Heaven to all creatures, without affectation, yielding a passage to them as glass does to the light. I should also desire that all the honours and all the praise which we receive from beneath should pass on from us to God, without being arrested in us, just as the clear crystal would give a passage to the light proceeding from torches below it; so that, by purifying them, we may send them on with more luminous brightness to Heaven. For it is thus that we ought to render to God the honours and the praise which are given to us. He alone merits honour and praise : He it is who has placed in us that which men praise in us, and He has placed it there, not that the praise should stop short in us, but that it should pass from us to Him, and that He may be blessed and lauded.

"Moreover, we must observe that if nothing is presented to the glass to receive the light which passes through it, the light is not manifested. In vain might the sun shine on the one side and lighted torches on the other; so long as there was no object to catch and reflect the splendour, it would remain only in the glass. In like manner we may receive heavenly light and an abundance of graces, but if we draw near neither to God nor to our neighbour, to give to the One what is His right, and to the other what charity owes to them, we shall, it is true, possess this light, but only in ourselves and as hid under a bushel, where, being thus straitened, it cannot produce its effect, which is communication, and where, after a time, it will perchance run the risk of being stifled and extinguished.

"Consider also that when the sun illuminates a clear mirror there is no object which so well displays its light, nor which gives back its rays with such brilliancy ; moreover, that between the sun and the glass these rays do not appear, but as soon as the sun strikes and penetrates the glass, immediately we behold a splendour so pure and so vivid that it dazzles our eyes, and can even burn if the glass be so arranged : this teaches us what takes place between God and ourselves, which is a secret affair, not to transpire until it has wrought its effect on us.

"Let us, therefore, suffer our souls to be penetrated with the graces of God, that we may afterwards, by the brilliancy they will give forth, enlighten and warm all that shall come within our reach.   Let us imitate the clear crystal, which, solid as it is, yields a passage only to light ; let us, like it, be impenetrable to all save to what comes from God and returns to God ; and let us avoid what is only too common, the permitting ourselves to be led by our senses and immoderately to covet earthly things : this would be like daubing a glass with mud, which, though beautiful in itself, nevertheless, in consequence of the filth in which it is encased, is no longer capable of light, and the light illuminates it no more than it does the mud ; so that, in order to render it capable of receiving light and emitting splendour, we must keep it clean ; the same must we do with regard to our souls thus soiled, washing them often in the pure waters of penance. Wherefore let us offer ourselves to our Lord, in order that we may fail in nothing regarding the graces which He gives us, in respect either to ourselves or others, and may not bury His talents. In fine, let us imitate the crystal, which allows itself to be penetrated by light alone, and then distributes it. Let us raise our visor before men, and proclaim openly to them by the language of our actions, ' My Beloved is mine, and I am His,' like the spouse in the Canticles ; and by our example and our endeavours let us increase the number of loving souls, opening and facilitating to them the way of love. O blessed be the God of Love, in whom I am, &c."

Of his prudence little need be said after all that has been implied in what we have already related. His frankness in no way interfered with or intrenched on his prudence. Circumspect by nature, grace had perfected this quality in him, and given it a supernatural sphere for exercise. He was never deluded into a precipitate confidence by some little show or appearance of good ; he first weighed all the circumstances of the case, the dispositions of the persons themselves, and the actual existing necessity for the kind of frankness of which we have seen him speak ; and, indeed, in the very letter from which we have quoted he gives his correspondent much wise advice concerning the order and measure to be observed in this communication of spiritual things. "We must," he writes, "lay our heart open to some, and give them what is most choice; with others we must practise more reserve, and approach the subject somewhat more distantly and coolly; and with others, again, we must lock up altogether and hide our secret, when we discern no dispositions in them to make a good use of it." The prudence which is also needed in the progress and conduct of any affair was also eminently displayed in him; he had light to choose the best way to go about a matter, prevision to anticipate obstacles, wisdom to know how to apply a remedy to what was capable of cure, always choosing the least violent and painful, so as it was effectual, and sometimes refraining from applying any remedy at all when it might produce a worse disease than that which it was designed to cure. He always looked at the two sides of a question, and not all his zeal for promoting the most cherished objects could avail to blind him to any grave inconveniences which might possibly result from active interference. The following example may suffice. He was requested to procure, in favour of a young man convicted of homicide, what were called "letters of abolition," whereby the effects of a judicial sentence were annulled by a superior authority, the mother of the delinquent having promised, if she could obtain his pardon, to give 8,000 livres, to be applied to pious purposes and in alms for the poor. De Renty demurred. There could be in itself no objection to interceding for mercy in a case which was not one of deliberate murder; accordingly, in his first letter, without committing himself to any decision, he inquired whether the criminal was truly penitent for his offence; but in his second, evidently after further consideration, he writes thus: "I have not thought it advisable to interest myself to obtain these letters, because it would look like procuring impunity for the sake of pecuniary gain, and defiling one's hands with the price of blood. In a word, although others might undertake the business without hesitation, and although I see that considerable alms would be the result, yet I cannot have any hand in it. God's Providence will never forget His holy poor."

If prudence is needed in the conduct of affairs for the guidance of the zealous man, it is equally necessary in order to moderate what he imposes on himself. The body ought not to be weighed down by excessive labours, nor the mind be overwhelmed by a multiplicity of business, so as to stifle or interfere with devotion. Charity is offended, not served, by neglecting our own salvation in order to attend to that of others; for charity's first duty is towards self. To give it the first place is not selfishness but the reverse; for selfishness really makes a man as uncharitable to himself as to his neighbour. Moreover, without denying that there are such things as holy imprudences, it is certain that in over-taxing ourselves we are usually indulging self in the form of over-eagerness, and allowing a certain confusion between the merit of the work itself and that of loving and pleasing God and seeking His will alone to gain entrance into our minds. God can convert the world without our help, but He will neither convert nor perfect us without our own co-operation. He will ask no account of the success of our labours for others, but He will require us to give a rigid account of ourselves. Hence it is that zeal requires the corrective guidance of prudence, lest on the one hand the bodily strength should be so exhausted as to render a man unfit for those very labours which God expects from him and to which divine charity impels him, or, what on the other hand would be still worse, lest his mind should be so overburdened as to distract him from due attention to the interests of his own soul. De Renty was alive to both these dangers; and we find him suggesting the first to which we have alluded in a letter to an ecclesiastic who was suffering under some ailment brought on by his exertions during a mission, and advising him to allow himself more repose. "Permit me," he says, "to tell you quite plainly what is one of my greatest apprehensions, namely, that you should attempt too much, and thus, for want of moderation, render yourself useless. The enemy sometimes, and very commonly, finds his profit in this way with those persons whose dispositions are the best. You no longer belong to yourself, but wholly to others, and are a debtor, like St. Paul, to all men. Preserve yourself, then, not by saving yourself up, but by not overwhelming yourself with toils and fatigues. I have heard how God is blessing you; forgive, for the sake of the interest I take in your work, this observation, which I have made with all respect and humility."

It may be said, however, that De Renty did not himself act on these principles, for we have seen that his severe austerities required to be checked, and it would be difficult to find any one who taxed his strength more unsparingly or burdened himself with a greater multitude of affairs than he did; indeed, it has been supposed that his life was shortened by his unremitting exertions in the cause of charity. Granting all this, we must remember that he shares with those saints who have been attracted to severe self-mortification the charge of pitiless rigour where the body was concerned, and we must also remember that when his director enjoined upon him certain modifications he submitted without remonstrance, and even deferred to the advice of a woman, Margaret of Beaune, because he believed that she was divinely enlightened. But in truth, if his health was injured and his death hastened by his charitable labours, we have no reason to suppose that the Holy Ghost prompts every one to live in a manner most conducive to health and longevity. Some chosen souls, on the contrary, are moved to sacrifice all such considerations, and simply to spend themselves for God, who is pleased to make them complete their work on earth in a brief period. But His grace never moves any one to do what is injurious to his own spiritual health; and in most cases, and in the absence of those unmistakable promptings which imply a pledge of assistance to carry out what they suggest, a reasonable prudence should be observed; for the spiritual as well as the bodily health is often irretrievably damaged by an inconsiderate and over-active zeal. This is why De Renty very generally recommended a moderation which many might think he did not himself observe; yet it was not so in reality. However little he may have spared himself, however numerous his occupations may have been, he always gave the interests of his own soul the preference and made them the object of first attention. He performed without fail all his devotional exercises, and employed a great portion of his time, by day as by night, in converse with God and prayer; besides, while passing to and fro in the streets, he used frequently to enter the churches, and sometimes would spend whole hours before the Blessed Sacrament when his occupations allowed him. Add to this, that by a special grace nothing distracted his mind from its continual application to God, particularly in the last years of his life, when his active charitable employments had become more than ever multiplied. Yet, although he enjoyed this high privilege, he nevertheless always devoted certain allotted times to prayer; for an intimate friend having asked him whether he was still able, so pressed as he was with business, to keep up his former habit of two hours' daily mental prayer, he replied, "When I can I give three, four, and five hours to prayer, but should some opportunity occur of serving my neighbour, I leave it readily; for God, in His mercy, bestows on me the grace to be ever His, and never to be separated from Him, whatever may be my employment."

CHAPTER VI.

Wonderful Fruits of De Renty's Zeal.

Although we could not speak of De Renty's zeal for souls, and of the qualities which accompanied it, without at the same time furnishing abundant proof that God singularly blessed his labours, it may be well to add here a few more examples of the wonderful effects of this zeal, effects which we must attribute to that power of grace which accompanies the words of those who are themselves replete with the Spirit of God. De Renty's very presence and appearance seemed to have in them a converting influence, often surprisingly sudden in its character. Wherever he went—into towns, villages, private houses, or convents, wherever, in short, Providence led him—he carried this gift along with him. Everywhere you might have believed that he was invested with an Apostolic mission, and with the Apostolic grace annexed to it, the grace of bringing light to men's eyes to give them the knowledge of God and of His Son, and of kindling the fervour of Divine love in their hearts.

The following incidents will serve as examples of this remarkable power with which he was gifted.

Being at Paris on one of the early days of Lent, as he was visiting a poor man, a loud noise as of people singing and dancing in the adjoining tenement came through the wall. Instantly his zeal took fire ; he rose, and, entering the next house, suddenly made his appearance in the midst of the riotous party. He looked at them without uttering a word, and so impressed and awed were they by the mere sight of him, that immediately the songs were hushed, the dance ceased, and they all waited in respectful silence for the intruder to speak. De Renty now remonstrated with them warmly on their dissolute life, and in particular on their desecration of that holy season. Tears at once filled their eyes, and many were so deeply touched that they went to confession the very next day.

His success in another case was perhaps still more remarkable, because it was not question only of careless ill-livers, but of a cold-hearted sinner. He found a poor girl, whom a villain had seduced and then abandoned, leaving her to face, not shame alone, but the extreme of destitution, and who, having fallen in consequence into a state of miserable despondency, had

at last determined to put an end to her life. His
words had their usual effect; they drew the poor
creature from the depths of despair, and encouraged
her to raise her heart again to God and cast herself on
His mercy. He then sent her to confession, and went
himself in search of her betrayer. To bring such a
man to better sentiments seemed an almost hopeless
task. What effect could the words of a stranger have
upon one who had not only hardened his conscience
by deliberate offences of the deepest dye against God's
laws, but had closed his heart against every natural
feeling of humanity. And, indeed, as might have
been anticipated, the young man in the first instance
treated all that was said to him with contempt. But
De Renty persevered so earnestly in setting before
him the loss of his soul, the justice of God, and the
severe judgment that awaited him, that at last the ice
melted, and he who a few minutes before exhibited
only cold indifference and insolent contempt now shed
tears of emotion. De Renty, or, rather, grace had
triumphed; and when once the sinner had been
moved to repentance he was ready to comply with all
that might be enjoined upon him. De Renty accordingly exhorted the penitent young man to make the
only reparation in his power for the wrong he had
done, by marrying the girl whom he had seduced and
deserted. He consented, and De Renty had the happiness of seeing them live in peace together and persevere in the fulfilment of their Christian duties.

There is, perhaps, nothing more difficult than to
restore such as have fallen into a state of despair to a
right state of mind. Despair is peculiarly a temptation of the devil, and, when yielded to, gives him a
power over the unhappy soul almost akin to possession.

Despair also resembles insanity, upon which it often borders, and to which it very frequently drives, by rendering the person who has become its prey all but inaccessible to reasonable appeal. De Renty had a special gift for rescuing these victims of Satan's malice from his clutches. While at Amiens, he fell in with a poor woman who had gone wild with grief from the loss of her means of living. She had brought this calamity on herself, having been detected in an illicit traffic in salt; those were the days of the "gabelle," the detested tax on that necessary article of consumption. Brooding over her affliction, she fell into a state of gloomy despair, and conceived an intense hatred against those who had reduced her to her present misery. Thus sick in mind she fell sick unto death also in body, yet could not bring herself to forgive her enemies, as she held them to be, and was therefore unfit to receive the sacraments. De Renty went to her with three other persons, and spoke to her for a considerable time, but all in vain. Perceiving that his words made no impression, he ceased, and, kneeling down in the middle of the room, he invited those who had accompanied him to unite in supplication to God. After praying awhile, he said to the woman, "Will you not join us in begging mercy of God ?" He then recited certain acts, and she complied so far as to repeat them word for word after him ; but such a change came over her, while she was doing so, that no sooner had she finished than she protested before all present that she forgave every one with all her heart, and then listened attentively and calmly to the instructions which De Renty gave to assist in preparing her for the worthy participation of the sacraments.

T

Another similar instance is recorded in which this holy man had a like success.　While he was engaged one day in preparing the sick at the Hôtel Dieu for confession, a Religious came and told him that a man had been just brought in who had been run through the body, without having, as it appeared, given his assassin any cause of offence.　He was in consequence so enraged against his assailant that he could not endure that any one should speak to him of forgiveness; but no sooner had De Renty represented to him what was the duty of a Christian upon such occasions, than he became perfectly gentle, and declared that he cordially forgave his enemy and was quite ready to see and embrace him.

As we have already observed, the hope which fed and supported his charity was so strong in De Renty that he persevered when most persons would have drawn back discouraged.　He would not be baffled; if one means failed, he tried another; and it was seldom he was disappointed, for if hope in the natural order is a condition and the frequent harbinger of success in any great and difficult enterprise, so in the supernatural order it is one of its surest pledges. Some ecclesiastics of note, with others, were engaged in giving a mission at Pontoise; and De Renty, who was intimate with most of them, was there also. According to his usual practice, having gone to the prison without notifying his intention to any one, he found that a culprit was in confinement there who was an old offender, and so obstinate that the missionaries, who had exhausted all their efforts to move him, could make no impression.　They had tried severity, they had tried gentleness, they had tried threats, they had tried entreaties, but all in vain; nothing could induce him to dispose himself to confession. De Renty's measures were soon taken; but meanwhile the hour when the ecclesiastics of the mission dined had arrived, and they sent to apprise him, that he might join them at their repast. After he had been sought for fruitlessly in several places, the prison was thought of, and there accordingly he was found, sitting at table with all the inmates of the gaol, to whom he had given a dinner, and had remained to partake of it with them; thus following the example of Jesus, of whom he was so close an imitator, who sat down with publicans and sinners and, when reproached with this condescension, said, He was not come to call the just but sinners to penance. There, then, sat De Renty, conversing amicably with the prisoners, consoling them and animating them to live good lives, but ever directing his conversation with an eye to him whom he specially designed to win, addressing much of his conversation to him in particular; and this he did with such adroitness, that before the meal was over he had secured his captive. As it may be supposed, he followed up his victory without delay, and the hitherto recalcitrant criminal was speedily brought to make a firm resolution to change his life with a good confession of all his sins; so that one of the missionary priests was fain to declare that De Renty had accomplished in three days what others would have had much difficulty in bringing about in as many years.

The following testimony of a person to whom De Renty had been a channel of benediction will confirm what has been said of the grace which seemed to accompany him like an atmosphere. Just as touching or kissing .devoutly the relics of saints will work miracles of healing—the Spirit of God thus honouring

T 2

the mortal tabernacle in which He had dwelt, even at
times preserving it from decay and imbuing with
a heavenly fragrance those remains which in the
course of nature would have been reduced to corruption and to dust—so also will the very presence of
those in whose souls He peculiarly dwells ofttimes
work marvels of grace.   It is as if these divinised
souls exhaled a sweet odour of sanctity and exercised
a constraining power of conversion on those who are
brought near to them.   De Renty had been requested
to see the person just mentioned, who was enduring
one of those excruciating interior trials through which
some souls are called to pass, and was also at the same
time afflicted exteriorly.   Light to discern the loving
hand of God in these sufferings, and strength to bear
up under them, seemed to be failing, when De Renty's
visit acted as a complete restorative.   This is the
account given by the sufferer a few days after the
interview : " The effect I experienced from the conversation I had with this servant of God was such,
that no sooner had I been able to prevail upon myself
to speak to him, in order to manifest my interior, than
our Lord communicated Himself to me so powerfully,
that I was quite penetrated by the effects of His presence.   I felt a very particular assistance given to me
by the Blessed Virgin, whom the holy man was
moved to invoke at the beginning of our conversation,
and I can with truth aver that I instantaneously received great succour in my needs ; so that every word
he uttered made an impression on my mind and
worked a great effect, which has continued ever since,
and I feel it still at the moment that I write this
And although my sufferings are not changed, yet I.
myself am so changed in my disposition, that I seem

to be quite another person, and as if all within me breathed no longer after anything but the fulfilment of the Will of God and the accomplishment of His purposes at any price and whatever it may cost to nature, which must be taught to yield to grace and to serve, not resist it. My sufferings are not changed yet I must confess that I no longer suffer ever since I have been content to suffer. It is true that what is weak in me suffers; I suffer in my sensitive and inferior part, but the superior portion of my soul cannot be, and indeed is not, it would seem, susceptible of suffering, by reason of its conformity to the Will of God. My sole desire in this my willingness to suffer is that I may make a good use of my sufferings, labour after solid virtue, and abandon myself entirely to the disposal of God."

Although such a gift as De Renty has been here shown to possess must be esteemed very rare—as rare, indeed, as are souls of his eminent spiritual attainments—yet undoubtedly proportioned to the personal sanctity of individuals, and not to their eloquence or natural persuasiveness, shall we find their influence in drawing other souls to God. When we work by nature's powers alone the results are natural; the truly spiritual man does not work alone; he works in union with Him who is the author and giver of grace. We have seen how closely De Renty was ever seeking to unite himself to Jesus in all his thoughts, words, and acts, so that the life of Jesus should alone reign in him; but, moreover. whenever he was about to treat with any one on whatever matter it might be—and all the affairs he undertook had God and His interests for their prime object—he used to " give himself first to our Lord ".

(such were the terms he himself employed) in order
to speak in His spirit and in His power. What
wonder, then, if his Lord, finding him thus admirably
disposed, should have made him His instrument to
effect great things, and supplied him with rich and
powerful graces to that end? But more than this:
not only was he thus supernaturally assisted in all his
zealous labours for the good of others, but it pleased
our Lord also to give him at times a prescience
and anterior knowledge of affairs in which He designed to employ him, in order, as it may be believed,
to prepare him thereby to undertake them without
fear or hesitation, and to enable him to acquit himself
well of them. Thus, for example, when staying at his
château of Citry, towards the close of the year 1642,
our Lord made known to him that when he returned
to Paris a fresh burden of work for the benefit of the
poor would be laid upon him. At that time he had
already so much laborious occupation of this kind,
that reasonable prudence, apart from the circumstance of having received a superior light, would
have dictated a refusal to embark in more; but when,
two days after his return to the capital, it was proposed to him to assist in the distribution of funds
which had been collected for the relief of the bashful
poor, he knew that it was God's will that he should
consent. Accordingly he undertook the task of
visiting the fourth part of these indigent persons and
giving them alms proportioned to their needs, which
in so large a city as Paris would have been an occupation quite sufficient of itself to fill up the time and
exhaust the strength of any ordinary person. But
De Renty had many other engagements besides, as
we know, and, humanly speaking, he could not have

sufficed for all ; he needed some special divine assistance ; this, however, he was assured would not fail him, since He who had laid the command upon him was pledged to administer the ability to fulfil it. Upon another occasion we find him again having what we may call a supernatural presentiment of some approaching work for God. " Last night," he said to a confidential friend, " I was all bathed in tears in consequence of what our Lord showed to me." He then was silent for a short time, as though reluctant to say more, but soon, as if still penetrated with the grace he had received and impelled to manifest what had been imparted to him, he added that, while in prayer, he had been shown that the furtherance of a great work in Canada would be committed to him ; and this, in fact, turned out as he had foretold. For, besides other good service which he rendered to religion in that colony, he was chiefly instrumental, in conjunction with other devout persons, in the foundation of the church in the Isle of Montreal. Not only did he largely contribute by pecuniary aid, but his advice, his care, the credit he enjoyed, and his activity in stirring up others to liberality, were of the greatest assistance in this noble work.

Sometimes the light he received was not so full, and he knew only that he was about to be employed in some new way, and no more : as when, on one occasion, he felt himself inwardly pressed to go to Pontoise, although no particular business called him, and he had many affairs on his hands at Paris. Implicitly yielding, however, to the heavenly impulse, which with one who lived continually in the light of the divine presence, and with an ear ever attentive to the divine whispers, carried its own evidence with it and was clearly distinguishable from a mere human and natural impression, he hastened to Pontoise ; and there he met a gentleman of rank, who lived in a distant province, but who had come thither moved by our Lord, and in the expectation of meeting M. de Renty, who he was given to understand would teach him how to save his soul and also how to serve God perfectly, a matter in which his ignorance had been hitherto equal to his deficiency.   De Renty taught him the lesson he had been sent to learn from his lips, and then returned to Paris, never seeing or hearing more of his disciple, who seemed, as he said, to have vanished.   One is reminded, when reading such instances, of the solitary interview which the Spirit of God miraculously procured between Philip and the Ethiopian queen's minister and their subsequent sudden separation.   Thus it is that our good God leaves no one who sincerely desires heavenly knowledge without an instructor ; and thus also it is that He wonderfully employs in such work those holy souls which have surrendered themselves unreservedly both to His service and to His guidance.

CHAPTER VII.

DE RENTY'S GRACE FOR THE GUIDANCE OF SOULS.

ALLUSION has been more than once made to the special grace vouchsafed to De Renty for the guidance of certain souls who were moved to seek spiritual direction at his hands. This was indeed a very peculiar and exceptional grace, as also the office for which he, a layman, was thus frequently chosen was itself very peculiar and exceptional. We are not now speaking of the abundant light imparted to him, which enabled him to advise well, and to their great profit, the countless persons who were continually applying to him for counsel on a great variety of subjects, but of a particular illumination which he received with reference to certain chosen souls who had recourse to him for habitual spiritual direction, and whom he wonderfully helped to rid themselves of their defects and make rapid advances, not in the road of virtue only, but even in the strait paths of perfection.

Many of these persons being still living when Saint-Jure wrote De Renty's life, he forbore to name them ; of the others who were dead he selected for distinct notice one only, whose relations with De Renty might serve as a specimen of those which existed between him and others under his guidance. This was the Comtesse de la Châtre. Like so many of her class, this lady had been engaged in a frivolous life of worldly dissipation ; but God, who designed to lead her by the instrumentality of His servant to a state of high perfection in the course of a few brief years, inspired her with the desire to seek direction from De Renty, and moved him to consent to be her adviser in spiritual matters. She made such rapid progress that even he was surprised at the change which had been so speedily wrought. This young and delicate lady, accustomed to all those little luxuries and comforts which seem so essential to the rich, especially when their health is feeble and ailing, as was her case, put away from her all these self-indulgent alleviations, replying to one who was pressing on her something of the kind which she had formerly allowed herself, " Oh, how many things seem to us indispensable ! I have given all such things up for the love of God, and many more, and yet have experienced no inconvenience from their disuse. It is true that nature desires to take great care of itself whenever it can, and is easily deceived in this matter of its needs, believing them to be far greater than they are, whereas they are frequently only imaginary." De Renty was enlightened to discern her special vocation, and to teach her to follow it; to help her to die daily to herself, and to support her very sharp interior trials. He had also great freedom and energy in speaking out his mind to her, and she, on her side, received all he said with the most perfect docility, and strictly obeyed his directions. Her deference for him was so profound, that she always reckoned that she heard our Lord's own words and commands from his lips ; and she received a very remarkable confirmation of this her belief, for one day when she had recourse to him in one of those interior states of suffering to which we have alluded, and had not experienced any relief from what he said to her, she felt impelled to kneel down and give her will into our Lord's hands to enter into all His designs regarding her. Having made this act of self-sacrifice, she was rising, when behold ! she no longer saw De Renty before her, but our Lord Himself surrounded with light, who said, " Do whatever My servant shall bid you." These words instantaneously relieved her from her state of inward distress, and left her filled with a sweet peace, a lively sorrow for her sins, and a true contempt for both the world and herself.

Notwithstanding the manifest benediction which God had granted to his direction of this lady, and great as was the spiritual union thus established between them, De Renty always behaved towards her with the utmost reserve and discretion, never seeing her more often than the advance of God's work in her soul demanded, and in their interviews limiting himself strictly to what was necessary for this end. Madame de la Châtre, indeed, felt this conduct to be a little rigid, and would have been glad that he should have relaxed somewhat of this stiffness, as she confided to a person who, she believed, had some influence over this holy man, probably his director, Saint-Jure, who himself relates the circumstance. M. de Renty, she said, mortified her extremely by his civility and his distant behaviour. Not only could she not see him as often as she thought she required, but even, when they were together, he would not sit down, unless indeed he visited her when she was ill and unable to rise; but there he stood, hat in hand, like an inferior. " I pray you," she added, " to tell him what from respect I dare not, that I feel much pained by this demeanour, and that it distresses me to see him in this attitude, when I ought myself to be beneath his feet." On the message being delivered to De Renty, he made the following reply : "I remain in this attitude because it is in accordance with my duty to God and with what I owe to Madame de la Châtre; moreover, since our Lord constrains me to speak to her, I am bound to do so for her needs, but strictly for these alone, and then take my leave; now the position and behaviour I maintain keep us both in mind of this. Were I to seat myself, we might not limit ourselves to what was absolutely necessary, and

perhaps we might even pass on to useless things : this
is what both she and I must beware of. I am a layman and a sinner, and it is with extreme confusion
that I speak to her, although such is God's will, and I
have also been assured by persons of learning and piety
that I am under an obligation to do so."

Although De Renty alleges his condition of layman
as the ground of the guarded conduct he observed,
Saint-Jure evidently thinks that the rule he had laid
down to himself would allow of more universal application, and makes this comment on the subject : " All
who undertake to assist and to guide souls should
ponder this wise reply, and should feel convinced that
the good direction of a soul does not consist in speaking much to it, but in disposing it to speak much to
God, and, still more, in rendering it worthy that
God should speak to it, and produce within it His
substantial Word, His Son ; and, after having given
it counsels suitable to its state, disposing it to carry
them out courageously in practice. We must know
that virtue consists not in words but in deeds.'
Madame de la Châtre attained a high degree of virtue
under De Renty's direction, and entertained the purpose, notwithstanding her weak health and many
infirmities, of entering the Carmelite convent at
Beaune, but she died ere she had been able to execute
her design.

The following are some rules of perfection drawn
up by De Renty for other holy persons who had
sought his guidance. They, no doubt, embody his
own constant practice.

" I have protested before the Blessed Sacrament
my resolution to live according to the maxims and
counsels of Jesus Christ ; and for this end,

"1. Not to desire or seek, directly or indirectly, the augmentation of my fortune, whether as regards riches or honours, nor even consent to accept any of those advantages which my friends may wish to procure for me, except under obedience and by the advice of my spiritual father and director of my conscience.

"2. To study to acquire a contempt and hatred of worldly riches and honours, and never more to speak of them according to the mind of the flesh, but according to the spirit of Christianity; and, in order to establish these maxims in my mind, to shun as much as I can the society of those who follow the contrary maxims.

"3. Never to undertake a lawsuit either as plaintiff or defendant until I have tried every possible means of accommodation, without human respect; in all which I will act under advice.

"4. To retrench all superfluities both in my person and household, that I may have wherewith to assist the poor; and to examine myself strictly on this head every month after Holy Communion, as if I were on the point of rendering an account to God.

"5. Never to contend, but to yield as far as possible to every one, be it in the matter of honour and precedence, or of opinions, or of the will of others, which I must ever prefer to my own.

"6. To avoid all pleasurable things, and not even to do or desire anything from the motive of pleasure, never consenting to any such thing unless it be justly united with something which necessity, condescendence to my neighbour, bodily health, or mental recreation requires.

"7. To suffer with patience contempts, insults, contradictions, losses, unjust treatment, and affronts.

" 8. To do what I can with discreet zeal to hinder offences against God, the blaspheming of His sacred Name, and the laceration of my neighbour's character by backbiting and calumny.

" 9. To avoid and reject any kind of delicacy for the relief of my body, and even, so far as I can, curtail my comforts, without occupying my mind about health.

" 10. To receive with charity and readiness the requests of my neighbour, and to provide for his needs as much as lies in my power, either personally or through the instrumentality of others.

" 11. To administer fraternal correction with charity and humility, and with the utmost prudence, and myself willingly receive it.

" 12. Every month at the least I will examine myself as to my failures in respect of these resolutions; and every year those who have made them can meet to renew the present protestation and consult as to the means to be adopted for their fulfilment."

The knowledge of interior things possessed by De Renty admirably fitted him for the peculiar office to which he was called. His own experience, no doubt, greatly aided him, but he seems moreover to have received wonderful light from God to understand all the secrets of the interior life and its most hidden ways. He had a special grace to discern the true from the false, the safe from the perilous, and the movements of the Spirit of God from the suggestions of the evil or merely human spirit. He had a singular gift for calming minds, as we had occasion to see; for fortifying and inspiring them with courage; for detaching them from all things, and uniting them to our Lord Jesus Christ, in order always to act by His Spirit and according to His example. The following extract from some remarks in his handwriting, which were found among his papers, will give us an insight into his deep acquaintance with the mysteries of the spiritual life.

" There are three kinds of elevations and groanings of the soul to God which ought to be its abiding occupation, in order that it may fulfil our Lord's command to pray continually and without ceasing, lest, relaxing in this holy exercise, it should fall into forgetfulness of God and then into sin. The first is the elevation and groaning of penitents, who are beginning to purify themselves ; the second, that of the faithful, who are making progress, and are in the illuminative way ; and the third, that of the perfect, who have arrived at the unitive life.

" The first, renouncing sin and worldly vanities, bemoan their past life and seek God, sending forth their groans and sighs towards Him from a depth of fear and reverence: this is the beginning of life eternal. The faithful seek to know His Will through His Word, that is, His Son, and desire to accomplish it after His example, since this Word is our Way and our Truth. Such is the progress of the soul in this state. The perfect groan before God that they may attain to union with Him after the pattern of our Lord, and practise this union by acts of charity and by the fulfilment of the first and greatest of the commandments, wherein consist perfection and life in this world.

" There are souls in the first state which, renouncing sin and vanities, receive great sensible consolations from God, and taste of sweetnesses which ravish them. If they do not study to pass on to the second state, in order to learn the will of God by His Son, and to

execute it after His example, the devil will deceive
them by this bait, and will detain them in the search
for and enjoyment of these pleasures; so that, not
walking in Jesus Christ, who is their Way, they will
go astray, and will end by falling over precipices.
Their state will be a certain vague abandonment of
themselves to the desire of belonging to God, of doing
His will and loving Him, accompanied by a deceitful
interior tranquillity, in which they will believe themselves secure, but whence nevertheless they will fall
into a very perilous disposition, because they do not
establish themselves in Jesus Christ, whom God has
given to us for our sole guide. For if, after having
purified themselves from grosser worldly affections,
they do not further purify themselves from self, giving
themselves to Jesus Christ, with a resolution to imitate
Him and to enter into His sacrifice of self-annihilation, instead of receiving the Spirit of God they will
become confirmed in their own spirit, and, making to
themselves false lights, they will follow only their own
judgment and whatever is brilliant and soft which
corrupt nature may suggest, running great risk of
falling into the error of the *Illuminés*, who persuade
themselves that all that comes into their imaginations
proceeds from God, because it seems to them that they
desire, seek, and love God only, and no longer feel, or
feel very slightly, the reproaches of their conscience.

"If you closely observe those who enter on eternal
life in this manner, you will find that they have very
little faith or union with Jesus Christ; and, should
you ask them what they desire and what they aim at,
they will give you this general answer: 'All that
God wills.' Such persons ought to be set right, if it
be still possible, and, if the complacency they feel in

their sensible sweetnesses and the attachment with which they cling to their own judgment have not gone too far, moved to will, indeed, what God wills, but to will it after the example of our Lord and according to the maxims of His Gospel, which He has left us as Good Tidings and as His Testament, to be at once our light and the measure of our lights.

" Many stop short at this first step, and are nevertheless esteemed and admired even by persons who pass for spiritual, nay, sometimes by their very directors, and their state is called the mystical life ; whereas the deceitful spirit of nature and of the devil is disporting itself in the midst of all these darksome illuminations, these false tranquillities, these fine phrases, these sublime words, and this multitude of devotional writings, the worth of which is generally only that of the paper to which they are committed : whence it happens that we so often see those who have begun with pure intentions fall in the end into gross faults, when self has slipped into the soul in the place of Jesus Christ.

" There are other persons who attach themselves exclusively to the preaching of St. John the Baptist, to austerities and penance, placing their reliance on these, without applying themselves further to Jesus Christ, or acquiring His spirit, but, instead of this, indulging a certain interior satisfaction and confidence in their mortifications ; and here they rest. Others stop at Jesus Christ alone, as if He had no Father, and have a very tender devotion to His Humanity ; nothing but the sensible touches them, and they proceed no further. They know the Man, Christ Jesus, but not Jesus Christ the Man-God, who is our Way, our Truth, and our Life. Others centre all their

hopes in the Blessed Virgin and the Saints, and rely
on special devotions of their own, which are very
good when founded on repentance for sin and true
conversion of heart ; but they greatly delude themselves in hoping for the aid of the Blessed Virgin and
the Saints and for a participation in their merits, if
they will not give up their vices.

"These three states, as thus distinguished, furnish
much light for the guidance of souls in their beginning, progress, and perfection, and for the discernment
of the errors into which they may fall. Now each
state has its own proper work, its own suffering, and
its own prayer. The work which belongs to the first
state, that of beginners and penitents, is to discover
all that inclines to sin, is detrimental to salvation,
and estranges from God. Their suffering consists in
weeping for their sins, mortifying their passions, and
subduing their body in all that moves it to rebel
against reason and do injury to the spirit, as also
in chastising it for the disorderly movements of con-
cupiscence and its risings. Their prayer must be
directed to the begging for grace and strength to this
end. The work of the second state, or of the faithful
is to study Jesus Christ, His life, and His doctrine.
Their suffering is to bear the pains which result from
this imitation, as well as the contempt and persecutions which accompany all those who walk in His
steps. Their prayer is to beg a communication of
His life, His spirit, and His dispositions, in order
to act interiorly and exteriorly after His pattern.
The work of the third state, or that of the perfect, is
to do all by the movement of the spirit of Jesus
Christ and united to God. Their suffering is to
endure befittingly the corruption, grossness, and dark-

ness of the world, and the persecutions for justice'
sake which will be their unfailing portion. Their
prayer is to ask for an ever-increasing abundant participation of the spirit of Jesus Christ, a still more
intimate union with God, a more entire death to self,
a more faithful employment of the grace and talents
they have received, and final perseverance.

"To this I add that in the first state we must labour
to resist sin, to conquer our passions, and renounce
vanity, which beginners will not be able to do without
availing themselves of various exercises and without
doing much violence to themselves. But those to
whom God has given access to the two other states
can usually accomplish this by a simple turning away
of the mind, which, while it does not lessen humiliation, obviates eagerness and disquietude. In the
second state, a very strong correspondence on our
part is needed in order to follow Jesus Christ, that we
may no longer act according to ourselves but according to Him, that we may become simplified, and endure
with patience and longanimity the accomplishment of
our purification in Christ Jesus. We must bear the
secret storms and interior tumults which are roused
within us by our old habits, and by a spirit which,
acting by its natural movement, although according
to reason, is all full of images and forms. We must
with much patience lose our soul to find it again
clothed with Jesus Christ. In the third state the
work is of a passive order, as is also the prayer,
wherein the liberality of God does almost all, and the
soul enjoys a certain experimental satiety of the presence and of the truth of God, and of His charity in
Jesus Christ, in whom it abides. At times it is immersed in joy at the grandeur of God, His power, His

goodness and infinite perfections ; our alliance with
His Son ; His love, His ways, and the admirable effects
which are produced by the participation of His spirit ;
and in the possession of these goods it experiences a
peace, a gladness, and a force which transcend the
senses and are beyond all power of expression.
Fidelity to the two first states disposes the soul for
the third ; but we must remember that, while we are
in this temporal life, and are ever subject to change
by reason of our weakness, we have always need to
labour in order to make progress in these states, and
to renew our spirit that we may re-establish ourselves
and repair our losses."

Besides the light which De Renty thus habitually
received for the guidance of souls, it pleased God often,
as we have seen with regard to those works to which
He was about to call him, to vouchsafe him special
illumination on peculiar occasions.   We may instance
the case of a young lady in whom he had taken a
charitable interest, and who, desiring to become a
Carmelite nun, communicated her design to him, with
a view to obtaining his advice.   He saw great difficulties in the way, as indeed there were, and he gave
her several reasons why she had better dismiss the
idea from her mind.   However, God made known to
him subsequently in prayer that it was His will that,
in spite of all obstacles, she should embrace the religious life, and He even indicated the place where
His design should be accomplished.   M. de Renty
apprised her of the intimation which had been made
to him, and she received this communication with
great respect and the most entire confidence, which
the event justified, for, notwithstanding the apparent
impediments, she became a Carmelite nun, and

entered the convent which had been designated to her director.

Quite as remarkable as the supernatural illumination which was thus occasionally vouchsafed to him, was the habitual prompting he received as to the terms in which he should convey his communications to the persons who sought light and guidance from him. Here is his own account. Writing to Saint-Jure he observes : " As for what concerns myself, I have not much to say ; by the mercy of God I bear about with me a fund of peace before Him in the spirit of Jesus Christ, and so intimate an experimental realization of life eternal that I have no words to express it : this is my chief attraction. But I am so naked and barren that it is a matter of wonder to me when I consider this my state and the way in which I speak. I marvelled how, when speaking to this person "—he has been relating an interview with one who was suffering from great interior trials,— "I began to discourse without knowing how I was to proceed, and, as I uttered the second word, I had no idea what the third would be, and so on in all that followed. It is not that I lack a full acquaintance with these subjects, according to my capacity, but, as regards producing anything externally, it is all given to me ; as it is given to me, so I give it to another ; and afterwards nothing remains to me but the fund (of peace) which I have mentioned."

Our Lord promised His disciples that when brought before kings and governors for His sake it should be given them in that same hour what they should speak, for that it was not they who spoke but His Spirit who spoke within them. And we may well believe that this promise had a wider reach, and that in all emergencies they who, like De Renty, discarding trust in human prudence, eloquence, and all natural or acquired abilities, abandon themselves with childlike confidence to the direction of God's good Spirit, will receive all such substantial aid as they may require, although they may not be sensible of this assistance. De Renty's case was of course very exceptional, and he was himself a person of very exceptional sanctity; accordingly we see in him a very marked exhibition of this fulfilment of the Divine promise. But if laymen were to attempt to meddle with the work which De Renty was specially called to undertake, without a clear vocation to such employment, we need scarcely say that all their pious intentions and reliance on Divine promptings would be so much sheer delusion. De Renty, so far from intruding into the office of directing souls, had to do violence to himself, as we have seen, before consenting to accept it. He always felt it a heavy cross to have to advise those seculars who had recourse to him ; but when ecclesiastics and religious, drawn by the report of his great gifts and extraordinary sanctity, applied to him, as they frequently did, for spiritual counsel, then indeed did he experience the deepest humiliation. Amongst these applicants were even heads of religious communities, who also considered it a great advantage to be able to communicate with and consult him on affairs of the highest importance.

It was about the year 1641 that he began, properly speaking, to give himself to this work, but of all the employments with which our Lord charged him in His service, there was none which was so trying to him, or to which, had he heeded his own inclinations, he would have felt more repugnance. For he not only considered that he was thus raised to an office which was above his condition as a layman, but esteemed himself also as personally most unworthy of it. Accordingly, notwithstanding the inward movements, pressing him to accept it, which he continued to experience in spite of all the objections which his reason and humility suggested, he would do nothing in the first instance until he had taken advice. When he had been assured that such was God's will he hesitated no longer ; yet, although doubts were silenced, nothing ever availed to diminish the confusion which he always felt in the performance of this recognized duty, as his whole bearing on these occasions, full of bashful respect and humility, sufficed to prove. The blessing which attended the care he was thus led to bestow on souls set the seal of Divine approbation on the work.

CHAPTER VIIL

DE RENTY'S EXTERIOR BEARING AND MANAGEMENT OF AFFAIRS.

HAVING followed De Renty through the different avocations of charity which made up his external active life, it remains for us briefly to advert to his general bearing in the fulfilment of them. To say much on this head would be simple repetition ; yet our notice of this portion or aspect of his life would be incomplete did we not dwell awhile upon this important subject. And most important truly is the character of this outward bearing, for it is the sure measure of the benefit which others derive from our conversation and good services, as well as the index of the worth of the external act of charity. De Renty knew well that if we would make an impression for good on our fellow-men, if we would win them to ourselves in order to win them to God, which was the ardent desire of his heart, it is not the amount of what we do or say, the eloquence of our tongue or the energy of our exertions, that will prevail. It is we ourselves who influence. There is a natural power of influence, and there is a gracious power, by which we mean that which is the result of an indwelling grace; but both are in fact personal. In each case it is the man who influences. If what he says or does tells, it is because of the manner in which he does or says it; and that manner is the exponent of himself: it is in that capacity that he acts upon others. Now what was, perhaps, the most remarkable feature in De Renty's manner was his calmness, his modesty, his unalterable composure ; and one, indeed, who knew him well averred that it was these outward character- istics which first impressed him with the conviction of De Renty's extraordinary sanctity : " There was something," he said, " so reverential in his counte- nance, that it was easy to judge that he was ever abiding in the actual presence of God." No matter where he was, or how engaged, he was uniformly the same. Whether alone or in company, whether with friends or strangers, rich or poor, whether amongst his children or with his servants, in the solitude of the field or in the crowded streets of the city, or

sitting at table in his familiar circle, there was no
variation : his face wore the same expression, his
very gestures and movements underwent no change.
There was, in fine, a Presence with him which super-
seded all other presences, and was the controller and
regulator of his behaviour. Moreover, nothing that
occurred, however unexpected, and however unplea-
sant or perplexing, had the least effect in throwing
him off his guard or working any change in him. It
did not seem to reach him, so completely was he
shrouded in his sanctuary of recollection.

It certainly needs that a man should have obtained
a high degree of control over all his passions, and
even over their first movements, for him never to
lose his mental balance and equanimity for a single
instant, or betray the least disturbance in countenance, gesture, or so much as heightened colour; but
perhaps even this habit of self-control would not
suffice without the continual recollection of God's
presence ; if, rather, that recollection be not one of
the chief means of obtaining, and the only security for
preserving, this admirable composure. De Renty's
temperament, as we have already observed, was very
far from phlegmatic, and he had one of those active
and ardent spirits which naturally brook neither
delay nor opposition ; so that all had been the work
of grace, though it wore the appearance now of a
second nature : we mean as respects facility and
the absence of effort or constraint, for his serenity
produced impressions on others quite beyond the
power of mere nature to effect. Another witness,
speaking of the recollection and close union with God
which De Renty enjoyed, and the perfect peace of
mind which was its fruit and which beamed in his

countenance, says that the very sight of him inspired devotion. This union appeared to be uninterrupted; he never seemed to be distracted from it, whether by casual thought or outward occurrence ; never did he betray the least carelessness or levity, however harmless ; never did he speak a useless word. In society, where others habitually unbend, he was never led to pour himself forth in talk, for his eye was always fixed inwardly on God, and nothing could divert him from this attention. He was at the same time proof against all human respect : not but that he paid due civility to all, but it was plain to every one that he was chiefly occupied within himself.

Such was the account given of him by the last-mentioned witness; and it entirely coincides with that of the first-named, who also testifies that so engrossing was his inward application that no accident, however sudden, no object, however extraordinary, could move him or withdraw him from his state of recollection. "I never," he says, "saw him admire anything which the world values or with which it is charmed, nor did his eyes rest with curiosity on anything : he walked through the streets with a composed and modest mien, with an even and measured pace, looking neither to right nor left, for in fact he was so entirely occupied in all things with Jesus Christ, that out of Him and apart from what had reference to His glory nothing touched or interested him. De Renty was not easily attracted even by things which, having a colour of spirituality, might have seemed to justify curiosity. For instance, being much pressed one day to go and see a remarkable person who was reported to have miraculous gifts, and who enjoyed the reputation of being a saint, he replied gently, "Our Lord is in all our churches in the Blessed Sacrament; we can visit *Him.*"

By nature De Renty was not a great talker, and the movements of grace had reinforced this natural attraction to silence, so that he was a man of very few words. When he visited or was visited by any one, or when he attended any meeting for pious purposes where he was necessitated to speak, he would do so in his turn, but always with calmness and self-possession, in concise although very expressive terms. No one ever saw him eager to put in his word and give his opinion, or raise his voice to a louder tone, or betray hurry and excitement, even though often greatly pressed for time. If he had to relate anything, it was briefly, with no needless adjuncts or superfluous words; all he said was strictly to the point; so that, as one observed of him, it would have been difficult to find a man who talked less or talked better. When he observed the conversation trending off to worldly or trifling matters, he took his leave of the company or slipped away quietly; but even when speaking of good and holy things he was sparing of words; and he used to say that we ought to use moderation even when talking of God and of what was best; nor was there anything, he confessed, which annoyed him more, and which he had more difficulty in supporting, than the prolixity of some spiritual persons, who would pass whole hours in talking together about virtue in a vague, profitless sort of way, and who emerged from these conversations with empty, dry, and dissipated minds.

But though De Renty spoke little, and was even laconic in what he said, there was neither stiffness nor

coldness in his manner ; on the contrary, it was full
of deference, kindness, and cordiality. He was also
very patient and forbearing with the ignorances,
blunderings, awkwardnesses, want of tact, ill-temper,
and all other tiresome and trying faults displayed by
his associates, always ready to accommodate himself
to others, and to overlook many disagreeable things,
without seeming so much as to notice them. The consequence was that no one's company was more desired,
no one's conversation more valued, or opinion more
respected, while his modest air, his composed manner,
his look of heavenly peace, and his very silence inspired sentiments of devotion in those who beheld
him. Something, indeed, of his own spirit of recollection seemed to pass by a kind of happy infection
into the circle, for people had only to see him to be
prompted to greater self-restraint ; the very knowledge of his presence had a marked effect, so that the
belief that he was in a church would render those who
knew him more attentive to their prayers. Nor were
these effects merely temporary, for there were persons
who declared that after having been in his company
they have experienced for several days an attraction
to occupy themselves more than ordinarily with God.
Sometimes the desire which was so general to be near
him, to see him, to listen to 'him, would become so
evident, that it was impossible for him not to be conscious of it. Such consciousness always brought with
it a deep sense of self-humiliation, which was apparent
in his countenance ; but if he was made the subject of
praise and commendation for anything he had said or
done, he would remain, so long as the conversation
continued, in grave and profound silence, with his
eyes cast down, his body at times being quite bent,

like one filled with shame; thus clearly manifesting the inward displeasure he experienced. It is worth observing, because such is by no means invariably the case, that these peculiarities, as they may be called, never shocked or offended any one, but on the contrary produced general edification. Love, reverence, esteem met him everywhere. Such is the power of holiness when it pleases God to open men's eyes to see its beauty, and even the world itself will be fain to confess of the saint in his measure what once it was constrained to testify of the King of Saints, " He hath done all things well." It was perhaps ordered by a special disposition of God, for the purpose of supplying a divine counterpoise to this universal approbation and the better to secure his virtue amidst so many temptations to self-esteem, that this holy man met with no appreciation in the quarter whence his natural warm affections might have led him to welcome it to the prejudice possibly, in some slight degree, of his beautiful humility : we allude of course to the persevering coldness, censure, and even contempt which he experienced from his own mother.

The multiplicity of the affairs which claimed De Renty's attention and time has been so often alluded to that we need not here further dwell upon the subject, save to observe that he was enabled to transact them, not merely by the aid of great vigour of body and high mental capacity and energy, but in virtue also of his method of applying himself. This is well worthy of notice. Perhaps nothing fatigues mind and body more, and contributes more than aught else to disable persons from getting through a multitude of employments with any satisfaction, than the eagerness, hurry, and interior disturbance which so commonly

beset those who are thus burdened. An uncomfort-
able, excited, feverish state is the frequent affliction of
the individual who has his or her hands, as it is called,
full of business of a multifarious kind, a state palpably
painful where the body and nervous system are weak,
but none the less existent because the malady is confined to the soul. Another state equally inimical to
the perfection of work and to the good spirit of the
worker is produced by long wearying occupation of
an unvarying sort. This, on the other hand, tends to
produce what we may describe as the drudging temper:
the man labours like a horse in a mill, with this
difference to the disadvantage of the reasoning being,
that he knows that he is drudging, reflects upon it,
and is downhearted accordingly in proportion. Now,
without question, a pure intention of acting and
working for God will sanctify work of both kinds, but
a previous good intention will not suffice to keep the
wheels moving smoothly, if nature is allowed to inter-
pose with all its exciting or depressing movements, as
the case may be. We have seen how De Renty performed all his actions, not only for God, but *in* God ;
and we have now to observe the method which, under
that abiding influence, he pursued. He did each piece
of work simply, as if it were all he had to do ; he did
not, it is true, lose a moment, but he never grudged a
moment, if it was needed. The bustler is always
. sacrificing the present to the past or to the future,
which future, when it becomes the present, will share
the same fate. De Renty was never in a bustle. He
was never eager ; he acquitted himself of one thing, and
then he passed quietly to another ; and so tranquil and
collected was his mind that he could even attend to
two or three things at once, interruption never flurry-

ing him. Thus he would often be interrupted by unexpected applications when engaged on some necessary and pressing affair. Letters would have to be read, persons to be seen and spoken to, and answers returned on the spot; all this he would do, with brevity, of course, but with perfect clearness and perspicuity. No doubt his great mental powers enabled him to achieve in this respect what would not be possible to others, but no mental power, purely natural, will preserve a soul in peace and self-possession hour after hour and day after day at such harassing work. In one of his letters we find him alluding to this press of business which continually besieged him, and then adding, " Do not trouble yourself, however, on this account ; I do at once as much as I am able, and the rest in time, without disquieting myself. Our Lord vouchsafes to bestow on me His peace in all this, and never to feel embarrassed by it."

He used to reflect a good deal before coming to a decision ; but, although his opinion was thus maturely formed, nevertheless he was not attached to it as his opinion, and willingly gave it up if better reasons were alleged in opposition to it. He was not wedded to his own views, he was never in love with his own lights and ideas, and was ready to set them aside with perfect humility in deference to persons whose judgment he valued. But when once his mind was thoroughly made up, he was firm and persevering in carrying out his resolution, never wearying or flagging, but continuing as ardent and energetic to the close as he had been at the beginning. Yet this perseverance was in no way prompted by a natural ambition and desire of success, which will animate and sustain many persons in the face of great difficulties and under pro-

tracted opposition ; as was proved on many occasions
when, having set some good project on foot, he no
sooner saw it progressing well towards its accomplishment than he would commit it to the care of some
competent friend, in order that he might devote himself to some fresh undertaking, or, as there is reason
to believe, from a higher and more secret motive,
namely, to avoid the praise which is given much more
freely to those who terminate than to those who com-
mence a good work.

His boldness and assurance in all that regarded
God's service equalled his vigour and determination.
It was evinced, not in his words only, but in the
indescribable resoluteness of his countenance. This
expression no way interfered with or marred its
placidity and tranquillity, for there was in it no
passion. Its effect was marvellous. Passion sometimes carries away others by its fervour and impetuosity, but it is strength which commands assent.
Strength and sweetness are not opposed ; so far from
it, each is imperfect without the other ; but together
they are irresistible. It was on occasion of the meetings to which we have often alluded, when he had to
propound and maintain his opinion, that this power
of his was most strikingly exhibited. It carried all
before it. The cogency of his reasonings, the solidity
of his judgments, and the peculiar pertinence of all he
said, which seemed so precisely to hit the point which
called for solution, were enhanced and weighted, as it
were, by this force of character, made visible in his
countenance and in every tone of his voice, while his
sweetness rendered this superiority acceptable to all.
Acquiescence almost invariably attended his repre-
sentations. If some contentious person occasionally

stiffened himself in opposition, and De Renty, after supporting his own view by the powerful reasons he knew so well how to state, failed to satisfy him, he would instantly become silent, but his face still bore that remarkable expression of firmness, and, strange to say, that alone had often so much effect as to silence the opponent in his turn, and not silence only, but convince him; so that it not unfrequently occurred that when the assembly broke up he would go up to De Renty and humbly apologize to him for his factious opposition. The good man would then gently explain how his own pertinacity had sprung simply from regard to God's interests, which he believed to be implicated; except for this he was ready, with all his heart, to yield to others and give up his own view. If De Renty's determination of character did not clash with its gentleness and sweetness, so neither did it interfere with his humility. Speaking before an audience was with him no occasion for display. When begged to attend a meeting in order to give his opinion of a matter under discussion, he went at the appointed hour (always punctually, it may be observed), and having taken his place, which, when he could choose, was ever the lowest and least prominent, he listened with the closest attention to all that was said; and when he had himself delivered his own view in a few modest but energetic words, and the affair which had required his presence was settled, he at once retired. No one could prevail on him to linger a moment longer, so economical was he of his time, and so little desirous was he to put himself forward in public under any pretext however specious.

It has been already remarked that he never neg-

x

lected his own exercises of piety, however occupied
he might be, and that the affair of his own perfection
was his great affair : for this very reason other affairs
were conducted with a corresponding perfection. He
had received in recompense for this fidelity to God
two great graces. Not only was he as solitary and
as collected in the midst of the turmoil of business as
a hermit in his cave, but our Lord seemed graciously
to have relieved him of all anxious toil, and to do
the work for him and in him. The other grace was
to have all, in a sense, effaced from his memory as
soon as it was done : a great grace truly, for who
does not know from experience the teasing effect of
the mind being full of anything on which it is
engaged, not only before but even after the transaction, and the great impediment such pre-occupation
puts in the way of inward and simple attention to
God, nay, even of common attention at fixed times of
prayer ? "I do not act less," he writes to his director,
"however great my recollection may be ; indeed, I
act more, for I have a desire to do everything ; but I
act in such wise that I have clearly no part in what
I do, for it is our Lord who does all." And again,
" As respects my intercourse with the world, things
are as usual : when it is question of writing or speaking to those who ask advice, I seem to be furnished
with all knowledge and able to enter fully into whatever is said, and then it is all blotted out ; the doors
are closed, and nothing remains of it." In another
letter he alludes to this same grace, and is apparently
speaking of the first time it was conferred, at least
in such a remarkable degree. "One day," he says,
"finding myself burdened with divers affairs, which
involved both writing and acting, I was moved to

separate my mind entirely off from them, and instantly I felt that the burden was removed, and ever since nothing has cost me any trouble; nevertheless I do more, but without reflecting on it. This grace has been often renewed to me, though in various ways, and I know that it is a great grace, and that I ought to be very thankful for it, because it serves to keep me simple in the midst of multiplicity." But to this subject we shall have again to refer when we come to speak more particularly of his interior and mystical life.

Notwithstanding this peculiar assistance, he did not presume upon it, but used all prudence and diligence in whatever matter he had in hand, while still continuing to rely much more on God's blessing than on any human means; and this was why he always assiduously recommended all he undertook to God, and in the choice he made of persons to assist him had regard far more to the qualifications of grace than to those of nature. The promotion of God's glory and the salvation of souls is God's own work, and, as such, must be principally the work of grace; moreover, knowing that the work of God is ever contradicted and opposed in the world, he expected both opposition and contradiction, and was very patient under them. He persevered courageously, undiscouraged by difficulties, and if he failed after doing all he could, he was perfectly satisfied, acquiescing in the will of God, who for His own inscrutable purposes often allows the holiest undertakings to be thwarted and defeated. He was, besides, so well aware that God's great purpose in us is to subdue our self-love and natural will, that he was neither surprised nor displeased at either crosses or failure.

X 2

" Our nature," he writes, " is a pitiable thing when it meets with approbation, even in the things of grace : this is why I reckon it a great mercy to be able to execute a solid good work, approved and recognised as proceeding from the Spirit of God by those whom He has placed in His Church to judge, and that the accomplishment should be brought about amidst contradictions and crosses." And another time, " We may, indeed, have good and holy projects, and they may proceed from God's inspiration ; nevertheless, when He permits them to fail we must adore His secret dispensations, which prove a greater mercy to us by traversing our plans, than if they succeeded to our great consolation ; we must always fear lest our own spirit should attach itself to anything." Again, he makes the following remark : " The good Jesus has His designs, which He pursues by ways which we should never choose ; and the reason of this is that He desires to break our wills and prevent us leaning upon earth : this is why He thwarts even the most righteous undertakings, being more jealous of the sacrifice of our hearts than of all else besides, however specious it may be."

In fine, his great rule in all affairs was not to regard either their own apparent importance or their successful conclusion : this was God's affair, not his. His affair was to look simply to the will of God in them ; hence, there was with him absolutely no difference in their respective value, save such as that holy Will conferred upon them. Hence also it was that he never intruded himself into anything without the call of God, signified to him in some manner, and was never either precipitate or anxious. Hence again, he readily withdrew from what he had begun if

he felt an inward movement warning him to do so.
As his eye was always directed towards his Lord for
guidance, so he never failed to receive it, either in the
form of light communicated to the understanding, or
by an impression on the will, both imparting the
certainty which God is able to give, and will infallibly
give when needed, to the soul which thus waits for
His orders.   And truly De Renty was always as one
waiting for orders, day by day, hour by hour, and even
minute by minute.   Some one having asked him once
whether he would do such or such a thing at some
particular time, he replied, " Do you not know that I
have no to-morrow ? " and on another occasion, he
said, " I see five or six things necessary to be done,
but I could not say to which I shall give the first
place, nor when nor where I can bring them about ;
for by God's mercy I am quite indifferent about
everything."   His director's injunctions were a frequent guide to him, as we gather from his letters.   " I
will premeditate nothing," we find him writing on one
occasion, after placing himself at the disposal of his
spiritual Father, whom he was expecting shortly to
meet in Paris, " save to go there in order to obey our
Lord and follow His guidance through you, doing
everything to the best of my ability.   I have found
that in places where I have expected to do the most,
there I have done nothing.   This has taught me to go
as one bare of everything, and when I am expecting
the least and am only abandoning myself to God, it is
then that He does the most ; this is why I leave it to
Him to do as He pleases, and to you in Him."
Speaking to another person who was full of great
designs for God's service, but which were not season-
able as yet, he said, " Let us apply ourselves to things

only from day to day ; the thoughts you entertain are holy, but we must abandon ourselves to God as regards the future, and employ the time He gives us in loving Him and following whatever He manifests to us as His will, keeping ourselves always before Him, in a spirit of sacrifice with Jesus Christ our Lord."

A letter written by him to his director in the year 1646 will serve to illustrate his sentiments on these kindred subjects in the closing years of his life. We think it worth giving at length.

"I will tell you something," he says, "of what took place in me yesterday ; it will show you what is my present state. As I was hearing read the Gospel for the Assumption of the Blessed Virgin, where Martha and Mary are spoken of, much of the impression which I received formerly from this Gospel was revived in me, namely, that prayer and simple occupation with God are very preferable to all exterior exercises, however holy they may be, since Martha, who was engaged in the holiest and best of exercises, was reproved for being troubled, while Mary was praised for her repose. Those words, " *Turbaris erga plurima* —Thou art troubled about many things," served for a long time to separate me from external things, and even from interior things which, although good, were not absolutely necessary : such as going to visit and instruct the poor, reading or writing something devotional, and the like. I knew that at that time it was expedient for me to quit these occupations, with the view of forming and fortifying the soul in the inaction of self, and to attain to the renunciation of the will and of natural vivacity, in order to await the Divine direction, and to follow it with wise simplicity by the Spirit of Jesus Christ, who vivifies and lives in those who hearken to Him with reverence. But I must observe that during these last three or four months that I have been in Normandy I have been almost perpetually busied with external things : speaking to numbers of people, doctoring the sick who come to me, going about composing differences, building, constructing a great church, which required taking down and enlarging, and for which a great many plans are needed, and even models, because there is no one in these parts who understands architecture, with which I was formerly conversant, and so I have had to recall my old ideas, and to set to work in good earnest. Yesterday, after having been engaged the whole morning, as I was listening to the aforesaid Gospel and dwelling particularly on those words, *Turbaris erga plurima*, an interior light came to me, and it was said to me, '*Non turbaris erga plurima.*' I knew then, and that in an evident manner, that those things which we do by the order of God, whatever they may be, do not disturb ; and I saw clearly, at least so it seems to me, that St. Martha is reproved, not for doing a good work, but for doing it with eagerness ; and our Lord, by these words, '*Turbaris erga plurima*,' shows that she was performing her action in a solicitous manner, and with a disorderly agitation of spirit, although it had for its pretext a most praiseworthy end ; that what is chiefly necessary is to listen to the Eternal Word ; so that, like as His Human Nature, whether it were to act, preach, or do aught else, received Its movements from the Divine Nature, according as He said, " *A Me ipso facio nihil : sicut audio, hæc loquor*—Of Myself I do nothing : as I hear, so I speak "—so also should we take our direction from Jesus Christ, who is this

Word of Eternal Life : that is why we ought not to do anything with a troubled mind, but do all in peace in this spirit. I received at the same time a great help in all those little external occupations to which my duty binds me, and I had no difficulty in abandoning myself to this order holily disordered, in which I feel that God wills me to be, that He may accomplish by my means what cannot otherwise be done. For these last three months I have perhaps not once been able to make three or four hours' uninterrupted prayer on my knees outside the church, and if I could pray only in this way I should have done my duty so far very ill. And no doubt I have done it very ill; nevertheless, I know that God amid the employments which He lays upon me, makes me feel His presence and His power to bind the soul to Himself in the closest manner, and that the external work may be done with the fingers' ends while the heart enjoys the true union of the children with their Father by the Spirit of His Son, whereby we are brought into communion with Him, and with the Blessed Virgin, the Angels, and the Saints, and with a whole Heaven, if so we will : so large an opening does this Lord give to the soul when it pleases Him and as it pleases Him.

"I had at that time so sensible an impression of God, and nevertheless so much transcending sense, because it takes place in the noblest part of the soul, which is the spirit, that I might have been rolled about like a ball without losing sight of my God. Everything here, however, is transitory, for our Lord rolls the ball after a strange fashion when He so wills; and these various modes are designed to aid the soul, and make it perfectly ductile, leaving it nothing which looks towards self or is according to self, but all for its God and according to its God.

"Moreover, I saw clearly that a person whom God employs in lowly things and who applies himself with as much fidelity as if they were high, keeping himself in his allotted order from obedience and self-annihilation, is in no wise less pleasing to Him than another who is occupied in brilliant employments. The question does not regard the works, but the fidelity with which the person abandons himself to God, to do what He wills. Who would not love to convert a thousand worlds and bring all souls to God? nevertheless, you shall only haul stones, or even do nothing at all. There is much call for sacrifice in patience, and much consolation in the other employments; and I believe it is beyond comparison more rare to meet with souls faithful to patience and willing to do no more than God desires of them, than to find them faithful in those actions which are of a striking nature. I know well that in all things it is God who does all, but the sacrifice of patience and inaction is greater to a heart which has love and zeal for His honour, and which, besides, being disposed for work, has to exert more force to restrain itself than it would require to act.

"We cannot feed upon nothing, and that hunger which is ready to devour the four quarters of the globe is constrained, as if perpetually circulating within a reverberatory furnace, to limit itself to a continual round of I know not how many different kinds of self-oblation, until it finds an issue in the consideration that God is sufficient to Himself, that He has no need whatever of us for His glory, and that He is doing us so much the more honour in employing us in that it is not for the advantage of His service, for we are never so pure but that in some way we tarnish His work and make it lose a portion of its brightness ; so that we are not only unprofitable servants, but hurtful ones.

" I will add one word more to give you the information you ought to have, that you may be able to correct me : I have a true and heartfelt shame at doing nothing for God ; sometimes I experience so great a grief on this account, when I consider His dignity, His love, His gifts, and His communications through the alliance of Jesus Christ and His Spirit, that it would arrive at being excessive and insupportable, seeing in myself nothing but powerlessness for good, misery, and sin, if I did not calm myself by what I have just been saying, that God is sufficient to Himself, and does with us what He pleases, keeping us in obedience and abjection."

That great master of the spiritual life, Saint-Jure, after quoting the above, makes the following observation : " Here is his letter, from which there is much to learn ; " and we cannot do better than to adopt his simple comment and add none of our own.

PART III.

INTERIOR AND MYSTICAL LIFE.

CHAPTER I.

MARGARET OF THE BLESSED SACRAMENT.

THE reader will have incidentally gathered much
information concerning the interior life of M. de
Renty in the first two parts of this biography. It
was indeed, impossible, as well as undesirable, to
speak of his perfect conversion and of his active life
of charity without often adverting to his peculiar
interior attractions and to the character of his sanctity,
a character which results from the inward impress
which the Holy Spirit imparts to the soul. But we
have reserved to this concluding portion of our picture
of this holy man a more direct reference to this subject, and a closer view of his interior and mystical
life.

We have already intimated more than once that
his grace and attraction led to that form of sanctity
which is produced by devotion to the Sacred Infancy.
This bent was manifested from the very beginning of
his entire conversion of heart to God, which dated
from the mission given by the Fathers of the Oratory
in the year 1638, when he came under the direction
of P. de Condren. Devotion to the Sacred Infancy
was that Father's own special devotion; the Infancy

was the mould in which, as we may say, his inner life was cast, and according to which he was fashioned and modelled; and it would appear that, with his keen spiritual insight, he discerned it to be God's purpose to lead De Renty by a path analogous to his own. Hence we find De Condren founding his penitent solidly in the principles of self-abnegation, inculcating an entire renunciation of self in every form, and drawing him to the practice of a childlike humility and simplicity. Above all, he urged upon him the maintenance of a close union with our Lord in every thought, word, and action, not only in order that they might by this means possess full merit and value, but also that the soul might thus be in the attitude and condition to receive passively the likeness of Jesus imprinted on it, with those characteristics and lineaments with which it was His pleasure to impart it. We have seen how rapidly De Renty advanced in the school of littleness and humility, in the imitation of his Divine Model and in interior union with Him, during the two years he had De Condren for his director, and afterwards under the guidance of Saint-Jure; but, as we have before observed, it was a nun of the Order of Carmel, that Order which has been so prolific in saints, who was to be the instrument in God's hands of giving a fuller development to that devotion to the Infancy which already formed his leading attraction; a development which was to be accompanied by a corresponding moulding of his soul into a more perfect resemblance to the Babe of Bethlehem.

It is along the line of our attraction that graces lie thickly strewn, like a kind of milky way in the inner firmament; they are strewn there as they are

nowhere else, and the soul which, by some mistake or
neglect, or some secret and subtle revolt of self-will,
wanders aside and endeavours to advance heavenward by any other road, will be stinted, if not starved.
Its sanctification, its perfection, if not its salvation,
are attached to its fidelity to this way, which is God's
way for that soul; just as in His eye that soul is
foreseen according to an appointed model in Christ,
the Son of His love, and according to no other.   By
that mysterious, inscrutable, and marvellous gift of
free-will, we may say that He has put us in possession of the same power to thwart, more or less,
His gracious purpose as He, the Omnipotent God,
had to form it, since He has made that purpose
conditional on our acceptance.   Wonderful and awful
thought!   We may thwart God Himself, but we can
thwart Him only to our loss; for there is one thing
we cannot do : we cannot attain to the perfection
of our foreseen sanctity, the only perfection within
our competence, by any other road than that by
which the Holy Ghost would lead us to it.   It was
because De Renty had so faithfully surrendered himself to the leadings of divine grace, and had set
himself so valiantly to work to silence nature within
him, that he had made such signal and rapid progress
in perfection.   But God has, moreover, placed, as
it were, along the path He has traced for us certain
stations, at which the soul which punctually follows
His guidance receives extraordinary increments of
light and strength, so as to be enabled to pursue
its way with a plenitude of grace which causes it
scarcely to recognise itself.   It was a station of this
kind to which De Renty had arrived when he took
his road to Beaune.   "I was but as a stone," he said,

"before I received help from my sister Marguerite." Without accepting in its literal sense this account of himself, which in all sincerity he gave, we may well believe that at that time he received one of those powerful illuminations and impulses which constitute an epoch in the interior life, and make a man by contrast believe that hitherto he has not advanced a step, or at best has crawled, and that now only he begins to run; a persuasion which results, not only from the sensible increase of grace vouchsafed, but from the brilliant light which illuminates the path divinely marked out for him, and which enables him to keep still more closely along that track which is studded with graces ready prepared, and to concentrate all his spiritual energies in the right direction.

A brief account of the remarkable woman who exercised so great an influence on De Renty's inner life, and was the instrument of the astonishing spiritual progress of his later years, will not be considered out of place.

Marguerite Parigot was a native of Beaune, and was brought up in all the comforts and luxuries which surround the children of the rich; but God early marked her for His own, and she gave those precocious signs of future sanctity with which we are so familiar in the lives of holy men and women. She lost her mother while still a child, and was received as a novice by the Carmelites at the early age of eleven, upon her own pressing solicitation and by the interest of her uncle, who had ceded his Priory of Saint-Etienne to establish a convent of that order in Beaune. The house was poor, and often almost destitute of the necessaries of life; but the daughters of St. Teresa had drunk deeply of the spirit of their foundress, and, esteeming their poverty to be their greatest riches, were as studious to conceal it from the knowledge of their wealthy relatives and friends as others might have been to make known their wants.   Here was the true spirit of Bethlehem and Nazareth.   The Prioress, the Mother Elisabeth de la Trinité, and the Mistress of novices, the Mother Marie de la Trinité, both women of eminent holiness, were the instruments ordained by God to train her whom the Holy Child designed to be a miracle of His grace.

And severely was the young novice tried by the mistress to whose care she was committed.   Although Mother Marie tenderly loved Marguerite, or, rather, because she so loved her with the truest love, she did not shrink from treating her during the whole of her noviciate with a harshness which would have been more than injudicious in any ordinary case.   In that of Marguerite it was but proportioned to the graces which the Infant Jesus showered upon her, and it was the occasion of calling forth the exercise of those special virtues which are the fruit of the devotion of which we are speaking—humility, simplicity, and obedience.   Marguerite was like a sweet infant in her hands.   The mistress might make her do and undo, and then reproach her with idleness before the whole community, derange and overset the preparations which Marguerite with an innate love of order had made for her work, and then lay the blame on the young novice—she might interrupt her at her meditation by calling her to execute some absurd commission, nay, she might give successive contradictory directions—without exciting, not only the least remonstrance, but even the least reflection upon

X

what was done or ordered. Marguerite went and came, did and undid, even as feet and hands follow naturally and readily the movement of the will, and have no office to judge. Like a child, she always deemed herself in the wrong, and humbly asked forgiveness for offence taken, as if for offence given. Once only, when a ridiculous, impossible act was commanded, she burst into tears and said, " My mother, force me to obey," and then, raising her eyes to Heaven, exclaimed, —" My God, I conjure Thee, enable me to obey ; let me die and obey, since Thou, O Lord, didst live and die, by obedience." Mother Marie even threatened once to expel her from the convent, adding, " And what could you do elsewhere with your continual bad health ? "   " I would do whatever the Holy Child Jesus wished," was Marguerite's simple reply.   Her hardest trial was being forbidden Communion, for which she was ever thirsting with ineffable ardour ; yet her sweet submission was never at fault, and when her mistress caused some of the Sisters to question her, in order to ascertain whether this loving soul would permit herself any complaint, she would reply, " My mother knows better what is necessary for me than I do myself : it is the Holy Infant Jesus who guides her."

But these and such as these were not her only purifying trials.   She had to suffer the assaults of the powers of Hell, torturing her body and terrifying her soul by the most appalling manifestations.   She repelled them by her Crucifix, which she calmly clasped to her bosom, and in the power and strength of the Holy Child.   These demoniacal attacks were succeeded by the most afflicting maladies.   The doctors, who, it must be confessed, have not seldom, in those days at any rate, been rather inflicters of penance than ministers of healing, added their own scientific tortures, with no result but the exhibition of the superhuman patience of their victim. She was cured at last by holy obedience. The Prioress, following a divine impulse, took the *camail* of the Cardinal de Bérulle, and, laying it on the sick girl, "My sister," she said, "be healed by obedience to our holy patron." Instantly Marguerite beheld the devils taking their flight, and was relieved at once from all pain and from the blindness which she had also suffered. They returned to the charge, however, on the morrow, when, after interrogating the physicians as to the possibility of their science effecting anything for the relief of the patient, the Prioress, having called the community together to join with her in prayer, repeated the same act and command, forbidding the malady ever to return, which, although Marguerite suffered subsequently from other ailments, it never did. One of her afflictions, as we have noticed, had been total blindness, partially removed, however, in presence of the Blessed Sacrament, and especially when It was exposed, upon which occasions Marguerite could always distinctly perceive It. Her pains were also suspended in Its presence, and she seemed to draw life and strength from the Source of Life in the Tabernacle. To procure her this temporary relief, the sisters used to carry her into the chapel. Those moments, so full of joy to her soul and of ease to her body, the sufferer never desired to prolong one moment beyond the appointed hour; and once, when the Sisters designedly left her a little longer, she was seen, in spite of her paralytic state, to pass with astonishing rapidity through the cloister back to the Infirmary, where she was found in her bed, none of the inmates having observed her entrance. Such was the miraculous force of the virtue of obedience in this disciple of the Divine Child.

The annihilation of her will was modelled on the same Type. Marguerite met all the accidents of life and submitted to them as the Holy Babe submitted to be wrapped in swaddling-clothes, lifted up, or laid down, at His Mother's pleasure. "Is it so very difficult to serve God?" she would say. "We have only to give ourselves into His hands simply and without reserve. We cannot imitate the perfections of our Father in Heaven, because we cannot see Him, but we can look at the Child Jesus in the manger, and He has all His Father's perfections."

Marguerite made her profession on the Feast of the Presentation of the Blessed Virgin in the year 1632. On the vigil she was seen raised in the air in an ecstasy before an image of our Lady, during which she received instructions from the Mother of God concerning the perfect abandonment with which she was to consecrate herself to God upon the following day. It was during the ceremony of her reception that, rapt in a vision, she beheld the Infant Jesus with a countenance of inexpressible loveliness, and surrounded by hosts of angels and saints. He seemed to pour on her a celestial dew, which arrayed her in a nuptial robe of innocence and simplicity. He then, before all the assembled court of Heaven, bestowed upon her the title of Spouse of the Holy Infant of Bethlehem. These mystical espousals were afterwards renewed more than once. From this moment so completely was Marguerite estranged from earthly things that she lost, so to say, almost the idea of her own personality; and, notwithstanding her humble dread of singularity, she persevered for some time in speaking of herself as "she who belongs to the Infant Jesus." When sharply reproved by her mistress, who bade her desist from this practice and call herself by her name, Sister Marguerite of the Blessed Sacrament, she deplored with tears what, indeed, seemed to be a physical inability to comply, and the name of Jesus was heard as if issuing from her throat. "What can I do, my mother?" she exclaimed; "It is not I who speak, but Jesus. I do not belong to myself; the Infant Jesus has become my whole life and being." From this time she never appeared to notice any conversation which was not directly addressed to her; she was deaf to everything and blind to everything which had no connection with the Divine Object of her perpetual contemplation. Her angel-guardian opposed any diversion of her attention. Whenever, in particular, any frivolous conversation took place in her presence, or was addressed to her, so long as it continued she was powerfully attracted to complete absorption in God. "I cannot explain it," she said, on being questioned, "but when people talk to me about external things, my brothers, the angels, make me glorify God with them, and these words alone occupy my mind: 'God only is great, holy, adorable.'" Her angel also effaced from her memory all the admirable words which she might have uttered. This abstraction of mind, however, never interfered either with her occupations or with the charitable attention which might be claimed from her; but she answered always in the fewest possible words, and then returned to her silence of love and inarticulate prayer.

We may just mention here a circumstance which is intimately connected with our immediate subject. To Marguerite was vouchsafed a participation of the same grace with which St. Frances Romana had been honoured, that of beholding her guardian-angel, as well as of frequently seeing and conversing with many other of these princes of the heavenly court, who assisted her in her work and drove away the spirits of darkness. Having asked our Lord what was signified by the diversities which she observed in the appearance of many of the angels, He told her that those on whom she saw the form of the Cross especially honoured His Passion, while such as were distinguished by a whiteness surpassing in splendour anything to be seen on earth were devoted to honouring His Infancy. He also told her that the last angel whom He had assigned to her belonged to that order. What an insight is here afforded us into the loving dispensations of God, ordained to conduct us on to perfection and to the crown He has laid up for us, as well as into the offices which these glorious spirits perform in our regard, aiding us in prayer and helping us by their inspirations to follow the promptings of grace! We are perhaps in the habit of too exclusively regarding our faithful invisible companion as our protector and guardian from evil, and comparatively seldom advert to the invaluable assistance he can render us in prayer and in keeping close to our particular vocation.

Marguerite's very outward form bore the stamp of the Holy Infancy. Up to her twenty-ninth year, which was that of her death, when she entered upon her last tremendous sufferings connected with the Passion, she

had preserved, in despite of all her maladies, the peculiar beauty and grace of early childhood.   Diminutive
in stature, with pure and delicate features, and a voice
of infantine sweetness, you would have supposed her
to be barely twelve years of age.   Such was the outward appearance of Jesus's " little spouse," a name by
which the Holy Child often designated her.   The
following is the description given of her by one of the
Sisters in the deposition taken after her death :—
" There was in her at once the simplicity of a little
child and a marvellous wisdom, enlightening the minds
of others and inclining them to follow her counsels,
in spite of contrary inclination ; in short, the sanctity
of her state made me apprehend the dignity and
grandeur of the divine and adorable state of Jesus in
His humble Infancy more than all that I had ever
been taught upon the subject."   This same Sister
spoke in the most rapturous terms of Marguerite's
humility and of her charity, the one causing her, notwithstanding the beautiful innocence of her life, to be
perpetually bathed in tears for her sins ; the other,
which was an image of the boundless love of her Lord,
impelling her to charge herself with the sins and sorrows of a multitude of souls for whom she was ever
pleading with the Divine Infant ; and, all the while,
not only was her own peace undisturbed, but she had
the gift of rejoicing the hearts of others, and of ele-
vating them to God by the mere sight of her.   So
exquisitely tender was this charity, that she could not
endure to see the slightest suffering in another : " her
little heart," says the same Sister, " was immediately
touched with compassion, although she never betrayed
the least sensibility for her own."   The same tenderness of charity was exhibited if any observation was

made before her to the prejudice of another. Generally speaking, as we have observed, she did not hear what was said in her presence ; but upon these and similar occasions the Child Jesus, who moved and directed her faculties, would often suffer her to notice it, and prompt her to say that such observations were displeasing to Him.

The assimilation of Marguerite to the Infant of Bethlehem and Nazareth was, however, to be succeeded, as already indicated, by a conformity to the Victim of Calvary. Bethlehem and Calvary are never severed. The Crib leads to the Cross. The Babe lying in the Manger is the Victim prepared to be nailed to the Tree. And thus it is that those eminent souls who have been called to exhibit a marvellous devotion to the Sacred Infancy, are so far from being designed to give less attention to the Passion, or to be absorbed in the contemplation of the Child Jesus, to the exclusion of their Crucified Lord, that, on the contrary, it is amongst them that we meet with some of the most remarkable instances of conformity to the Sufferings and Death of the Redeemer. The Crib, it is true, has been their mode of approach to the Cross ; but so it was with Jesus Himself. When Marguerite was called to tread the dolorous road of Calvary, our Lord, in preparation, inspired her with a burning desire to suffer for sinners, filling her with the spirit of sacrifice, penance, and charity. "Come," He said to her one morning, after she had received Communion, "come and learn the science of the Cross." At the same moment she had a vision of a Cross, the foot of which was in the abyss below, while the summit reached to the heavens above, and the arms were extended to the furthest confines of the universe.

From this moment she entered on the Way of Sorrows, the path which her Saviour had trod, that she might lead, like many other saints in all ages of the Church, a life of expiation in union with the expiatory sacrifice of the God-Man.   This is not the place to give details of the mystical wonders manifested in this holy nun ; suffice it therefore to say that, after being called to the supernatural life of a voluntary victim for the sins and offences of men against the majesty and holiness of God, and for the outrages offered by them to her Heavenly Spouse, as well as to that of a continual intercession for sinners whose special needs were revealed to her, for whom, as also for certain souls in Purgatory, whose state was shown to her, she inflicted upon herself the most cruel mortifications and penances, our Lord was pleased to vouchsafe to her a sensible participation in the sufferings of His Passion.   "The Divine Child," says one of her biographers, " whose image our dear sister so well reproduced, in order to give us the example of all the virtues of Christian childhood, had grown in Marguerite ; He was arrived at the fulness of His age, and it only remained for Him to undergo a last and supreme transformation before arriving at heavenly joys : He must become in her the Man of Sorrows, ascending all the steps of Calvary, laden with the weight of the Cross."

It was in the Lent of 1634 that Marguerite was first led through all the different stages of our Lord's sufferings, beginning with the forty days' fast in the desert, which she passed in a state of continual ecstasy, neither eating nor drinking for the whole of that time.   During Holy Week all the impressions of our Saviour's Passion were reproduced in her, not mentally only, but in external bodily manifestations,

followed on Easter Sunday by a rapturous participation in the joys of the Resurrection Festival, which
she celebrated in spirit with the whole court of
Heaven.   This application of Marguerite to the
Passion of Jesus and to the joys of His Resurrection
was renewed several times in successive returns of
that holy season.   The extraordinary mystical sufferings she endured were ever followed by a corresponding wonderful increase of graces.   They were also
alternated by visions of glory, when she would often
behold bands of saints and angels rejoicing round the
Crib of the new-born Babe of Bethlehem ; and the
dereliction of soul in which she had been previously
immersed would then be succeeded by the most tender
and familiar testimonies of God's love.   During these
days of heavenly joy and consolation Marguerite, says
her biographer, " was all-powerful."   Happy they
who commended themselves to her prayers !   It was
no longer a few individual sinners of whom she would
obtain the conversion : her sphere was now widely
extended, and she had become the protectress of whole
towns and provinces, for which her intercession was
sought by persons who had heard of the marvels of
grace operated in her and the wonderful efficacy of her
prayers.

France was at that time passing through the last
melancholy years of the reign of Louis XIII. Menaced
on all sides by foreign armies, torn by internal dissensions, and ravaged by a devastating plague, nothing
seemed wanting to complete the measure of her calamities.   Meanwhile a humble daughter of Carmel was
praying unknown in the poor convent of Beaune, and
her prayers were mighty to stay the chastising hand of
God.   It was by her compassionate Lord's desire that

she thus stood between His anger and her guilty
country. She had repeated revelations to this effect
during the year 1636. "Hasten, my daughter," He
said to her in one of these visions, when He had displayed before her the miseries with which France was
threatened, "hasten to draw upon the treasures of My
Infancy; it is by Its means that you will obtain
pardon for this guilty people." He on this occasion
taught her how to honour Him from His Incarnation
to His twelfth year, and promised that this devotion
should, in calamitous seasons, be the safeguard of those
who practised it. The 25th day of each month was
to be specially consecrated to the memory of His
Birth, and a little chaplet of fifteen beads, which
Marguerite called the Corona of the Infant Jesus, was
to be said. But, above all, Marguerite pressed on
the associates the necessity of becoming penetrated
with the spirit of the Hidden Life of the Child Jesus,
and to copy in their domestic interiors that of the
Holy House of Nazareth. And now from mouth to
mouth, far and wide, spread the knowledge of the
revelations made to Marguerite, and, as its result, came
an ever-increasing number of applications from persons
desirous of joining the new devotion. Soon the
highest names in the land had been enrolled in the
Confraternity. Marguerite desired to profit by this
general movement of minds to erect a chapel dedicated to the Holy Child, and presently gifts flowed in
apace for the work, which was rapidly completed, and
the Divine Infant renewed to her His promises to show
mercy to France.

The truth of these promises was soon to be tested
by the rapid advance of the hostile armies. The alarm
was general, and so great in the capital that the

Parisians believed the ferocious John de Wert was
already at their gates, while in the unprotected town
of Beaune, more immediately menaced by his pitiless
German bands, consternation was at its height. The
churches were crowded day and night with suppliants,
and the clergy caused the Blessed Sacrament to be exposed. Amidst the universal terror Marguerite alone
preserved her tranquillity. "Fear nothing," she
said, "the Holy Child is now honoured in this city,
as He required. Can we believe that He will not
protect His little Nazareth?" That was the name she
loved to give to the new chapel. She even upbraided
her sisters with their want of confidence in God, telling them that a straw from the Manger of the Divine
Child was sufficient to turn back the most formidable
army. On the 25th of August, when fear had reached
its climax in the little city, the Infant Jesus appeared
after Communion to Marguerite, and told her that on
the morrow the enemy would begin their retreat;
which actually took place, most unexpectedly, as had
been foretold. Marguerite, however, was bidden to
continue her supplications, for that the justice of God
was not yet satisfied, and that, if the people did not
repent and amend, but relapsed into their evil ways
as soon as the danger was past, the foe would assuredly return; and, in fact, a new army of Germans
poured into Burgundy with overpowering force in the
month of October following. From the ramparts of
Beaune, the flames of burning villages could be de-
scried, illuminating the horizon, and the panic was
aggravated every hour by the crowding in of the
neighbouring peasants, whole families, which had
barely escaped with their lives after seeing their
homesteads and cottages destroyed. All the rich

women in the place were hastily quitting it, and such
as had relatives in the convent urged the Prioress to
adopt the same prudent course ; but the confidence of
Marguerite, who pleaded the promise of the Infant
Jesus, prevailed.   The Carmelites remained ; and
some days later our Lord again announced to His
spouse the retreat of the enemy, adding that, because
of their excesses, this army would not leave Burgundy without chastisement or without experiencing
the terror it had itself inspired. All was accomplished
according to the divine promise.   On the 3rd of
November, the enemy, crediting a false report as to
the numbers of an insignificant body of troops which
had thrown itself into the town of St. Jean-de-Losne,
which they were beleaguering, hastily raised the
siege and made a precipitate retreat, which was
rendered disastrous by a sudden rise and overflow of
the waters of the Saône. Tents, baggage, artillery were
submerged or carried away by the stream, while the
Germans fled in-dismay; and this army, lately so insolent and confident of victory, reached the frontiers
diminished by three-fourths of its number.   The mind
instinctively turns, while reading of these chastise-
ments and mercies, of God's tender love for France,
of the prayers of saints staying His uplifted arm, and
of the prompt deliverance following upon the people's
repentance, to the present condition of that unhappy
land.   Here, in times gone by, we see afflictions like to
those we have witnessed in our day, visitations
brought on by like causes ; and the curtain is, as we
may say, drawn aside to show us the salvation ready
at hand, if France would but, as a nation, turn as,
when Marguerite prophesied, the city of Beaune
turned, to her offended God.

The fame of this deliverance greatly increased, as may be supposed, the devotion of which Marguerite was so zealous an apostle. All ranks and classes sought her prayers, and the reputation of her sanctity, as well as the report of the countless graces and favours obtained by prayers offered to the Infant Jesus in the Carmelite church, began to attract to Beaune a prodigious concourse of pilgrims. All were desirous to see and speak to Marguerite, if possible, but, as this was certainly not possible, they at least would assist at the conventual Mass, during which, we are told, the very knowledge of her presence, although to the general congregation she was not visible, made an undefinable impression on them. The pious would eagerly await the moment of giving Communion, in the hopes that she might leave the choir reserved to the nuns, to come and kneel at the altar-rail ; and those who were not disappointed of their wish testified afterwards to the emotion produced upon them by the sight of her countenance, when receiving her Lord, which at those times was super-naturally illuminated and shone with an angelic beauty. This was no popular delusion, for the truth is confirmed by the Prioress, herself one who might have been no unworthy claimant of the honours of canonization, if Carmel had not produced so luxuriant a growth of saints. If Marguerite's presence, and the mere sight of her, made so deep an impression, what was not the effect experienced by those who were able to converse with her ! All confessed to the ascendancy she exercised over them, and their assertions were corroborated by their acts. Rancour was expunged from hearts, injuries were forgiven, souls filled with a spirit of abnegation, and the meekness, gentleness, and all the other virtues of which Jesus was the Teacher and Example, implanted in them. Numbers of persons who were unable to repair to Beaune were constantly writing to Marguerite to recommend themselves to her prayers. Some informed her that they had had chapels built and dedicated to the Child Jesus ; others, that they had resolved to watch in His honour on the night of the 25th of each month, or that they would give abundant alms, or perform special mortifications on those days ; others promised Communions, and the like ; but all were determined to change their lives, expiate their sins, and renounce the vanities of the world.

The devotion to the Holy Infancy thus spread rapidly through France ; hearts were softened and purified from the deleterious influences of war, and of the incessant civil struggles which had distracted the land for so many years ; and thus was ushered in the great religious revival which took place in France at the middle of the 17th century. It is scarcely necessary to add that foremost in taking up the devotion propagated in a house of their own Order, were the Carmelites ; who were followed by the other religious communities in the kingdom, which thus became so many fresh focuses of devotion to the Holy Child. It is wonderful to notice how Marguerite, in the midst of the multitude of affairs and of souls recommended to her prayers, never forgot any, never omitted any. One of her confessors having asked her how this could be, she replied, "It is because I always find in the Heart of the Divine Infant the persons for whom He permits me to pray, as if I saw them in a mirror which reflected all objects without confusion or admixture." Notwithstanding the countless applications which made inroads on her time and attention, whether in the form of visits or of letters, she received or replied to every one with a sweetness which made each feel to be an object of particular interest. With an untiring patience she listened to the repeated recital of the same miseries and the same wants, consoling, encouraging, and fortifying all, and never allowing any one to suspect the fatigue which must so often have oppressed her. "Our sufferings," she would amiably say, "are only for ourselves; others ought never to perceive them." Not repentant sinners alone or the newly-converted votaries of the world sought her counsel; souls of the most eminent sanctity rejoiced in being associated with her prayers, and every day brought pilgrims distinguished for their virtues to renew their humility or their fervour by an interview with the "little spouse of the Infant Jesus."

With all these visitors, whether illustrated, as were many, by earthly rank, or by a nobility far higher, we have no concern here; our attention must be concentrated on one who, in his own person, combined both, —the Baron de Renty. In the following chapter we shall consider the development of his leading attraction, which was the immediate consequence of his connection with Marguerite of Beaune.

CHAPTER II.

Spiritual Alliance between De Renty and Margaret.

The keynote of De Renty's devotion and sanctity had always been, as we have abundantly shown, union with Jesus. The love of God in Christ has been seen to have been the motive power of all his actions ever since his full conversion. We hear little, in connection with him, of the sense of duty, or of any such abstract motive, however good as embodying a true and sound idea, but much and at every turn of this personal love of God. Father Faber tells us that two different schools of spirituality arise from the manner in which respectively this sense of duty or personal love of God has the leading prominence. "All are agreed," he says, "that as the proof of love is the keeping of the commandments, so the sense of duty, the brave determination to do always and only what is right and because it is right, must go along with and be a part of personal love of God. Personal love of God without this would be a falsehood and a mockery. They who dwell most strongly on the sense of duty do not omit personal love of God; and they who lay the greatest stress on love, both imply and secure the keen sense of rightfulness and duty. But much depends on which of the two we put foremost." Without being blind to the danger that, by dwelling exclusively on love, religion may be made " too much a matter of mere devotions, an affair of sentiments and feelings, highly strung and therefore brittle, over-

z

strained and so shortlived," we must also bear in mind
that "by laying all the stress on duty, the true
motive of duty may not have fair play, and the
peculiar character of the Gospel be overlooked or
inadequately remembered."

These two motives of Christian holiness—the sense
of duty and personal love of God—are thus stated by
the same great writer :—"We must pursue such and
such a line of conduct because it is commanded,
because it is right, because it will win us respect,
because it will enable us to form habits of virtue,
because it will edify, because we cannot otherwise go
to Communion, because we shall be lost eternally if
we do not pursue it. This is quite intelligible, and it
is all very true, but not particularly persuasive. . . .
We must pursue such and such a line of conduct
because it is the one which God loves ; and God loves
us most tenderly, and has loved us from all eternity ;
and God yearns that we should love Him, and He
catches at our love as if it were a prize, and repays it
with a fondness which is beyond human comprehension ; and it grieves His love, and He makes it a
personal matter, if we swerve from such conduct, and
if we only love, all will be easy. This also is intelligible and very true, and also very persuasive, and has
a wonderful root of perseverance in it." While both
views are true, they nevertheless, as the same writer
goes on to observe, "form quite different characters."
Without ignoring the fact, however, that "religion
comes to persons in different ways," and while we take
heed never "to throw the slightest slur on any method
which succeeds in securing the continuous keeping of
God's commandments upon supernatural motives," we
cannot err in pronouncing the way of personal love to

be in itself the more excellent way. Moreover, it is
the way which the saints have followed. "Doing
what is right because it is right is not a sufficiently
perfect or robust motive to carry a man all the way to
perfection. Love alone can do that." The principle
of the sense of duty, "although it is thoroughly
Christian and lives on Christ, appears to have but a
weak tendency to produce that nameless indescribable
likeness to Christ which is the characteristic of the
saints ; it has not enough of self-oblivion in it, and is
very deficient in its sympathies with the mystical
operations of grace."*

Sanctity is not a mere character ; it does not
essentially consist in a compendium of virtues, still
less in a multitude of good works. These are its
fruits and its attendants ; but sanctity itself is something higher, deeper, more transcendant: it is nothing
less than union of the soul with God, the Source of all
sanctity and Very Sanctity Itself. Holy, holy, holy
is the Lord of Hosts, the Triune God ! To this union
men are called in Christ, the God-Man, and it is by
incorporation with Him, the Head, that this union is
contracted. It would seem to be an obvious consequence that this union must be most easily and most
fully perfected by whatever process keeps it continually
before the mind, renders it the immediate object of the
soul's aspirations rather than the mere following of a
rule, and thus draws it to live upon it, and make progress
in it daily. But to be thus led implies one necessary
condition—a deep persuasion of the tender love of

* For the full treatment of this question, see some admirable pages in the concluding chapter of Father Faber's
work, *The Creature and the Creator*, from which the above
quotations are taken.

z 2

God towards us. We love Him because He first
loved us. It is true that all Christians know in a
certain way that God loves them ; they could not be
Christians did they not know, believe, and confess
this. They know and believe that God so loved man-
kind as to give His Only-Begotten Son to die for
us, and that He who bestowed such a gift will, as
St. Paul argues, keep no good thing back, but will
freely give us all things. But there are two ways of
knowing anything and of giving it our assent : of this
we are all well aware ; and so, in spite of what we
have just said, nothing, perhaps, is more difficult than
to acquire a real heart-felt conviction of the exceeding
love of our God towards ourselves personally. It is a
fact that, "for some reason or other," as Father Faber
observes in the passage from which we have already
quoted, " it is very hard to persuade a man, or for him
to persuade himself, that God loves him. The moment
that fact becomes a part of his sensible convictions a
perfect revolution has been worked in his soul." The
spirit of the Son, whereby we say Abba, Father, then
takes possession of it, superseding, or, rather, absorbing that of the servant by converting the service of
duty into the devoted manifestation of love.

This spirit of the Son we note in De Renty from
the moment of his conversion, and from his letters to
his director we gather what strong interior lights he
had received concerning the ineffable union of God
with His creature, man, in the Incarnation. "I
have had the grace vouchsafed to me several times,"
he writes. " of very intimate knowledge of the inef
fable mystery hidden in God for all ages, and now
manifested to His saints, of which St. Paul speaks : I
mean the alliance which He has contracted with us in

Jesus Christ. This knowledge causes as much astonishment as love ; and I hold that the man who is enlightened and penetrated with these truths no longer continues to be a man, but is annihilated, and his whole desire is to be lost and dissolved, that he may change his nature, and enter into the spirit of Jesus Christ, in order in Him henceforth to act through Him alone. I have conceived such great things of the Humanity of Jesus Christ united to the Divinity, that it is certain that words cannot express them. How profoundly has this divine alliance plunged this Sacred Humanity into self-annihilation, and into the sacrifice of love, at the sight of the greatness of God ! What honour to human nature to have such a Predestinate, and what a glory for us to be called and chosen in Him to enter into the favour of God, and through Him to ascend to God and to the enjoyment of Him ! It would consume the whole day if I were to undertake to write what I have seen of the wisdom and the goodness of God in this mystery of love, which He has revealed to us in His Son."

De Renty had great interior communications touching all the mysteries of our Divine Redeemer ; but the greatest of all had reference to His Infancy, to which our Lord drew him specially to apply his soul after his visit to Dijon in the year 1643. The reader will remember the occasion of that visit,—the unhappy lawsuit which his mother insisted on prosecuting before the Parliament of that city. It was seven years since the fame of the marvellous sanctity and graces of Marguerite of the Blessed Sacrament had spread far and wide through France. The accidental excitement on the subject which peculiar circumstances had fostered had probably now sub-

sided. The world does not occupy itself long about
anything, but its attention is quickly caught by something fresh, good or bad, as the case may be. The
true children of the Church are not excited even about
those marvels which are ever taking place within her
bosom, so that although the holy Carmelitess was still
as much as ever an object of veneration to them, and
her prayers were as eagerly sought by devout souls,
yet, as time had rolled on, she was probably less talked
of generally, at least at a distance; anyhow, it would
appear that it was not until De Renty found himself
in the neighbourhood (Beaune is about twenty-one
miles from Dijon) that he heard of the very extraordinary favours which this holy nun had received
from our Lord, and continued to receive, living a life
altogether supernatural, and exhibiting a pattern of
the most solid and sublime virtue. Accordingly, he
conceived a desire to repair to Beaune, and recommend
himself to her prayers. He did so, but was not able
on this first occasion to have a personal interview with
her. For some years past, Marguerite had not been
in the habit of seeing or conversing with seculars;
in which, as in all else, she followed the course pointed
out to her by our Lord; nevertheless, De Renty derived great profit even from this first visit. Yet
Marguerite had only sent him a simple message; but
when God has a grace to bestow, He is often pleased
to choose what seem most inadequate vehicles for the
conveying of it. The effect, however, is none the less
perfect, if the soul opens with faith and humility to
receive it. Writing after his return to Dijon to the
Mother Prioress of the Carmelite Convent, he says,
" I have no words to express to you the mercies of
which I have been the recipient, through the jour-

ney I made to Beaune. My sister Marguerite points out to me in the Holy Child Jesus so perfect a severance from this world, that it seems to me that here is my appointed place for despoiling myself of all."

It will be observed that he calls her, not "sister Marguerite," but "*my* sister Marguerite," marking thus the spiritual friendship which had already begun to bind these two souls to each other, although they had never met. These spiritual unions, which it has pleased our Lord at times to knit between certain persons in Him, as they differ altogether in their characteristics from natural friendships, so also are they not subjected to the same conditions. Nevertheless, the effect produced was far deeper after De Renty had been admitted to a personal interview, as he was the following year on his return to Dijon, when, his own eminent virtues and gifts having become better known, and calumny having been shamed into silence, or, rather, converted into praise, the Mother Prioress had good reason to judge that it was fitting to accord him this privilege. It was then that he truly contracted with Marguerite the alliance of grace which was to be the channel to him of an abundance of gifts. Every Catholic is familiar with the idea of the mutual communication and intercommunication of good things subsisting in the Church, the mystical Body of Christ. It is included in and is a result of that great dogma which we profess in the Creed, when we say, "I believe in the Communion of Saints." This mutual participation in spiritual things, so rich a source of profit to souls, but which, through a kind of supineness, indifference, or feebleness of faith, many scarcely realize, or do not realize in its fulness, and fail accordingly of the great advantage

they might reap therefrom, has been prominently set
before us in recorded instances in the lives of persons
of eminent holiness.   We are not now speaking of the
peculiar sympathy existing between individual souls
and certain glorified saints, who have thus become to
them special channels of grace, as, for example, we
find in the life of P. Ravignan, whom a tie of this
nature connected with the great founder of his order,
St. Ignatius, but rather of cases in which the two souls
thus bound together are as yet both "in the way."
Of this character was the union contracted between
De Renty and Marguerite of the Blessed Sacrament.
There was a transfer and communication to his soul
of the gifts which this holy nun possessed ; the chief
of which, as it was indeed the root of all the rest, was
a close and most intimate application to the Mystery
of the Holy Infancy, of which the distinguishing
marks and features began henceforth to be imprinted
on him and developed in him in a most eminent
degree.   It is not to be believed that the few words
which the Carmelitess addressed to him during their
necessarily very limited meeting could have worked
this result in the ordinary way, viz., by informing the
understanding, convincing the reason, moving the
affections, and thus deciding the will to follow the
advice given, and embrace the devotion recommended.
Great as was the unction which accompanied
Marguerite's every word, strong as was the attraction
of grace which seemed to radiate from her whole
countenance and surround her like a heavenly atmosphere, it is hard to imagine that she could say
much about the Divine Babe which was in one sense
new to De Renty, already so devoted an adorer of the
Sacred Infancy, and to whose heart, in the stillness

of his long meditations, the Holy Spirit must have already spoken ineffable things on this subject in voiceless words, more impressive than those of mortal tongue, however eloquent. We are led, then, to believe that the communication of grace between Marguerite and De Renty was something of an altogether superior and transcendant character, which, like all supernatural facts, belongs to an order above the reach of the human understanding to fathom, or of human language to express. It is best, perhaps, represented by a simile, itself taken from the supernatural order; but analogy is often the best clue to such comprehension as we can attain to in these mysterious subjects. This transfer of the special and exalted graces of one soul to another may be compared, then, to the illustration which we are told the higher gradations of angels impart to those beneath them in the heavenly hierarchy, an illustration whereby the lower in dignity and capacity are given to participate after a manner in the sublimer gifts of superior ranks. No impediment subsists in these glorious spiritual beings to the free or full reception of this influx, which gladdens Heaven with a multiplication of light and love at the bare thought of which we are filled with admiration and delight. Similar to this, we may conceive, is that intercommunion in the mystical Body of Christ of which we are speaking. It is a kind of supernatural circulation; and just as the free circulation of blood in the human body maintains it in health, nourishes, fortifies, cheers, and exhilarates it, and any impediment or obstruction to that circulation keeps the system in an oppressed and languid state, and hinders the process of nutrition, so is it with this spiritual circulation. Did our souls offer no obstacle to its blessed inflowing, if self did not block up, so to say, almost all our spiritual pores, and thus isolate us from these mutual influences, it would be impossible to imagine what a different spectacle the Church of Christ, the assembly and body of the faithful, might present on earth. True, it is union with the Head which is the primal source of our sanctification, as He is indeed the only Source of Grace,—all besides are but channels,—still, even as in proportion to the closeness of our union with Him, the Head, is our intimate union with the members, whether they be glorified saints in heaven, or holy persons still on earth, so do they in their turn become to us so many feeders of our grace, and enrichers of our poverty, and thus draw us nearer to the Head, because in the Church of God there is a true and heavenly " Socialism," all things there being in common. " Behold," says the Royal Psalmist, " how good and how pleasant it is for brethren to dwell together in unity ; like the precious ointment on the head, that ran down upon the beard, the beard of Aaron, that ran down to the skirt of his garment."* It is in the unity of the Body that this plenitude of the unction of the Head circulates and spreads, even as the very skirts of his garments received a share of the oil that streamed down from Aaron's sacred head. How dry, sapless, and unfruitful is the self-sufficient soul which keeps apart from this health-giving contact and proudly strives to live upon itself!

Far different, as we have seen, was the spirit of De Renty ; hence nothing was lost to him, and he absorbed into his spiritual system, if we may be permitted such an expression, every sanctifying influence

* Ps. cxxxii. 1, 2.

which approached him. His interior senses, quickened by divine grace, perceived and seized on their nourishment; and, while charity made him always ready to impart, humility made him ever prefer to receive. The attitude of disciple and learner was far more congenial to him than that of master and teacher so often forced upon him. Hence he who had reluctantly become the guide in spiritual matters of so many persons distinguished alike by their piety and high position, took his place joyfully at the feet of the poor Carmelite nun, and reverenced her counsel as that of a heaven-sent director : nay, so intimately convinced was he of her wonderful lights, especially in his regard, that he used to call her "the oracle of Heaven." "I am no longer surprised," we find him writing, "that the Holy Child should have permitted me to become acquainted with this incomparable sister, since He makes use of her to produce such powerful impressions on my heart. Ah ! how admirable are the dealings of God with this His beloved one ! What light, what grace for those who perceive this brightness ! I this morning read something which she deigned to write to me. It contains as many miracles as it does words. She is a prodigy of grace !" And again, contrasting himself with her : "Good God ! how many graces on the one side, how much misery on the other ! How reconcile all this ? "

In imitation of Marguerite, M. de Renty desired to make a solemn consecration of himself to the Holy Child, and to make it through her hands, that it might be the more agreeable to Him. Here is the form, which he wrote with his blood : "I have consecrated myself this Christmas Day of the year 1643 to the Holy Child Jesus, referring to Him my whole being, my soul, my body, my free-will ; my wife, my children, my family, the goods He has bestowed upon me ; in short, all that may concern me ; having besought Him to take possession, as His entire property, of all that I am, that I may henceforth live only in Him and for Him in the quality of His victim, separated from all that appertains to this world, taking no part in it save according as He shall apply and permit me. So that from this time forward I must regard myself as an instrument in the hand of the Holy Child Jesus to do whatsoever shall please Him, with great innocency, purity, and simplicity, without reflection or retrospect on anything, without taking part in any work, without rejoicing or sorrowing about anything that happens, not regarding things in themselves, but in His will and in His guidance, which I will endeavour to follow by taking up my station at His crib and keeping close to the divine states of His Infancy. I this day, therefore, lose my own being, to become entirely the slave of the Holy Child Jesus, subsisting upon Him, to the glory of the Father and the Holy Ghost. I sign in the hands of the most Holy Virgin my Mother, my Patroness, and my Protectress, and in the presence of St. Joseph.

" GASTON JEAN-BAPTISTE."

This consecration, which he sent to Marguerite, was accompanied with a letter to her, in which he said, " I present myself to the Holy Child Jesus through your hands, in order that He may vouchsafe to make me His property in consideration of the prayer which I hope you will offer Him to that effect." Marguerite replied, " The Holy Child is willing to give Himself wholly to you, but you must on your part be wholly His. Just as, in respect of your body, you are continually breathing the material air, so must you, for the life of your soul, breathe everywhere the innocency, purity, and simplicity of this Divine Model." In imitation also of Marguerite, M. de Renty built a chapel dedicated to the Child Jesus, to which on the vigils of all the 25th days of every month he repaired at ten o'clock in the evening, there to remain in prayer until midnight, the hour of the Saviour's Birth. He also, further to honour the Infant Jesus, took some poor child and entertained him in his house for the whole of the day, and had three poor people to dinner, that he might pay homage in their persons to the Holy Family of Nazareth.

As De Renty had thus consecrated himself entirely to the Infant Jesus, so also, in return, did the Divine Child give Himself liberally to His servant. Marguerite, who was by grace brought into such close communion with him, had often a clear sight of De Renty's interior and of the dealings of God with his soul. Our Lord told her that henceforth he should be led and animated by the spirit of His Infancy, and that He gave Himself to him to be his teacher, his light, and his intelligence. Manifesting to her His Heart one day, he said, " Behold the abode of My servant." She often saw him, in a ray of light, so penetrated and filled with the grace of the Holy Infancy that words failed her to describe what indeed was inexplicable, and she sought for some similitude whereby to convey a notion of his state. "He is," she said, "in the grace of the Infancy of Jesus like a sponge in the sea ; nay, he is, beyond comparison, more utterly lost in the inexhaustible ocean of the infinite riches of this Divine Infancy." The abundance of favours he enjoyed is further corroborated by his own testimony, for, writing to an intimate friend at this period, he says, "The Divine King of the Crib, the Holy Child Jesus, shows me such great favours that I entreat you to thank Him for them. They are *inexplicable*." De Renty, who, as we know, did not willingly speak of himself, never lost an opportunity of acknowledging the graces he had received through the intercession of Marguerite. It was he, as we have already mentioned, who induced M. Olier to become acquainted with this holy soul ; and it would be difficult to calculate the effects of this one recommendation. M. Olier's grace, like that of De Renty and of his first director, P. Condren, was the grace of the Infancy. In sending him therefore to what we may call the fountain-head of that devotion in France at this time, he was the instrument of increasing and developing it in the soul of the Founder of Saint-Sulpice, and thereby, through him, powerfully influencing the spirit of that seminary which was to train so many holy priests and devoted missionaries for the Church of God. It was only a year before Marguerite's death, which occurred in 1648, that M. Olier paid this visit to Beaune. He was at that time so exhausted by his labours, that the physicians declared that his life could only be prolonged on the condition of his leaving his parish for a time and allowing himself a season of relaxation. He consented, and took the opportunity of visiting holy places and holy persons, thus converting his "tour," as we should call it in modern parlance, into a pilgrimage, and, while, like

the bee, he was gathering honey for his hive, and collecting a spiritual store for his personal edification, carrying
the fragrance of his own virtues wherever he went.
Before quitting Paris, De Renty was very urgent with
him not to leave Burgundy, whither he intended to
direct his steps, without seeing the Carmelite nun at
Beaune, whom God was leading in ways of grace so
extraordinarily exceptional. To prepare the religious
of her convent to receive him and treat him with the
favour he merited, De Renty wrote in these terms to the
Prioress, the Mother Elisabeth de la Trinité :—" My
Reverend Mother, I believe that you will hear with
much joy that the Providence of God is leading the
Abbé Olier into your neighbourhood, on his road
to the tomb of the Blessed Bishop of Geneva, Francis
de Sales. I have begged him not to pass without
seeing you; he informed me that such was his
purpose, and requested me to write to you and to my
sister Marguerite, and this I do rather to obey him
than to recommend to you one who is a saint, and a
very great saint, of our time. You will soon perceive
this. I hope that our Lord will cause His blessing to
abound at your interviews; and, if I had any advice to
offer you, it would be this,—that you should make him
fully acquainted with my sister Marguerite, for there
is no one in whom you may place more confidence,
or who has greater grace and experience to be a
support to you before God and before men, as much as
you may need. I should be wrong were I to say
more on the subject. It is for the Holy Child Jesus
and His grace to regulate everything. I entreat you
to get the community to request M. Olier to give them
some conferences. He is always full; you will see a
great vessel of grace, and a pure light."

As soon as M. Olier reached Beaune, after visiting
first, as he was wont, our Lord in the Blessed Sacrament, and next in the persons of the poor of the hospital, he went straight to the convent. It had been
revealed to Marguerite, who as yet did not know him,
that God designed to unite her, by devotion to the
Infant Jesus, to a soul which would be given to her
as a guide in spiritual ways ; and she no sooner saw
M. Olier than she was seized with so profound a sense
of veneration that she could not refrain from falling
on her knees and adoring the Infant Jesus present in
His servant, just as if she had beheld Him in the
manger with her bodily eyes. Here was another of
those spiritual alliances knit by the Spirit of God for
the mutual advantàge of souls ; only, as Marguerite
was a quasi-director to De Renty, the priest of God,
whom her disciple sent to her, was to become *her*
director. Yet they both received great spiritual
benefits from each other, and experienced on this occasion of their meeting many interior favours from God.
To this M. Olier bore witness when he wrote, " The
divine operation of the Holy Ghost in souls is a thing in-
comprehensible to the human mind." Marguerite, over-
joyed at having found the promised guide, after returning thanks to God for His goodness, gave him a picture
on which she had inscribed these words: "My Reverend
Father, the Infant Jesus, who is our bond, our life, our
all, will perfect and consummate the grace which to-day
He has vouchsafed to us." M. Olier, on his part, presented her with the crucifix of the Mother Agnes de
Langeac, which he always wore about him ; and he
could have given no stronger proof of the high esteem
in which he held the Carmelite nun.* He continued

* Agnes of Jesus was Prioress of the Convent of St.

to direct her by letter during the short remainder of
her life. We have related these incidents because
their effect was not limited to the advance in grace
and in the paths of perfection of the two eminent
persons thus brought into connection by De Renty;
their meeting having been fruitful in blessings to a
whole religious house, whose fervour was sensibly
renewed by communication with M. Olier, for each
of the nuns desired to see and converse with him
personally. But more than this : the great founder
of St. Sulpice, already a fervent adorer of the Divine
Child, returned from Beaune so imbued with the spirit
of the Sacred Infancy that the abundance of his grace
overflowed upon his own community, with results
which were not to be of a mere temporary character.

The death of Marguerite, which took place on the
26th of May, 1648, did not interrupt the sensible
union of grace subsisting between her and De Renty,
and he continued to receive great assistance from her,
as he himself averred. He thus writes to his director
on June 18th of the same year : " The Holy Child
Jesus has called to Himself our good sister Marguerite

Catherine de Langeac, and has been commonly called Agnes
de Langeac. This Dominican nun was bidden by the Blessed
Virgin to pray for M. Olier, then Abbé of Pébrac, and for
three years offered prayers, tears, and rigid mortifications for
his perfect conversion and sanctification. She appeared to
him three times; and this was not a mere vision, but a case
of bilocation, for when he recognized her at their first meeting, and said that he had seen her before, she confessed that
so it was, mentioning the several occasions and the reason
for which she had been directed to pray for him, God having
chosen him for the work of founding ecclesiastical seminaries
in France. The crucifix of Mère Agnes, which he gave to
Margaret, was restored after her death to M. Olier.

2 A

of the Blessed Sacrament, in dispositions entirely con-
formable to her life and miraculous grace. I have
had an intimate experience of her presence and union
with me, and have also received great assistance from
her since her death ; I have had a renewal of her
grace" (he means the grace of the Sacred Infancy),
" enabling me to enter into it afresh, so far as my condition and infirmity permit ; I have a deep appreciation of its solid value." He seems, indeed, not merely
to have had a frequent sense of Marguerite's nearness
to him, after her departure to glory, but to have beheld
her, on one occasion at least, in a vision of the intellectual order ; for such would appear to be the import
of the following passage in a letter to his director
written a month later :—" Yesterday, by a singular
favour of God, I had a sight of the Divine Majesty, of
St. John Baptist, and of my sister Marguerite, who
were represented so vividly to my mind that I cannot
doubt of the reality of what I beheld. Oh, what
effects do such presences produce, and what love is
kindled by their looks ! I find myself all renewed in
veneration for that great saint, my patron, and for that
worthy servant of God who honoured him while she
was on earth, and, no doubt, has begged him to protect me. Most true is it that the work of God in her
is a continual prodigy of grace and a masterpiece of
His hand."

CHAPTER III.

The Grace of the Sacred Infancy.

The peculiar grace of De Renty, as we have already said, was, like Père Condren's and M. Olier's, that of the Sacred Infancy ; and it had impressed its stamp upon his whole Christian character in proportion as it had been developed. The new man in him was emphatically moulded on that type, beyond what he was himself apparently cognisant ; for, although conscious of his attraction to this special devotion, it was not always present to his mind as that upon which his whole spiritual life was formed. But when he had been brought into communication with Marguerite, and particularly after his second journey to Beaune, it was far otherwise. Devotion to the Infant Jesus, as we find him telling the Mother Prioress of the Carmelite Convent, was now his main and chief nourishment. " I find all in the Infant Jesus," he says, " and am referred to Him for all." His lights kept pace with his impressions, becoming more and more perfect and vivid, and he was in consequence charged by his director to give him in writing the results of his experience, and the knowledge which had been vouchsafed to him on this subject. We alluded to this letter in our Introductory Chapter, when speaking of the difference, or, we might more correctly say, the relation existing between devotion to the Infancy and devotion to the Passion, and we quoted a passage from it in which De Renty explained how it seemed to him that *of ourselves* we should primarily seek the humiliation of the Crib rather than the sufferings of the Cross, in

2 A 2

which there might be a certain presumption, seeing
that it was the office of the Holy Spirit to lead us
from Bethlehem to Calvary, in imitation of our Divine
Redeemer, who, when taking on Himself the form of
a servant and choosing the Crib, came to do the will
of His Father by obedience. In obedience to this
will, as He Himself said, He did and suffered all,
even to the Death upon the Cross ; His choice of the
Crib including His acceptance of all that followed and
was involved in it. "I saw, then," writes De Renty,
"that in order to conduct ourselves well in all our
internal states, whether of light or of obscurity,
whether of Thabor or of the Cross, we ought always, in
order to receive, preserve, and increase our grace, to
begin by the Infancy of our Lord, who teaches us the
annihilation of ourselves, docility to God, silence, and
innocency, without any eye to self, without any pretension, but with the abandonment of a child of grace,
a child of the Child Jesus." It was in this spirit, as
we have seen, that he had always acted, but, now
that so much additional light had been vouchsafed
to him concerning this mystery, he was more than
ever established in this state of childlike dependence on grace and on God's appointments regarding him. He remained habitually with his eye
fixed on his Lord, waiting for the signification of His
will, not from day to day only, but from moment to
moment ; never aiming at anything, never aspiring to
anything, of his own movement, but in humility and
simplicity allowing himself to be guided and led like
an infant, who never thinks of having a will or choice
of its own in the disposal or management of itself.
He thus expresses his views on this subject, in the
letter to which we have just alluded :—" The Infancy

of our Lord is a state in which we must die to all, and in which the soul, in faith, in silence, in reverence, in innocency, purity, and simplicity, awaits and receives the orders of God, and lives day by day, and all the day, in a state of abandonment; in a certain wise looking neither before nor behind, but uniting itself to the Holy Child Jesus, who, annihilating Himself, awaited all His Father's commands: to be visited by the shepherds and the Magi, to be circumcised, to be carried to Jerusalem, to go and dwell in Egypt, to return, to take His way to the Jordan in order to be baptized, to preach, and then to die upon the Cross, to be afterwards raised from the dead and consummated in glory. On these traces, my Father, we must follow, so it seems to me, Jesus Christ our model, by the grace of His Infancy."

Besides the great lights he received concerning the mystery of the Sacred Infancy, he was inwardly illuminated to discern in a wonderful degree the beauty and perfection of those virtues which are the most closely connected with it, and are its peculiar fruits. Purity, Innocency, Simplicity,—these constitute what may be called the distinguishing spirit of this mystery, and are its special product in souls attached to its contemplation. These virtues were sometimes represented to his mind in a figure. At the head of a little writing which he composed on the subject were these words :—" I beheld my soul enclosed within a rampart of innocence, on a foundation of death, nothingness, and nudity, in order to live in divine purity with the Holy Child Jesus." Of this passage he gave a further development in a letter to his director. He told him that by the state of death in which he contemplated his soul, he understood its complete purgation from self and from all created things. When the soul is thus, as it were, suspended in a desert, beholding no object whatsoever, and leaning upon nothing, it was shown to him that God from above draws it to Him by the end of the cord of pure love, as St. Catherine of Genoa said, and that this cord was the Infant Jesus, in union with whom we must in every way surrender ourselves, to fulfil the part of a victim which in purity, innocency, and simplicity, sacrifices and consumes itself for His glory. This state was repeatedly presented to him as that to which God called him. He was no longer to act in anything save by the leadings of the Infant Jesus. His holy and divine operations; His pure love for His Father; His sacrifice of Himself for His glory and the destruction of sin; His submission to all His successive orders, which He clearly beheld, awaited with patience, and executed in their appointed time, doing nothing by his own movement, were proposed to De Renty for his imitation so far as his infirmity permitted. Now, in order to enable him to act with the purity of spirit thus required of him, and to preserve it unimpaired, innocency and simplicity were given to him to serve as his two ramparts of defence. This innocency he described as a luminous crystal, through which he was to look at things innocently,—that is, without applying his mind to the evil which his eyes beheld, and without receiving any impression from the vices and disorders of men, nothing of all which was to abide in his recollection. "This innocency," he goes on to say, "inclines us to a great benignity, and a great sweetness towards our neighbour, and it is an incredible aid to me in my occupation, on account of the number of evils and sins of all sorts of which I am daily cognisant, and about which it seems that our Lord wills that I should occupy myself in order to remedy them in some measure. Innocency, then, interposes itself between me and all before me, that purity may not be disturbed in its operations ; that is to say, in directing its eye to God." It was thus that innocency fulfilled the office of a rampart, enabling him to look as an angel might look on all the folly, vanity, wickedness, and impurity of the world, as well as on all the beauty and attractions of exterior objects.   But the parallel which we can best understand, and which is most closely analogous to the model set before him, is that of the infant.   An infant sees everything which passes before him with a pure and innocent eye ; he views things superficially and does not penetrate into their malice ; he forms no judgment, he makes no criticism, he retains no subsequent image in his mind ; so, in like manner, the child of grace looks innocently at all things without receiving any malignant influence or contracting any contamination which might soil his purity ; no object leaving any trace behind it, or so much as creating a mental impression.

But how is this possible ? we may be inclined to say ; how is it possible for one who is so divinely enlightened to know the malice of sin, and whose spiritual vision has been sharpened by that self-knowledge which furnishes a key to the reading of the hearts of others, thus to pass through the world, not only without contamination (for this, by God's grace, he may hope to do), but without receiving an impression, or even formulating a severe judgment on much that he is forced to see ?   Is not such innocence more like ignorance ?   To the child, in the natural order, this is possible, because he is ignorant, and his igno-

rance blinds him; but the child of grace is not
ignorant: on the contrary, none can see so clearly as
he, none can form so sure a judgment. Now it must
be allowed that the state which De Renty describes
and which is similar to what we find recorded of many
saints, is certainly above ordinary attainment; we
cannot, without a special grace of God, enjoy such
an immunity as he did; it was a particular favour
granted to him, that he should know and remember
at proper times whatever was necessary to action,
but that he should make no reflection upon it, and
that all should be effaced and sponged out, as it were,
on the instant. But we must remember that he had
made it the diligent study of years to cultivate in
himself the temper of the little child, and this
diligent study had rendered him a not unworthy
recipient of a gift which no one could, strictly
speaking, merit.

Yet, not only is the temper itself attainable, but a
certain degree of it is a condition of salvation, although
its higher degrees are seemingly rare. The importance
of these, however, to Christian perfection cannot be
overrated. De Renty's natural disposition,—haughty,
decisive, penetrating, with those frequent concomitants,
a critical judgment and a satirical turn,—furnished
peculiar obstacles to the acquisition of the temper in
question; yet, by God's grace, he had completely
triumphed. How hard to achieve this triumph it is, in
most cases, is attested by the best spiritual writers; and
if our own hearts do not always bear the same witness,
it is because we have never, perhaps, seriously set ourselves to work to acquire the childlike disposition—
never, perhaps, clearly perceived the need we have of it,
—nay, possibly have even in our blindness valued our-

selves on qualities which are its opposite, and on abilities which have proved to be amongst the greatest hindrances to its attainment.

It is thus that a great master of our own day has expressed himself with reference to a propensity more inimical, perhaps, than any to the acquisition of childlike innocency, that of judging and criticising : " The habit of not judging others," says Father Faber, in his *Spiritual Conferences*, " is one which it is very difficult to acquire, and which is generally not acquired till very late in the spiritual life. If men have ever indulged in judging others, the very sight of an action almost indeliberately suggests an internal commentary upon it. It has become so natural to them to judge, however little their own duties or responsibilities are connected with what they are judging, that the actions of others present themselves to the mind as in the attitude of asking a verdict from it. All our fellowmen who come within the reach of our knowledge, and for the most retired of us the circle is a wide one, are prisoners at the bar ; and if we are unjust, ignorant, and capricious judges, it must be granted to us that we are indefatigable ones. Now all this is simple ruin to our souls." And again, " The habit of judging is so nearly incurable, and its cure is such an almost interminable process, that we must concentrate ourselves for a long while on keeping it in check, and this check is to be found in kind interpretations. We must come to esteem very lightly our sharp eye for evil, on which, perhaps, we once prided ourselves as cleverness. It has been to us a fountain of sarcasm ; and how seldom since Adam was created has a sarcasm fallen short of being a sin ? We must look at our talent for the analysis of character as a dreadful possibility of

huge uncharitableness. We should have been much
better without it from the first. . . . Sight is a great
blessing, but there are times and places in which it is
far more blessed not to see. . . . Of course, we are not
to grow blind to evil, for thus we should speedily
become unreal. But we must grow to something
higher and something truer than a quickness in
detecting evil."

There is, then, something higher and truer than
this penetrating discernment and quick appreciation
of evil. De Renty had laboured unremittingly to
attain to it, and the grace to which he alludes was
the rich reward which God had bestowed upon him.
Akin to the habit of judging is the disposition to take
scandal. "To give scandal," says the writer from
whom we have just quoted, "is a great fault, but to
take scandal is a greater one;" and further on he
tells us that it is a very common one amongst the
superficially pious. "I find," he proceeds to tell us,
"great numbers of moderately good people who think
it fine to take scandal. They regard it as a sort of
evidence of their own goodness, and of their delicacy
of conscience, while in reality it is only a proof
either of their inordinate conceit or of their extreme
stupidity." He adds this striking observation: "I
do not remember to have read of any saint who ever
took scandal." This is nowise surprising when we
consider that to take scandal implies the forming of
an unfavourable judgment and the deliberate entertaining of it. "Is it often allowable," he asks, "to
judge our neighbour? Surely we know it to be the
rarest thing possible." That the proneness to take
scandal is altogether opposed to the saintly mind may
be at once inferred from noticing its repugnance to

the interior spirit. "The supernatural grace of an interior spirit," he says, "among its other effects, produces the same results as the natural gift of depth of character; and to this it joins the ingenuous sweetness of charity. A thoughtless or a shallow man is more likely to take scandal than any other. He can conceive of nothing but what he sees upon the surface. He has but little self-knowledge, and hardly suspects the variety or complication of his own motives. Much less, then, is he likely to divine in a discerning way the hidden causes, the hidden excuses, the hidden temptations, which may lie and always do lie behind the actions of others." Hence it is that the judgments formed of others by the man who is wanting in an interior spirit are not only rash, but, as F. Faber expresses it, have a "coarseness" and "vulgarity" about them. "Sometimes he only sees superficially: this is if he is a stupid man. If he is a clever man, he sees deeper than the truth. His vulgarity is of the subtle kind. . . . . He cannot judge of character at all. He can only project his own possibilities of sin into others, and imagine that to be their character which he feels, if grace were withdrawn from him, would be his own. . . . . He is cunning rather than discerning. To clever men charity is almost impossible, if they have not an interior spirit."

This passage satisfactorily answers the difficulty which we supposed might be raised as to the acquisition of the uncriticising spirit of the child, who can look upon evil innocently and without taking scandal, a difficulty grounded upon the increased knowledge of the human heart possessed by the spiritual man. That increased knowledge, while it deepens his own humility and self-contempt, makes him as respects

others only ingenious in framing excuses. This implies both a knowledge far deeper and a wisdom far
higher than any which natural cleverness and penetration can impart, a knowledge and a wisdom as
superior to that of the world as the character of
Christian perfection is to the highest ideal of goodness which it can entertain. That perfection is
summed up very pertinently to our present topic in
the following short passage from the same gifted
writer: "In what does perfection consist? In a
childlike, short-sighted charity, which believes all
things; in a grand supernatural conviction that
every one is better than ourselves; in estimating far
too low the amount of evil in the world; in looking
far too exclusively on what is good; in the ingenuity
of kind constructions; in an inattention, hardly
intelligible, to the faults of others; in a graceful
perversity of incredulousness about scandals, which
sometimes in the saints runs close upon being a
scandal itself. This is perfection, this is the temper
and genius of saint-like men. It is a life of desire,
oblivious of earthly things. It is a radiant, energetic
faith that man's slowness and coldness will not interfere with the success of God's glory. Yet all the
while it is instinctively fighting, by prayer and
reparation, against evils which it will not allow
itself consciously to believe."

The description of charity in St. Paul's first Epistle
to the Corinthians had been the study of De Renty
for years; and, although he invariably carried a New
Testament in his pocket, he had written this passage
out on a separate piece of paper, that he might often
take it out and make it matter of continual meditation and reflection. Here he had conned his daily

lesson of the charity that thinketh no evil, that hopeth all things, and believeth all things ; it had sunk deep into his soul, and God had now recompensed his perseverance by giving him a shield which preserved him even from temptation to those failings which he had so heroically resisted and overcome.

The other rampart of his purity was, as he told his director, simplicity. This simplicity protected him from all multiplicity, or doubleness of motive and aim ; from all reflections on the past, as to what he had said or done himself, or what others had said or done ; from all those retrospects which are prompted by the anxieties of self-love, in which the mind re-enacts the scenes through which one has passed, awakening thereby corresponding impressions of complaisance and self-satisfaction, or of disturbance and regret at the part one has played, and provoking inward comments on the defects exhibited or sins committed by others. It protected him also from all solicitude as to the present employment, or concern about the future. In every employment, however varied, he found but one—the employment simply of loving and pleasing God. Multiplicity, as all know, is reckoned to be one of the greatest obstacles in the spiritual life ; and although too great a multiplication of even good occupations, whether exterior or interior, may and does often lead to it when such are not dictated by the Spirit of God, nevertheless it does not essentially consist in this multiplication, but in the multiplication of motives and their corresponding acts. No one can well have been immersed in a greater multitude of affairs than was De Renty, yet no one had cultivated more devotedly singleness and unity in mind and purpose. The one motive of God's will was

ever, as we have seen, the sole spring of all he did;
and when persons thus act from the unmixed view of
pleasing God, they are strengthened, by this concen-
tration of their faculties on one object, to apply themselves, when needful, to many things without falling
into the vice of multiplicity. "Persons of little
spirituality," says P. Surin,* "are deprived of this
grace" (the grace of enjoying the presence of God in
the midst of external occupation) ; "for, seeing themselves burdened with affairs, they divide their forces,
and allow themselves to be occupied with the particular
motive of each thing to which they apply themselves.
Hence arises a confusion of divers sentiments, each
thing making its own impression : one of joy, another
of sadness ; one of desire, another of fear. The trouble
which this excites is felt, but the principle is not
perceived, which is this multiplicity dividing the
mind." The gift of simplicity of which De Renty
speaks was, as in the case of the innocency bestowed
on him, something over and above the quality which
he had meritoriously acquired as a habit, and could
only find a fitting comparison in the simplicity of
childhood, which has no afterthoughts on what it has
seen or done, or carefulness as to the future, but lives
in the present impression alone. Thus was De Renty's
purity of intention guarded on all sides; innocency
and simplicity acting as his protection and bulwark
against past, present, and future. Nothing, according
to our limited means of judging, could approach more
nearly to a confirmation in grace—which, without a
special revelation, cannot be pre-supposed in any case
—than being thus arrayed in a divine panoply, which
rendered all temptations alike innocuous, whether they

* *Dialogues Spirituelles,* tom. ii. liv. iv. p. 178.

came from the world, the devil, or from the carnal heart, or, rather, did not suffer them to reach or come in contact with the soul. And this marvellous and surpassing grace was a gift, as De Renty himself confessed, which he derived from the Infant Jesus, to whom he had been called to dedicate himself in so special a manner. What can be said to recommend more strongly a devotion the matured fruits of which proclaim it to be at once so safe and so salutary?

CHAPTER IV.

DE RENTY'S DEVOTION TO THE MOST HOLY TRINITY AND HIS EMINENT FAITH AND HOPE.

IT is assuredly not without a deep significance that the Church, after honouring the Eternal Father for sending His Only-Begotten Son into the world to take our nature and to die for us ; the Son for His Incarnation, Passion, precious Death on the Cross, and glorious Resurrection; and the Holy Ghost as sent by the Father and the Son at Pentecost to be her informing and guiding Spirit, sums up all these mysteries with the celebration of the Festival of the Most Holy Trinity. A special illumination and insight into this central and crowning mystery of the faith, and a close application to the contemplation of its inscrutable depths, seem to belong to the climax and, what may be called, the culminating point of the mystical life ; and this is so far intelligible that, a perfect union with

God being the goal to which this path is leading chosen souls, it would follow that that goal is attained in the bosom of the Eternal, the Ever-Blessed Triune God. It is hard to deal adequately with so high a subject: not only is it out of our power to treat worthily of sublime states so far above our conception, but we even fear lest we should use inaccurate language in speaking of them. We willingly fall back therefore on that of the saints, who have had experimental knowledge of these exalted regions, and who yet found it so difficult to put into words satisfactory to themselves what they were able to tell concerning them. St. Teresa, in her *Castle of the Soul*, compares the soul to a vast palace, containing, like Heaven, many mansions or abodes—some higher, some lower, some on one side, some on the other, with a central apartment, which is the chief of all, wherein takes place what is most secret of all that passes between God and the soul.

This figure of St. Teresa, we may remark in passing, recalls to our mind the old Temple of Solomon, which, being built according to the express plans and directions given by the Lord Himself, could not aim simply at magnificence and artistic beauty, but had doubtless in all and each of its details a mystical and spiritual meaning. Now that temple was built in concentric portions, the outermost circle being, as all know, the porch of the Gentiles, while the innermost was the Holy of Holies, into which the high priest alone entered once a year, with the blood of the Paschal lamb. This Holy of Holies was, as the Apostle tells us, a figure of Heaven, but this does not interfere with its being also the figure of the central depth of our own souls, where the most secret and sublime operations of grace take place. All God's works are reflections and expressions of Himself in some measure or degree, and the soul of man in particular resembles a microcosm of the universe. Thus there is a Heaven within us : are we not indeed told that the Kingdom of God is within us ? Hence the saints sought God by a retreat into self rather than by an external aspiration. It might be interesting to carry out the parallel between the ancient Temple, with its service, and the human soul, as the scene of the wonders of the New Law ; but this is not the place.

To return, then, to St. Teresa's image of the Castle. The central abode of which she speaks is classed as the seventh, in which the spiritual marriage of the soul with God is accomplished. " When it pleases our Lord," she says, "to have compassion on what this soul, which He has already taken spiritually for His spouse, is suffering, and has suffered, through her longings for Him, He places her, before consummating the spiritual marriage, in His chamber, that is, in this seventh abode. For, as He has in Heaven, so He must needs have in the soul, a place where His Majesty dwells alone, and this place we may term a second Heaven . . . . We ought to regard the soul, not as something put away in a corner and limited, but as an interior world, containing in itself all those beautiful abodes which we have seen ; and it is very just that so it should be, since the Creator of heaven and earth deigns to dwell there." She then goes on to indicate what ensues on the introduction of the soul into this central abode. " The most Holy Trinity," she says, "by an enkindling, which first comes upon her spirit, after the fashion of a cloud of exceeding brightness, shows Itself to her,—all the Three Persons, and these

2 B

Persons distinct; so that, by a marvellous knowledge
granted to her, she understands with the greatest certainty that all the Three Persons are one substance, one
power, one intelligence, and one only God : so that
it may be said that the soul knows and sees, as with
its eyes, what we know here only by faith, albeit it is
not with bodily eyes that she beholds this, since this
vision is not representative." (She had previously
stated that the vision was *intellectual*.) It seems
scarcely necessary to observe that the saint does not
mean to assert that the soul in this state has a direct
intuition of God, for this would imply an admission
to the beatific vision. Visions of the character here
described she elsewhere defines as beheld neither
by the eyes of the body nor by those of the soul.
"Though I use the term 'sees,'" she says, "the soul sees
nothing, and this vision is not of the kind I have called
imaginary or representative : it is an intellectual
vision, which causes the soul to know how things are
seen in God, and how they are in God." She does not
say, therefore, that the soul sees God by direct intuition, but understands by means of this exalted vision
"how things are seen in God, and how they are in
Him." Perhaps this kind of vision may be the nearest
approach to the beatific, being made to the pure intellect,
and as such more inexpressible in human words, which
are sensible signs, than are the inferior kinds of vision,
in which the senses, either external or internal, play
a part ; indeed, it would be hard to conceive of any
nearer approach to the beholding of God unveiled.

The saint proceeds thus with her account of the
vision of the Blessed Trinity in the seventh abode:
" These Three Divine Persons, then, communicate
Themselves to the soul, speak to her, and cause her to

understand the meaning o. the words of our Lord in
the Gospel : that He, His Father, and the Holy Spirit
will establish Their abode in the souls that shall love
and keep His commandments. " O my God," she
continues, " what a difference there is between hearing and believing these words, and comprehending, in
the manner I have related, how true they are ! Wonder goes on progressively increasing in this soul, because it seems to her more and more that these Three
Divine Persons never leave her, but that she is continually in Their company, as she clearly perceives in
the manner I have stated, that is, in the inmost part
of herself, which resembles so deep an abyss that,
ignorant as I am, I cannot well describe it."

Such is the language used by the saint in speaking
of the hidden central region of the soul, in which this
mysterious meeting with the Blessed Trinity takes
place, a region hidden from our very selves, " that
innermost sanctuary of the soul," as Father Faber
terms it, " which so few reach on this side of the grave,
the secret cabinet, where the Holy Trinity dwells
blessedly, in the very centre of our nature, up from
whose secret recesses joys shall one day break and
flow such as we never dreamed of, such as would look
to us now far beyond the possibilities of our nature."

We will now compare what we are told of the
interior spiritual state of De Renty in the concluding
years of his life with the foregoing remarks of St.
Teresa, and we think it would be difficult to avoid
coming to the conclusion that a grace very much resembling what she describes as vouchsafed to those
happy souls who attain to the seventh abode was
enjoyed by him. On this subject we do not presume,
however, to express an opinion, and will limit our-

2 B 2

selves to retailing Saint-Jure's account. He tells us, then, that De Renty's special attraction, for a few years preceding his death, was the Adorable Mystery of the Blessed Trinity, the final term of all. It was not merely that he had a special devotion to that mystery: certainly it is very possible for souls to have that attraction, sublime as it is, in earlier stages of their spiritual progress ; but something more than this is indicated by Saint-Jure and evidenced in De Renty's own words, which he quotes. For instance, in the exposition of his interior state which he gave to his director in the year 1645, he says, " I have generally within me an experimental realization and a plenitude of the presence of the most Holy Trinity." In another letter he says, "All things are blotted out of my mind as soon as they are done ; nothing remains except God, by a naked faith, which, causing me to abandon myself to our Lord Jesus Christ, imparts to me much strength and great confidence in the Divine Trinity, because the operation of the Three Divine Persons is distinctly shown to me therein : the love of the Father, who reconciles us through His Son, and the Father and the Son, who give us life by the Holy Spirit, who causes us to live in communion with Jesus Christ, which communion effects in us a marvellous alliance with the most Holy Trinity, and at times produces in hearts sentiments which are inexplicable."

To a confidential friend, who was also much drawn to the contemplation of this mystery, he wrote, "The proper and particular effect of Christian grace is to make us to know God in Trinity, uniting us to the Son, who makes us operate by the Spirit : The truth is, we are by baptism dedicated to the worship of the Most Holy Trinity ; we are consecrated to Its glory ;

we receive Its impression, and we bear Its mark, to
apprise both ourselves and all creatures that we belong
to It." We find him writing again to this person on
the same subject in the year 1648, when his own
course was well-nigh consummated : " The Feast of
the Most Holy Trinity inclines me to write to you,
to renew you in reverence and dedication of yourself to this incomparable mystery. I unite my
heart to yours, to venerate that which I cannot express ; let us be melted with gratitude and fortified by
the virtue of faith, that through Jesus Christ we may
be consummated in this adorable mystery : things infinite, which our hearts feel in the expansion of grace,
but which we cannot render into words. Let us
adore God, let us adore Jesus Christ, let us adore the
Holy Spirit, who reveals to us the work of love and
mercy of the Divine Persons in us, and let us profit
by it."

In the same year, the last of his mortal life, he
declared very positively that the sole application of
his mind at that time was to the Most Holy Trinity ;
that his soul was very intimately united to the Three
Divine Persons, from whom he received illuminations
surpassing human intelligence ; that he lived a life of
perpetual retirement and enclosure with the Son of
God in the bosom of the Father, where this Divine
Son was his life, his light, and his love, and the Holy
Spirit his guidance, his sanctification, and his perfection ; that he bore within him the kingdom of God
—which he explained by reference to that which the
blessed spirits in Heaven enjoy—by reason of the
vision and supernatural knowledge of the Most
Blessed Trinity communicated to him, and the pure
love with which he felt himself burn, and which

transformed him into God, in whom he possessed a
joy and a peace transcending all sense. Again, that
in this state he was conformed to the Son of God in
that union of beatitude and suffering which He had
while here below, and that through His Divine Spirit
he accomplished in himself all the mysteries of our
Lord's life on earth, which put him in the abiding
state of a victim offered to the Most Holy Trinity,
and aspiring to the resurrection and full consummation in glory. Such were the interior dispositions
of this saintly man towards the Holy Trinity, as
described by himself.

In this state he passed the last years of his life,
and in it he died, thus completing his sacrifice. No
spiritual change came over him after he had reached
this term ; nor did he himself, it would seem, look for
any ; for on one occasion he used these remarkable
expressions : that when a person was called to this
state he ought to remain therein, and not change any
more. The only change which took place in him was
one of advance, a daily progress in perfection ; and we
have his own testimony that he received admirable
impressions of grace from Each Divine Person, marking him with the individual character of Each in a
wonderful manner. " The Divine Goodness," he
wrote to his director in the year 1647, " effects in me
what I cannot express : I possess the Most Holy
Trinity, and I feel distinctly the operations of the
Three Divine Persons." Doubtless on some other
occasion he had entered into fuller details with respect
to this mysterious operation of grace, for Saint-Jure
thus describes what he could have learned only from
De Renty's own lips : " The Father," he says, " kept
him retired and recollected in His bosom, giving him

a large share of that infinite inclination which He has
to communicate Himself, and of His divine fecundity
to generate children, not according to flesh and blood,
but according to the Spirit, and kindled in his heart
the love of a father and mother united for all men,
whence flowed that marvellous charity towards them
which we have witnessed.   The Son made him a faithful image of God by the expression and resemblance
of His perfections ; He imparted to him a filial spirit,
in order to acquit himself towards God of all the
duties of reverence, belief, confidence, love, and
obedience of a good son to his father, and put him in
a state in which God might speak to him interiorly,
producing in him His Word, accompanied with that
mighty power of which St. Paul speaks, to touch souls
and operate great effects of salvation in them.   The
Holy Spirit, the infinitely pure Love of the Father
for the Son, and of the Son for the Father, cleansed
him from the impurities of self-love and all self-
seeking, and inflamed him with a perfect love towards
God ; He taught him to spiritualize all material
things, to sanctify such as were indifferent, to draw
good from those which were evil, and to live a life of
the Spirit after the pattern of our Lord." Such is
the account given by De Renty's own director of the
sublime interior state to which he had been advanced,
and in which, after he had attained to it, he rested
until the day when he was summoned to enter into
his true and eternal rest.

It seems almost superfluous, after speaking of an
interior state so sublime as that which is indicated in
the account which De Renty's own director has left on
record, to add that this holy man was distinguished
by his possession, in a most eminent degree, of the

Theological Virtues of Faith, Hope, and Charity. Indeed, they may be said to shine forth in every action of his life ; little, therefore, need be added.

De Renty had early been penetrated with a deep conviction of the all-importance of faith as the root of the Christian virtues, which, severed from it, cannot flourish, and which depend for their growth and luxuriance on the firmness and strength of the root which supports and feeds them. It may seem that all Christians hold this truth as an axiom of their belief, and that there was therefore nothing remarkable in this persuasion. But herein lies the difference. Universally recognized truths are apt to be, so to say, shelved by the careless multitude, almost, one might suppose, because they are so recognized. They are acknowledged or, rather, implicitly accepted, and lead to very little in the way of action. So well aware of this propensity is our holy Mother, the Church, that she stringently urges on her children the daily recital of acts of Faith, Hope, and Charity, although every action of a Christian's life ought virtually to be such : yet it is to be feared that with many of us the practice degenerates into something of a routine. What we may call *reality* was a striking feature in De Renty's character,—the joint result of sincerity and decision. There seemed no interval with him between knowing and doing, resolving and executing. With him truisms were vital, important truths, which, as such, rendered a certain line of action imperative and pressing. To that line of action he instantly addressed himself with all the energy of his soul, and in it he unflinchingly persevered. In this manner he had laboured to acquire faith, and had reached to so high a degree of this virtue, that the evidence of sight would to him bear no comparison with it. He was far more intimately persuaded of the presence of God and of the truth of our holy mysteries than of the shining of the sun in the visible heavens. He lived by faith, walked by faith, saw everything through its medium ; judging of everything by its standard, and never looking at the externals of anything.

Our delicate repugnance to many offices in the service of the poor and sick we are apt to lay to deficiency of charity : if we had the love of the saints, then we think we could without disgust address ourselves to the most repulsive employments ; and this is certainly a truth, but it is truth imperfectly stated. Our repugnance probably proceeds full as much from the want of faith as of love. Faith enlightens the eyes, and gives vigour and robustness to both hands and heart. To the man who lives by it every action in which he is engaged assumes a different complexion, and takes another form ; not that which the senses convey, but that which he knows it to be through faith. So it was with De Renty. Another result of the strength of this virtue in him was that he was independent of all those vicissitudes of mind and feeling which so afflict and depress many good persons. If it pleased our Lord at times to withdraw sensible consolations and leave him in dryness, he was not in the least distressed ; fortified by faith, he passed on cheerfully and manfully as usual. To a defect of faith, indeed, he attributed the disquiet and impatience which are so often experienced under similar privations. In one of his letters we find the following observations :—" You will rarely meet with persons given to prayer who bear well interior abandonments, and who will wait any length of time at the door of light and sensible realization without gaining entrance and yet without growing wearied, and who do not look this way and that way, and make some effort to obtain this relief for themselves, seeking some support besides faith, which alone ought to suffice the spiritual man. The sensible consolation which God gives us is a supplement to our meagre faith ; but the just man ought to live by faith, and sustain himself on that stable foundation, without waxing impatient, but abiding in expectation of his Lord. The mischief arises from our lack of faith, which makes us very ignorant of the things belonging to the light, although we are only too ready to act the part of connoisseurs in these matters." Other letters of his contain passages of the same import, deploring the rareness of the Centurion's faith ; all desiring that Jesus should come and make His presence sensible in the mansion of their soul, for the healing of their disquietudes. " Such persons," he says, " seek a peace which they will never acquire ; for abiding peace is only to be procured by making a sacrifice of ourselves in faith. This draws the Spirit of Jesus Christ into our hearts, who will henceforth be our strength in the midst of every trouble and in death itself."

Hence he was by no means curious concerning visions or extraordinary ways, interior words, miracles, and the like : not that he was incredulous concerning such things, or did not put a due value on them, but because he did not set store by them or lean upon them, but went straight to God, even as he was led by the way of pure and naked faith. These sentiments are evidenced in one of his letters to Saint-Jure, where he alludes to some person of extraordinary sanctity,

who, it seems, had upon various occasions made certain communications to him regarding his own state.
These communications had evidently been closely
tested by De Renty, for he tells his director that what
gives him experimental proof of the presence of God
in this person is, that she had never spoken of anything to him without his having been disposed
interiorly for its reception. This circumstance, in his
estimation, set a kind of seal upon their truth and
genuineness ; nevertheless he adds, to qualify his
reliance, " One must not rest on such things as on
certainties, but must be in a manner dead to them
and to all reflections regarding them, in order to
follow without curious scrutiny, in simplicity and in
faith, what our Lord impresses on the soul at the
present moment, whatever the subject may be." And
this was his own practice. When he went to Beaune
to see Sister Marguerite of the Blessed Sacrament, as
he had been specially moved to do, he did not allow
his wishes to run an inch in advance of the movement
on which he acted : he said that he should not ask to
see her or speak to her ; that if our Lord caused him
to know that such was His will, then he would speak
to her ; otherwise he should not himself seek for an
opportunity. An anecdote is related of him which
recalls what we are told of St. Louis, king of France.
De Renty was at Dijon when the miraculous Host,
which had been sent by Pope Eugenius IV. to
Philippe le Bon, in the year 1430, was exposed to
public view. Being pressed to go and see It, he
replied that he did not require to see in order to
believe, and that he believed more than his eyes could
show him.

    Where faith is strong, it follows, almost by a kind

of moral necessity, that hope is also vigorous. Nevertheless, the great importance of a lively hope is, perhaps, less perfectly realized, speaking generally, than that of faith and charity. Of course we all know that hope is essentially needful as a Christian virtue, and its acts find their place in a Catholic's devotions along with those of faith and charity; but we are speaking of eminent degrees of this virtue. Little that is heroic can be acomplished even in the natural order without a very strong proportion of hopefulness in the character, and this for the very simple reason, if for no other, that the want of it lowers aims, and, moreover, deprives resolutions of their firmness and action of its energy. But many more reasons combine to render it an imperative condition of great achievements in the supernatural order. A feeble amount of hope, when applied, say, to some projected good work for the glory of God, is often set down to a due regard for prudential considerations, which are not obvious to the precipitate; or it will wear the guise of humility; but such humility is of a spurious kind, and is not seldom the form which reliance on self assumes in the diffident. The diffident man mistrusts his powers, just as the self-confident presumes on his; yet each is looking to self. Not but that prudence should on all occasions have its proper weight; neither is it to be supposed that every one is to think himself fit for everything because God can do what He wills in spite of every obstacle, and by instruments naturally the most incompetent. God, by His Providence outwardly, or the movements of His grace inwardly, or by both combined, is sure to make clear to those who wait on Him for light and guidance what it is He requires of them; and what it would be beyond their capacity to attempt. Still it cannot be denied that good men are to be found who will attempt nothing great whatsoever; who recoil from everything arduous ; who never see any project for God's glory save under one aspect, the difficulties which beset the undertaking ; who in the required agents, be those agents themselves or others, regard only their inadequacy, their infirmity, their imperfection. After making all due allowance for temperament and constitution, it is obvious that there must here be not unfrequently a deficiency of hope in its eminent degrees, and God's work loses, and the perfection of individuals loses thereby.

The Christian virtue of hope, on the other hand, pays a magnificent homage to God, and especially to His attributes of Power, Fidelity, Mercy, and Condescension. The Divine condescension to prayer, in particular, is one, it would seem, of the most valued attributes, if we may allow ourselves such an expression, as it is among the most beautiful, in the character of our Ever-Blessed God. He is continually putting it forward, reminding us of it, urging it upon us, reproaching us for not relying on it, for not availing ourselves of it. There is, perhaps, not a single virtue more frequently enforced in Holy Scripture than hope in God. Let any one who questions this take up the Psalms and read anywhere at random, and he will be surprised to find how often the encouragement to hope in God occurs. The marked displeasure, also, which the Almighty has shown at the absence of hope and confidence in Him, or their deficiency, is another evidence of its value, a displeasure which to a superficial observer seems sometimes almost startling, and would scarcely have been anticipated. Witness that king of Judah, whose victories over the Syrians were to be limited because he had struck only thrice on the ground :— " The man of God was angry, and said, ' If thou hadst smitten five, or six, or seven times, thou hadst smitten Syria even to utter destruction, but now three times shalt thou smite it ;' " * and again, the punishment which Moses, along with Aaron his brother, incurred from faltering in confidence when bidden to command water to flow from the rock : " Because you have not believed Me, to sanctify Me before the children of Israel, you shall not bring these people into the land which I will give them." † The not believing is here plainly want of confidence. It is not to be supposed that he who had witnessed all the great things which God had done for His people, and had himself been the chosen instrument in so many of these marvellous works, who had been forty days on Sinai with God, and had seen as much of His glory as mortal eyes might behold and yet live, could be deficient in faith, or doubt that He who had divided the Red Sea and made it stand like a solid wall, and who had rained down bread from heaven, could not also cause water to flow from the hard rock and give His people to drink in the desert. But he looked off from God to man, from the magnificent power and promises of God to the unworthiness of the people, and then he faltered. ‡

* 4 Kings xiii. 19.   † Numbers xx. 11.

‡ The Douai version has the following note on the passage :—" The fault of Moses and Aaron on this occasion was a certain diffidence and weakness of faith ; not doubting of God's power and veracity, but apprehending the unworthiness of that rebellious and incredulous people, and therefore speaking with some ambiguity."

The firm confidence in God which De Renty always evinced was a grand act of worship which he was perpetually paying Him, for it was grounded on the firm faith he reposed in the power, goodness, mercy, and liberality of God, and the infinite merits of our Lord. Looking to these, he hoped all things, and believed he could do all things. If he regarded himself, he said, he could not do anything, however trifling, but casting his eyes on God he was persuaded that nothing was impossible to him. Thus neither his humility nor his mistrust of himself inspired pusillanimous or desponding thoughts, but quite the reverse. They threw him entirely and simply on God. God was his hope, and he knew that whoever places his hope in God shall never be confounded. He was convinced, moreover, that in order to keep up that unwavering confidence in God, we must carefully maintain ourselves in this state of self-distrust. We must, as it were, be always despairing of ourselves. Every grain of reliance on our own powers, which is so ready to creep in along with success, is a kind of larceny and treachery to Him who is our shield and our defence, and who, as David, that great preacher of confidence and hope, expresses it, covers our head in the day of battle.

Writing on this subject to a friend, De Renty observes that the Church, by placing at the beginning of all her offices these words : *Deus, in adjutorium meum intende : Domine, ad adjuvandum me festina*, would remind us of the importance of never placing any trust in self. The soul, it would seem, is ever to regard itself as on the edge of a precipice without support, and to be always crying out for mercy to preserve it from falling. " And, in fact," he adds, " we should fall continually if we were not continually succoured; and as the Office is divided for the seven portions of the day, and the number seven comprehends all time, because it comprehends the weeks, and the world also has been created under this number, the Church would thus teach us that we ought to have this foundation of self-mistrust and expect with confidence all our help from God." He followed this rule faithfully in his own practice; and, while using all the means which prudence dictated and duty required, he committed the result to God without eagerness, without anxiety, without impatience. A man who waits for God must wait for Him at His own good time. God is not our servant; we are His; and, if He deigns to employ us as His instruments, we must never forget our place, or take His affairs into our own hands. Impatience and restlessness more or less render us guilty of this serious fault, and are adverse to the full perfection of Christian hope. De Renty cast himself on God for the future, as well as the present, without reserve. "As for my children," he said, "I place them in the hands of the Holy Child Jesus; I determine nothing, I am ignorant what may happen to-morrow, but He gives me a great reliance on His protection, which renders me blind, and deprives me of all will, while it yet leaves me ready to will anything."

We need scarcely say that with such dispositions De Renty knew not what fear was. He was naturally very resolute and courageous, and upon this was now superinduced a supernatural valour, which made him utterly pass over every consideration which caution might suggest to the boldest. He feared nothing, in short,—nothing except to offend God; sin being the only thing which, properly speaking, can injure a Christian. He went about in town and country (both very unsafe in those unsettled times), not only unattended but unarmed, and that at all hours of the day and night. A friend of his consulted him one day on the subject, observing that he was afraid of traversing the streets of Paris by night without a sword, lest he should be suddenly set upon; and this was by no means a groundless apprehension. De Renty, who had long given up that appendage, replied, "Follow whatever inspiration God shall give you after you have prayed, and remember that He assists us according to our confidence in Him." In one of his letters to his director, we find these words: "With confidence, faith, and love I fear neither devil, nor hell, nor any of man's devices; and I think neither of heaven nor of earth, but to do in everything and everywhere the will of God." We have all Gaston de Renty condensed in these few lines.

But it was in hours of spiritual dryness and abandonment rather than on occasions of bodily danger, to which he literally did not give a thought, that his sublime hope and confidence in God were most remarkably displayed. Job said,* "Though He kill me, yet will I trust in Him;" and truly De Renty might have taken these words for his motto. "It is when we are in a state of dereliction and privation of sensible grace," he writes to an intimate friend, "that heroic abandonment of ourselves to God is to be found; it is like hope in the very midst of despair. Let us be children of the true Abraham; Isaac shall not die although he seems already slain; and, if the true Isaac

* xiii. 15.

2 c

is at last crucified, it is in order that we should find our life in crosses and death."

As hope and confidence impart boldness, so also they minister strength and courage to endure. Words would sometimes be presented to De Renty's mind before he fathomed their full bearing, or, at least, before he recognized the particular impression which at the time they were designed to make upon him. Commonly these were Scripture words, but sometimes he did not recollect whence they came. Thus he says that for a considerable time the words *longanimiter ferens* were continually occurring to him; he could not remember where he had seen them, and scarcely knew what they were designed to tell him, unless it were patiently to wait on God without any proper action of his own save fidelity in seeking grace; when, taking up his New Testament one day, he opened in the 6th Chapter of the Epistle to the Hebrews, where the Apostle speaks of faith and patience, and of their reward, the heritage of the promises : "qui fide et patientiâ hæreditabunt promissiones," alleging the example of Abraham : " *Et sic, longanimiter ferens, adeptus est repromissionem.*"* These words brought great consolation to his soul, as did also the following passage from St. James, which almost immediately caught his eye : " *Patientes igitur estote, fratres, usque ad adventum Domini : ecce agricola exspectat pretiosum fructum terræ, patienter ferens.*"† " I remain thus in

---

* "Who through faith and patience shall inherit the promises" (v. 12). "And so, *patiently enduring*, he obtained the promise" (v. 15).

† "Be patient therefore, brethren, until the coming of the Lord. Behold the husbandman waiteth for the precious fruit of the earth, patiently bearing" (v. 7).

peace," he concludes, "on the foundation of abandonment and confidence." And truly peace was his, an
immovable peace, for it depended on nothing con-
tingent and dwelt in the supreme region which
storms cannot reach. Yet this peace, he would tell
others, is attained through storms, or what bears their
appearance ; for God, to lead us to aspire to it, and to
acquire as well as preserve it, sends us trials and
temptations, that He may place us in the necessity of
seeking Him as our haven of repose and safety.
"Think you," he once asked, "that it was without a
particular Providence that our Lord suffered His
Apostles to put to sea alone in a boat, and permitted
a contrary wind to arise? Who does not know that
it is thus that He fashions the souls of the faithful by
His absences and probations ; that He may afterwards, by coming to show His power over the sea and
the tempests, vivify our faith, manifesting Himself as
the Messias and the true Liberator of the world?"
But many persons, he said, like the Apostles, take
fright when they see Jesus thus walking on the
waters ; everything terrifies them, both within and
without, and Jesus himself is mistaken for a phantom,
unless He makes Himself known still more evidently
to them, and imparts strength and confidence to their
souls.

2 c 2.

CHAPTER V.

WHAT shall we say more of De Renty's love of God?
His whole life was the expression of it; we will here,
then, only add a few remarks as to his interior state
in connection with this queen of virtues. Into this
we obtain some insight from letters to his director.
"The Lord," he writes in 1648, "fills my soul from
time to time with His light, which vivifies it in Him,
and this in so many ways, that what passes in a few
brief moments would take so long and would need so
many words to express, that I do not venture to
attempt it." He sums up all, therefore, in one view,
the same which is in substance constantly recurring,
in one way or another, in his letters, and which
appears to have formed the staple of the vision he
was always inwardly contemplating, and upon which
he was ever feeding his soul. All this light, in short,
converged in the one grand mystery of "the charity
of God in Jesus Christ, His communication of Himself to us by the Incarnation of His Word, and our
communion with Him by the same Word, become our
brother, conversing with us, and bringing us into
society with Him, to be one only in Him, and to
experience what is the charity of God towards us."
Penetrated and inebriated with this truth, he could
see nothing but charity, and feel no impression but of
charity, in every line he read of Holy Scripture:
charity, the end and design of Christianity, "charity

from a pure heart, the end of the commandment."*
"But this charity," he said, "is acquired through
faith in Jesus Christ,—' unfeigned faith,' as the
Apostle designates it,—which binds and unites us to
Him, in order that we may sacrifice to God our souls
and bodies through His Spirit ; which same Spirit
leads us on to this perfect end of the commandment,
and thus gives us to God, and God to us, in charity
and in a most dear, inexplicable union : may He be
blessed for evermore ! "

His fervent aspirations after this perfect union of
love are all marked with the practical stamp of his
character. With his eye ever fixed on the true vocation of man in this world, which may be divided into
the three progressive steps of knowing, loving, and
serving God, it was in the last that he recognized the
full completion of that vocation. " Desires are the
flowers," he would say, " but works are the fruits of
love." But by these good works he did not so much
mean what ordinarily pass by that name, though of
these, as we have seen, his hands were ever full,
but a more inward work, our own self-destruction.
Without this, he said, love was never pure ; " for we
must know "—these are his words, taken from a letter
to a friend—" that our love for God does not consist
in receiving many gifts and graces from Him, but in
much renunciation of self, in forgetting ourselves,
and suffering for His sake, and that perseveringly
and courageously." And who, in fact, ever said or
thought that love consisted in receiving ? Do we not
always rather test it by what it bestows ? The heart
that loves is led, according to the measure of that love,
to think of the object of its love, to seek the interests

* 1 Tim. i. 5.

and procure the glory of the loved one, to do all that can please, and avoid with extreme care all that can offend him.

Love of this kind was the soul and motive of all De Renty did; for, though he performed acts of other virtues, yet they all had their origin in that furnace of charity which burned perpetually within him. Such was the testimony of those who knew him most intimately. One of these observed that the ardour of this love not only was revealed in the glowing words in which at times it found utterance, but would even manifest itself in his external appearance. To this friend it was that De Renty confided that, when he pronounced the Name of God, he tasted on his lips an indescribable sweetness, and was filled with heavenly delights; and to another he wrote, as much as ten years before his death, that he could not conceal from him that he felt a fire in his heart which unceasingly burned and consumed him. What must it have have been as time went on, and he advanced with rapid steps in the ways of divine love! At times, indeed, its transports would be so irrepressible, that he was as one beside himself; and he confessed to an intimate friend that he would have wished to cast himself into a fire to testify his love of God. In his letters to those confidential friends with whom he had frequent communication on spiritual matters, burning words on this subject would often fall from his pen; and so ready was the fire to kindle, that if any strong expression concerning the love of God occurred in the letters of his correspondents, it was like a spark falling upon tinder. "I know not why you insert those words in your letter—*Deus meus et omnia*," he writes to one of them; "but you move me to say to you and to all creatures, My God and my all, my God and my all, my God and my all! If you take them for your device, and send them to me to express the fulness of your heart, can I be silent on receiving them, and not give vent to my own feelings? Know, then, that with me also it is *Deus meus et omnia :* and if you should doubt this, then would I write it a hundred times over. I say no more, for all else is superfluous with him, who has an insight into *Deus meus et omnia.* There I leave you, then, in all jubilation, and conjure you to beg for me the solid grace of these holy words."

De Renty's zeal for God's honour had its pure source in love : this is why there was no hastiness in it, no asperity, no impatience, no indiscretion. Of its extraordinary activity and ardour some notion may have been gathered from what has been related of him ; but much, his director says, remains unknown, either because it was purely spiritual and found no outlet, or because his humility concealed so many of his good deeds even from his most trusted friends. The following passage from a letter to Saint-Jure, written as early as the spring of 1641, will give some idea of the inward transports he so often experienced, leaving him to express desires some of which have a paradoxical sound in our ears, as do similar utterances recorded of the saints. " One day," he says, " moved by a strong wish to be wholly God's, I offered Him all that can be or that cannot be ; I would have willingly given Him all the heavens and all the worlds, if they had been mine ; while, on the other hand, I desired to be beneath all men and in the lowest possible state, and even, supported by His grace, to suffer, with the devils, eternal pains, if He might be more glorified thereby. When in this disposition of tranquil fervour, there is no species of martyrdom, no kind of greatness or littleness, no ornament or despoilment, which, as it passes through the mind, the soul does not accept in order to render honour to God. One would wish to be a king to rule everything, and the lowest of the poor and miserable to suffer everything, and this beyond all reason through excess of reason. It is impossible to understand how, in so short a space of time, one can see so many different things, and it would require a very long discourse to explain any one of them circumstantially. All I could do in this state was to give my liberty to God, recording on paper the gift which I made Him, and signing it with my blood."

If zeal for God's honour is a form which love assumes, and a proof of its ardour, conformity to His holy will is a still more convincing evidence of its strength, and may be reckoned as an infallible token of love. This disposition was most remarkable in him from the very beginnings of his conversion. He did not seem, according to his own testimony, to have had to labour to attain to it gradually; it was a singular grace, with which we find him at once enriched, as part of his special vocation, although he may have been led to manifest it more peculiarly in the latter years of his life, when his will was shown to be entirely absorbed and, so to say, lost in the Divine Will. This conformity was strikingly evinced on all those occasions which are most trying to the affections, when it requires an effort even in excellent Christians to practise so much as the virtue of a loving resignation. De Renty went far beyond this. He not only acquiesced at once in every dispensation

of God, however painful to him, but the Will of God
was so entirely his will that he not only desired it
should be done, but desired it as God desires it : that
is, it became his pleasure as well as his will.   For
God, who is infinitely Blessed, can only will what
He does will with an infinite joy and satisfaction.
Into this joy De Renty entered in all his sorrows.
When, in the year 1641, news was brought to him of
the death of a beloved child (an affliction to which we
have already alluded), he did not utter a word expressive of his own feelings, neither did he manifest
anything except the most entire complacency in God's
holy Will, who had disposed of his child as was best
in His eyes.   Again, in 1643, when he was threatened
with a misfortune which would have tried him far
more severely, the loss of his wife, whom he tenderly
loved, he exhibited like sentiments.   When she had
been given up by the physicians, had lost the use of
speech, and seemed about to expire, his perfect conformity to the Divine Will remained unshaken.   " I
cannot deny," he said, " but that nature in me suffers
great pain at this loss ; but my spirit is filled with so
much joy at beholding myself able to sacrifice to God
a thing so dear to me, that, if a sense of propriety
did not restrain me, I should manifest it outwardly,
and make open demonstration of it."   Such a demonstration, however, he knew well would be greatly
misunderstood, and might shock even good and pious
persons.   Only the saintly mind which has arrived at
feeling that its meat and drink, not its duty alone, is
to do God's will, can fully realize such a combination
of joy and sorrow.

But De Renty's conformity to God's will was carried
into higher and sublimer regions.   Even in the affair

of his own perfection, although he aimed with all the
concentrated powers of his soul to advance in holiness,
nevertheless here also his desires and aspirations were
strictly limited by God's will in his regard. He
desired to be holy only in the manner and degree
which God desired. The sense of adherence to this
Will which he ever carried about with him was
deepened exceedingly after he had given his liberty to
God, and signed the act with his blood; so that he
averred that he not only felt an impossibility of
willing anything save what God willed, but that he
could not so much as conceive how any one could be
otherwise minded.

Love, says St. John, casts out fear, but the fear of
which the Beloved Disciple spoke was servile fear,
not the holy filial fear of God. In the early portion
of his life we noticed the deep sense of abasement
which De Renty felt continually before the Majesty
of God. His inward reverence was so intense that,
in speaking of Him, he was sometimes observed
even to tremble. When walking by himself in the
country, and alone with God, this feeling would often
lead him to uncover his head, and walk exposed
either to the burning rays of a summer sun or to the
chill of winter blasts. Though never without this
abiding sense of reverential awe, he had sometimes
special impressions of this kind, which would last
a considerable time. In June, 1647, we find him
informing his director that he had been for a month
in this state, always occupied with his own meanness
and littleness, like one before the throne of the
Majesty of God, who from confusion and awe does
not dare to lift his eyes. In another letter to a
friend he describes the attitude we ought to preserve

before God by the similitude of a courtier in the presence of his earthly prince, a comparison which had much more appropriateness and cogency in those days than in our own. "These men of the world," he says, "furnish us with an example; for although they may have their heads full of affairs and, moreover, be persons of intelligence and high abilities, yet there they stand, head uncovered, eyes cast down ; their demeanour is modest, they do not utter a word, and think only of observing an attitude of attention ; they have forgotten all else ; and mere human respect produces all this in them with regard to a person who is often their inferior in talents and in natural qualities. How much more ought the holiness, the majesty, and the infinite greatness of God to transport us out of ourselves, and put us in a state of extremest awe !"

The combined reverence and love which thus actuated De Renty gave him that horror of the least offence against a God at once so infinitely good and great which we have witnessed in him. This horror produced great purity of conscience. They who had heard his confessions testified, after his death, to the wonderful tenderness of his conscience. He had, as may be inferred, little of which to accuse himself; and it appears that he experienced in consequence some inconvenience in confessing to any but his ordinary confessor, which, as he explained to a person with whom he was intimate, proceeded from their ignorance of his state, which prevented them from understanding so well what he said, and because he was often himself embarrassed what to say. He was in the habit, as we know, of writing an account of his state to his director ; and to this he added a catalogue of his faults, whether of commission or omission, despatching a letter regularly every month during the last two years of his life. A glance at the contents of some of these reports, preserved by Saint-Jure, will show us how very slight was the nature of his sins, and how few he could recall within the space of a month. In this very circumstance, however, he finds matter for self-reproach, condemning himself for his blindness in not being more fully alive to his failings, of the greatness of which he has, notwithstanding, a profound general impression.

Here is the sum of his offences for one of these months. He had on two occasions said a few ill-humoured words to two of his servants, and he had twice from inattention omitted the *Angelus*. Passing on to another month, we find him recalling two faults of the tongue : they scarcely wear that appearance in our eyes, since not a shadow of detraction or malicious intent can be attributed to them ; but he condemns them. Consulting with some others as to the means to be used for removing some orphan children of heretics into other hands, he " without reflection named two gentlemen, related to them, who would be unwilling to aid in the matter." The other transgression was the letting a person see that he had knowledge of some faults of another, of which, however, he was aware that the individual he was addressing had also cognizance. He does not clearly explain the circumstances, but, from the terms he uses, it would seem that his object was the encouragement in good of the person with whom he was conversing. Yet he says that he instantly felt an inward reproach, as he knew that it would have sufficed to speak well of one without alluding to the defects of another; adding, "it was going too deep into the matter." Clearly with him an unnecessary allusion to the faults of any one, although prompted on the instant by what appeared a good motive, was akin to detraction or, at any rate, a culpable indiscretion.

In another of his monthly reports he has but one solitary offence to record, which, however, he prefaces with a general lamentation on his dulness and obtuseness which intercept the divine light, and on his vileness and ingratitude. He had been occupied the whole day with accommodating some affairs, and towards evening he saw a man come in who, as all were persuaded, had obstinately persisted in a falsehood, upon which he said, " through inconsiderateness and want of recollection, ' There is the man of the lie.' "

We will conclude the list with the two following faults. The first he had felt very much : it was the having made a · remark, which in itself was but trifling, namely, that he had placed a servant in some great house. " I had been moved," he says, " not to mention it, but afterwards it escaped me. I feel it deeply, for we ought to be faithful to the Spirit of God." As he was incapable of going out of his way to say anything which either savoured of vanity or might bear even the appearance of self-satisfaction, it was probably a remark naturally suggested by the subject of conversation, but which his delicate conscience, ever listening to catch the faintest whispers of divine grace, had prompted him to suppress. It was with the disregard of this secret inspiration that he here reproached himself so strongly. The other offence was the having taken precedence of a priest at table. True, he evinced much reluctance, but he says he cannot think how he could have yielded, not to the priest, but to the person of rank who pressed him. He viewed this compliance as being in himself a culpable instance of human respect. Such were the faults, and the worst faults, of this man of God, and truly it requires a spiritual microscope of no little power to detect the grain of evil in the greater number of them.

———

CHAPTER VI.

DE RENTY'S REVERENCE FOR HOLY THINGS AND DEVOTION TO THE BLESSED SACRAMENT.

DE RENTY's veneration for holy things, and for all that appertained to the Divine Service, was the necessary consequence of his love and reverence for God. The eminent degree in which he possessed what is called the virtue of religion was continually shining forth in all his acts and words; and first, he had the deepest reverence for all holy places, and in particular, for churches, a reverence to which his whole bearing as soon as he entered the sacred precincts bore sensible witness. Nothing could exceed the modesty and recollectedness of his behaviour; he would never sit down, not even during the sermon; but as he usually sought those parts of the church frequented by the poor, he was able to avoid any show of singularity while indulging the bent of his piety. He would remain for hours together on his knees; sometimes on great festivals so long as seven or eight consecutive hours. He did not like being addressed while in church; no matter how high the individual's rank might be, he would cut the conversation short; and if more required to be said, he would take the person outside the door, or in some other manner adroitly disengage himself. His veneration for the clergy was unbounded. The inferior ecclesiastical orders shared this respect, but that which he entertained towards priests was truly admirable. He never liked in company to pass before one; it required a species of compulsion to induce him to do so; and we have already seen the sorrow he felt at having allowed himself on one occasion to take precedence of a priest. On meeting one he always humbly saluted him; and, if he were riding, he would alight from his horse; in short, he lost no opportunity of doing honour to the consecrated ministers of the altar. In his own house he welcomed them with mingled cordiality and respect; always gave them the place of honour, and never failed to accompany them to the door at parting.

When a mission was given on any of his estates he had the table' of the priests served with silver plate, reserving pewter for the gentlemen and nobles who visited him. One day a lady and gentleman of high rank came to see him; they were accompanied by a priest who was living with them in the capacity of tutor to their children. As De Renty was conversing with them he espied this priest at the lower end of the hall, where he had remained with the nobleman's suite. Instantly excusing himself civilly to his

distinguished guests, he left them in order to go and
bring forward the priest, and pay him the honour due
to one whom he regarded as the most honourable
person in the company. There was nothing ceremonious or artificial in all this outward reverence. It
came straight from the heart, and was the spontaneous
expression of the high esteem in which he held the
Priesthood. He venerated a priest, not only on account
of the grace of consecration which he had received, but
because in him he beheld one who was able to procure
the greatest glory of God. Of this he was so deeply
convinced that, although contented with the condition
in which Providence had willed to place him, he would
certainly, had it pleased God to dissolve the tie which
bound him to secular life, have desired to embrace
the ecclesiastical state, as he acknowledged to some
one, probably Saint-Jure.

The desire he felt that all ecclesiastics, and priests
especially, should appreciate and live up to their high
vocation was intense ; as was also the pain he suffered
at seeing many even among those with whom he was
personally acquainted, and some of them in places of
much authority and influence, who were very far from
corresponding with their obligations. He could do
nothing but groan in spirit to our Lord, whom he was
continually beseeching to send Apostolic men. " Our
poor sinners, our poor sinners, give us our poor
sinners," was all he could at times ejaculate over and
over again ; by which, as he himself explains, he
meant, " Send us Apostles," for his whole mind was
so full of these sinners that he could find no other
words to express his longing desire for their conversion. He had before his interior eye a vision of what
the Apostles were, and what those must be who, after

their example, would "catch men." "I saw them," he says, "simple externally, but inwardly great Princes, who, though their life and appearance were mean in the eyes of men, and far removed from all pomp of this world, converted souls by their sanctity, by their prayers, by their vigilance, and by their labours. And I also marked a very common delusion, which is this : that people fancy that exterior grandeur and show serve much to accredit a man, and render him more capable of aiding his neighbour in the matter of his salvation ; but this is a gross mistake, for it is grace which has power over souls, and it is a humble and holy life which wins hearts." He deplored exceedingly the slovenly, hurried way in which so many ecclesiastics performed the offices of the Church, without devotion, and often even without outward decorum, while others assisted thereat in a like spirit." "What a pity !" he exclaims, after witnessing an example of this indifference ; "where is our faith ? My eyes were ready to pour forth a torrent of tears, but I had to restrain them and do violence to myself."

He had also great love and reverence for persons who had embraced the religious life, and aided with . all his power such as were desirous of devoting themselves to that state ; encouraging them to hold firm their vocation in spite of all outward opposition, which will sometimes, by the noise it makes and the clouds of perplexity it raises, arrive at obscuring, if it does not stifle, the inward light which God is vouchsafing to the soul. "I pray our great God," he writes to one whose vocation met with much opposition, "to deliver you from the process of human reasoning, which often in these matters is perfectly endless ; at

the same time assuring you that, if you give no heed
to it, He will manifest Himself to you ; I mean that
He will console and fortify you in faith concerning
your call, and in the experience of the gifts of the
Holy Spirit ;" those gifts whose teaching and illumination transcend all human reasoning. To another he
writes in similar terms, " Blessed for ever be the Holy
Child Jesus for the entrance into religion of those
two good souls of whom you speak. I rejoice in their
perseverance, which denotes a strong vocation. If
that other person you know of had a little more
confidence and strength to break her bonds, she would
strike a good blow for herself. So much wisdom and
examination is not wanted for dedicating ourselves to
the foolishness of the Gentiles and the stumbling-
block of the Jews. The world is a strange deceiver
and trifler; it is to be met with everywhere, and infects
almost everything. God has no need whatsoever of
our fine parts and excellent qualities ; it pleases Him
sometimes to confound the wise by His choice of the
little. Happy littleness, which is often reckoned as
meanness, and which nevertheless vanquishes all the
might and prudence of the flesh ! "

He was so impressed with the blessedness of the
religious state, that sometimes, when talking to nuns,
he would suddenly burst forth in a strain of heartfelt
congratulation. " Oh, my sisters, how happy you
are ! " he would exclaim ; and would then proceed
to speak to them in language so impressive on the
subject of their vocation as powerfully to excite them
to increased gratitude to God and courage to advance
in well-doing.

He was very devout to all the Saints, but he had a
special devotion to St. Joseph and St. Teresa, the

latter of whom, since the year 1640, he had chosen as his mother and mistress in the spiritual life. Far greater still were his love and veneration for the Queen of all saints, the Blessed Mother of God, to whom he had consecrated himself at Ardilliers, when, while yet a youth, he ran away to become a Carthusian. In the same year he joined a Congregation erected to her honour in the professed house of the Jesuits of Saint-Louis. He wore on his arm for several years a signet, on which was engraven an image of our Lady with her Divine Son in her arms; in memory, no doubt, of those words of the Spouse in the Canticles : " Put Me as a seal upon thy heart, as a seal upon thy arm ;" * and he usually sealed his letters with it. He reckoned that, even as we can give no greater pleasure to Mary than by loving her Son. so can we render no more agreeable service to Jesus than by loving His Mother. He delighted in speaking of her by her title of "Mother Most Admirable;" and amongst many other testimonies of his love, we may here record that he gave to the Image of Notre Dame de Grace a heart of gold enclosing one of crystal, intended to represent his own, which he had dedicated to her.

We have already had occasion to observe the great love and honour with which this good man regarded the Spouse of the Lamb, the Holy Catholic Church, reverencing all that came from her, all that apper-tained to her, to the very fringes of her garments. Words could not express the veneration in which he held her rites and ceremonies, and all that she had touched and blessed. He confessed to experiencing a special grace and virtue in the prayers employed in the ritual of the Church, and rejoiced to conform himself

* Cant. viii. 6.

to all her usages and partake in all her exercises.
When he assisted at High Mass in his parish church
he never omitted going up at the Offertory with the
common people; he made a point of assisting at all
religious ceremonies, even at those not usually much
frequented, such as the Blessing of the Font on Holy
Saturday, for he would miss no opportunity of finding
himself in the health-giving atmosphere and amidst
the scattered benedictions of Holy Church. It was
the same with respect to the popular processions, so
numerous in those days; he always followed them
whenever he possibly could, without regard to distance
or weather. In a letter to a friend we find his sentiments recorded on this subject. "Our procession,'
he says, "goes to-day to our *faubourg*, and we must
follow its standard, since our Lord has shown us
this great mercy in causing us to belong to His little
people. I regard it as a singular honour to follow
the Cross in their company whithersoever the Church,
our Mother, may lead us; for there is nothing in her
but what is great, seeing that all is done in the spirit
of religion before God, and represents great mysteries
to those who are lowly and reverential."

Honouring as he thus did all the ceremonies and
devotional practices of the Church, and rejoicing that
she should be surrounded with all that could pay
her homage and worthily adorn her, he was very
solicitous that Christians, while witnessing her
external pomp, should not satisfy themselves with
mere external honour, or with that superficial admiration which does not go beyond the imagination and
the senses. No one could be more deeply penetrated
with the conviction that God, to be worshipped
acceptably, must be worshipped "in spirit and in

truth." Something has been said already of his fears lest even the magnificence of churches and the beauty of their decorations should arrest the vain gaze and attention of men, instead of carrying them on to the interior worship of the God of all glory, thus diverting them from their true end instead of helping to direct them to it. "We must remember," he writes to a friend, "the simplicity in the midst of which our Divine Mysteries were accomplished, that we may not be engrossed with the display which now attends their celebration. This thought was suggested to me as I heard the music and the organs, and beheld the splendour accompanying the performance of the divine office : we must seek amid this pomp the simple, pure, and lowly spirit with which these Mysteries of our religion were first instituted. Not that all this ceremonial is not holy, but we must pass beyond it to the simplicity and poverty of Bethlehem, of Nazareth, of Egypt, of the Desert, and of the Cross."

What he had peculiarly at heart, was to unite himself in spirit, in will, and in intercommunion of good things with all the faithful in all places,—in fine, with the whole Church, on earth and in heaven ; thus realizing the Communion of Saints, an article of the Creed for which he had a peculiar spiritual relish. This gave him a large-heartedness which embraced all with an equal love, as belonging to Christ's mystical Body, no matter what their nation or profession or state of life might be. He had none of those narrow partialities from which pious persons are sometimes not entirely free, none of that disposition to balance praise of one thing or one person by dispraise of another, a subtle form of detraction not always easy to detect. He was averse to comparisons, never

a very safe exercise ; his love for one Order in the
Church, for instance, did not diminish his esteem for
the rest, but he entertained a general approbation and
affection for all in their several degrees.

Whoever is familiar with the writings of M. Olier,
with whom, as the reader knows, De Renty was
closely united in good works, and with whom he had
many spiritual affinities, will have observed how
intimate was the realization of the Communion of
Saints which the great founder of St. Sulpice habitually enjoyed. In this respect, as in several more,
they remind us of each other. De Renty's sensible
union with the saints underwent, however, at one
period a certain suspension, or, rather, absorption,
caused by the special application of his mind at that
time. This subtraction was in the first instance a
subject of distress to him until he was favoured with
further light. In a letter to his director we find his
own account of how this sensible realization of the
Communion of Saints and of their presence with him
was withdrawn, and how restored ; and how, also, it
was explained to him that by union with God we are
drawn into unity with His saints, and that by union
with the saints we are united in God, the two unions
being one in Him. "The operation," he says, "which
I have experienced for two or three years has always
constrained me to follow our Lord Jesus Christ, and
to find in Him life eternal in the presence of His
Father through the homage of His Spirit, of which I
have from time to time given you an account ; and I
must tell you that although I continued all the while
to honour in the depth of my heart our Lady, the
Saints, and the Angels, and although I desired to
testify the same on every occasion, nevertheless their

presence was obscured, and, as it were, set aside in my mind. I must confess to you that this thought frequently occurred to me, and I said to myself, " I honour our Lady so much, and I have also a special honour for certain Saints and Angels, and yet I feel not to know where they are. I used to raise my heart to them, it is true, but I had no sense of their presence, at least none like what I seem to experience now : for some months ago I had a great opening and light afforded me, accompanied with powerful impressions with reference to charity and precious union, causing me to conceive things inexplicable of God, Father, Son, and Holy Ghost, who is Charity ; and this came to me, not by reasoning and intellectual apprehension, but by a most simple view, and by a touch penetrating the heart with love ; and I knew that the Son of God, our Lord, came by His Incarnation to bring us this charity, and that He has united Himself to us, to make us all to be one in this intimate and dear union, until He shall have consummated us all in Himself, to be one day all one in God, when He shall give up the kingdom to Him,— *ut sit Deus omnia in omnibus*—and we shall enter into this dear unity of the Father, Son, and Holy Ghost. About ten or twelve days ago, having begun my morning prayer to God as usual, I felt within me that I had no access to Him : there I remained in a state of humiliation. The sight of the Father, access to the Son, with whom I usually speak with as much confidence as it He were still here on earth, and the assistance of His Holy Spirit, all seemed to be removed to an exceeding distance from me ; and I experienced such a sense of my own unworthiness, so genuine and so penetrating, that I could not venture to raise the eyes of my soul any more than those of my body.

"Then was it made known to me that I was indeed unworthy, as I felt myself to be, but that I was to seek access to God and our Lord in the Communion of Saints : instantly I was seized with an inexplicable feeling of veneration, love, and union with the Blessed Virgin, the Angels, and the Saints present with me. I cannot tell you the greatness and solidity of this grace ; for it is Life Eternal, it is Paradise ; and it is this union with the Saints in heaven and with those on earth of which I always, or almost always, enjoy the perception and the presence. Then I knew that our God and Lord has not made us that we may be alone and separate, but that we may be united to others, and by our union compose with them a divine whole. As a fair stone, such as might form the capital of a column, is useless if it is not in the place destined for it, and until it is laid therein and cemented into the body of the building lacks both its meaning and its beauty—in a word, has not attained its end—even so this grace has left me in the love and in the true experimental bond of communion and communication with the Saints, in the order, however, of those with whom I am the most closely joined, which is my life in God and in Jesus Christ our Lord."

We need scarcely say that one who loved Jesus so entirely, and who thus lived for Him and in Him, was most tenderly devout to Him in that dearest pledge of His love which He has left us on our altars, even Himself to abide with us for ever. The Blessed Eucharist, both as sacrifice and as sacrament, was indeed the object of his deepest devotion and continual adoration. He not only heard Mass every day, at which he considered it a high honour to be allowed to act as server, but he also communicated daily unless some urgent work of charity happened to interfere ; and per-haps he could give no stronger proof of his love than by thus leaving Jesus for Jesus. The Blessed Sacrament was the magnet which kept him fixed in the church for hours on his knees ; and to a friend who wondered how he could remain there for such a length of time, he replied that it was there he found repose and re-freshment to his spirit and renewed his strength.

This repose and refreshment, however, was not always to be acquired without a previous struggle. In June, 1647, he thus writes to his director :—"I have been very poor the whole of this month, and I do not know that I have been ever more so, as respects sensible devotion, or that I was ever more heavy in body and mind than I was during the whole day on the Festival of the Blessed Sacrament. I went through all like a veritable beast,—Office, Procession, Mass, Communion, Sermon, Vespers, Compline ; I did not know what to do with myself, whether standing or sitting. I had a fidgety feeling in my body; and in my mind a sen-sation of vagueness ; nevertheless, I knew that at the bottom of my heart I desired to honour God in our Lord Jesus Christ. After Compline I felt so extremely heavy that, finding myself unable to remain before the Blessed Sacrament, for I was ready to drop down, I wanted to prove whether I might not be the better for retiring aside for awhile, and giving way a little to my drowsiness ; but I became in consequence only worse harassed and more oppressed in body and mind, so that I felt quite capable of laying myself down flat on the floor. I then recalled to mind some-thing I formerly read in a paper you gave me, of a

certain drowsiness which overtook a person of much
virtue; immediately I rose and repaired to the foot of
the Crucifix which is before the Blessed Sacrament,
being determined to honour our Lord in whatever
state I might find myself.   I had no sooner knelt
down, and by God's help had won the victory over
myself, than my mind was opened, and I received a
light from the Blessed Sacrament, instructing me that,
in order to be moulded into a bread having some
similitude to It, I must first be ground like grain,
then kneaded with water, and finally baked by fire,
and that such was the means whereby one has to
become incorporated with the mysterious Bread, Jesus
Christ; and at the same instant that He showed me all
this at one glance, I experienced so ardent a desire to
undergo this process, that it has remained with me
ever since.   The corn, the breaking, and the bruising
in the mill have proved a good nourishment to me;
the water of afflictions is excellent for kneading and
giving a fresh form to the flour; but the crowning
perfection is the oven of divine love, which imparts
consistence and colour."   He then goes on to develop
and enlarge upon the comparison which had been so
forcibly suggested to him, between the material and
the super-substantial bread, and adds, that during the
whole octave of the Blessed Sacrament many things
were shown to him concerning It.   He thus concludes :—"Jesus Christ, broken and ground by His
Passion, gives Himself to us to eat, in order that we
may announce and express His death, His charity,
and His virtues in our lives.   Here I abide all
enamoured of Jesus Christ, desirous to be wholly His
and to render Him back by affection all that He has
given to me, my goods, my body, my soul, my time,

and my eternity. I feel a great thirst to serve Him and experience desires which I reserve to tell you when I shall have the honour of seeing you."

His great love for the Adorable Sacrament made him write in large letters over the mantelpiece in his Castle of Citry, " Praised for ever be the Blessed Sacrament of the Altar," and impelled him to visit on foot all the churches in the neighbourhood, to see in what manner the Blessed Sacrament was reserved. To many poor churches he presented silver ciboriums, as also tabernacles, which he had himself made and gilded, for he was wonderfully skilful at all handicraft. On the 26th of December, 1646, we find him writing to Saint-Jure, " I have begun this Advent to do what I have long desired, viz., to fill up the time not demanded by any urgent affairs with some manual work : this time generally occurs between supper and the hour for prayer. To carry out this design, I have arranged a little work-room, where I carve tabernacles for the Blessed Sacrament: supposing I should make only one a month, the time would be usefully employed, and some necessitous church supplied."

As early as the year 1641 this love, always active in him, had led him to form an association of ladies in his parish of St. Paul, who should, each in their turn, pray an hour before the Blessed Sacrament. He also wrote a little treatise to encourage this practice, showing that, as our Lord is continually present in this Adorable Mystery that He may communicate Himself to us, it was most reasonable that there should always be some persons in the churches where He abides to render Him their homage and so satisfy the desire He has to communicate Himself to us. We see De Renty here aspiring after that Devotion

of the Perpetual Adoration which our day has seen
carried out so widely. He modestly presented his
little work to the parish priest for his approval; and
Saint-Jure tells us that the devotion which it encouraged still continued to flourish years after De
Renty's death, and that it spread to other parishes.
It took root, also, at Dijon, where this indefatigable
man succeeded in establishing it in the face of
many difficulties. His devotion to Jesus in the
Blessed Sacrament also led him to persuade many
persons in his parish to adopt the practice of following
Him when borne to the sick and dying; and he
might himself be continually seen, with lighted candle
in his hand, thus honouring our Lord as He passed
along the streets. Notwithstanding his pressing
occupations, and no matter what the inclemency of
the season, he did not grudge giving a considerable
portion of the morning to this pious act; and in a
large and populous parish such occasions must have
been of constant occurrence. One day, when the
weather was very bad, and he had himself a severe
cold, some friends urged him to forego his usual
custom, for, ill as he was, he was almost certain to
suffer from remaining so long exposed, bare-headed,
to the chilling wind and rain; but nothing could
restrain the ardour of his devotion: go he must, and
he did go, and, strange to say, returned freed from his
cold—and yet perhaps not strange, for what in another
would have been an act of rash imprudence, was in
him a simple correspondence with the great grace
with which he was favoured. Grace, not impetuous
nature, prompted these holy indiscretions: what
wonder, therefore, if, as in the previous instance just
related, when he refused to succumb to the bodily

oppression and fatigue which was bowing him to the earth, the grace which prompted his heroic refusal to yield to nature should also triumph over nature !

We will conclude with another example of his ardent love for the Blessed Sacrament, and of the zeal which consumed him for Its honour. One day, as he was accompanying our Lord in the streets, the procession was met by a nobleman's carriage drawn by six horses. As the occupants of the vehicle, probably Huguenots, neither caused it to stop nor so much as prepared to salute the King of kings, De Renty's indignation burned hot in his bosom ; in spite of all his meekness, the spirit of the soldier was not dead within him : it was as strong, indeed, as ever, only it was now enlisted in another and a holier cause, and he would not tamely behold his Lord thus grossly insulted. Without a moment's hesitation, therefore, he rushed forward just as the carriage was rapidly passing, and, seizing the reins, headed back the leaders. God rewarded his generous daring. The horses all stopped short on the instant, and De Renty held them fast until the Blessed Sacrament had passed by, thus, to the great admiration and delight of the spectators, compelling these people to pay the act of respect they had so insolently withheld.

CHAPTER VII.

DE RENTY'S DIFFERENT STAGES OF PRAYER.

PRAYER is the feeder of the soul's spiritual life in all stages of its progress, because it is the conduit of grace. De Renty was a man of prayer. Prayer, indeed, may be said to have been his one occupation, for with him every act, every word, every suffering, every thought was a prayer, because all was directed or offered to God. Hence what may be called the nutritive process of his soul was always going on, the channel of supply was always full and flowing. All this has been already abundantly proved, and it is not necessary to demonstrate it afresh. Neither do we purpose to speak of his vocal prayers : these have already been noticed sufficiently ; it is to mental prayer exclusively that we intend to advert.

It is possible certainly to be a good and pious Christian by the devout use of vocal prayer alone,*

---

* It is, of course, not meant to be here asserted that vocal prayer *necessarily* excludes mental : the rosary, for instance, is intended to combine meditation with vocal prayer. Still less would it be safe to lay it down as a rule that none can attain the perfection which God designs for them without practising mental prayer, as it is usually understood. St. Teresa tells us that she knew an aged and a very virtuous and penitent woman, whom for her excellence she would have been glad to resemble, who spent her whole time in continual vocal prayer, without ever being able to practise meditation. In such cases it is evident that there is an incapacity for any other form of prayer. The Holy Spirit is not restricted to any rule, and prayer is a means, not an end. Speaking generally, however, it would be true, we suppose, to say that

but it is hard to conceive any one who is capable of mental prayer arriving at a high degree of perfection without cultivating the habit of it—we mean in some form or other, for we are speaking of the practice itself, not of any particular methods, which, after all, are only helps thereto. For it is by mental prayer we come to know ourselves truly, to realize more deeply the mysteries of the faith, to extract the hidden manna from the words of Holy Scripture, and to elicit interior acts of virtue, thus becoming prepared for a more familiar and intimate access to God, to which He does not fail to raise those who humbly and perseveringly seek His face.

Saint-Jure, when entering on this matter of prayer, observes that, having to treat of difficult things, it might be desirable for him to give a few words of preliminary explanation. If one who was himself so deeply versed in the science of mystical theology spoke thus, we might well draw back from touching at all on the subject, had we to do anything more than follow closely in his steps. To this we shall, therefore, limit ourselves, and simply reproduce briefly the substance of what he says. M. de Renty, he tells us, had experimental knowledge of all the different modes of mental prayer, having ascended its four degrees, the first of which is the prayer of reasoning and discourse ; the second, which is superior to it, being affective prayer ; the third, the prayer of union or contemplation. Now, contemplation is of two

if a soul would advance in the spiritual and interior life its first step must be the cultivation of the practice of medita-tion ; and that total incapacity for anything above ordinary vocal prayer—that is to say, for either meditation or con-templation—would seem to indicate an ordinary vocation.

sorts: the active, which may possibly be acquired;
and the passive, which is infused, and counts as the
fourth and highest degree of prayer.

The prayer of reasoning, or discourse, is commonly
called meditation, and is an exercise familiar to
devout Catholics. It consists, as all know, in the
application of the mind—the imagination, memory,
and understanding—to some subject, whether it be
an incident in our Lord's life, a mystery of the Faith,
some passage of Holy Scripture, some Christian virtue,
or other like matter, with the view of moving the
will, through the consideration of motives thus elicited
and presented to the intellect, to entertain good affections, and form good resolutions. The different aids
to meditation, of which we possess a rich variety, and
which are usually grounded on the method taught by
St. Ignatius, are chiefly directed to facilitate the practice of this mode of mental prayer, which is the most
common and the most general, and that through
which, in the ordinary way, those even must pass
who are destined to attain to higher degrees. God,
we know, can raise a soul at once to a state of contemplation, but these are exceptional cases; at any
rate, we cannot thus raise ourselves; consequently, if
not otherwise attracted by grace, we must begin at
the beginning. De Renty, then, commenced by this
kind of prayer, mostly selecting his subject of meditation from the Life or Passion of our Lord.

After having been faithful and assiduous in the
practice of this first degree for some time, he was
raised to the next in order, affective prayer. This
prayer consists in a familiar and affectionate interior
conversation with our Lord, without preliminary discourse of the reason, and employing but few words.

It is a communication with God present and abiding in the soul, which, quitting considerations and re-searches, which before were needed by it in order to find God or to realize some verity of the faith, now, at the simple thought or remembrance of Him, is attracted towards Him, and pours itself forth in interior acts of praise, blessing, adoration, thanks-giving, oblation, petition, but, above all, in acts of charity, which most closely unite us to our Sovereign Good. The previous discourse of the reasoning faculty is dispensed with, because it was but the means em-ployed for the enlightening of the understanding in order to the moving of the will; but the intellect at this spiritual stage finds itself sufficiently enlightened through its previous meditations, and needs not to go over the ground again, or to seek fresh motives to excite the affections. The method, then, pursued is simply to retire into the secret depth of the heart, and turning to God, present there, not by a chain of reasoning, but by faith, which at once apprehends Him, thus to remain in His presence under the im-pressions of reverence, adoration, self-humiliation, and filial love, which faith in that presence produces, mak-ing acts of the several Christian virtues and affections, according as grace shall move thereto. This kind of prayer is sometimes called the prayer of the presence of God, on account of its initiatory act ; or the prayer of faith and of affection, because of the second act pro-duced by the soul, in which it exercises faith, and pours itself forth in affections of various kinds, accord-ing as it is prompted or finds most facility. Variety, however, is not needed, one affection sufficing, if it should furnish sufficient occupation for the whole time.*

* We have followed the explanation of affective prayer

2 E

De Renty practised affective prayer for some years,
during which he gathered a large store of spiritual
riches.   He thus speaks of this kind of prayer in one
of the papers he left :—" This prayer does not proceed
by the way of reasoning and research, but by a loyal
love, which is ever tending rather to give than to
receive. Faith, in its obscurity, brings more certainty
than all the lights it can receive, of which lights,
however, the soul must avail itself with reverence and
thankfulness, without indulging in self-complacency
or becoming attached to them.   This prayer requires
no mental effort, and does not try the head ; it is a
state of modest presence before God, in which you
maintain yourself, looking to His Spirit to suggest
what He pleases to you, and receiving it in simplicity
and confidence just as if He spoke to you."   It was
De Renty's way to begin his prayer by humbling
himself to the dust in the presence of God, regarding

given by Saint-Jure in his Life of M. de Renty.   He does not
aim at entering into the subject with any detail, but is only
giving a general and comprehensive idea of its character.
Other spiritual writers will be found to divide the prayer of
affection into two degrees, to the higher of which would perhaps more properly belong the appellations of the prayer of
the presence of God and the prayer of faith.   Indeed, it
seems a little difficult to draw a rigid line of distinction between the more advanced stages of internal affective prayer,
as described, for instance, by Father Baker in his valuable
work, *Sancta Sophia*, and *active* contemplation.   (See Treatise III. on the Degrees of Prayer.)   A passage subsequently
quoted from Saint-Jure would seem also to imply as much.
Internal prayer of the will and affections may thus, as he in
common with other spiritual writers represents it, be regarded
as a preparation — more or less remote, according to the
degree at which the soul has arrived—for the prayer of contemplation and union.

himself as a mere atom, and less than an atom ; then straightway to excite in himself perfect confidence in His Infinite goodness and mercy, from which he hoped all things. Those whom he thought fitted he often encouraged to adopt this method of prayer, which required neither penetration nor intellectual power, nor intense application of mind, a thing difficult and, indeed, impossible to so many : all that was needed was simply to believe and to love. The profit derived was also far greater.

He considered it to be most desirable that, when praying, persons should give themselves more to the operations of the will than to the speculations of the understanding, and allow much greater scope to the action of faith than to that of reason. As reason was given to us to discern natural things, so faith is imparted to us to make us acquainted with divine things, which are seen by the light which grace imparts, not by that of the understanding. We discourse with men by reasoning, but with God by faith. He needs not our much speaking, which here is not only superfluous, but out of place. The light of faith is very superior to that of the natural understanding. Not only does it reveal things to which the reason cannot attain, but even those which reason can comprehend are reached by its means circuitously and with labour, while faith realizes them at a glance. Besides, the knowledge acquired by reason partakes of the imperfection and inferiority of the medium by which it has been obtained. " Whatever knowledge we may have on earth," observes Saint-Jure, " of God and of spiritual things, this knowledge is always in some manner deceptive, for it does not represent things as they truly are, because our mind cannot here below conceive anything which has not first passed through the senses, where spiritual things contract a kind of materiality, and take a form, thereby becoming falsified and disguised ; but faith shows them as they are." Hence the prayer that proceeds by the way of faith is much superior to that which avails itself of the discursive reason.

If the number of those who pass on from meditation to affective prayer is comparatively limited, particularly of those who solidly attain to it (for many more enjoy touches of it, and make occasional approaches to it, while still remaining in the lower degree), the number of those who mount higher is still smaller, whether it be that God does not invite many to these sublime states, or that He meets in very few with sufficient correspondence to His invitations. De Renty, however, was of that happy number. From the prayer of affection he was attracted and raised to the prayer of contemplation and union, in which he was elevated to a very high degree. Contemplation, as we have observed, is of two kinds. The active, as it is usually called, may be acquired with the aid of Divine grace,* but the passive is altogether beyond the power of the holiest, most diligent, and most faithful soul to attain, for it is the pure gift of God, infused by Him into the soul, which contributes nothing of its own save the consent wherewith it receives this divine operation ; and for this reason it is called passive. God gives it as He pleases and when He

* It is not meant here to assert that all indiscriminately may attain to active contemplation, for which certainly all are not fitted, and to which all are by no means attracted, but that it *is* attainable, if God so will ; whereas passive contemplation can in no case and under no circumstances be acquired.

pleases, and withdraws it in like manner, no effort
availing for its retention any more than for its acquisition. All that a person can do is to dispose himself
for the reception of so high a favour, should God be
pleased to bestow it; but as there is no use in striving
after it, so also are we enjoined not to aspire to it.
It is otherwise with active contemplation, at which
persons who are capable of it, and are attracted
towards it, may be encouraged to aim.

Active contemplation, then, consists in a simple
regard, or view, of the soul directed towards God or
some spiritual truth, resulting in admiration, love,
and other divine affections, and preceded by no previous discourse of the reason. This definition may
readily be understood by a comparison with natural
contemplation, which is the quiet viewing and
regarding of any object, either externally or mentally
present, with the accompanying impressions and
sentiments resulting therefrom. For instance, when
you behold one dear to you in pain and suffering, the
sight elicits in you feelings of pity, of sympathy, of
desire to console and relieve him, and the like, without any accompanying process of reasoning. The
same may be said of the image of such a sight recalled
by the mind. And so it is with the soul in contemplation, say, of our Lord, in the different stages of His
Passion : whereas in meditation it made use of
reasoning to produce considerations which might
move it to acts of the affections and of the will, and
even in affective prayer it had to use some effort to
elicit these acts,* it now produces them at once by a

* Father Baker calls these acts "forced immediate acts
of the will." "In forced immediate acts of the will," he says,
"especially at the beginning, there is some degree of medita-

simple regard. Even these acts themselves cease to
be multiplied, and become more simple and subtle.
The soul also, like Magdalen at the Saviour's feet,
tends rather to listen to what God may inwardly
speak than to speak much itself, even in the form of
affections. Hence our Lord bade His disciples, when
praying, not to speak much, by which speaking He
intended not merely the utterance of the tongue, but
also that of the understanding and the other mental
faculties. He Himself is called the Word, and He
desires us to listen to Him—a desire expressed in that
often-recurring phrase: "He that hath ears to hear
let him hear." Father Avila, who wrote a treatise on
the words: "*Audi, filia*—Hearken, O daughter," from
the 44th Psalm, tells us that we ought to address
ourselves to prayer rather in order to listen than to
speak; and he confessed to F. Lewis of Granada,
who wrote his Life, that, when about to enter on this
holy exercise, he used to tie up his understanding as
if it were a maniac, that he might hinder himself from
being loquacious.

"There are certain souls," observes Saint-Jure,
"who when at their prayers are always talking, their

tion, which is the thinking on the object and thereupon producing the act or affection itself, and quietly continuing and
resting in it till all the virtue be spent. There is likewise
always some use of images, and in the beginning these images
are more gross, but afterwards, by practice, they grow more
pure, and all manner of discourse ceaseth; yea, the soul will
begin to reject all distinct images, and apprehend God without any particular representation, only by that obscure
notion which faith informs us of His totality and incom-
prehensibility; and this only is truth, whereas all distinct
images are but imperfect shadows of truth."—*Sancta Sophia*,
tom. iii., s. iii., c. i.

persuasion being that the secret consists in being always speaking to God, unceasingly employing their faculties in producing acts, and never listening ; without reflecting that what God would say to them would be far better and more profitable to them than what they can say to Him, and that in conversation and when talking with anybody we do not keep speaking to him, but first we speak and then we listen : so also in your prayers, speak to our Lord and then hearken to Him, attending silently and respectfully to what He may have to say to you." Such is the practice followed in active contemplation, and here Saint-Jure points out wherein the first three degrees of prayer differ from each other. "The understanding," he says, "acts more than the will in discursive prayer, the will more than the understanding in affective prayer ; although it must be noted that beginners are not at their first entrance entirely without discourse, but this discourse diminishes gradually, until it ceases altogether.* Moreover, they at first abound in a variety of acts of affection, but in the end they make much fewer. In the prayer of union " (by which he here means active contemplation and union, not passive) "the will predominates also over the understanding, but with more simplicity than in the prayer of affection ; moreover, God now operates more and man less, and His operation is of a purer and more spiritual and divine character : this is why he ought to await in peace and confidence the action of God, without eagerness."

De Renty reckoned that the great imperfection of souls commonly consists in their not waiting suffi-

* This is precisely what Father Baker says, as quoted in previous note.

ciently for God. Unsubdued nature is very busy, and never wants for specious pretexts to bestir itself; besides, it thinks that it is doing wonders when it is simply hindering the operations of God in the soul by the agitation and disquiet it creates; for, in order to receive divine impressions, tranquillity and silence are needed. Such was his opinion, and he acted upon it. It may occur to some, that by thus suppressing all inward discourse, and simplifying internal acts, the soul is really doing less than it did previously, and is in danger even of losing its time. "This would be an error," says Saint-Jure; "it is, on the contrary, employing its time very well, since by retrenching the action of the senses and inward discourse it removes that which keeps it at a distance from God, who is infinitely above all discursive reasoning, and still more above all that belongs to the senses; so that in going by the way of faith and the affections of the will the soul draws nigh to Him. To proceed by this road is to advance and make great progress."

We find among De Renty's papers passages which also reply to the objection raised above. "Some one will say," he writes, "'often nothing comes to me in prayer; I fear to lose my time in idleness.' Know, however, that you do not lose your time when by losing yourself you place yourself in reverence and confidence before God to offer Him your homage. He cannot take such a proceeding amiss. Another will say, 'I have had distractions, I have found myself in great dryness of spirit, and I am harassed by many other troubles.' I reply, Persevere, notwithstanding all these difficulties, as much as you can in your regard of faith and reverence, and in your affections; keep yourself close and shut up in the cabinet of your heart; let all these tempests growl outside without heeding them, after the example of Noe, who was so peaceful, as his name itself imports, in the interior of his vessel, although it was beaten on all sides by the waves and rocked by the storms. The soul needs this to purify it and dispose it for the operations of God. As the green wood before flaming exudes and throws out its humidity, and has to go through this purgation in order to be fit to kindle, in like manner distractions and all kinds of imaginations assail us, according as God pleases. But do not let us disquiet ourselves on that account, or withdraw from the holy exercise of prayer; let us simply turn away our attention from these miseries when we perceive them, and continue quietly making our oblation, being assured that we shall not have to support the Lord's absence long without His coming to us."

He had himself experimental knowledge of such states, and sometimes, when alone, he would protest aloud to God that His he would be, in spite of all these distractions and aridities. "I am Thine," he would exclaim, "and will be Thine for ever without reserve. Thou hast created me, and I will love Thee for ever." Sometimes he would trace similar ejaculations on the ground with his finger, sometimes on his heart. "I am content," he would say, "with all that God wills and orders for me, and I desire nothing beyond. I will not strive either after consolation or to free myself from dryness; my determination is to bless God at all times." To his director we find him writing, "I am sometimes an hour or two at prayer before anything comes to me; sometimes I suffer through dryness, distractions, and lassitude, but, in

whatever manner it may be, I never end without
being willing to begin again, and without a renewed
desire to pray. Sometimes my bodily lassitude will
all at once vanish through an interior strength communicated to me, which disposes me to continue my
prayer out of the time and place of prayer and in the
very midst of conversation and business ; and I can
sincerely tell you that, although I do everything very
ill, nevertheless as regards prayer I experience no
difference at any time, for I find myself recollected
whatever may be my employment." To another
person he wrote as follows : " I remained the other
day three or four hours in church in a state of great
dryness, without anything coming to me whereon to
fix my mind. Meanwhile I heard a good servant of
God behind me reciting a chaplet of Glorias, and the
like. I offered what he said to God, until all of a
sudden it was shown to me that when the soul is
alone in a desert, where she has nothing created on
which to lean, then it is that the cord of the pure
love of God. is given to her, being thrown to her
from heaven to attract her ; and I experienced something of this kind. Although nothing may be suggested to me, yet, when I have finished my prayer, I
should always be quite ready to recommence."

Thus did this holy man labour to turn to account
and cultivate the talent he had received, the gift of
active contemplation ; and God rewarded him by the
bestowal of the passive and infused. In this state
the intellect is illuminated by great lights, and the
will filled with ardent affections, and specially with
love, without any labour or contribution of its own.
Indeed, it must forego all activity of that nature
in order to enjoy it. " Even as Moses, that perfect

image of contemplatives," says Saint-Jure, "in order to fit himself to ascend the Mount of Sinai, there to hold converse with God, left the flocks, and the people, small and great, his very brother Aaron, and even Josue his minister, who was his constant attendant, and thus all alone sought the summit of the mountain, where he entered into a sacred cloud in which God abode—*accessit ad caliginem in quâ erat Deus*—as the Scripture says, and remained there forty days in contemplation and intimate converse with the Divine Majesty, so also must the soul leave the senses, the reasoning powers, things sensible, and things intelligible, in order to be admitted to true contemplation, which takes place in the clouds of faith, where God indubitably is, and by faith to receive light and love." The test of the goodness of all prayer, however seemingly sublime, is, after all, its practical effect, since with this object is it bestowed; all else is illusion. "All these high contemplations and grand communications," says Saint-Jure, "must have for their end to render the contemplative soul more careful to observe the commandments of God and more attached to His Will, even as those of Moses issued in the giving of the Tables of the Law which were consigned to his hands, but which, nevertheless, he afterwards broke, to teach us by a figure that the soul in these holy dispositions will be liable to fail and be ready to stumble, in spite of all its lights, if not upheld by God."

De Renty was, after the pattern of Moses, elevated to the summit of the mount of infused contemplation. He had arrived at this sublime degree of prayer as early as the year 1645, for we find him at that date writing thus to his director :—"For a long time, I have had during prayer no use of the understanding or the memory; nor, indeed, much more at any other time. I see nothing, I feel nothing; I have neither inclination nor repugnance for anything, I only feel my will alive and ready for all that God may point out to me." These expressions prove how deeply he had penetrated, or, rather, had been led into that luminous darkness of which the mystics speak. In another letter he says, " For some time I have experienced that my prayer is no longer according to any rule. I possess the Most Blessed Trinity with a plenitude of truth and of light, and that with so simple and so strong a view in the superior part of the mind, that I am in no way distracted thereby from my external avocations." This combination of contemplation and action,—this union of Martha and Mary,—seems to bespeak a very high spiritual state. At another time he writes, " Jesus Christ operates the experience of His kingdom in my heart, and I feel that He possesses it, and that I am all His. I have now a greater opening, but it is withal so simple, that it is impossible to render it in words : all I can say is, that it is a simple and true view of God in Trinity, with an accompaniment of praises, benedictions, offerings, and other homages, but all with such simplicity, that no sound is heard below; and even above it would be indiscernible, so far as to be able to describe it in detail, except for reflection. I do not even know whether what I say is quite accurate." Who that is familiar with the observations of saints, when speaking of the more sublime degrees of prayer and of their confessed inability to render them intelligible in human language—such, for instance, as are so frequently made by St. Teresa—can fail to perceive a striking resemblance to them in the account which De Renty here gives of what was taking place in his soul?

Through this intimate converse with God, and union in prayer with the Eternal Truth, he received wonderful illuminations, and specially with reference to the sense of Holy Scripture. He writes thus to his director : " With one word which I may read in the New Testament there will sometimes come to me knowledge of our truths in a manner so penetrating and abundant, that I can feel my body quite replenished therewith ; I mean that my whole being seems penetrated by it." To another friend he made a similar avowal :—" When I read the Holy Scriptures I collect all my energies to enter into the effect which they produce ; which is a plenitude of God, satiating the soul solidly and experimentally." Saint-Jure, who was the depositary of his papers, tells us that he had made comments upon all the Gospels read during Lent, which strikingly set forth, not his piety alone, but the abundant lights with which his mind was favoured. Little more need or can be said on this subject. It was one upon which he, as other holy souls, was ordinarily very reserved : " My secret to myself." Doubtless in the sanctuary of his soul much took place which ear never heard, and which could not have been rendered intelligible in human language had he attempted to reveal it. Suffice it, then, to say, in conclusion, that so powerful was his attraction to prayer, that he arrived at that point at which it became unceasing ; so that he was fain to confess to a confidential friend that he no longer needed either special time or place for his devo-tions, since it was impossible for any circumstances to abridge or interfere with his prayer, which was continual, wherever he was, or however he might be engaged.

———

CHAPTER VIII.

De Renty's State of Mystic Death.

"Mystic Death," says P. Surin, "is the extinction of our life as respects the world and ourselves, so that we may no longer live save for God." * "He that hath suffered in the flesh hath ceased from sins, that now he may live the rest of his time in the flesh, not after the desires of men, but according to the will of God;" † and to this sacrifice the Prince of the Apostles exhorts us by setting our great Head and Model before us. "Christ, therefore," he says, "having suffered in the flesh, be you also armed with the same thought." Christ, who was the Most Holy One, and knew no sin, but was made sin for us, bore in His sinless flesh the burden of our transgressions, and offered it on the cross. Our imitation of His sacrifice, and our conformity to Him, consist in the mortification and destruction of the fleshly nature we have inherited from the first Adam, and which we bear about us even after our regeneration. When this martyrdom is complete, the soul enters into a state which is called mystic death. But thus to die

* *Dialogues Spirituels*, l. iii., c. iv.　　† 1 Peter iv. 1, 2.

is to begin truly to live, for this mystic death renders the soul capable of intimate union with God, in which union consists its perfection. "The soul must die," says Saint-Jure, "in order to live its true life, and it must annihilate itself in order to become anything great." As the poison of sin has insinuated itself into every portion of our natural man—even, as Isaias says, "from the sole of the foot unto the top of the head, there is no soundness therein"—so must all this corruption be expurged from all parts by mortification, and the old Adam destroyed so far as is possible on earth. Then it is that the life of Christ, the glorious redeemed nature which we possess in Him, develops and manifests itself, and takes possession of all the faculties, spiritual and corporal, which are no longer swayed and ruled by human motives, but act in all things by and according to the movements of grace.

To this blessed state De Renty attained. It had been, as we have seen, the one aim of his desires and struggles ever since his conversion; and God gave him much illumination regarding its value. We find him, in one of his letters, saying that, while singing the *Magnificat* in church, he received an inward light when the choir came to the verse, "*Deposuit potentes de sede et exaltavit humiles*—He hath put down the mighty from their seat, and hath exalted the humble." He seemed to behold a soul in the plenitude of itself, rich in the possession of strong natural faculties, full of its own natural devices and discoveries, all alive in the use of its senses, exterior and interior, desiring to see everything and hear everything—in fine, replenished with self and empty of God. And then our Lord made him understand, through the

intelligence He gave him of this verse, that He de-
spoils this soul of its own proper spirit, "arrogant and
rich in iniquities;" that He humbles, simplifies, and
annihilates it; and that by this means He exalts the
humble—"*Exaltavit humiles*,"—raising this soul to a
marvellous state. In this state he beheld it reduced
to what he calls a rich nothingness, empty of itself
and of all that it had from the senses and from its
human nature, as well as of all the gifts with which
it had been endowed, that it might follow God in
perfect nudity, and become, as it were, only an ear to
hearken to Him. He perceived that when it has
arrived at this complete state of abandonment and
denudation, God works what He wills in that soul,
and it becomes wonderfully clearsighted, discerning
afar off the most minute things, as one might discern
a small shrub in the midst of a bare, flat plain. He
had special lights on this subject after he had solemnly
resigned his liberty to God, and it was then shown
him to what a point this self-annihilation must be
carried in order to render the soul capable of union
with God. "I beheld my soul," we find him telling
his director, "contract itself as it were into a little
point; I saw it shrinking up, diminishing, and
reducing itself to a nonentity; I also saw myself
simultaneously as one surrounded by all that the
world loves and possesses, and a hand seemed to
remove all this away from me and cast it into the
abyss of nothingness. First, I saw external things :
kingdoms, governments, superb buildings, rich furniture, gold, silver, amusements, pleasures, all which
hinder the soul from going to God, and whereof
for that reason He desires to see it despoiled, that
it may attain to that state of nudity and death

which is to put it in possession of solid riches and true life."

The subject of this first step in the mystic death, the death to what is exterior, is well illustrated by P. Surin in his explanation of that state in the passage from which we have just quoted. After describing the courtier's life of devotion to these externals—the Court and the great world being in those days synonymous terms—and how he languishes and dies of ennui when separated from this sphere of all his enjoyments, he goes on to speak of worldly ecclesiastics, who, though they must of necessity spend a portion of their time in their benefices, are consumed with melancholy and sadness if they, too, cannot go and take an occasional turn at the Court. These men also really live in those things ; and when this vain inclination is eradicated from the heart, they die to that external object : this is a part and a beginning of mystic death. So, too, the Religious who has his preferences with respect to the place he is in, or the employment allotted to him, lives in those objects ; " and when he entirely stifles this affection, cultivates a perfect indifference, and gives himself to prayer, seeking only to please God, he dies to them mystically." It is the dying voluntarily to these things in order to seek God alone which gives to this death the character of mystic, but the total separation constitutes in itself a kind of death. How true this is will at once be perceived if we reflect how men will consider themselves as good as dead, wretched ciphers, moral corpses, as soon as that which filled their minds, constituted their social dignity in their own eyes, and gave them a sense of usefulness or a pride of position and importance, is irretrievably taken from them, or

2 F

they are themselves compelled, from whatever cause, to relinquish it. "Every one," says P. Surin,* "has something in which he finds his life. With Monsieur So-and-so it is to be a counsellor, or to have a place in Parliament. When he has sold his office he feels like a dead man ; he is no longer besieged by persons coming to solicit his patronage, for he has ceased to hold the office which gave him consideration ; and it seems to him as though he were no longer in this world. It is, perhaps, for the interests of his family that he has divested himself of this office. If he had quitted it for God, and to give himself more perfectly to the service of God, this would be a kind of death, which would put him in a condition to become a spiritual man." It is because men do not value what is spiritual, and because their ambition is limited to earth, that we hear them talk so pitiably of being laid on the shelf and put by when their earthly career is closed ; for they fail to perceive that their compulsory deprivation and consequent inaction, which comes to them like a death-stroke, might, if accepted in the right spirit, be the portal to a far higher life of unimaginable grandeur.

To return to the vision which De Renty had of his own soul. After beholding himself thus despoiled of all that is external, he saw himself, in the next place, stripped of what is still more highly prized by us, as being more intimate to ourselves, and seeming, indeed, to be part of our very selves : our internal possessions, whether natural or acquired, our knowledge, our manifold experience, and all the subtle operations of memory and understanding ; all these, also, De Renty beheld as though purged away, that the soul might

* *Dialogues Spirituels,* l. iii., c. iv.

die to its own natural mode of acting. "I saw," he says, "that we must become like simple and innocent little children, separated, not only from evil, but even from our own manner of doing good, applying ourselves to those things which Divine Providence sets before us ; thus going by things to God, instead of to God by things." Thus the soul is never diverted from God, and sees Him only ; in a certain way not even regarding what it is doing, having in its different occupations neither choice nor desire, and being neither elated nor depressed by good or ill success, but remaining equable under all circumstances, because God is always contented, come what will. " We must," writes De Renty to a friend, " be annihilated to everything, that we may follow in simplicity, without a look, without a reflection, what our Lord works in us or orders for us, be it this or that : it is the road pointed out to me, by which I am to go to Him ; whence it comes that all things are to me without any savour of their own. Such is my ordinary state."

In this second stage of the mystic death, the will is resigned still more perfectly than in the first. P. Surin, speaking in the person of a soul in this blissful condition, uses language similar to that of De Renty. "All is indifferent to me," he says ; " I abandon all I will or desire, all my employments, all my actions, to the disposal of Divine Providence, and to the discretion of obedience. I prefer to do what others will to what pleases myself. A soul, thus dead, takes no satisfaction save in conversing with God, pleasing God, and seeing His will accomplished. The holy Bishop of Geneva said, 'I wish very few things, and, moreover, the things I wish, I wish very little.' A soul which is not in these dispositions

cannot fail to have many distractions and dissipations of
mind." "I assure you," says De Renty, writing to a
friend, "that there is no safety save in nothingness
and death.   He who is baptized ought to be dead in
Jesus Christ, in order to lead a life of annihilation ;
the rest is not all bad, but it is always dangerous,
particularly any action which we perform of ourselves ;
so let us divest ourselves of all, that the Holy Child
Jesus may give movement to all."

How completely he had thus divested himself—how
dead he had become, not to the world alone and to all
external things, but to himself, to his own will, judgment, affections, temper, and even to the natural bias
of his disposition—the previous narrative has shown,
and it would be superfluous to recapitulate.   But
there is a third and further stage in the mystic death,
which is wanting to its full perfection.   There is an
intimate life in the depth of the devout Christian's
heart, in which are treasured up all his most sacred
affections.   Here he enjoys sweet colloquies with our
Lord, experiences the delights of sensible, divine consolations, and all the ineffable effects of grace.   To
this life also he must die, for holy and good as all this
seems to be, and, indeed, is in itself, being the boun-
tiful gift of God, yet self-love is apt to mingle with it,
and there is danger often of mistaking attachment to
God's gifts for the love of God Himself.   The soul
which would attain to the perfect mystic death must
be reduced to the pure love of God's will, as respects
both these spiritual favours and all else, living for Him
only, even while enjoying His most precious gifts.
But as this is extremely difficult, and requires the
highest degree of disengagement, God, when he calls
a soul to such heights of sanctity, commonly makes it

pass through very searching and painful trials. When
the soul is moved to make an entire sacrifice of itself
to God, "He accepts the sacrifice," says P. Surin,
"and sends it drynesses, pains, and agonies, which
operate in it this mystical death."

We have already noticed how De Renty had
subdued in himself all attachment to sensible devotion, of which pious souls are apt to be so greedy.
He had so completely mortified himself in this
respect, that not only did he not complain or murmur,
or suffer himself to be cast down, at the subtraction
of sensible consolations and of the sweet experimental
realization of the Divine Presence, but he did not so
much as regret it : we do not say he did not feel it—
that would have been impossible—but it neither
distressed nor disturbed him. He set a much higher
value, in fact, as he himself averred, upon those
graces in which the senses have no participation than
on such as are visible and sensible. He even feared
the latter much, for he considered that among spiritual
persons there were a great many who were "rich in
spirit" to a very culpable degree. Sad it was, he
said, to know that few indeed were entirely free from
this fault, because we esteem and love these things so
much. "Man," he said, "naturally loves to see;
hence he seeks the light ; and, not yet having had experience of that of God, which we cannot well receive
save by extinguishing our own and putting ourselves
to death, he seeks that which he finds within himself,
and this he mistakes for the divine, because he figures
and represents this light to his imagination after his
own fashion. "As for obscurities, derelictions, and
other spiritual pains," he writes to a friend, "one
suffers them, cost what it may, and one throws oneself

headlong into them, as it were, with the most complete abandonment, like a fish into the water, which is its element : God on all sides of us ; ourselves in God for ever, and for all things."

But not only was he dead to sensible consolations ; he was also dead to what comes in the form of a more subtle temptation, namely, an eager aspiration after perfection. This may seem a contradiction to much which has already been stated, but it is not really so. What he sought with all the ardour of his soul was, not any abstract idea of perfection of his own, but that degree of perfection to which God called him : thither he tended, as to his goal, loving and willing only this or that good thing, this or that virtue, as God willed it, and in the degree He willed it. "Self-love," he said, "so much fears to see itself despoiled, that it cares not to what it holds on, provided it retain the means of subsisting and maintaining itself in its little right of property ; and this obliges us to labour incessantly to annihilate all our desires, even those which seem to us only to tend towards the virtues; I say, which seem to us, because, if God afforded us light, we should doubtless perceive that what appears to us to tend to self-despoilment is often, in truth, a desire to possess something and to retain ourselves, whereas we ought always to tend to nothingness, in which alone we can find God. Oh, how happy are they who are poor in spirit !" Hence he never aspired to any-thing great or extraordinary on account of its great and striking character ; neither was he dazzled or attracted by anything of the kind. A person of much holiness and high spiritual attainments having once intimated to him, on the part of God, promises of high gifts in store for him, he thus refers to this communication when writing to his director : " The things which have been intimated and promised to me are what they are, without my stopping to think of them, or being able to dwell upon them; we must live by faith." And again, being confidently assured that a signal favour had been accorded him by our Lord, the only effect of this assurance was to impress upon him a great contempt of himself, and a deeper sense of abasement; and, as the whole subject had been detailed to him in writing, he would not allow himself to retain this or any other similar documents bearing on what was most secret and intimate in his spiritual life, including even those which he had written in his own blood. These last he might well prize, but this was with him a reason for getting rid of them, knowing well how the heart, divorced from all else, will wind itself insensibly about all its little devotional furniture, and how such affections are the more difficult to remove, because it is not easy to detect any evil in them, or to understand their character ; nay, they even appear to us most just and commendable, on account of the profit we imagine ourselves to derive from the objects on which they are fixed, and which at a less advanced stage of grace we probably did derive. " I should desire," said De Renty, " if I had to form a desire, to possess nothing save my God : this is the satiating food of the soul and the rich treasure of the heart."

The love of God impels those especially who are actuated by it in no ordinary degree, to labour, or at least to desire to labour, continually for the promotion of the Divine honour and glory ; and we have seen how the life of this true servant of God was devoted to these aims. There is an imperfection, however, which is apt to mingle even with so holy an occupation, namely, an over-solicitude for the success of works undertaken for this end, an imperfection often difficult to detect, because this very solicitude wears the appearance in our eyes of intense zeal for the Divine interests ; yet, in order to die mystically, this anxiety for success must also be laid aside and merged in a higher aim, which entails no disturbance of mind because it cannot fail of its attainment, the accomplishment of the Will of God. Some one having closely questioned De Renty as to whether he did not desire anything, and at least the success of those works in which he was engaged for the glory of God, he replied, that he had no other desire in all his actions and enterprises than the fulfilment of God's Will ; and although he used his best endeavours to make them succeed, he nevertheless habitually abandoned himself to all that His Divine Majesty should decree. So completely dead was he to all those things which God worked by his means, that when they were accomplished, not only had he not so much as a passing feeling of self-complacency, but he thought no more about them, and took no greater interest in them, than if they had been done by another person. He seemed, indeed, not to possess the faculty of remembering aught except God ; so void was his memory of all the things of earth, that that faculty appeared incapable of suggesting any idea which could distract him from this one thought. Hence he never made any of those imperfect reflections upon the past which so often intrude themselves to tarnish our good deeds ; nay, God had given him the singular grace not to be occupied with these actions even when employed in them ; and no sooner were they done than

they were effaced from his memory, and never returned to trouble or distract him. But not only was
he thus entirely dead to his own share in the good
works in which he was employed, but he would have
been equally satisfied, had his Lord so willed it, to
be reduced to a state of complete inaction; for he
told one of his friends that God by His grace had
placed him in a state of so much indifference, that he
would have been quite content to remain paralyzed
and bed-ridden, powerless to move, for the whole of
his life, without any regard to the services which he
was at present able to render to his neighbour, but
from which in such case he would have been pre-
cluded, all being alike to him in the Will of God.

It may be thought that there was one exception to
the complete state of death which we have here
endeavoured to describe. Surely there was one point
upon which De Renty still betrayed sensitiveness:
he was pained by expressions of the value and esteem
in which so many held him. But this pain was nothing personal; it arose entirely from his zeal for
God, and for the growth of souls in holiness. He
was jealous for his Lord, and desirous to see Him
fully occupy the hearts which He was attracting to
Himself. Hence we find him writing to one of those
persons who sought direction from him, "I cannot
without pain endure the value you set on seeing and
speaking to me. Let us see God much, let us bind
ourselves without ceasing to Jesus Christ, that we
may learn in Him and from Him a profound self-
annihilation." Yet so far as he himself was concerned, praise had arrived at affecting him as little as
dispraise. Such is not the case in earlier stages of
the spiritual life. The soul still engaged in battling

with her interior enemies dreads the very shadow of
a commendation, as men dread a poisonous exhalation;
whereas the hatred of praise displayed by saints, or
persons of saintly character like De Renty, is more
often grounded upon the motives to which we have
just alluded than upon the abhorrence of it as a peril
to themselves. A very intimate and confidential
friend having one day, either for the purpose of
sounding him on this point, or simply giving utterance to his own impressions, said that he was pained
at seeing him surrounded with so much honour and
esteem, De Renty rejoined, with much simplicity,
that certainly he had very good reason for feeling thus, for that there was no ground for these
favourable sentiments. His friend now ventured to
ask him how he was affected when he heard himself
praised. "I pay no attention to it," he replied, "and
give it no heed; it does not move me more than if
I were the stock of a tree: by God's grace I am insensible both to praise and to contempt; neither the
one nor the other makes the slightest impression on
my mind; I do not so much as bestow a thought
upon it."

We must content ourselves with a concluding quotation from De Renty's letters, which sums up his
views with reference to the conditions of perfect
union with God, conditions which imply nothing
short of the mystic death of which we have
been speaking: "I see very clearly that the means
to arrive at union with God is to be stripped of all
which is not God, and dead to all creatures and to
self. Ah, how well I know the importance of this
denudation and of this death! What is it, indeed,
which interrupts the abiding union of love which we

ought to have with this Divine Majesty, this Sovereign Beauty, but a slight attachment to some created object? And shall we suffer a thing so trifling and unworthy to occupy us instead of God, and hinder His Divine Spirit, which is a fire of all-consuming love environing us on all sides, from having the power to effect in us what the element of fire operates in wood? Shall I, vicious and ever dissatisfied because I am filled with my wretched self—I who can never be perfectly happy save in the possession of my God—not fill myself nor occupy myself with God? This I can do with His grace, gently separating myself from all things by a simple and loving application of my soul to Him." Souls thus annihilated and become nothing to themselves are, as Saint-Jure observes, " rare master-pieces in God ;" and the contemplation of them may serve this purpose, if no other, to give us some conception of the admirable purity required for perfect union with God, and to inspire us with very serious reflections as to the amount of Purgatorial cleansing the best of us may require on leaving this mortal life. We think much, it is true, of the punishment due to us from the Divine justice for unexpiated separate transgressions which stand out in dark relief in our memories, but our very imperfection and imperfect mortification (which grace, and a high grace, can alone reveal to us) conceal from us our general unfitness at death for the Divine union ; yet this may constitute a far more powerful obstacle to release than what we justly regard as our worst sins. How often are people styled saints by their unreflecting acquaintance, and almost canonized by their loving and mourning relatives, who are perhaps all the while stretching forth their hands for help instead of this cruel and profit-less laudation? The consideration of the complete and entire mortification of the natural man which is the necessary condition of union by grace with God in this mortal life, may thus serve profitably to suggest to us the corresponding purity needful for union with our Supreme Good in glory hereafter.

CHAPTER IX.

LAST ILLNESS AND DEATH OF DE RENTY.

DE RENTY, thus mystically dead, as we have seen, was ripe for Heaven, and God was about to call him to his reward. On the 11th of April, 1649, the indisposition from which he had already suffered for some days, but which, as was his wont, he had con-cealed, was so much aggravated that he could no longer bear up under it. After having employed the whole day in works of charity, he was obliged towards evening to take to his bed, when he was seized with a general torturing pain. Even his mind had a share in this suffering, for he said that he had such strange and grotesque imaginations—a tendency apparently to delirium—that, but for grace inwardly enlightening him, and enabling him to restrain himself, he would have uttered more extravagances than a madman. Hence, he observed, his illness was of a very humilia-ting character; "but it is needful," he added, "that the sinner should honour God in all the states in which He places him." While enduring these pains, bodily and mental, and, indeed, throughout the whole course of this his mortal sickness, he was habitually employed in raising his heart to God in affectionate aspirations, blessing and praising Him, and making acts of submission to all that He ordered or should order for him; while from time to time he would give utterance to these sentiments aloud with much devotion. Nothing could exceed the sweetness he manifested to all who attended upon him, or the more than childlike obedience with which he acquiesced in whatever was prescribed for him, seeming to think everything well done, whether it was so or not.

The patience for which he had been so remarkable never failed him in these last trying hours of life; and amidst those inexplicable dolours which so often assail the dying, but which they are powerless to explain, he did not attempt to describe them, nor did he ever utter a single complaint, or allow others to commiserate him. The Sister of Charity who nursed him —the same who had so often visited the poor and the sick in company with him, and whose experience at the bedsides of the dying made her well know how acutely he suffered—pressed him to confess as much to her. "O my Sister," he replied, "how much suffering does the love of God extinguish! the servants of God suffer nothing." Being asked by another person if he suffered much, he answered in the negative; and the other having rejoined that to all appearance this was not the case, he then said that it was true that his sickness weighed heavily on him, but that he did not feel it, because he did not advert to it. When pressed to take some little agreeable palliative, he refused, saying that such things would not help to make a man either live or die, and were not necessary. But his medicines, nauseous and bitter as they were, he accepted with a cheerful and satisfied air, and, though he swallowed with much difficulty, he would finish them to the last drop. He only once evinced a shade of reluctance : this was on the day before his death, when, being told of an " excellent remedy which was to produce the most beneficial effect," he replied that " patience was an excellent remedy," plainly signifying that he had small inclination to make proof of that which was so highly recommended to him. Nevertheless, when it was brought he took it without making any objection, not even asking what was being given to him, so dead was he to all that concerned him.

Though he daily grew worse and worse from the time of his seizure, he never asked for anything to relieve his sufferings. Once when his attendants had been changing his sheets and had added a pillow, which previously he had refused, he did not reject it —probably not to distress the feelings of those whose tender care had provided it—but it was with a countenance of some confusion and humiliation that he laid his head upon it, for he thought he was being made too comfortable, and observed, " Here is Monsieur, very much at his ease !" Feeling a little natural joy at seeing a person with whom he had intimate spiritual relations, and who had come from the country to visit him, he instantly repressed it, repeating energetically three several times, " I desire nothing but God." To this person he strongly recommended the work of the Missions, begging him to promote it with all his power, as being a work which exceedingly glorified God, and, of all those with which he was conversant, was the most profitable to the Church. "Promise me," he said, "that you will use your strenuous endeavours and procure their multiplication to the utmost of your power. Oh, how pleasing is this to God!" His beloved poor were not forgotten, and he said to his wife, "I recommend the poor to you. Will you not take care of them? You will do it better than I; and never fear: whatever you may give will not diminish what remains." Indeed, for the greater part of the first week of his illness, and during much of the second—for it lasted a fortnight —he was occupied about different works of mercy, directing alms to be distributed, and dictating letters, concerning the many charitable affairs of which he had the management in the provinces, and as to which he also rendered an exact and detailed account.

The respect with which he was so generally regarded caused many persons to come and see him when they heard of his serious illness. He received them all with much sweetness and kindness, but these visits cost him an effort, for many who came had only the commonplaces of worldly civility and the compliments of polite and empty condolence to offer. He who was so silent under all his sufferings complained to some one of this infliction, saying, "They come to talk their philosophy to me, which is not what I need." On a similar occasion he briefly observed, "A Christian requires few words." Among his visitors was a lady of high rank and also great piety, who said, "Sir, I would willingly give my life for yours." These were not vain words on her part, but were dictated by her deep regret at the loss which she was about to sustain. He knew it; but, raising his eyes to heaven, with a smile of joy on his face, he replied, "To die is not to separate from each other; our conversation and our union will be more intimate than ever." But she, still clinging to the hope of keeping him on earth, rejoined, "But, sir, if God should be pleased to restore you to health and leave you in this life some time longer, would you not desire it? St. Martin was willing to live on this condition." "Ah! Madam," replied De Renty with much confusion, "let there be no comparison between a sinner and a saint: the Will of God be done."

He had not been ill more than three days, when he begged to see his confessor; upon which, being asked if he felt worse, he replied that he did not, but circumstanced as he was, with a disorder in which the mind and the judgment might at any moment be affected, it was well not to procrastinate, or allow oneself to be taken by surprise; it was therefore highly reasonable for him to do what he had so often recommended to others. On the following day he made his confession, after which he asked for his relics, that he might enter into more particular communion with all the saints. On the morrow he again confessed, and continued to do so almost daily until his death. The Curé of the parish came to give him Communion, and seeing him, after receiving, fall into a state of deep silence, which he only broke to ejaculate with profoundest humility, "My God, my God, pardon me; I am a great sinner!" he asked him why he said so little, and did not for their satisfaction address a few words to those around him: to which the sick man replied that it did not become him to speak in presence of the Incarnate Word whom he had just received, and that it was not fitting that he should occupy any place in hearts which ought to be filled with God alone. He told him, however, that his mind was much fixed on the joy which a creature ought to feel when on the point of being united to its First Beginning and its Last End.

In the afternoon of this day, his state of interior recollection and contemplation still continuing, some one told him that he ought to divert his mind from this strong inward application, and that the physicians even judged that his malady arose from a melancholy temperament. To this he replied, " I never felt joy equal to what I have experienced to-day ; " and the person addressing him having inquired the cause, he said, " It is the thought that I am going to unite myself to my God." This ardent desire to depart and be united to his Lord he also testified to another, saying, like St. Paul, " *Cupio dissolvi et esse cum Christo*—I desire to be dissolved and to be with Christ ; " * with those other words of the Beloved Disciple : " *Spiritus et sponsa dicunt, Veni ; et qui audit, dicat, Veni ; et qui sitit, veniat. Etiam venio cito : Amen. Veni, Domine Jesu*—The Spirit and the bride say, Come. And he that heareth, let him say, Come. And he that thirsteth, let him come. Surely I come quickly : Amen. Come, Lord Jesus ; " † abandoning himself, nevertheless, always for life and for death to the Will of God. One afternoon he begged that the windows might be opened, that he might better contemplate the light of heaven, and when the rays of the sun streamed in, " O beautiful Day of Eternity ! " he exclaimed ; " how I love this brightness, which helps me to think of that day which no night shall follow ! "

* Phil. i. 23.   † Apoc. xxii. 17, 20.

2 G

The more he suffered the more he strove to turn his mind to God and to pray to Him, imitating his Divine Master, who, in the very height of His Agony, prayed the more earnestly ; and whenever, from time to time, the violence of the malady so oppressed him that he had to make a greater effort to think of God, he would say aloud, " Courage ! courage ! Eternity approaches ! " Several other ejaculations he also uttered with much fervour, but he could not pronounce distinctly, by reason of the excessive dryness of his mouth, caused by the fever.   Suddenly he became quite silent, looking upwards fixedly ; and thus he remained for near a quarter of an hour, all which time he had a smile on his face, as of joy mingled with admiration, like to one who is contemplating some grand and beautiful object. At last, summoning all his remaining strength, he made a supreme effort, and, sitting up, uncovered his head ; in which attitude he continued for a while, still gazing upwards, with a rapt look of intense love and homage, which seemed to seek expression in aspirations, choked in their utterance, partly by the ardour of his soul and partly by the weakness of his body, but amidst which these words were distinctly audible : " I adore Thee, I adore Thee."

When the Curé judged the fitting time to be come, he administered Extreme Unction to him.   De Renty received this sacrament with much devotion, responding to all the prayers, and all could see that he was closely occupied with the words of the ritual, which, indeed, he was heard repeating to himself for some time afterwards.   On the priest's asking him if he would not wish to bless his children, he said, " What ! bestow a blessing in your presence ?   I am too happy to receive one."   Nevertheless, being urged to give it, on the ground that the Church approved the practice, he raised his eyes and hands to heaven, and said, "I pray God to be pleased to grant you His blessing, and to preserve you by His grace from the malice of the world, that you may have no part in it; and, above all, my children, that you may live in the fear and love of God, and obey your mother."

On the morning of the Saturday, which was to be the day of his death, he fell into strong convulsions, and it was thought he would not rally from them; but at half-past ten o'clock the spasms left him, when, having looked attentively for a moment at those around him, he fixed his eye on one of his intimate friends, a nobleman high in authority, and, with that attractive smile which was natural to him, signed to him to draw near. On his friend approaching he said, "I have a word to say to you before I die;" then, pausing a moment to gather strength, he testified his affection for him in words too indistinct to be altogether audible; after which, in a firmer tone, and with a more articulate voice, he proceeded, "The perfection of Christian life is to be perfectly united to God in the faith of His Church, and we must not concern ourselves with novelties. Let us adore His dealings with us, and be faithful to Him to the end; let us attach ourselves to a God crucified for our salvation; let us unite all our actions and all that is in us to His merits; and let us hope that, being faithful to Him by His grace, we shall have part in the glory of His Father. I hope we shall see each other again in a day that shall have no end." His friend wishing to reply and to thank him, De Renty laid his hand on his lips, and, bidding him adieu,

2 G 2

added, " That is all I had to say to you ; pray for me."

Near upon an hour later, raising his eyes as if he had seen something, he said, " The Holy Child Jesus —where is He ?" They brought him a picture of the Divine Infant, which he pressed to his lips ; then, asking for his crucifix, he took it in his hands and lovingly kissed it. He now entered into his agony, which lasted a full quarter of an hour, but for more than half of this time he ceased not to pronounce the Holy Name of Jesus, and to make to the best of his power acts of resignation and abandonment to God. Then all was still, and he sweetly and peacefully expired ; his pure soul going, as all who knew him had good reason to believe, to the place of its rest in the bosom of his Lord. Nor was evidence wanting to confirm this, in his case, most legitimate belief. He died at twelve o'clock, the hour on which the Saviour of men was raised on the Cross ; and there was a person, Saint-Jure tells us—we cannot help thinking, from the wording of the passage, that it was himself—who received some intimation that its merit was specially applied to him by our Lord at the moment of his death, so that this application, joined to the acts of abandonment and death to self which he had himself produced, and wherewith he had so devoutly honoured the Cross, completed the purification of his soul and fitted it, on leaving the body, to enter at once into beautitude and the enjoyment of God. Others, it was said, had visions and revelations of his glory. It was asserted that he was seen at the moment of his death rising like a globe of light from earth to heaven. Miraculous cures through his intercession, as well as aids and commu-

nications made to the souls of others for their spiritual profit, were also confidently related. "All
this," says Saint-Jure, "is by no means unworthy of
credit: on the contrary, a life so holy as was his,
and the heroic virtues which made him one of the
great wonders of our day, recommend it to our belief,
and induce us to accept these assertions readily.
Yet, since I have not the same certainty of these
things as I have of those which I have narrated, and
seeing that holiness and Christian perfection do not
consist in them, and that we cannot imitate them, as
we may the rest, I do not dwell any further on the
matter."

De Renty died at Paris on the 24th of April, 1649,
before he had quite completed thirty-eight years.

The words with which his director, who has been
our guide and authority throughout, concludes his
biography of this holy man, may fitly close our
own :—"I shall only observe in conclusion that we
have great reason to admire in this death the counsels
of God, who has removed from the world one who
was doing so much good in it, and who might yet do
more. For, being in the vigour of his intellect and
the flower of his age, and enjoying as he did so high
a degree of general esteem, credit, and influence, he
might have been of marvellous service, greater than
even he had yet been, in furthering the honour of
God and the welfare of his neighbour. But what
can we say ? It is God who has done it ; and that
is to say all. He has willed thereby to show us and
to teach us that He has no need whatsoever of us for
the promotion of His glory and the execution of His
designs, and that He will accomplish them without
us ; and this, that we may ever be humble in His

presence. Moreover, He has called him to a place and to a state in which he glorifies Him much more perfectly than he could here below—a place pre-eminently, therefore, styled the place of glory; by which we are to understand, not merely the glory which the blessed receive there, but still more that which they render to God. We might add that sometimes He takes from us these holy men before the time, men who are as the pillars of His Church and the support of the faithful, to punish us for the ill use we make of their conversation. and the little profit we draw from their example.

"But after all, when I was apprised of his illness, and of the danger he was in, it came into my mind, knowing as I did his consummate virtue and holiness, that, despite all considerations of the good which he was capable of doing on earth, it might well be that he would die, because he was a fruit ripe for Heaven: so that, even as one gathers a fruit when it has arrived at its maturity—for to gather it sooner or later is to injure it,—in like manner, God had taken M. de Renty at the maturity of his grace and at the height of the virtue for which He had designed him, as one who was perfected and finished, in order to be-stow upon him in Heaven the reward due to his merits; where also He desires to have us, that with him we may adore, glorify, and love perfectly God the Father, Son, and Holy Spirit, to whom be honour, praise, benediction, and all homage now and for ever. Amen."

Now Ready,

THE LIFE OF HENRI-MARIE BOUDON,

ARCHDEACON OF EVREUX.

Being Vol. VII. of the "Library of Religious Biography," edited by EDWARD HEALY THOMPSON, M.A. . Cloth, 5s.

In the construction of this Biography, the writer has carefully compared the previous Lives, and studied the collected works of this saintly man, including his numerous Letters.

WORKS OF M. BOUDON

WHICH HAVE APPEARED IN

SELECT TRANSLATIONS FOR SPIRITUAL READING.

I.—THE HIDDEN LIFE OF JESUS, A LESSON AND MODEL TO CHRISTIANS. Translated from the French by Edward Healy Thompson, M.A. Second Edition. 3s.

"This profound and valuable work has been very carefully and ably translated."—*Weekly Register.*

"The more we have of such works the better."—*Westminster Gazette.*

"A book of searching power."—*Church Review.*

"We earnestly recommend its study and practice to all readers."—*Tablet.*

"We have to thank Mr. Thompson for this translation of a valuable work which has been long popular in France."—*Dublin Review.*

"It is very satisfactory to find that books of this nature are sufficiently in demand to call for a re-issue; and the volume in question is so full of holy teaching that we rejoice at the evidence of its being a special favourite."—*Month.*

II.—DEVOTION TO THE NINE CHOIRS OF HOLY ANGELS, AND ESPECIALLY TO THE ANGEL GUARDIANS. 3s.

"It may be doubted whether any other devotional writer of the French Church, not marked for reverence by authority, is more highly or more justly revered than Boudon. . . . Faith assures us that we are surrounded on every side by a world of spirits, which, by the permission or by the command of God, interfere in earthly events and in human interests, and with which, therefore, we are in truth much more really concerned than with the great majority of those earthly events which we so often allow to engross all our attention and all our thoughts. We need, then, hardly say how valuable are works like this in the present day and in our own country. They show us how near the invisible and spiritual world appeared to men who believe only what we believe, but who lived in a country and an age where faith was more universal and more fresh. We do not know any English book which in any degree supplies its place, and are heartily glad to see it put within the reach of English readers."—*Dublin Review.*

"We congratulate Mr. Thompson on the way in which he has accomplished his task, and we earnestly hope that an increased devotion to the Holy Angels may be the reward of his labour of love."—*Tablet.*

"A beautiful translation."—*Month.*

"The translation is extremely well done."—*Weekly Register.*

III.—THE HOLY WAYS OF THE CROSS; or, A Short Treatise on the various Trials and Afflictions, interior and exterior, to which the Spiritual Life is subject, and the means of making a good use thereof. 3s. 6d.

"If some of our statesmen out of work could spare a little time from their absorbing occupations of blowing up the embers of insurrection abroad, or of civil discord at home, for the study of this little publication, they might learn, even in their old age, some plain truths about Christianity, and avoid the sad blunders that overwhelm them whenever they attempt to deal with any question that has a supernatural bearing. . . . If this work becomes as well known as it deserves, its circulation will be very wide."—*Dublin Review.*

"Boudon is fortunate in his English translator, and we may feel sure that these little volumes will long hold their place among our spiritual classics."—*Month.*

"The author of this little treatise is well known as a master in spiritual life, whose writings have met with the strongest commendation. . . . It comes to us with the best introduction, and with no slight claims upon the attention of every one."—*Tablet.*

"An infallible guide-book, to be commended to every Christian pilgrim."—*Weekly Register.*

"A perfect gem of safe devotion, and of priceless value as a sound spiritual book."—*Universe.*

"Precisely one of the very best kind for spiritual reading."—*Catholic Times.*

"Eminently adapted for spiritual reading, and beautifully translated into terse and vigorous English."—*Catholic Opinion.*

In preparation.

IV.—THE REIGN OF GOD IN MENTAL PRAYER. With a Preface by the Rev. F. Sebastian, O.D.C.

V.—THE SPIRIT OF BOUDON : Being Selections from his Letters, of which 387 have been included in his Complete Works published by the Abbé Migne.

LIBRARY OF RELIGIOUS BIOGRAPHY.

EDITED BY

EDWARD HEALY THOMPSON, M.A.

I.—THE LIFE OF ST. ALOYSIUS GONZAGA, S.J.
Third Edition. 5s.

"The life before us brings out strongly a characteristic of the Saint which is, perhaps, little appreciated by many who have been attracted to him chiefly by the purity and early holiness which have made him the chosen patron of the young. This characteristic is his intense energy of will. . . . We have seldom been more struck than, in reading this record of his life, with the omnipotence of the human will when united with the will of God."—*Dublin Review.*

"The book before us contains numberless traces of a thoughtful and tender devotion to the Saint. It shows a loving penetration into his spirit, and an appreciation of the secret motives of his action, which can only be the result of a deeply affectionate study of his life and character."—*Month.*

II.—THE LIFE OF MARIE-EUSTELLE HARPAIN; or, The Angel of the Eucharist. Third Edition. 5s.

"The life of Marie Eustelle Harpain possesses a special value and interest, apart from its extraordinary natural and supernatural beauty, from the fact that to her example and to the effect of her writings is attributed, in great measure, the wonderful revival of devotion to the Blessed Sacrament in France, and consequently throughout Western Christendom."—*Dublin Review.*

"A more complete instance of that life of purity and close union with God in the world of which we have just been speaking is to be found in the history of Marie-Eustelle Harpain, the sempstress of Saint-Pallais. The writer of the present volume has had the advantage of very copious materials in the French works on which his own work is founded, and Mr. Thompson has discharged his office as editor with his usual diligence and accuracy."—*Month.*

"Marie-Eustelle was no ordinary person, but one of those marvellous creations of God's grace which are raised up from time to time for the encouragement and instruction of the faithful, and for His own honour and glory. Her name is now famous in the Churches; . . . and her writings have imparted light, strength, and consolation to innumerable devout souls both in the cloister and in the world."—*Tablet.*

III.—THE LIFE OF ST. STANISLAS KOSTKA, S.J. Second Edition. 5s.

"An admirable companion volume to the 'Life of St. Aloysius Gonzaga.' It is written in a very attractive style, and by the picturesqueness of its descriptions brings vividly before the reader the few but striking incidents of the Saint's life. At the same time, it aims at interpreting to us what it relates, by explaining how grace and nature combined to produce, in the short space of eighteen years, such a masterpiece of sanctity."—*Dublin Review.*

"We strongly recommend this biography to our readers, earnestly hoping that the writer's object may thereby be attained in an increase of affectionate veneration for one of whom Urban VIII. exclaimed, that, 'Although a little youth,' he was indeed 'a great saint.'"—*Tablet.*

"There has been no adequate biography of St. Stanislas. In rectifying this want, Mr. Thompson has earned a title to the gratitude of English-speaking Catholics. The engaging Saint of Poland will now be better known among us, and we need not fear that, better known, he will not be better loved."—*Weekly Register.*

IV.—THE LIFE OF THE BARON DE RENTY; or, Perfection in the World Exemplified. Second Edition. 6s.

"An excellent book. We have no hesitation in saying that it ought to satisfy all classes of opinions. The style is throughout perfectly fresh and buoyant. We have great pleasure in recommending it to all our readers; but we recommend it more especially to two classes of persons: to those who, because the dress of sanctity has changed, think that sanctity itself has ceased to exist; and to those who ask how a city man can follow the counsel, 'Be ye perfect, as My Heavenly Father is perfect.'"—*Dublin Review.*

"A very instructively-written biography."—*Month.*

"We would recommend our readers to study this wonderful life bit by bit for themselves."—*Tablet.*

"A good book for our Catholic young men, teaching how they can sanctify the secular state."—*Catholic Opinion.*

"Edifying and instructive, a beacon and guide to those whose walks are in the ways of the world, but who toil and strive to win Christian perfection. We earnestly recommend these records of the life of a great and good man."—*Ulster Examiner.*

V.—THE LIFE OF THE VENERABLE ANNA MARIA TAIGI, THE ROMAN MATRON (1769-1837). With Portrait. Third Edition. 6s.

This Biography has been composed after a careful collation of previous Lives of the Servant of God with each other, and with the "Analecta Juris Pontificii," which contain large selections from the Processes. Various prophecies attributed to her and to other holy persons have been collected in an Appendix.

"Of all the deeply-interesting biographies which the untiring zeal and piety of Mr. Healy Thompson has given of late years to English Catholics, none, we think, is to be compared in interest with the one before us, both from the absorbing nature of the life itself, and the spiritual lessons it conveys."—*Tablet.*

"We thank Mr. Healy Thompson for this volume. The direct purpose of his biographies is always spiritual edification. The work before us lets us into the secrets of the Divine communications with a soul that, almost more perhaps than any other in the whole history of the Church of God, has been lifted up to the level of the secrets of Omnipotence."—*Dublin Review.*

"A complete biography of the Venerable Matron, in the composition of which the greatest care has been taken and the best authorities consulted. We can safely recommend the volume for the discrimination with which it has been written, and for the careful labour and completeness by which it is distinguished."—*Catholic Opinion.*

"We recommend this excellent and carefully-compiled biography to all our readers. The evident care exercised by the editor in collating the various Lives of Anna Maria gives great value to the volume, and we hope it will meet with the support it so justly merits."—*Westminster Gazette.*

VI.—THE LIFE OF MARIE LATASTE, LAY-SISTER OF THE CONGREGATION OF THE SACRED HEART. With a Brief Notice of her Sister Quitterie. Cloth, 5s.

"The narratives of Marie Lataste are marked by a wondrous power of language, which is so vivid in its simplicity, and bears so much the impress of truth, as to leave on the mind of the pious reader no doubt at least as to the subjective reality of the things related."—*Tablet.*

"Experienced religious, keen theologians, and prudent bishops have testified to the virtues and approved the writings of Marie Lataste. . . . The Life is very valuable, as giving an insight into the exceptional operations of the Holy Spirit in a human soul, and cannot fail to do good in those who read it with the prepossessions of faith."—*Dublin Review.*

"From time to time we are allowed to lift the veil which hides the interior life, and to see the operation of grace in some chosen soul. If the results are beyond the intelligence of worldly men, the working out of the results is still more wonderful, and we may be permitted to suppose that God finds a special satisfaction in perplexing self-reliant philosophers. . . . A life of our nineteenth century sanctified under the personal direction of our Blessed Lord is meant by Him for our instruction, and will not be allowed to pass into oblivion."—*Month.*

"The life and writings of this saintly religious have, during the last fifteen years, excited great interest in her native country, France, and we cannot doubt but that her very enthralling and most edifying biography, now for the first time presented to English Catholics, will meet with many readers and admirers."—*Weekly Register.*

(5)

In immediate preparation

VII.—THE LIFE OF M. LÉON-PAPIN DUPONT, THE HOLY MAN OF TOURS.

VIII.—THE LIFE OF ARMELLE NICOLAS, the Servant Girl of Campcnéac.

IX.—M. ORAIN, Parish Priest of Fcgréac during the Great Revolution.

OTHER LIVES WILL FOLLOW.

Shortly will be published, uniform with the Life,

THE LETTERS AND WRITINGS OF MARIE LATASTE, with Critical and Expository Notes by two Fathers of the Society of Jesus. Translated from the French by Edward Healy Thompson, M.A. 2 vols.

No Life of Marie Lataste would be complete without her writings, because they form the one special and distinctively supernatural element in it, containing, as they do, not merely in substance but in detail, the instructions imparted to her by the Saviour Jesus.

The Letters, which are eighty-seven in number, are partly biographical, and partly of a doctrinal and practical character.

The Writings include papers on the following subjects:—God and Creation ; the relations of God with men ; Jesus Christ, His functions in the Divine economy ; the principal mysteries of His life ; the Blessed Virgin, her intercessory office, her mysteries ; the good angels ; the devils, and their relations with men ; the sacerdotal ministry ; the Christian and his duties ; religion in general, and the great acts of religion : communion, confession, and prayer; the law of probation and of mortification ; grace, its divisions and operations ; the theological, cardinal, and moral virtues ; the gifts of the Holy Spirit ; sins, their causes, their species ; the duties of different states in life ; religious vocation ; spiritual direction ; the four last things.

In preparation,

A NEW AND ENLARGED EDITION OF

THE LIFE OF JEAN-JACQUES OLIER, FOUNDER OF THE SEMINARY OF ST. SULPICE, with Notices of his most eminent Contemporaries. By Edward Healy Thompson, M.A.

This new edition of a work which received the special approbation of the late Abbé Faillon, author of "*La Vie de M. Olier,*" and
of the late Very Reverend Paul Dubreul, D.D., Superior of the
Seminary of St. Sulpice, Baltimore, U.S., is founded on the more
extended biography which the Abbé Faillon left completed at his
death, and enriched with extracts from the recently-discovered
memoirs of Marie Rousseau, which contain interesting details,
not previously known, concerning the first years of the foundation
of the Community and Seminary of St. Sulpice.

THE WYNDHAM FAMILY : A Story of Modern Life. By the Author of "Mount St. Lawrence." 2 vols., with frontispieces. Cloth, 10s. 6d.

" It is not mere praise, but simple truth, to say of these volumes that
in them the author has succeeded in combining the solid and edifying
instruction to be expected from a Catholic tale, with the interest and
amusement usually sought for in the fashionable novel or 'story of modern
life.' Its plot is excellent, and each one of its varied range of characters
is conceived and described with a power which displays a close and intimate knowledge of human nature in many and very different phases."—
Tablet.

" We heartily welcome the writer's reappearance among us as a caterer
for the amusement as well as instruction of our Catholic youth. In the
' Wyndham Family,' however, there are excellent lessons to be found for
all ages, and we are glad to see the honest vigorous attacks made upon the
worldliness, selfishness, and frivolity which are now eating so largely
into Catholic society, and which, although they are habits of the most
pernicious sort, are singularly ignored, merely because they may not
amount to mortal sin."—*Dublin Review.*

"The tale is very charmingly written, and the various incidents are
detailed with a verisimilitude and particularity which gives an air of
intense reality to the whole. The author of 'Mount St. Lawrence' may
be congratulated on a work which will add to the reputation deservedly
acquired by that much-admired production."— *Weekly Register.*

" The book is well planned, the characters well conceived, and the
English undeniably good and accurate. It is evidently the work of a practised writer, a writer of good taste, religious thoughtfulness, and knowledge of the world. If it is not as popular as a hundred books of very inferior workmanship, it will be because the public taste has been vitiated
by the overflowing stream of trashy sensationalism. The book before us
is on the reactionary side, and on this account we heartily wish it success."
—*Month.*

"This is a novel of the good old sort, in the style of Miss Austen or Miss
Edgeworth, wherein characters are depicted as they are in real life, without exaggeration."—*Catholic Opinion.*

"The book is admirably written; it is interesting, instructive, and
amusing. The story is well told ; the characters are good ; in a word, it
is an admirable work for the present day."—*Ulster Examiner.*

"This is a semi-religious story, cleverly designed, and beautifully
written."—*British Mail.*

By the same Author, .

MARY, STAR OF THE SEA; or, A Garland of Living Flowers, culled from the Divine Scriptures, and woven to the honour of the Holy Mother of God. A Story of Catholic Devotion. New Edition. 5s.

" A beautiful dream, the ideal of a holy life, every incident and character in which was natural, and, strange to say, in the highest degree practical, and yet with a certain mysterious, imaginative air thrown over it, which it is difficult to describe. . . . The recollection of it hovers about a reader after he has forgotten the details, as he might remember a glimpse of some religious and secluded household, made romantic by its distance in memory, in which it seemed

> ' That airs of Paradise did fan the house,
> And angels offic'd all.' "

—*Tablet* (1850).

"Years ago we read an exceedingly pretty little book, and its pleasant and most useful, as well as cheering, lessons never left our minds in all the ins and outs and ups and downs of life. It was called ' Mary, Star of the Sea,' and certainly it was a general favourite in every Catholic circle into which we knew it to penetrate."—*Catholic Times*.

" A pleasing and instructive story, leading the reader along through a very good exposition of Scriptural evidences to Mary's dignity and privilege."—*Month*.

" An old and well-established favourite."—*New York Catholic World*.

" The design of the volume is to defend and promote devotion to the Mother of God, the Spotless Bride of the Holy Ghost. . . . It is a commentary on the Litany of Our Lady of Loreto, and, as such, full of instruction and incentives to devotion."—*Brownson's Review*.

A FEW REMAINING COPIES OF

THE UNITY OF THE EPISCOPATE. By Edward Healy Thompson, M.A. Cloth, 4s. 6d.

" It is impossible by any abridgment or extracts to give any fair or adequate idea of Mr. Thompson's argument, which is the most masterly and the most completely worked out that we have met with for a long time."—*Dublin Review* (1847).

" The book which made altogether the most decided impression on my mind was *The Unity of the Episcopate*. The *principle* of unity was there unfolded in a way that was new to me, and which, I think, does away with a whole class of passages (and they the strongest) which are usually alleged against the Papacy."—The late F. Baker, Paulist, quoted in the Memoir of his Life by F. Hewit, p. 95.

THE SUFFERINGS OF THE CHURCH IN BRITTANY DURING THE GREAT REVOLUTION. By Edward Healy Thompson, M.A. (The 24th Number of the "Quarterly Series" published by the Fathers of the Society of Jesus.) 6s.

"Mr. Thompson has done his work well. His narrative is clear, even, calm, and filled with facts; and, in carrying his readers through the revolutionary history of the most Catholic districts of France, he has enlarged the body of evidences upon the great laws of spiritual rebellion, which, while occupying fresh fields and offering new varieties of evil, leads inevitably to the most disastrous results."—*Dublin Review.*

"An excellent history. It carries us from the beginning to the end of the Revolution, and places before us striking pictures of the principal events which took place during the struggle between the faithful Bretons and the vile fanatics who vainly endeavoured to stamp out Catholicism from the land where some of its noblest children have lived and died."—*Cork Examiner.*

"Another page from that bloodstained record at once so enthralling and so terrible, so full of heroism and of ruthless tyranny . . . a clear and admirable explanation of the causes of the Revolution, masterly sketches of those princes of evil, Voltaire and Rousseau, records full of thrilling interest: hairbreadth escapes, and heroic professions of faith and patient endurance of suffering."—*Weekly Register.*

"Mr. Thompson gives us the true history of the Civil Constitution of the Clergy, an inquiry to which he has devoted much zealous labour."—*Month.*

"A work no less useful than interesting, for it enables us to perceive the fatal mistakes that were often made even by good men in those trying times; and thus it is a guide to us even in the contests of the present day, when the faithful have to contend for all that we hold most dear against the same false principles."—*Tablet.*

"Mr. Thompson has in his judicious preface pointed the moral of the story in a manner which gives it a special significance and a direct bearing on contemporary events."—*Irish Monthly.*

LONDON: BURNS AND OATES.

www.ingramcontent.com/pod-product-compliance
Lightning Source LLC
Chambersburg PA
CBHW052331110726
47901CB00005B/1200